D1105315

THE AFRICAN SAFARI PAPERS

This book is dedicated to anyone who's had cold, grinding, grizzly bear jaws hot on their heels.

Acknowledgements

With thanks to:

Dad for being there in '84;
Mom for telling me the Robert the Bruce spider story;
Libby for keeping a warm home to come back to in Canada;
Caitlin for providing the initial inspiration;
Wendel, Kim, Adam and Rowan for reading the early drafts and being so helpful and supportive;
Bill Hicks for proving that courage and integrity don't have to be compromised;
Joe Kertes, Timothy Findley and Jim MacDonald; and Margaret Hart for storming the castle;
John and Kendall for the shearing, shaping and shepherding.

Note to the Reader

In the summer of 1983 I took a safari to Kenya with my mother and father. The book you are about to read is a work of fiction. It should not be confused with my actual safari, which, by comparison, was reasonably uneventful. Likewise, the characters set forth here should not be confused with actual persons, living or dead.

Dad has us sitting in different parts of the plane. It's in case we crash. He has a plan for everything. This way, one of us will presumably survive, proudly pick up the fallen torch and carry on.

I hope it's me.

Checked on mom. She was crying. Jesus. Wouldn't say why. Just stared out the window. Dad was sitting in the back, drinking scotch. He didn't seem too happy when I told him. He got up right away to see what was wrong.

I went and smoked a bowl in the bathroom. *What about the smoke alarms, Richard?* No problem. Designed for the uninspired . . . not the desperate. *How do you do it?* I smoke with a small pipe and haul every last burned leaf and stem deep into my lungs. I exhale through a straw into a sink full of water. A few wisps curl into the air but not enough to set off those pesky alarms. Any remaining odour gets zapped with a tiny room freshener I carry. Fresh orange fragrance . . . made from real oranges. Mom swears by the stuff. *Spritz, spritz.* So do I.

I left the bathroom humming nicely. Like the big furnace gran had in the basement of her old house. Warm and buzzing. It didn't matter that the plane was getting bounced around like a pop can tossed from a moving car. I passed mom and dad. He seemed agitated. She kept staring out the window watching those wings dip and dive.

"There's nothing to be afraid of," said dad, trying hard to be compassionate but wanting nothing better than to get her in a head-lock and run her forehead into a pole.

"Then why aren't we sitting together?"

"It's just a sensible precaution."

"A precaution for what, Ted? Crashing. If you didn't think it was possible, we'd be sitting together. I hate you for putting these thoughts in my head."

"Janet, the odds of being killed in a plane crash are one in four million. You've got a better chance of winning ten million dollars in the lottery."

"What are the odds of a freak of nature, a blast of sudden and catastrophic wind shear?"

Yes dad, what about that?

"Wind shear does not bring down planes at 37,000 feet."

"Oh no? What about rolling thunder?"

"Rolling what?"

She had already told me about this. I have to admit that she succeeded in twisting a knot in my stomach, a knot that had remained tied until my visit to the latrine.

Mom began her account sounding like a somber narrator on a disaster documentary. "Mount Fuji. British Airways. March 5, 1966. Boeing 707. Perfectly clear day. Suddenly, wham! The plane disintegrates. 124 dead. The crash investigators determined that a rolling mass of air, something like horizontal wind shear, smashed into the plane and blew it to pieces." Mom took a deep breath and her voice dropped to a whisper. "Do you know what happens when a plane breaks apart at 37,000 feet? All your clothes get ripped from your body. Shoes, socks, underwear. Everything. You fall to the ground completely naked."

Dad was left mute. There are certain images you don't want interfering with the dull and reassuring drone of those big engines. I don't think he was affected by the image of plummeting to his death. He was probably thinking about the embarrassment of being found by a Sudanese search-and-rescue team, spread-eagled in a field, without a stitch.

Mom wrenched her eyes from the wobbly wing and reached into her purse. "I need a cigarette."

Dad grabbed her wrist. "You can't smoke here," he growled.

Having the three of us scattered about the fuselage might have been a good idea for a runway crash but it left mom in a non-smoking seat. She had already been back to my section to smoke several times. She didn't like dad's survival plan and by the look on her face she liked his grip on her wrist even less.

Mom whipped her hand free, snagged a cigarette, lit it, and blew an anxious plume into the cabin. Dad's momentary courtship with compassion was over. He spat out a barely comprehensible "Goddamn it," before standing too quickly, hitting his head on the luggage compartment and swerving back to his seat.

It was a matter of seconds before the protests began.

A loud American woman behind us made a sorry-ass attempt to get mom's attention with her coughing. Just once I would like to meet a quiet American abroad. I realize I have a better chance of seeing a hairy frog but I have hope.

Defeated in her effort to stop the clouds of smoke with her coughing, and undeterred by mom's comment that she had quite a cough and it was a good thing she didn't smoke, the loud American woman leaned forward. "There's no smoking."

Mom was thoroughly enjoying her cigarette. She glanced at her fingernails like she often did at home in our living room. "Says who?"

"It's the law."

"Fuck the law."

That's when I left. Good for mom. Yes, it's a non-smoking seat, but it's not the complaint, it's the attitude that travels with it, like a magpie splashing wet shit on your head. Fuck off. Find something worth getting excited about. I like anti-abortion activists more than I like anti-smokers. At least pro-life fanatics get excited about something that matters.

Oh I know, all those tests warn us about the evils of second-hand smoke. But if anyone thinks that brief exposure to one cigarette is going to give them cancer, then they had better save their money and purchase one of those plastic bubbles that John Travolta lived in for that TV movie in the 70s. Because that's the only place they're going to be safe. Anyone who thinks they can get cancer so easily is insane. They should be locked up.

I agree with one gloomy forecast. If you're locked in a small basement room with no ventilation with a person who smokes two packs a day, and you never leave that room for forty years, you *might*, not for sure, not a guarantee, but you might run the risk of getting cancer.

But let's say the scientists who live off government grants are right. If someone has that weak a constitution, is so frail in spirit and health that brief exposure to a burning cigarette is going to give them cancer, then so be it. Let them die. We'll end up with a stronger herd. Let's weed out the weak ones. The cranky ones. The pathetic ones who always complain. It's survival of the fittest. Just like fucking Africa. Any anti-smoking fanatics stealing a peek at my journal? Stop now. This journal is for snoops with dirty hands. I mean it. Put the journal down.

The only reason that people don't like smoking is that it reminds them of their own mortality. It's like I'm standing there, dressed in a black robe with the big hood, and I've got a cigarette in one hand and a scythe in the other . . . and they're cringing . . . and they're thinking . . . what do you mean this doesn't last forever? What do you mean I have to die one day? And with a deep voice I chuckle from inside the hood.

Because that's really what this anti-smoking crusade comes down to. A fear of dying. Come to think of it, that's what all crusades come down to.

11:17 p.m.

Managed to close my eyes for a bit. Everybody on the plane is asleep. Everything is peaceful. This is when the bomb would go off. Life's cruel that way. I'd be thinking just what those college students on Pan Am 103 were thinking, "Gee, it'll be nice to get back home for Christmas. I wonder if Melanie will meet me at the airport?" Thinking of sleigh rides and carolers and how sweet Melanie's pussy was going to feel, slipping and sliding under that big comforter. There would be the soothing voice of the pilot announcing the flight time to New York and maybe mentioning something about the constellations I could see on this clear night, if I happened to be sitting by a window. Reaching slowly for my tray table because the idea of sipping a brandy suddenly appeals to me. Turning serenely to the flight attendant and opening my mouth to speak and then . . . BOOOOOM! Plane disintegrates. Clothes blown off. Still strapped in my seat. Still conscious. Floating. Stars bright. Holy night. Upside down. Freezing air squeezing my balls. My ears bleeding.

Jesus. Why do I write this shit when I'm flying?

I checked on mom. She had put out her cigarette when the flight attendant asked if she'd be so kind as to do so. Good for Air France. Nice and civilized.

Dad had mentioned before I arrived in Paris for the safari that mom was having some troubles. What kind of troubles? He wouldn't say exactly. Which was surprising because he's always so thorough. I was too self-obsessed to pursue the matter. I needed to borrow some money from him so I wasn't worried about her troubles.

Can't believe they've been in Paris for a year. She never wanted to move to France in the first place. She quite liked our two-storey house and small backyard with a birdbath for the robins. Her flowers. Her shrubs. Her badminton.

According to mom, dad had wanted to live in Paris ever since he read Hemingway in college. She says he put in his transfer request seven years ago. I'd never seen him so happy as the day he came home and announced that he and mom were going. I'd never seen mom pretend so hard to be happy.

The timing was perfect. Maggie was at university. I was due to finish high school. Dad would go over early and mom would join him after I'd graduated. They would rent out the house and get a condo for Maggie and me to live in.

I remember our final morning together in the house. It was a week after my last day of classes. Mom had come up to my room to do laundry before her flight. Her last domestic duty as a mother. She asked if I needed anything washed. I didn't hear a word. I was so hungover. I remained sluggish until I realized she had taken my jean jacket downstairs to wash. Gradually I pieced together the sequence of events taking place down in the laundry room. She was feeling in my pockets to see if there was anything that needed to be removed. Things that would be ruined by the warm, soapy water. Things like a candy bar. My wallet. My pack of cigarettes . . . my . . . I jumped out of bed and bolted downstairs. I was too late.

Mom was standing beside the dryer holding a vial of hash oil. She had tears streaming down her face. I would have expected a demonstration of disappointment. But she wasn't just disappointed. She looked shattered. Her expression was so extreme, so ridiculous, I almost started to laugh. She held that small vial as though it were a bullet I'd shot into her heart and, through some miracle of self-surgery, extracted it with her fingers. She was holding it out for me to see. Dark, red blood dripping on the cement floor. She told me she thought I was a drug addict. She said she was going to take the vial to Paris and show dad. She never did. Good old mom. Protecting her youngest.

Maggie drove her to the airport. I was too sick. Poor mom. Standing at the bottom of the stairs, saying good-bye to the house, and the only sound is me in the upstairs bathroom puking. That was the last time we stood under the same roof until I came to Paris for this safari.

She's got to learn not to be so hysterical. She read a story in the newspaper once about a mother on LSD who had cut out her baby's heart with a broken beer bottle. She thought that's what all people did on LSD No mom, just those people that are nuts in the first place. Nuts should not take LSD. Mom doesn't know I've taken it. She would spontaneously combust if she knew how often. And guess what? There's not a single baby's heart on my floor. Lots of shattered illusions. Lots of lies. Lots of preconceptions about time, death and glass onions. But, so far, knock on wood, no baby hearts.

I don't take drugs as an escape trick, like some cheap magician on a cruise ship. I take drugs to find gold, like a greedy prospector in the backcountry. There are those who take drugs to be cool and those who take drugs to expand. I am not James Dean. I'm a balloon. And god has a mouth on my hole. And is blowing. And filling me up. And filling me up. One day I will explode. And then I will be free.

I am so grateful that mom and dad never mentioned god in our house. The closest I came to a church was when a school chum got me interested in the Boy Scouts. I joined for the badges and the camping trips and the roasted marshmallows. My chum was a Latter-day Saint, a Mormon for those not in the know. He and his family ate whole-grain cereal for breakfast, and they set aside every Monday night and called it Family Home Evening. They talked and laughed and sang — even when Monday Night Football was on. They were aliens to me.

The Scout meetings were held in a room in their church. It was around the second or third meeting that my Latter-day Saint chum started showing up with his dad a half hour early. This meant we got to the church a half hour early. The father said the same thing every week. "I see Bishop Ballantyne's car over there . . . wonder what the heck he's doing here on a Wednesday night . . . oh, what do you know, there's a worship service in the chapel, shhh, well, let's not just stand around twiddling our thumbs for twenty minutes, why don't you grab a seat beside us on the pew here, Richard."

This went on for months. I didn't hear a fucking thing that that old bishop said. But then one day I figured it out. This wasn't about camping at all. This wasn't about marshmallows and lighting your farts on fire. This was about saving my soul.

I quit right there and then. And from that day forward I waited, coiled and tense like a mountain lion, for short-haired missionary boys in smartly pressed white shirts and ties who came to my door with a divine smile, a firm handshake and a plan.

I'd greet them in my underwear. With nasty holes in my ass. I'd smoke cigarettes and hash oil. I'd drink beer and whiskey. I'd flip through *Hustler* magazine and ask them what they thought of a particular photograph of a particularly juicy snatch. I'd scratch my balls. I'd belch, break wind, rate the stench, pick wax from my ear. In spite of all this, they'd still get around to asking if I knew who the "king" was. I'd say it was Elvis. They'd tell me that my soul needed an eternal friend. I'd say that my soul was already spoken for, wrapped in the warm embrace of the Dark Prince. Most of them left after that. The persistent ones stayed. I guess they liked the nude pictures lying on the coffee table.

Never a mention of god in our house. So when I was ready, when I started asking questions, that's when I turned to drugs. And they gave me colours that no church in the world could provide. Mom and dad gave me a blank canvas upon which to paint. They can be a pain sometimes. But there's one thing I'll never forget. They never touched my soul. God bless them for that.

I'm looking at the other passengers sound asleep. I wonder if this is what enlightenment feels like? Awake and no one to talk to.

Later

We have begun our descent into Nairobi airport. The sun has risen. The air is calm. My ears are hurting. I wish they'd pop. Just hit a big air pocket. No doubt mom is gripping her armrests like some poor slob getting gum surgery with too low a dose of freezing. That's it for now. Welcome to Africa.

Friday, August 12
10:45 a.m.
Norfolk Hotel
Room 26
Nairobi, Kenya

Customs was a joke. Didn't even open a bag. Not that I was worried because I put all my goodies in one of mom's travel bags. Yes, I am a bastard. *So tell me, young man, just what would you have done if your good mother had gotten busted?* I would have confessed. But then again I've got a slippery, cowardly side.

In grade six we broke into a bookmobile that was visiting our elementary school. The bookmobile was just a school bus filled with books that came around once a year. I assume its mere presence in the parking lot was supposed to get us interested in reading.

Me and Kurt Hutchison forced the door open so tiny Alex Cooper could squeeze inside. He wasn't there to steal. It was enough of a victory to see him inside the bus. We had parachuted a soldier behind enemy lines. Alex was great. He kept running from the front of the bus to the back, with his arms in the air, yelling. He must have done this about forty times. We laughed until we almost peed ourselves.

We didn't know it but we had broken the bus door. We got called down to the office and Mr. Harris, our principal, pulled out his big leather strap and smacked it down on his desk. I was the only one who flinched.

"Alright boys, I'm calling your parents, let me have your phone numbers."

Alex and Kurt gave their numbers quickly, and quite bravely, I thought. And me? Well, I had a problem. The bookmobile break-in occurred on a Tuesday. My birthday was that weekend. And we had a double-sleepover planned. One-night sleepovers were common enough. But a double-doozie? That was pretty special.

All I could think of was that mom would get the call, tell dad and I'd be grounded. No double-sleepover. No nothing. I cracked and began to sob. "Mr. Harris, I didn't have anything to do with the bookmobile. I swear it."

I cried and cried until finally Mr. Harris turned to Kurt. "Is Richard telling the truth?"

Kurt shot me a disgusted look. *Please, Kurt. You know your parents aren't going to give a shit. My dad will go nuts. C'mon, buddy, cover me.* Finally, Kurt shook his head.

"He had nothing to do with it."

"Alright, Richard, you can go," said Mr. Harris.

I left the office feeling like a complete loser. What a coward.

But the weekend was great. Kurt and Alex came over. We ate pizza and watched nude movies at midnight. For some reason, before the prigs took control, Channel 4 showed adult movies on Fridays at midnight. The movie that night was an instructional film about how to make love to a pregnant woman. I can still see this naked woman lying on a bed with her big belly, and her butt pulled right to the edge of the bed (this was the special technique) so her significant other could fuck her without putting any weight on the baby. And fuck her he did. We were stunned. Not by the sight of a pregnant woman getting fucked. By the sight of any woman getting fucked. Amazing.

They say you don't get interested in sex until puberty. Bullshit. We were bald as walls and small as worms, but that didn't stop our little peckers from rising up to salute the midnight movie. Those birthday parties were primitive. Or obscene. Take your pick.

We spent most of the time running around the basement naked. If someone had to fart they would yell, "Wait, I've got one." We'd gather around the person silently, like he was going to sing us a song or read a poem. He'd bend over, spread his cheeks and let 'er rip. We'd all fall back laughing, shocked and amazed at the wonders of the human body.

Was my cowardly denial in Mr. Harris' office worth it? You're damn right it was. Would I do it again? In a second.

We took a cab in from the airport. Dad was his usual preoccupied self and I think mom was a little perplexed by my interest in, and possession of, her travel bag.

I looked around at the drab countryside that passed by. "Is this it? This is Africa?"

Dad shook his head. "We just left the airport, shithead. What do you expect? Elephants on the highway?"

He swung a hand around and patted mom on the knee. "We didn't crash, Janet."

Mom was staring stoically out the window. "We still have to fly back, Ted." she said.

"That's the spirit. Ruin three weeks of safari worrying about the flight back." Dad cracked his knuckles. "This trip is costing me five thousand dollars. I suggest the two of you start making more of an effort."

Dad always has to let us know how much things cost. Everything has to have a value. He got me a watch for high school graduation. Told me not to lose it because it was a good watch . . . an expensive watch. He fought the temptation but was eventually overwhelmed. He blurted out that it cost him three hundred dollars. Every damn time. A value. A number. Jesus Christ.

"We're tired, dad. We've been flying all night," I said.

Dad sneered. "What a couple of babies."

We got to the hotel. I jumped out of the cab and almost landed on a beggar. The man had no arms and no legs. Unbelievable. *Weebles wobble but they don't fall down.* Somehow he managed to roll himself down the sidewalk. A long string was clutched in his mouth. The string pulled a cardboard sign that read, "You will know the truth, and the truth will make you free — John 8:32."

Dad was hoisting suitcases out of the back of the cab as I made my way to the lobby entrance with mom's travel bag under one arm and one of my own bags, a small one, under the other. "How about some help with the rest of the luggage?" asked dad.

"Let the professionals handle that," I said. "This is, after all, where slaves came from. They've got more experience than I do."

I heard him cursing under his breath. I'm terrible about winding people up. I always make comments I shouldn't. You'd think he'd know me by now. I can and will find humour in anything. It's my silver lining. It keeps me from abandoning myself to vicious deeds.

The hotel is awesome. A five-star deluxe model. I'm pleasantly surprised. Most of our family road trips took us to the States and were spent in a Motel 6, with dad and me in one bed and Maggie and mom in the other. Dad has really opened the wallet for this trip. God bless him. But then again, he didn't have a choice. There's not a Motel 6 to be found in Nairobi.

12:15 p.m.

Once I got to my room I transferred all my goodies from mom's bag to my own. My small pipe, cigarette papers, two lighters, two cartons of du Maurier cigarettes, a safety pin, an ounce of big buds from Humboldt County, California, three vials of hash oil, half an ounce of Lebanese hash, six grams of jude in a sandwich bag and a small roll of tin foil. Poor mom. She would have gone to prison for life. Or maybe they would have chopped off her head. Who knows. Anyway, no such problem going back. Everything will be smoked by then — the evidence destroyed in fantastic clouds all over the Kenyan countryside.

The one piece of contraband I was courageous enough to smuggle in my own bag was an issue of *Penthouse* I had purchased before flying to Paris. I don't know why I get in such a state buying these magazines. Actually, that's not true, I know exactly why I get in a state. I'm thinking about what others are thinking when they see me buy it. They're thinking about me taking the magazine to a dark room and masturbating with it.

The little Indian man at the Mac's smiled at me when I asked for the *Penthouse*. The smile looked patronizing. It wasn't. Well, probably wasn't. But it set me off. *Look at the loser boy buying pornography because he can't get any on his own.* Fuck you, Indian man.

Penthouse is my favourite. *Hustler* is too explicit. Who gets off on seeing pictures of girls that look like they're posing for their gynecologist? Not me. And *Playboy?* Too clean and wholesome. They're trying too hard to make the magazine seem respectable. I honestly don't care if a nude model supports world peace. I love *Penthouse* girls. They strike the perfect balance between the transparent tramps in *Hustler* and the salubrious sluts in *Playboy.*

Some women say they don't understand how a man can masturbate to a photograph of a naked woman. It's actually very easy. You flip through the magazine until you find a picture that catches your eye. It's the pose. The look on the model's face. *Penthouse* does a fabulous job of capturing models in the "throes of passion," the parted mouth, the eyes. I know it's not real but that's why god gave us imaginations.

Once you find the picture, you begin playing out the scene. In mine, the model starts out fully dressed. I'm usually in her house for some professional purpose. I'm a plumber or a newspaper boy or I'm delivering groceries. She always seduces me. I never seduce her. I'm always a little shy, a little reluctant. She's usually married, unhappy, really horny. She teases me. Perhaps she has to change her clothes to go out. She does so with me there. Why not? We start to have sex. Oh my. Until, finally, on the brink of ejaculation I arrive at the moment that the photographer captured. Click. And then I get out some toilet paper or a sock.

I remember the first time I ejaculated. What a magical night. I knew something was different because my cock was suddenly a lot bigger than it had been. But not that big because I could still fit it inside a bottle of shampoo. I got it stuck there once and had to wait twenty minutes for my erection to die down. I decided I better stick with my hand. I spent many a night in the bathroom. I stroked myself for hours. But still nothing. Mom and dad knew exactly what the hell I was up to. You don't have that many baths in one evening.

Finally, on the fourth night of frantic and prolonged masturbation, it happened. My legs started to shake. A soft, warm wave passed upward and then suddenly a wonderful white sap erupted and gooped all over my stomach. I sometimes forget what an intense moment that was. Much more intense than losing my virginity. So, that's ejaculation, I thought. Marvellous. Simply marvellous.

I never had another orgasm like that first one but it hasn't been for lack of trying. I figure I've masturbated at least six thousand times. No joke. I could have fathered six thousand freaks (not counting the twins and triplets). Started a town. Named myself mayor.

In fact, I was just whacking off on my bed here in my hotel room. Had the magazine open. Was nearing the dramatic end to the scene. Had the model bent over a desk. Just like in the photo. I was doing her like I really knew what I was doing. And she was saying all the right things. Telling me how big I was. Telling me to do it harder. Deeper. I felt that warm wave begin boiling and rising. I didn't hear the footsteps. Didn't see the door open.

Now dad is a very manly man. He prides himself on being tough. He used to box when he was a teenager. He also forced me to join contact sports like hockey, to be hurt and to hurt other people. In hindsight I'm grateful. I'm sure I'm stronger as a result.

I hated playing hockey but dad bundled me off to games on bitterly cold nights anyway. In between periods, all the other sons would cry and their fathers would rub the feeling back into their frozen feet. Not me. I kept my skates laced up and fought back the tears. You had to be tough around him. One frail expression and you were toast, you were a fag.

I have to admit, seeing me lying on that bed with my pecker in my hand did not conjure up images of Bobby Baun scoring the overtime goal in game six of the 1964 Stanley Cup finals on a broken ankle.

The sound dad made was unexpected. It should have been a low growl. Instead, I got a yelp. The sound a small terrier makes when you accidentally step on its foot. The yelp was followed by a skip backward like a schoolgirl in a pretty dress jumping awkwardly back into a hopscotch square.

All this was quickly followed by an exclamation that we sang as a duet. "Jesus Christ."

I quickly threw a sheet over my embarrassed and shrinking member.

He turned his back and found his low, steady voice, "We've got a meeting with the travel rep." He bumped into the door frame and left.

My face was flushed. I surprised myself, yelling at the closed door, "Do you think you could knock next time, asshole?!"

There. At least a little of my dignity was restored. I slid off the bed, pulled up my pants and tucked the magazine under the mattress. There was a light tap at the door.

"What?" I said.

"Are your pants up?" dad asked.

"Yes," I said.

The door burst open and he stormed inside like the Mangler from that *Flintstones* episode where Fred testifies against the Mangler, the Mangler escapes from prison and bursts into Fred's house, *Flintstone! I'm gonna get you!* But he trips on Pebbles' roller skate and is knocked unconscious. Unfortunately, there was no roller skate for dad to trip on. Before I could move he had me pinned up against the wall with his forearm on my throat.

"I paid for the goddamn room. I don't have to knock."

I think he might have crushed my windpipe if my eyes hadn't

betrayed my young man's swagger and revealed the terror I felt. He released me.

"I don't want any stunts on this trip," he said.

I wanted to ask him what the hell he meant but my throat was still burning and I wasn't sure I could speak. He stalked out, shutting the door behind him.

It's strange. You think you're grown up. You think you're a man. And all it takes is one quick forearm to the throat to remind you that you're just a kid, a weak little kid.

8:49 p.m.

Piss, gloom and the fuck of it all. We had our meeting with the travel rep from Wimpole Tours. Boring as all hell. I was so tired I could barely keep my eyes open. Mom was distracted. I don't think she paid attention to a word the rep was saying. Dad was getting irritated. I know what he was thinking. He's paid five-thousand dollars for this trip and mom is staring off into space and my eyes are at half-mast.

After the meeting I came back to my room and masturbated. I wasn't really into it but I can't fall asleep if I don't. I slept until five o'clock and went down for dinner.

Me and dad scooped potatoes and peas onto our forks in between mouthfuls of roast giraffe, which tasted like deer, which is another way of saying it tasted like shit. I found out later I could have ordered a hamburger. Goddamn it.

Mom's plate was full. Her fork dipped into her mashed potatoes, did a few lazy pirouettes and then stopped.

Dad was on his third glass of wine and had lapsed into a fine depression himself. "You can't work at an oil rig for the rest of your life," he blurted out. "You should be starting university in the fall."

I knew it would come. *The talk.* About my future. But I thought it was going to be later in the trip. I hadn't had time to prepare.

"I don't know what I want to take."

"It doesn't matter. You don't go to university to get a job. You go to get an education."

"Next year."

"Maybe my offer won't be good for next year."

"Why are you putting all this pressure on me?"

"I'm not. I just don't want you to waste your life away in the oil patch. You're losing valuable time."

"I'm happy there. It pays great. The food's awesome. It's beautiful country. I work an eighty-hour week and then I get a whole week off. I like that."

"And what do you do on your week off?"

He knew what I did. I'd already answered this question on the telephone several times.

"Read books, hang around. Stuff like that."

"Your sister said you've been drinking a lot."

Thanks, Maggie.

"I drink some. I work hard up there. I deserve a week of rest."

He was getting himself worked into a nice lather. He turned to mom. "You haven't touched your food."

"I'm not hungry," replied mom. She didn't want an interrogation so she quickly pulled a cigarette out of her purse, hoping to divert his attention.

"I'll have one," I said. Mom handed me a cigarette. Dad sat back in his chair, startled. "I've never seen you smoke before."

So now there's two things you've never seen me do before.

Dad pulled a mint wrapped in plastic from his pocket. He's been popping mints in his mouth for as long as I can remember. He looked at it. His shoulders sagged a bit. My sad-sack future. My smoking. Mom's lack of an appetite. Too much. He pushed his chair back and stood up. "The van leaves at eight. We'll meet here for breakfast at seven." And with that he was gone.

I turned to mom. "I hate him."

"Why?"

I laughed. Mom's face remained set. It pissed me off. "Are you deaf?"

"No."

"You heard him. He's a prick."

"Please don't use that language around me."

"I'm sick of him bugging me about stuff. I've got a great job and I'm fine."

"He's just worried about you. We're both worried. You've started to drift away from us."

"I'm in Canada. You guys are in Paris. There's a big body of water between us. It's called the Atlantic Ocean. You might have heard of it."

"You get that from your father."

"What?"

"Your sarcasm. It's so childish."

If there's one thing I hate it's being told I have a mannerism like him. Fucking hate it. *Fuck you, mom.*

"What were all those drugs in my bag?"

"What bag?"

"My suitcase. The one you took to your room."

"I gave it back to you."

"I know you did. But what kinds of drugs were those?"

"I don't know what you're talking about."

"There was an awful lot of them wasn't there?"

What the hell was I supposed to say? I had to deny. Why was she being so poised about it? When did she find them? And why didn't she throw them out?

"It's just some grass and stuff," I said.

"And hash and hash oil."

"You couldn't tell the difference between hash oil and motor oil."

"What is the tin foil for?"

Oh shit. We were speeding down a narrow, dark road, she and I, alone in the car, coming around a tight corner, seconds away from a collision with the 'H' word.

"I don't even remember putting tin foil in there."

I tried to stare at her blankly like she was making a big deal out of nothing. *You crazy old coot. Tin foil is for wrapping cheese after you've taken the plastic off. Keeps it fresh in the fridge. You taught me that.* A big drop of perspiration fell from my eyebrow and landed on my wrist. She held up a dinner napkin to demonstrate.

"Don't you put heroin on the tin foil and then hold your lighter below it until the heroin burns so you can inhale the smoke?"

"I don't do heroin, mom."

"Then why do you have the tin foil?"

"Where are you getting all this from? Since when did you become such an expert on drugs?"

"You don't have to worry. I won't tell your father."

"You can tell him anything you want. I don't care."

"That's not true. He still sends you money. And I know you want to go to university. Maybe not this year. But eventually."

"I don't need his money. I'm not a prisoner like you."

She looked at me like I'd smashed her shin with a four iron. I couldn't tell if she was going to cry or scream.

"I'm sorry," I said. "Why the hell don't you leave him?"

"Because I'm a coward. And I'm a failure."

"You're not a failure."

"You don't know what you're talking about."

And with that she got up and left. I watched her move slowly through the restaurant. I regretted calling her a prisoner. It was pathetic of me. I'm just as much a prisoner as she.

I made a stupid decision. When I got back to my room I started throwing out my goodies. I flushed two vials of hash oil down the toilet before I calmed down. What a fucking waste. That's sixty bucks down the drain. The old girl is getting too smart. I'm going to have to be more careful.

11:07 p.m.

I just smoked half a joint and I am calmly sipping a glass of brandy. Dad left my room only moments ago.

Mom must have been quite upset after our conversation at dinner. Because shortly after I'd finished writing that last entry, dad came pounding in. He looked wild. I thought for sure she had told him about the drugs.

I was sitting in a chair at one end of the room. He stood at the other end. I think he didn't want to get too close or he'd start swinging. "What did I tell you about upsetting your mother?"

"I didn't," I exclaimed.

"Bullshit."

"She's been in a coma since we landed. I've got nothing to do with that."

"I'm warning you," he said as he came closer with his finger wagging. "If you kill her, Richard, I'm coming after you."

That caught me completely by surprise. What in the hell was he talking about? I wanted to be ominous and cool and say something like, "You go ahead. But I promise, I'll do great harm to you." Well, maybe that would have been lame. But it was a hell of a lot better than the shrill, "What'd I do?" that escaped me like a high-pitched fart.

I tried to stare at him — without blinking — but at the same time, I hoped he didn't notice I was shaking. I waited for him to take a swing. I would have gone for it. I was crazed. I wouldn't have cared if he'd beaten the shit out of me. I think I could have hurt him at least a little before he hurt me really bad.

He seemed surprised that I stood my ground. Well, from my chair. At least I stared at him. He smiled but it was an awkward smile. I think he was trying to intimidate me. His smile said, "You have no idea how close you just came to getting wasted." But he was trembling a little, like he wasn't so sure of himself anymore.

I decided to give him a chance to retreat with grace. I dropped my eyes to the floor. It worked. He turned and left the room. I still can't believe it.

There's a big missing piece here. How did we go from sniffles on the plane to me causing mom to kill herself? I have to assume that his concerns are real because dad is not prone to hysteria. If he weren't such a prick I would ask him what is going on.

I have visions of mom killing herself and him tracking me across the ice floes past Tuktoyaktuk like Dr. Frankenstein.

I am troubled tonight. I am on the outside looking in. I'm suddenly very suspicious about the past year. They had two chances to come back home and they didn't.

There was Christmas. Dad explained that it made no sense to come back to Canada so soon after arriving in Paris. This must have been his decision because mom would have wanted us all together at Christmas.

Then there was Maggie's wedding. Even though I know they were disappointed that she got pregnant, quit university and got married, they could have come back. I ended up giving her away. And I was drunk when I did it.

And where are the bride's parents?

In Paris.

Oh.

How can you not come back for your only daughter's wedding? Unless, of course, there was stuff going on with mom in Paris. Big, ugly stuff. And dad was worried about a scene at the church or maybe on the airplane.

I'm quite angry tonight. All these secrets. What the hell is he hiding? And what the hell is going on with him? Barging into my room. Putting a forearm to my throat, threatening to kill me. Christ, he's wigging out.

I don't remember him acting this way when Maggie and me were growing up. He was more predictable. Even when he was putting the house on edge with his moods, his temper. But he was never beating the family up or anything, threatening to kill people. And even mom. She was pretty goddamn stable.

One of the few times I ever saw mom wig out was after an incident with one of Maggie's friends in grade seven.

That was a big year for my discovery of the repulsion most people feel about the anus. It seemed the one part of our anatomy that no one wanted to talk about and so it became the one part that I wanted to celebrate. I went on a mission.

As mission control manager I used to organize all the guys in the class (the girls thought it was immature) and we'd form an anal train. Our poor grade-seven homeroom teacher would come back to class and find all the guys, perhaps fifteen of us, in a long line simulating anal intercourse, and of course, I'd be out front blowing the horn.

I have a theory. Before we were born into human form we were spiritual beings. We loved the fact that we didn't have human forms and human functions. We were free. It was a beautiful existance. And then grunt, grunt, sigh, push, oh my god, we suddenly found ourselves trapped in these organic shells. And in order to keep these shells alive we needed to consume a variety of substances. And what was consumed, of course, needed to be expelled.

We think we are angels descended. We think we are stardust. And we were. Or maybe we still are, deep inside. But every time we take a dump and wipe our asses we are reminded that, even though our thoughts may be divine, our bodies are no different than a dog's when it squats in the park. Somewhere, deep in our minds, is a memory of days without eating and shitting. And we get depressed and angry when anyone reminds us that we aren't so lofty, aren't so divine. That was my mission. Even if I didn't know it then.

The incident in question occurred at lunchtime. I was waiting with Maggie and her friend for mom to drive us back to school. Maggie's friend bent over to tie up her shoelace and I was on her like a shot. I started pumping her from behind. Maggie screamed and ran upstairs. Her friend was startled but not traumatized. Maggie came back down and told me in a grave tone that mom wanted to see me.

I walked up the stairs to where mom was standing. I awaited her reprimand with a big, sloppy grin. Not a word was spoken. But she looked possessed. She raised her hand and slapped me six times across the face. Three on the left. Three on the right. It stung like a motherhummer. I remember she licked her lips afterward. And that was it. I turned and walked back down the stairs using every ounce of willpower not to burst into tears.

That was one of the only times I saw her wig out. But this is different. That was wigging out for a single moment. And it wasn't even a real wig-out because she didn't even yell or anything. I think her wigging out this time is more of a week-at-a-time thing, or maybe a month. Or maybe longer. And maybe she'll start yelling.

We start the safari tomorrow. I'm quite excited.

3:30 a.m.

Just had a really scary dream. There was a rabbit about the size of a bear cub, hopping around my room. It jumped up on my bed and crawled onto my chest. It was purring like a cat, acting sweet. I raised my hand to pet it. Suddenly it went for my throat and began tearing through my skin. I was helpless. Blood spurted everywhere. I got dizzy. But felt euphoric. I knew I was dead. And then I woke up. I was still on my bed. The rabbit was gone and there was no blood. But above my bed was a door floating in air. It was a magnificent door with a shiny knob and a sense of something magical on the other side. I reached out to the knob. And then I woke up. A double dream. I've never had one before. Very cool.

Saturday, August 13
6:30 a.m.
Norfolk Hotel Garden
Nairobi, Kenya

I raided my fridge last night. Drank three beers, two brandies and a whiskey. I wonder if it'll show up on the hotel bill? Dad will be pissed. I don't have a hangover this morning. In fact, I feel great. I'm going to try and stop drinking on this trip. Or at least not drink to the point that I get wasted. I want to stay alert.

I just made some coffee in my room and I've found a big garden behind the hotel. I still have half an hour before breakfast. The garden is great. Big grass pathways, lots of flowers and the faint morning light is fantastic. I know the sun is going to come along and ruin it eventually by putting too sharp a focus on everything. I like hazy. I like distortion. It's soft and it's comfortable.

I am sitting on a bench. There is morning dew on the wood but I don't care. I am all alone and I like it this way. I hear voices coming down one of the pathways. Germans?

A couple just walked past me. They must have been in their fifties. He was in a suit and tie and looked distinguished. His wife was really good looking. Why do I get so horny for older women? She stared at me. And was that a trace of a smile across her face? I'm usually good about maintaining eye contact but she won this one. I looked away. That German woman's got me thinking about Mrs. Turner. I think I've spilled five litres of sperm thinking about Mrs. Turner.

Poor Dave Turner. He had no idea what a horny mother he had. I used to see her driving aimlessly in her car. Where the hell was she going driving around like that? She was probably going to Mac's to get garbage bags but I convinced myself that she was out cruising, looking for young men to fuck.

Mrs. Turner was not like the other moms. Even at fifteen I knew that. She was bold. Her eyes would drift below my belt when

I went by to pick up Dave for school. And this wasn't a quick peek. She would stare. We would continue talking and her eyes would stay fixed on my zipper. God, I loved her for that. So fucking obvious.

That summer, Dave went to camp for a month. There was no one to cut the lawn so Mrs. Turner asked me if I'd do it. On my third visit I decided to show her Mr. Happy.

I was trimming the edges around the flower beds when I heard the back door swing open. I was down on my knees and slipped my cock outside my shorts so it was resting against my thigh. A couple of quick strokes and it was hard, exposed and twitching.

Then doubt set in. What if she called the police? I was just about to tuck myself back in when I saw her shadow pass across my knee.

Mrs. Turner stood over me. I couldn't look at her. I imagined her hands rising to her face like a heroine in a monster movie. I waited for the high-pitched scream of horror. I waited for her to order me off the property and tell me what Mr. Turner would do to me after she told him. But none of that happened. She started talking. I didn't hear a word. It was like I had seashells over both ears. *She's looking at my cock.* My blood was pounding through my veins. But before I could take another laboured breath she was gone. *Did she even see it?* I looked down to see that my cock was already starting to shrink, turning back into a weenie. I felt completely pathetic.

I continued my trimming. I ended up beside the patio outside the Turners' bedroom. The patio door suddenly slid open. Mrs. Turner stood there with her shirt unbuttoned to her navel. I could see the soft curves of her breasts, pushed up and out under a white bra.

"Oh, Richard, I didn't see you there. I was almost naked," she said matter-of-factly.

I don't remember what I said. But I'm sure it was stupid. I continued with my trimming, oblivious to the fact that she had just seen my erection, and she slid the door shut. And that was it. I blew it. Would there have been any better way to lose my virginity than to fuck Dave Turner's mother while he was away at camp? But I was a coward. No, I take that back. I was unprepared. I can't believe I didn't take a peek through her patio door before she opened it. I would have seen her slowly unbuttoning her shirt. I would have been horny and ready for when she came out. Knowing she was horny and ready for me. I would have had a response to her saying, "Oh, Richard, I didn't see you there. I was almost naked." Two of my favourites:

That's okay, Mrs. Turner, don't stop on my account.

That's okay, Mrs. Turner, I've always wanted to see you naked.

And then on that hot summer day Mrs. Turner would have led me to her bed and ravaged me. We would have done it all. And we could have started meeting at hotels and she could have called me over to her house when she was alone. Instead, I will be tortured until the day I die for my hesitation.

My life would be different if I had responded when Mrs. Turner opened that patio door in her bra. I really believe this.

10:26 a.m.
Lake Naivasha Hotel
Room 11
Kenya, Africa

We got in about an hour ago. The air is damp and delicious. I don't understand it. I thought Africa was supposed to be hot and dry. Lake Naivasha is about two hours northwest of Nairobi. We're in another deluxe hotel. I'm not complaining though. I don't want to be out in some dinky tent. My room is sweet. There is a mosquito net over my bed.

After I finished writing this morning I smoked a bowl and started to stroll through the garden at the Norfolk. The surroundings were becoming more defined by the sunlight. It was time to go back to my room. I approached a figure slouched forward on one of the benches. The person hadn't heard me coming, and as far as I could see, was busy chattering to no one. I stopped when I realized it was mom.

She had birds all around her. It was odd because she wasn't feeding them. And yet there were twenty or thirty of them. Not pecking around for food. No, they weren't moving at all. They seemed to be a captive audience to her ramblings, which I couldn't quite make out. Her fingers were locked at grotesque angles as if frozen in some kind of arthritic attack. Her right leg bounced up and down like she was providing a percussion accompaniment to her words. But it was her eyes that scared me the most. They were what told me not to approach her. I knew if I did, those eyes would look at me and wouldn't know me. So I stayed back and watched.

So, this is it, I thought. This is mom when no one is around. I got a tingling in my neck. This is why there was no visit at Christmas. This is why Maggie's wedding was avoided. She is insane. Not in a funny way. No, not crazy in a funny, kooky way at all. She was scaring me.

We all had breakfast together at seven at the Norfolk. And guess what? She was fine again. And thus is revealed a consistent problem with drug-users and reality. How much of what I saw in the garden was mom and how much was the bowl I had smoked?

Dad was in good spirits. He had already gone for a four-mile run. He's always telling me how far he jogs. Says he does ten miles on Saturday mornings in Paris. He had forgotten the confrontation of last night. I like that about dad. He can be a complete asshole the night before and by morning he's pouring orange juice for you and cracking hard-boiled eggs and jokes at the same time.

We went outside at eight o'clock and met our guide. His name is Gabriel. He is a local Kenyan. I would guess he's in his thirties. All smiles and handshakes. What else would he be? He's getting paid to be nice to the white man. He walked up right away and shook dad's hand.

"Mr. Clark, my name is Gabriel. I'll be your guide."

Dad turned to mom and me. "This is my wife, Janet, and my son, Richard."

We all shook hands. I circled the white van we'd be travelling in and then peeked around for the other slobs that would be joining us. "Where's everyone else?"

"There is no one else," said Gabriel.

Finally, some good news. I thought we'd be sharing the safari with other groups. Wow. This was going to be better than I thought. A private safari. I was so glad that dad was rich. Well, not stinking rich. But well enough off to afford a private safari. Yee-ha.

We loaded into the van. I was ready to go. But we weren't moving. Gabriel was waiting. Dad noticed something outside the van.

"Richard, you didn't load your bag," said dad.

I looked outside and there it was. *Yup. That's my bag.* I thought I'd save Gabriel a little embarrassment so I shot him a quick look and nodded for him to go outside and get the damn thing.

Gabriel looked at me and smiled a huge smile that swallowed me whole. "I get paid to be the best safari guide in all of Kenya. I don't get paid to load bags for young men who are strong enough to load their own."

What the fuck are you talking about, Mister Safari Guide? I sat there for a moment.

"Richard, for Christ's sake," exclaimed dad.

I got out slowly and loaded the bag. I sat back down. I didn't like Gabriel. He tried to make eye contact with me through the rearview mirror. I wouldn't let him. He smiled again. This time at mom.

"Let's start the safari," he announced.

And with that we swerved out onto the busy streets of Nairobi. I was sulking. I'm such a baby sometimes. But when I dive into a good sulk there's nothing that's going to pull me out. Not Gabriel's big smile and certainly not the excitement of leaving Nairobi behind and entering the wilds of Africa — the real Africa.

It wasn't long before paved road gave way to a bumpy dirt road. Dad got out his video camera. He knows I hate the things so he won't be asking me to shoot. I've also asked him, kindly, not to include me in any of the shots. I hate video cameras. And I hate home movies even more. Still photographs are better. As long as I'm not in them.

We saw our first native villagers. Walking along the side of the road with big sacks on their heads. Just like in the nature shows. It was a reflex action. The three of us waved like idiots. I can't believe I participated but I got caught up in the moment. The villagers just stared right through us. There was anger on their faces. Hostility even. I dropped my hand. Why the hell would they wave back? They see this thirty times a day. Rich, white families blasting down the road in safari clothes, waving like morons. If I were them I'd probably throw a clump of dirt or a bottle. At least we're not wearing safari clothes.

"They hate us," I said.

"They don't hate us," said dad. "They just . . ."

"Want to kill us," confirmed mom.

"Nobody's going to kill you, Mrs. Clark," said Gabriel.

I looked at mom. She had started nibbling at her nails.

I managed to sneak a few cigarettes in the back of the van. I don't feel comfortable smoking around dad. When he's happy like he was then, I want to keep him in a good mood. Dad sat in the front with Gabriel. Mom sat in the middle row.

I have this image of myself as this free spirit, cartwheeling through life, thumbing my nose at "the man," but I still think I have to sneak cigarettes behind my father's back like a fourteen-year-old.

The van has an observation hole in the roof and I spent some of the journey with my head sticking through it. The cool air felt great. We drove through some corn fields. Not my image of Africa. I expected grasslands. Television sure gives you a perverted view of the world.

Dad looked around at the rolling hills with a lazy smile. He was thinking, *I'm a good man. Janet has always wanted to come to Africa and unlike so many suburban housewives, here she is. I've worked hard. My family has benefitted from my hard work.*

What a conceited bastard I am. How the hell do I know what he was thinking? But he was definitely in a mood for a chat. I was all the way in the back and mom was not talking. So that left Gabriel.

"How long have you been doing this?" he asked.

"This is my fifth season," replied Gabriel.

"Did you grow up in Nairobi?"

"I was born on the coast, a little town called Kipini. Two brothers. Two sisters. We moved to Nairobi when I was seven."

"Why did you move?" asked mom.

Dad turned in his seat a little bit, pleased that mom was joining in. The gesture was corny. But I was glad to see it.

"It wasn't that we wanted to move. My father and brothers were out fishing and they got caught in a bad storm. Their boat capsized and they were drowned."

We all chimed in with condolences and the van filled with mutterings of "I'm sorry" and "That's awful" and other things you're supposed to say when you hear something bad like that.

Gabriel seemed a little uncomfortable. Dad tried to rescue him.

"So your father was a fisherman?"

"A lawyer."

Dad wrinkled his brow a little. *A lawyer? I thought you people either chucked spears at animals or gathered vegetables?* Mom leaned forward in her seat. She always leans forward to tragedy.

"My mother thought it best to make a fresh start somewhere else. We moved to Nairobi and I stayed there until I went to university."

"University?" asked dad.

Which department? Custodial or security?

"In London. I studied medicine for eight years."

None of this made any sense to anyone. Including me. "So what the hell are you doing driving cracker around in a van?" I asked.

"Richard!" yelled mom and dad.

Gabriel started laughing. "My passengers are people who have come to Kenya to explore the land of their ancestors. The fact that they are predominantly white means nothing to me. They are curious and I am here to guide their curiosity."

Guide our curiosity my ass. Behind that big smile he hated this. He hated us. He had to.

"That all sounds really good," I said. "But why aren't you working as a doctor? Helping your people?"

"I never finished my studies, Richard."

"You quit? You must have been close to getting your degree."

"Two weeks."

"You're two weeks away and you just up and quit? Why?" I asked.

"Alright enough," said dad.

"It's okay, Mr. Clark. The boy is direct. I like that."

Dad shot me a look. *No more.* Mom was still shaking her head from the news about Gabriel's father and brothers. I decided I liked Gabriel, even if he did call me boy. Anyone who studied for eight years and then quit fourteen days before graduation was okay.

I was lucky I even finished high school. Grade twelve was a slow year for studying. Too much time spent smoking oil in the parking lot. I realized in May I didn't have a chance of passing my finals. Drastic steps were needed. The finals were kept in the school safe and I decided I was going to get them.

I arranged to have Kurt pick me up behind my house at two in the morning. He drove me to the school parking lot and dropped me off. I was dressed in black with a knitted navy watch cap on my head. Even if I was inexperienced, I was going to look the part. I climbed onto the roof with fifty feet of rope and a bag full of burglary gear.

At first I thought I'd go down one of the air vents. I managed to get one of the vent covers off with a screwdriver, which was no mean feat because I was never very mechanically inclined.

That all started with dad. He never gave me any confidence with tools. He couldn't fix a thing. Tools were his enemy. The three words that threatened to ruin every Christmas were "Some Assembly Required." Mom was usually the one to stay up on Christmas Eve and build the presents that required a screwdriver. Dad had tried one year to assemble a small pool table and managed to destroy half the basement in a fit of rage. The pool table never had a chance. I remember seeing it on Boxing Day outside in the alley beside the garbage cans, a small pile of splintered wood.

Dad was much better at cleaning the patio window, which he did religiously every Saturday. He'd scrub that window all day. And if you were forgetful enough to leave a finger smudge on it, he'd curse under his breath, or if he was in a bad mood, he'd tell you how stupid you were, and within minutes he'd be back at the window with his rag and his Windex. Mom handled the repairs in our house. Dad maintained the windows.

I sure could have used mom up on that roof. I was having a heck of a time trying to break in. I paced around for awhile just like a proper burglar, plotting the entry phase of my *break and enter*. And then I remembered. There were sky windows overlooking the library. And the library had a door that led to the office. And the office had the safe where the exams were kept. There was a two-storey drop from the sky windows to the floor of the library but that's why I'd brought climbing rope.

I got out my glass cutter and went to work. An hour later I had managed only to scratch the glass. It was ridiculous. I had a small utility glass cutter and this was half-inch industrial glass. I could've scraped for ten hours and I still wouldn't have made it. It's probably just as well. I might have fallen from the rope and been paralyzed on the library floor, where I would have stayed, crumpled in a ball, until they found me on Monday morning. It's one thing to get paralyzed in a motorcycle accident or a football game, but I would never have lived down the notoriety of being found paralyzed on the library floor, having tried to steal the exams. Come to think of it, though, it wouldn't have mattered. If I was paralyzed, who would give a shit how it happened? I would be pitied, not teased. Which is almost more cruel.

I darted home through the alleys in the wee hours of the morning. I wasn't disappointed at all. I had risked a lot going up on that roof. That had to count for something. And besides, I wasn't ready to give up.

Plan B was less ambitious. Kurt helped me again. He walked past the janitor's office and pretended he was having a fit. The janitor rushed out to help him. I dashed into the janitor's office and swiped his keys. That was easy.

Later, Kurt and I loitered around outside the main office until it was closed. Kurt tried several keys until he got inside. I was supposed to be the lookout in the hallway even though we didn't have a plan or a signal should there be trouble. I heard the awful squeaking of the cleaning cart being pushed down the hallway. And I knew where it was headed. Kurt was done for. I whistled once, for the hell of it, and waited around the corner expecting Kurt to be led out of the office in a headlock. It didn't happen. Fifteen minutes later, the cleaner emerged. Seventeen minutes later, Kurt walked out with a bunch of papers under his arm. Sweet.

We had every final exam but one. I failed social studies but passed the others with flying colours and got my nice watch from dad. Did I feel guilty that I had cheated? No. I think if I'd looked over someone's shoulder during the exam I would have felt shitty. That's cheating. But using our brains and our balls to beat the provincial examination department? That's something else.

Besides, grade twelve is when I started my spiritual quest. I didn't have time for restrictive clauses and atomic weights. I stole those exams so dad wouldn't have to be stigmatized by a son who failed high school. And also so he wouldn't have to return the expensive watch. I wonder if Gabriel's mother thinks he's a loser for quitting medical school.

Dad just came by the room. We are going on a boat ride this afternoon. Yippee.

4:12 p.m.

We just finished our boat ride. Gabriel didn't come with us. The lake was great. There's something neat about being on a big lake, surrounded by rich vegetation, here in Africa. It's not like some dumb lake back home with all the water skiers, power boats and boom boxes blasting Supertramp.

The water was a little choppy but I didn't get sick. We fished but caught nothing.

I have bad memories of dad and water. It's because of a ferry ride we took to Vancouver Island when I was seven. I was standing on the deck a good sixty feet above the water. Suddenly dad picked me up under my arms and held me over the edge. I was convinced he was going to let go. I was crying and screaming. I don't think I was scared of drowning. It was the anticipation of falling that freaked me out. Dad laughed so hard I thought he was going to pop a blood vessel.

I think he got that sadistic side from his father. Mom told me that grandpa and grandma had a cat before I was born. Grandpa refused to get her fixed because it would cost too much. She'd go into heat, get pregnant and deliver a litter. Grandpa would scoop up the kittens, put them in a burlap sack and attach the sack to the exhaust pipe of his car. Vrrrooom! Vrrrooom! Little paws pushing, pawing at the hemp. But only for a short time. Then the kittens got tossed in a garbage can in the alley. He kept the sack.

Poor grandma would just about snap from the sound of that mother cat calling for her kittens.

I remember driving out to Vancouver to visit the two of them every summer. Grandpa would sometimes chase me after he saw me take my shirt off. I'd run but I was never fast enough. He'd carry me like a prize tuna over to the holly tree and toss me into it. I'd claw my way out, bare back and bare arms bleeding. He had the same wheezing laugh. The same red face. The same vein ready to burst. Sadly, I have inherited the same gene. The proud tradition of cruelty passed from father to son. And if all goes well, my boy will pop the same vein, after he's pulled a stunt on some poor, unsuspecting sucker.

The hippos in the lake were awesome. Our first big animals. Dad has a list of all the animals we are supposed to see on the safari. The hippopotamus has now been dramatically checked off.

We got within about twenty yards of the hippos. The boat guy said that hippos were real aggressive. They'd snap you in two if they got the chance. They got several chances with us. Whenever we got too close the hippos would submerge. That was the cue for our boat guy to gun his engine. We'd fall backward as the boat lifted off and sped away, leaving a frothy wake behind us. And then we'd look back. Those damn hippos would come rising up like Moby Dick, in the exact spot we'd just vacated. The bastards were trying to capsize us. It made me nervous. It made dad nervous. All mom said was, "Incredible."

Huh?

We also saw some falcons and eagles and even a beaver. *A beaver? C'mon!* Yup.

On our way back there were all these tall, bony trees sticking out of the water. It was creepy. In the trees were the nests of giant birds. I was told what they were but I've forgotten. Vultures? Storks? The sun was dropping and these birds looked horrifying silhouetted against the darkening sky. The engine droned and I glanced at mom. She was fixated on the birds. Boy did she look serene. Too fucking serene if you ask me.

I am now going to take a bath.

8:33 p.m.

It is almost cold tonight. I love the mosquito net over my bed. Cocoon. The air is humid. Perfect.

After my bath I read for awhile, took a quick nap, then had dinner with the folks. Dad was in great spirits. I noticed he kept shooting looks at mom, assessing her, sizing her up and down. She ate all her dinner, which seemed to please dad to no end. He commented on it five times. Eventually mom said she was tired and went back to their room.

Dad and I went into a lounge room where they had a big fire burning. We sat down at a little table with three chairs. Dad was very comfortable after his third glass of wine. I was just finishing my fourth beer when the trouble started.

Some fat guy, must have been about three hundred pounds, came lumbering into the lounge. Loud and, yes, he was American. From San Francisco. He came in with his wife and went to the table right beside dad and me. There was only one chair at his table so he turned around and took our third chair. Didn't ask. Just took it. Dad, with his back to the fat man, didn't seem to notice. It was an insignificant action, but it was *our* chair. How did he know we weren't waiting for someone? Why didn't he ask if anyone was using it? He didn't say a word. He just grabbed the damn thing and sat his fat ass down at his own table.

I tried really hard to excuse him. Maybe he had a lot on his mind. Why bother with trivialities like asking dumb questions? After all, the chair wasn't being used. In all likelihood he was normally very polite and courteous. But that voice. That loud, complaining voice. He kept telling his wife how nothing was right on their safari.

I could see a bead of sweat trickling down from his ear. Fat pig. He took our fucking chair. He didn't ask. He just fucking took it.

I should have said something right away. I could have lied. *Excuse me, we're waiting for someone.* Or I didn't have to lie. *Hey! It's polite to ask if a chair is being used before you grab it. Where did you get raised? On an asshole farm?* My heart was pounding with the verbal uppercuts I was throwing in my head.

It took another beer and a bowl of cashew nuts to get the thoughts out of my head and into my mouth.

The fat man held up a bowl of nuts and called a hotel employee over. "These cashew nuts are stale," he said. "I want another bowl."

The employee smiled and bowed and took the bowl away. That's when I tapped the fat man on the arm.

"You travel ten thousand miles to a remote, unspoiled wilderness to see wild buffalo, lions, elephants, warthogs, all in their natural habitat. You travel ten thousand miles to experience the rich variety of another culture, to see tribes, to see native children, some of them starving. You travel to another world, the home of the missing link itself. You travel all this way to see all this . . . and you're worried about whether the cashew nuts are fresh?"

The fat man was taken aback for a moment.

"And you took our chair without asking," I added.

He recovered very quickly. Much quicker than I was ready for. "Listen, you little creep. Why don't you mind your own business?" he said.

I stood up. My knees could barely support me. "Why don't you make me?"

"Sit down, flat-face," he said and turned away.

"Yeah, right" was all I could manage. All I could think of. Shit. A red wave crashing down from my forehead and bathing my body in a sticky mess. Nothing else to say. Just "Yeah, right." Arms suddenly rubber. Tired.

I managed to make it to the bathroom. I splashed a handful of cold water on my face. My nearly handsome face, a face from which some might have difficulty detecting any signs of expression. Unshaven most of the time. Gentle, inviting eyes. Soft black hair curling up at my collar. Ears of normal proportion. Smooth complexion. Uneventful chin. Prominent Adam's apple. Sinewy neck. Veiny hands. Two yellow fingernails. Skinny legs. Bony feet. Everything okay. Not brilliant. But okay. And yet. There it was. The great betrayer. The remnants of the jagged ravine that carved its way between my lip and nose. Glacier. Rocky Mountains. Nature. Ice age. My cleft lip and palate. My harelip. Ha, ha, ha. All grown up now. Not a big deal anymore. Not like junior high school. Didn't have to worry about it anymore. Bullfuckingshit. Look at the fucking thing. Flat nose. Puffy lip. Making me look like an inbred, backwoods, banjo-playing, tobacco-chewing, sheep-fucking hillbilly.

The bastards wouldn't even have known what a harelip was except that dingleballs Dean Devlin let the cat out of the bag in grade seven. He had it in for me. I heard his father was a plastic surgeon. I suppose he must have asked him what the hell was wrong with the face of that Richard Clark kid. It started with "harelip" and, as the years passed, the villagers got more creative as they pursued me up into the burning castle with their pitchforks and torches. In the hallways, "Hey Bugs!" The locker room. "What's up, doc?" Yelled from a passing pickup truck, running home from school. "Wun, you wascawwy wabbit, wun!"

I felt my bowels moving. I ducked into the lone stall.

It's all okay. I did my share of teasing. There was Leslie in grade five with the big ass. Tormented her until she turned around and pitched rocks with tears streaming down her face. There was Trevor in grade seven. The little Englishman. We chased him home after school with snowballs.

The trick is to remember that Jesus was right. You reap what you sow. You tease and you get teased. I gave and I got.

Although with all due respect to the giant wheel of karma rolling around the universe and plowing people under I think I got more than I gave.

I heard someone come in the bathroom. Fuck it. Now I wouldn't be able to shit until they left. I hate that they can hear the plop of the water when my turd hits. I've waited for twenty minutes sometimes to get an empty bathroom. I know I'm an animal. I just don't like reminding myself when others are around.

The door opened again. I thought I was in the clear but it was someone else coming in.

The two men began talking at the urinals.

"How are you doing?" asked one. Christ. It was dad.

"Be doing better if this hotel had fewer punks," replied the other. Christ. It was the fat man.

"Yeah, you sure told him, alright," said dad.

I heard what sounded like water being poured on the floor and then the stamping of feet.

"Oh, hell, look what I've done. I'm sorry," said dad.

"You idiot!" said the fat man.

I heard both men do up their zippers.

"Listen, before you go," said dad. "That was my son you were talking to back there."

"I don't have time for this."

"No, no, wait a second. There's something you need to know. There are certain shortcomings you don't insult people about. Cripples in wheelchairs. Retarded kids. Guys with one leg. That kind of thing."

"What do you want?"

"An apology."

"Hey, you raised an obnoxious kid. It's not my problem. He should learn to keep his mouth shut."

"No, no, no. You're making this more difficult than it needs to be. Now you've insulted me. Now I'm going to need two apologies instead of one."

I could hear the fat man start to walk away. And then I heard struggling. Wrestling. Then a thump. A groan. Dad must have kneed him in the balls.

"Now repeat after me. I'm sorry about what I said to your son."

"Screw you," spat the fat man.

I heard gurgling. It sounded like dad was putting his forearm to the guy's throat. Jesus.

The fat man could barely speak. "I'm sorry about what I said to your son," he sputtered.

"And I'm sorry for accusing you of being a bad parent," said dad patiently.

"I'm sorry for accusing you of being a bad parent."

There was a great gush of air as the fat man was finally allowed to take a full breath. He staggered out. Dad went over to the sink, washed his hands, slowly dried them with a paper towel and left the bathroom.

I couldn't shit. I don't know whether I was more embarrassed by what the fat man called me or by the old man defending me like that.

I finally left the bathroom and found Gabriel. He was quite upset. Dad had been called into the hotel office. I guess the fat man had gone straight to hotel management.

Gabriel and I sat outside the office. I felt like I was back in high school.

"This is not good," said Gabriel.

Gabriel seemed really nervous. He asked if I had a cigarette. I gave him one. He didn't look like a person who should smoke. The cigarette was awkward in his hand — like how I look with a pair of pliers in mine.

"What did they tell you?" I asked.

"They're talking about bringing in the police."

"What?!"

"The man says your father assaulted him."

The door to the office finally opened and dad emerged. He didn't look at me or Gabriel. He didn't say a word either. He just walked on by. Jaw set. Oh boy. He looked like he'd been told he was going to jail.

Then the fat man came out. I wasn't going to but I had to. I grabbed my crotch and asked, "How's your nuts?" The fat man looked at me, spitting nails. *Go on, say it again, you fat fuck.* I'm such a lion in my mind. He disappeared into the hotel.

Gabriel got called into the office by a very stern hotel manager. I lit up a cigarette. I hoped the safari wasn't over.

Gabriel finally came back to me, obviously relieved.

"It's all okay," he said. "They managed to talk things out. The American wanted to sue. But it was his word against your father's. There were no witnesses."

Well, there was one. But he wasn't talking to nobody, no sir.

"And I'm going to bed," said Gabriel.

Gabriel started walking away from the hotel.

"Don't you guys stay here?" I asked.

"No massa. They got us down in the cages, chained at the ankles, with the chickens and the goats."

Gabriel laughed and was enveloped in the darkness.

It's a good thing dad didn't hit the fat man in the face. He'd probably have been arrested. I think I'll do a few sit-ups, have a bath, listen to some music and go to bed. I can't wait to masturbate under the mosquito net.

2:07 a.m.

I just got woken up. I can hear noises from the room next to mine. It sounds like fucking. There are many wonderful sounds on this spinning, green and blue jewel. Birds, fiddles, purring cats, frogs. But there is nothing that compares to the sweet sound of a woman approaching orgasm. Men are so controlled. Grunt. Grunt. And then a reluctant groan to announce the arrival of the semen. But not women. Their rising vulnerability. That coming release. That moment of complete and utter surrender. She's almost shouting now. I'm going to have to take a little break here.

Later

I started masturbating just in time. I came just as she came. The voices were foreign. Just as she started coming she yelled, "Christus, Christus!" Or something like that. She's probably Catholic. A foreign, Catholic woman getting fucked and having an orgasm. God I love hotel rooms. What I wouldn't give to own a hotel and have video cameras hidden in every room. That is my dream. I used to want to be a professional football player.

Sunday, August 14
12:01 p.m.
Lake Naivasha Hotel
Room 11
Kenya, Africa

Just waiting for dad to come by so we can go for lunch. Everyone was supposed to go on the lake again today to do some fishing. Dad ended up staying behind with mom. Apparently she didn't want to leave the room. He said he'd explain it all later. I wanted to have a father/son fishing excursion after last night. I wouldn't have brought anything up. But I was proud as hell. Defending me like he did. I'll never tell him I was in the stall. He'd just get embarrassed.

Gabriel ended up coming out for the fishing. I told dad that I would have been fine staying at the hotel for the morning but he insisted. He said he didn't want the day ruined by mom.

Gabriel seemed happy to be out on the lake and hinted that it was quite unusual.

"Why?" I asked.

"We just do the driving," he said. "We're really not supposed to be seen by the hotel guests until it's time to leave."

"Yeah, we certainly wouldn't want our safaris ruined by the sight of drivers wandering around unattended."

I told Gabriel about the beaver I saw yesterday. He said it was probably a water shrew, a hedgehog, a mongoose or a cane rat. No beavers in Africa. Well, whatever. It was a goddamn beaver. I don't care what he says.

We came upon a group of fishermen, standing in waist-high water, pulling nets out. Gabriel started conversing in his native tongue. I was impressed. I just smiled a stupid smile and nodded. Gabriel was probably telling them he was just showing another spoiled white guy around the lake. *He said he saw a beaver yesterday.* They all laughed. Go ahead, laugh at me, fishermen. They probably weren't laughing at me but what good is the world if it's not spinning around my head, taunting me.

Gabriel taught me the word for "hello." Jambo. So now when I pass the natives I can say, "Jambo, jambo," and feel like I really belong.

Gabriel and I found a quiet corner at the other end of the lake where he had been told the fishing was good. We baited our lines and cast them in. It was chilly. The sky was covered in one big grey cloud.

I pulled out my bowl and pinched in some hash. I took a big haul of smoke and handed the bowl to Gabriel. He smiled and shook his head.

"I think I'm in for a big adventure with the Clark family," he said.

I coughed out the rest of the smoke. "I think you are too."

He looked around at the lake. The boat rocked gently up and down. I'd try and describe the trees and the plants and the birds but I had no idea what I was looking at. It was certainly pretty but I'm not big on scenic descriptions. It wasn't the scenery that made it special, although it did make for a nice backdrop. No, it was just the mood. I felt very relaxed with Gabriel. I don't think I realized what a relief it was to be away from mom and dad for a short spell. The water lapped at the edge of the boat. Gabriel smiled. He smiled a lot. But the smile seemed genuine. Not like some people who pretend that everything's okay when inside you know they're all busted up and broken. Not Gabriel. His smile seemed like the real deal. Either that, or he had perfected the art of the graceful smile and was flying low and fast, right under my bullshit radar.

"Where are the hippos?" I asked.

"Good question."

"Maybe they're under the boat."

"They can't hold their breath that long."

Gabriel felt a tug on his line. He started reeling. In a moment he pulled in a fish almost a foot in length. Don't ask me what kind it was. It was just a damn fish. He pulled it off the hook and dropped it in the boat. It started bouncing around. It touched my bare leg. I screamed.

"What do we do?" asked Gabriel calmly.

"What?" I said. "You're the African. Kill the fucker."

"I've never killed a fish."

"Then what the hell are we doing out here?"

The fish skimmed against my leg again. I screamed again. "Get it out!"

Gabriel scooped his hands under the fish and tossed it back into the lake. I started reeling my line in.

"We're not doing that again," I said.

"No," said Gabriel.

Gabriel leaned back on his elbows and smiled up at the sky. I had two questions I was burning to ask him. We were in a boat so I asked the first one.

"How come you didn't go?"

Gabriel looked at me. This was a little test for him and me. If he knew I was asking about his father and brothers then it proved we were in tune with each other.

Gabriel started to lose it. He got tears in his eyes. And his lip began to quiver. He was on the verge of sobbing. I felt awful. I didn't want to see him get so upset. But then confusion set in. I couldn't tell if he was crying or laughing. I started to feel uneasy that I was out in a boat alone with him. Perhaps he was crazy. Crazier than mom even. Eventually, there was no question. He was laughing.

"I made it up," he finally blurted out. "There was no fishing accident. I still have two brothers and I still have a father."

I smiled. What a fucking weirdo. How could he invent something like that? Something so tragic. I didn't know whether to hug him or hit him. On the one hand, I felt I'd been duped and wasted the modest pouch of emotion I had invested in his story. On the other hand, I thought it was pretty damn cool. That he lied like that. And that he trusted me enough to tell me the truth.

"I've been doing this for five years. I take out twenty-two families a year. Do you have any idea what it's like to sit in a van with strangers for two weeks at a time? 'So, Gabriel, where are you from? What did your father do?' I decided I could either start hating all of you or I could start making things up."

"What did you tell the last family?"

"Crocodiles. Mother. Three sisters."

He covered his mouth to hide his smile. And then he got serious.

"You can't tell your parents."

"I won't. So all that stuff about medical school was bullshit as well?"

"The university story was true. I did quit two weeks before graduation."

I had my chance to ask the second question.

"Why?"

"I don't know."

"C'mon."

"I don't. I remember walking into the hospital and sitting down like I'd done for years. Watched a doctor walk in. Opened my briefcase. Got out my pen. Looked up. Something caught my eye. Saw a bird flying at the window. I saw the last few feet of its flight before it hit. It was a small, black raven. I was the only one who wasn't startled by the noise. It hit the window, sending cracks like a spiderweb through the pane, and fell from sight. I stood up. Left my books on my desk and walked out. I found the raven on the grass below the window. Still alive. Bundled it up in my jacket. Dropped it off at the zoo. Took a cab to Heathrow. Called the zoo from the airport. Heard the raven was going to survive. Got on a plane. Came back to Nairobi. What did the bird mean? It brought me back home. That's all I know."

"I want to shake your hand."

Gabriel took my hand and I shook it reverently.

"That took balls. But now you're stuck driving around rich, ignorant white folks who ask you boring questions about your family."

"I've found a solution for the boring questions. And I don't do this because I like driving."

A large heron swooped down low over the water. It turned near the boat and glided back into the sky. Gabriel's soul seemed to ignite and his eyes began to glow like the holes in a pumpkin with a flickering candle inside. He took a deep breath. It wasn't just the heron he was breathing in. It was the heron's connection to the sky, to the water, to the trees, to the other animals, well, pretty much to everything that was surrounding us. He took the whole batch in one breath.

I was going to say something stupid to spike it all to hell but I thought I'd leave Gabriel's moment alone. And besides, his "moments" didn't seem spikeable. They were pretty solid. And I know these things. I'm a professional spiker. He waited until the heron disappeared over the trees then started the engine.

On our way back to the hotel we passed a tiny island. Incredibly dark and mysterious. The foliage was so thick you'd disappear within ten feet of walking in from the beach. I would have loved two hours to go exploring. I asked Gabriel but he said that mom and dad were expecting me back for lunch. As we sped across the lake, I looked behind and watched the island get smaller and smaller.

Dad was writing postcards when I got back to the hotel. He's the only person I know who writes drafts of his postcards before he sends them out. He says it takes a few drafts to figure out exactly what he wants to say. And, more important, he's able to fit everything he wants to say onto the card without scrunching up his writing at the bottom. When he has a finished draft he writes these same words on the five or six cards he's sending out. No wonder I'm so lost.

5:25 p.m.

Had lunch with mom and dad. Mom was okay. Kind of. I think she felt bad that she was the reason dad had to stay in this morning. He would normally have reminded her about this fact all through lunch. But to his credit he never mentioned it once. It was mom who kept bringing it up. Apologizing for ruining the day. Dad patiently reminded her that the day was not ruined. It was only half over.

Dad left the table early to go get things prepared for our afternoon. This meant he had to go take a dump.

"So, you had fun this morning?" asked mom.

"I had a great time. Gabriel's a good guy."

"I didn't think you were a fisherman."

"I'm not. It's just an excuse to be out on the lake."

"I wouldn't have thought he'd go anywhere near a boat after what happened to his family."

"He made all that up."

"Nobody would make up something so terrible."

"I guess not."

Mom leaned forward and waited until I bent my head closer. *Leaning forward to tragedy.* She looked around and began to whisper.

"Your father thinks I'm crazy."

"Are you?"

"No. And don't let him tell you otherwise."

Her foot was tapping like mad underneath the table. I could hear it.

"Do you ever get the feeling that everything is crashing in on you? That no matter how hard you try, it's no use?"

I said not a word.

"Your father tried to get me to take pills this morning."

"What kind of pills?"

"Oh I don't know. Something to control my anxiety."

"Did you take them?"

"I put them under my tongue. And I spit them out after he left the room."

"Why'd you do that?"

"They make me nauseous."

"They might help."

Mom shook her head then she reached out and took my hand. We aren't a real physical family so I immediately jumped back like I'd been stung by one of her burning cigarettes, something that happened once or twice when I was a kid.

"Don't tell your father."

"About what?"

"The pills."

"Maybe you should take them."

"I won't take them. And I won't tell your father about your drugs if you don't tell him about mine."

First Gabriel. Now mom. Everyone's telling me stuff and then telling me not to tell anyone. Who the fuck do I look like? Father Mulcahy?

"Mom, you don't need to blackmail me. I'm a loyal son."

"I know you are. And you don't have to worry. I'm going to lick this thing. You'll see."

Mom got up from the table with a smile and started walking away. The smile lasted until she thought she was out of sight and then it disappeared as fast as a gopher down a hole.

Clearly I had let her down. She was looking for someone to tell her that they felt like she did. She came looking for me. She reached out to me. *Do you feel like I do? Do you get overwhelmed? Is it okay?* And what did I do? I gave her silence. Is this what we do to crazy people? We start shutting them off, making them feel different. We cut them off from those things they have in common with the rest of us. We push them away. And away they go. And, once they're gone, how do we bring them back?

People don't want to tell a crazy person that they know how they feel. Because it might mean that they're crazy too.

Of course I've felt overwhelmed. If mom had a half a brain she'd know that. What does she think my drugs are for? Not all the time. But some of the time. Maybe she knows this already. I should have said something. I should have told her I knew how she felt. But I fucking lied to her. My silence was a lie.

I can't believe what I'm writing. Things are moving too fast. Where did the pills come from? Is she so far gone that she's supposed to be on medication? Is she that crazy? I think I had a romantic notion about madness. There's nothing romantic about it. It's bad. It's bad to see someone slipping away, like a boat that's had its line to the dock cut.

We left for Hell's Gate after lunch. Gabriel told us it was a good place for viewing wildlife. He brought along a friend who had big holes in his earlobes and carried a rifle. I found out later he was a park ranger.

Gabriel dove into his description before we got there, sounding more like Vincent Price than a tour guide. He told us they call the area Hell's Gate for several reasons. The guy who used to own the area would kill anyone he found on his land and also the terrain is very desolate and when poachers were around they used to burn the carcasses once they took what they needed. You got your desolation, your killings and your fires. You got your Hell's Gate.

Dad winced and looked to see what effect Gabriel's words were having on mom. She wasn't saying a word but I could tell her anxiety was rising. Her jaw was tightening and her fingers were starting to ball up.

Along one of the dirt roads we slowed down for two tribesmen with spears. Now these were real Africans. Neither Gabriel nor the park ranger seemed interested in talking to these guys. They stopped by dad's open window and wanted to start a conversation. Dad was more than willing. I looked down and saw that both tribesmen had Nike running shoes, which ruined an otherwise primitive encounter. Gabriel sped the van away and explained that the Nike guys slaughter stray cows so the herdsmen can never leave their herd unattended.

Finally we came to a grassland. It was filled with zebras and gazelles, all of them grazing. This was the Africa I had seen on television. This got me excited. Gabriel parked the van and we all got out. Well, all except mom.

"C'mon, Janet," implored dad.

"I'm not walking out there," she said.

"It's perfectly safe, Mrs. Clark," said Gabriel.

"What about lions?" asked mom.

"Lions feed early in the morning," said Gabriel. "It's too hot during the day."

"Never mind," said mom.

"And besides," said Gabriel. "That is why I've brought along my friend with his gun. Just in case."

"No thanks," said mom.

"Jesus, Janet," seethed dad. "It's why we came here!"

I walked away from the van with Gabriel and the park ranger. It was exciting to be standing out on the grasslands. Even with the gun it was scary. There were animals out there that ate meat. They could sneak up at any moment and rip the flesh from your bones.

The conversation with mom at lunchtime had made me really depressed. I suddenly felt revitalized.

I stood and watched the zebras, maybe fifty yards away, munching on grass, tails swiping flies from their backs. It was so serene. Well, not that serene. I could still hear dad berating mom for not wanting to leave the van. I tuned them out and let the wind whip my hair.

Africa. This was Africa. Fucking zoos. I'll never set foot in another zoo as long as I live. This is where animals belong. In the wild. Not caged up for our amusement. Kids are the worst at zoos. Making all that noise. Yelling at the animals. Eating cotton candy. It's disgusting. If they have an animal that's injured and can't survive in the wild then fine, but otherwise leave the fuckers alone. And the sea aquariums. I remember when our family went to the marine thing in San Diego. Huge whales in those tiny pools. Fucking assholes.

Well they didn't get these guys. These guys were free. And we had money so we could see them. Fucking poor people. Let them look at pictures of animals in books. But don't build zoos for them. Or better yet, take a tiny portion of all the money all the nations spend on weapons and pay for each and every kid to come to Africa to see animals in the wild. For a month. Of course, it would make more sense to use this money to feed starving children but that's another good reason why I'm not running things.

I fucked a girl from England once. From a very wealthy family. She belonged to the Young Conservatives Society or some damn thing. She and her friends from the Society used to go out on weekends, drive into the bad neighbourhoods and throw rocks at the poor people. Imagine. I laughed my head off when she told me this. She was horrified with my jubilation. She thought she was confessing something terrible. I told her it wasn't terrible. It was honest. So many rich people pretend to be concerned with the plight of the poor but they're full of shit. They do fund-raisers and charity work but they're still rich fucks and they'll always be rich fucks. They pity poor people, and poor people don't need that. Better to be honest than a bleeding heart. Throw rocks not fund-raisers. Whew.

Mom eventually got out of the van. Well done, dad. She ventured about twenty yards but that was it. She wouldn't go any further. I ran over and said, "Isn't it great?"

"It's nice," she said.

Oh boy, did her face betray her words. She was terrified. Actually shaking.

"Mom! It's Africa! We're in Africa! Standing on the grasslands with zebra and gazelle!"

Mom nodded absently.

"That's enough," she said. Mom turned and walked back to the van. My enthusiasm drained quickly. She was like a vampire, sucking my spirit, swooping away. Dad came over.

"At least you got her out of the van," I said.

"Let's not let her ruin the trip, okay?" he said.

"Good idea," I said. We turned and watched the animals. Mom was back in the van.

"C'mon! Let's get going!" she yelled.

Dad and I ignored her.

"This isn't funny anymore! Get back in the van!"

I could feel dad's muscles start to tighten.

"Stop it!" she shouted.

She sounded panicked, but I didn't care. Dad sighed and started slowly back to the van. I stayed where I was. Mom was leaning out of the window, waving her hands, imploring me to return.

"Richard! You too! Get back here! It's too dangerous!"

I refused to move.

"C'mon, Richard," dad said quietly.

I finally turned and retreated to the van. I wanted to kill her.

There was much confusion during the drive back to the hotel. The park ranger thought he had done something wrong and was responsible for mom's outburst. Dad reassured him three times it was not his fault. I simmered the whole way. My sympathy for her was gone. She sat staring out the window. Her foot was dancing. She picked at her fingernails. And her frightened eyes searched the passing land for danger. I was disgusted with her. What a sorry excuse for a mother.

Riding back in the van, I was embarrassed that she was my mom. But when I was growing up, I was always so proud of her. Wanted to show her off. It was dad who I felt embarrassed about. He was the oddball, the weirdo. The guy who cleaned the windows every Saturday morning. And vacuumed the floors every Friday night. I never wanted him near me when my friends were around. I forbade him to come to my high school football games. But he snuck into the stadium once and I'm sure he regretted doing it.

It was a play-off game. The first one for our high school in ten years. I was a senior. I played defensive back. Or, more accurately, I sat on the bench and watched the other guys play. But there I was out on the field, while two injured starters sat on the bench, watching a ball that was tipped at the line. It was my chance to undo years of high school horror. I intercepted that ball. And I ran.

Eighty yards from the end zone. Our team down by four. Less than a minute left. Seventy yards from the end zone. Why did they pass it on second and one? Why didn't they call a running play? Sixty yards from the end zone. My teammates, my coach, yelling, swinging their arms like windmills. Fifty yards from the end zone. Was dad seeing this? Jesus, I hoped so. Forty yards from the end zone. Lungs burning. Legs getting weaker. Thirty yards from the end zone. Hearing footsteps behind me. Pushing harder. Twenty yards from the end zone. Remembering that statue outside Empire Stadium in Vancouver — John Landy looking over the wrong shoulder, Roger Bannister passing him. Ten yards from the end zone. Is this me?

Could this be real? Five yards from the end zone. This isn't me. Good things don't happen that easily. Right toe catching the turf. Left toe smacking into my right heel. Falling. An opposing player touching my shoulder. That's all he had to do because I was already down. Two yards from the end zone. Fourteen seconds left. Back on the bench. Two plays by our offence. No touchdown. It was over. We were seniors. We would never play football again. Nobody said a word to me. Not even the coach.

It started slowly. A drunken choir. At first I couldn't distinguish it. But gradually it grew louder and began cascading down from the stands. Guys started moving away from me on the bench like I'd shit my pants. The booze had loosened the tongues in the stands. The wobbly, wooden fence that held back the mean ones was busted down and cruelty surged across like hungry, meat-eating horses. Horses with smoke belching from their nostrils. Horses that crapped hot, orange coals. I didn't stand a chance.

Here comes Peter Cottontail,
hoppin' down the bunny trail,
Hippity, hoppity,
Easter's on its way . . .
One more time
Here comes . . .

I stole one glance at the stands. A small, surging sea of faces, singing, hands waving in the air. I thought I saw dad scuttling through one of the exits. Not a moment for the proud father to boast, "That's my boy."

The catastrophe at the two-yard line is like Mrs. Turner. Would my life be different if I had scored the touchdown? If I had been carried off the field on the shoulders of my teammates? They might have sung the song but they would have been celebrating and singing joyously. Maybe I would have been healed.

I never told dad that I saw him at the game. And obviously he never mentioned that he was there. It was our little secret. A lot of embarrassment in the Clark clan. And a lot of little secrets.

When we got back to the hotel everyone left the van quietly and we returned to our respective rooms in silence. I smoked some jude about fifteen minutes ago so I am now feeling cozy. And quite sleepy. Perhaps I will take a little nap and forget who I am.

7:43 p.m.

A couple of quick notes before I join mom and dad. Dad and I walked down to the lakefront at sunset (7:00 p.m.). It was so calm and peaceful. We heard the hum of a million mosquitoes. It may have only been fifty thousand but it sounded like a million. It sounded like bagpipes blown by an ancient wind, stuck on one note. Either wonderfully hypnotic or annoying as hell, depending on your point of view.

I could tell dad was taking me down to the lake for a talk. We tossed a few stones into the still water. I looked across the lake and saw the island that Gabriel and I had passed earlier in the day. It was even more tempting and magical hidden behind a shroud of mist.

"I wanted to talk to you about your mother," said dad.

I nodded and tossed another rock into the lake. I watched the tiny waves spread out in circles. This is what fathers and sons did at lakes. Tossed rocks. Shuffled around. Talked about stuff.

"I should probably have told you and your sister earlier but I didn't want you guys worrying and I thought it was something your mother could get sorted out on her own. But you're seeing it all first-hand now so there's no point in pretending."

Dad pulled a mint out of his pocket. Eyeballed it. Unwrapped it. And popped it in his mouth.

"Can I have one?" I asked.

"Last one," he said.

I knew he was lying. He always has extra mints. He just hates sharing them. He always says, "Last one." I've seen him say this to someone and then half an hour later, pull another mint out of his pocket.

"Your mother hasn't taken to Paris very well," he began. "She was okay for the first few months. She had lunches with the other wives, joined a pottery class, took tours of the city. But then about a month prior to Christmas I ran into one of the wives she'd supposedly had lunch with. This woman said they didn't have lunch, Janet had cancelled. Well there was something wrong with that, because the night before at dinner, your mother had given me a vivid description of her lunch with this woman — where they went, what they talked about, what she had for dessert. So I went home. It was early in the afternoon. Your mother was supposed to be at her pottery class. And I found her in bed. She said she wasn't feeling well. I asked her about the lunch. It bothered me that she had created such an elaborate lie. She said she did it to make me happy, so I wouldn't worry. She said this wasn't like before."

Dad paused here. I hate conversations like the one we were having. *If you've got something to tell me. Tell me! Don't make me feel like a newspaper reporter chasing down a story.* "She said this wasn't like before." Big pause. It was such an obvious manipulation. I was supposed to ask, "What did she mean by that?" but I didn't want to. I wanted him to just keep talking. But he wanted to be asked. So I did.

"What did she mean by that?"

"Your mother tried to kill herself after your sister was born."

Now, here was an appropriate place for a dramatic pause, for me to say, "What?" or, "Huh?" or, "Holy shit!" But he didn't pause at all. He had his little, leather flying helmet, his scarf, his goggles. He dropped his bomb and banked hard, picking up speed. I could see he wanted to get this over with.

"Her father had died while she was pregnant with Maggie and then after Maggie was born she got depressed. Clinically depressed."

"Why didn't you tell us?"

"There was no reason to. She got better and she's been fine since then. Until Paris."

I got up and walked away from him.

"You should have said something."

Dad followed me. He was getting angry.

"What was I supposed to do? Interrupt one of our Sunday bar-becues? Excuse me, Janet? Could you leave the yard for a minute? I want to tell the kids about your suicide attempt. They have a right to know you haven't always been the loving, devoted parent they think you are. Bullshit. You tell me. Have you noticed anything ter-rible about her in all your years growing up?"

"No."

I want to say I was devastated by the news about the suicide attempt. But I wasn't. I was buzzing. I was excited. Something hor-rible had been dredged up from the bog. It should have scared me. Or made me sad. But I felt none of that. Here was our family's dirty secret. Exposed. Released. You couldn't hate it. It'd be like hating a mangy dog that nobody wanted. You had to feed it. Love it. Dad was still smarting from my criticism of his years of silence. But I'd only told him he should have said something because that seemed the right response. I didn't really care that he'd kept it a secret. In fact, I kind of liked it. It was dark and dramatic — made me feel like I was in a movie.

"So don't you go questioning me about this. I only bring it up because of what's happening right now."

Dad wandered away from me. Now it was my turn to follow if I wanted to hear more.

"Your mother went missing in April for three days. I finally tracked her down. She was in a small hotel on the Left Bank. I found a half-written suicide note in the room. Another time the police picked her up wandering around on the rail lines of the Metro. She's not the type to seek attention. She certainly wasn't seeking attention when she tried to kill herself the first time."

"Who found her?"

"I did. I happened to come home from work that day."

"How did she . . . ?"

"Tranquilizers, sedatives. All the prescription pills she had for her depression."

"Why did you come home?"

Dad laughed. Not a happy laugh. An anxious laugh. The kind of laugh you expel after nearly hitting another car head-on at seventy mph. I asked the question because in all my years growing up he didn't come home at lunch once. Except for the day his father died, when he came home to pack for his flight.

"I spilled coffee on my pants. I came home to change."

What a fluke I was. I wondered, how did the coffee spill happen? Did someone knock into him? Did he trip? If that coffee hadn't spilled on his pants at exactly that moment, he would never have gone home, mom would have died and I wouldn't have been born. I owe my life to spilled coffee. I was going to ask dad about the details of the spill but he would have thought me insane, or at least selfish. I decided to ask him about Paris. That was sensible.

"What happened after the police picked her up?"

"We got her into a hospital. And she was there for four weeks. The doctors diagnosed her as having a chemical imbalance and pre-scribed medication."

"Is she still taking it?"

"She did until June and then she said it was making her nau-seous. So she got prescribed some anti-depressants and some pills to help her with her anxiety."

A question crawled out from under the debris of the dumpster. It smelled. But it begged. It pleaded. I took pity. . . .

"Can I ask you something?"

"Of course."

"What the fuck are we doing out here in the middle of Africa with her?"

I think my swearing provoked him more than the question. The back of his hand swung up. I flinched. He stopped himself. His hand dropped slowly and came to rest on his hip. His shoulders followed.

"This trip was for her. She's always dreamed of coming to Africa. She was better in May. Fine in June. By July she was really excited. Really looking forward to seeing you again. I was prepared to cancel as late as the night before we left. If I saw any signs that she was slipping I would have cancelled in a second."

"She started slipping on the plane."

"I know. And she may get worse. And if she does then we drive back to Nairobi and get the first plane back to Paris. In the meantime we'll just have to take it a day at a time. I've been giving her the anxiety pills in the morning and I think they've been helping."

They only help if you swallow them. I thought about telling him that she wasn't taking the pills. But I was damned if I was going to rat her out. But then again, my loyalty could cost her . . . her life. Very dramatic. Too dramatic. There's a hell of a lot more standing between her and suicide than those little pills. At least there better be.

"So I want you to help keep an eye on her. I'm not worried about the anxiety. It makes our little day trips difficult but at least she's not a threat to herself. However, if you start to see real signs of depression then you tell me and we'll get the hell out of here."

I nodded. Jesus. Mom really is nuts. This is serious. I was going to ask what signs of depression I should look for. But I didn't need to. Because I've got them. Not to that degree. And not all the time. But if I look at what I've got and multiply it by . . . three . . . no . . . two. . . .

"I know it's selfish but I want us to see as much of Africa as we can before we have to go back. Obviously it isn't worth putting your mom's life at risk but I think it's going to be okay and I think we're doing the right thing by being here . . . for her."

"What about Gabriel?"

"I don't want you telling him anything."

Dad stepped forward, paused, then patted me on the back. It was the closest he's come to giving me a hug in a long time.

"Your mother's still a kind, decent person and she loves you very much. She loves your sister, too. She's just having a tough time right now. And there's no need for her to know that we talked about what's been happening in Paris or the suicide attempt. Okay?"

"Right."

He stopped me and made very serious eye contact.

"I mean it. Not a word."

I was going to run an imaginary zipper across my mouth but sensed the gesture was entirely inappropriate. So I just nodded and returned the serious eye contact. This seemed to satisfy him. *Secrets with mom. Secrets with Gabriel. Load me up with one more, dad.*

"We're going to have to be as patient with her as we can, Richard," he said firmly before he trudged back up the path we'd come down. He passed Gabriel coming down from the hotel. They nodded at one another. What the hell was Gabriel doing in the hotel mixing with the masters? Dad looked so small and hunched over and tormented. His wife is mad. We are in Africa. And, like Shackleton, it is up to him when we abandon ship. The weight of all this was crushing his shoulders.

I have to admit there is a sick side of me that doesn't want to go back to Nairobi. I want to see what will happen. Part of me wants it to get dangerous. Wants it to get weird.

Dad just knocked on the door. It's time for our drinks before dinner.

10:06 p.m.

I'm on the little island. What a night. I'm actually writing by the light of the moon. How's that for a romantic image? Why do all my romantic images occur when I am alone? I'm looking at the faraway lights from the hotel across the water.

Mom came with dad for drinks. She was fine. It's almost like she knew dad had talked to me and she was proving to both of us she was okay. Whatever the reason, it was nice to have her back.

Now here's the strange thing. It started over drinks. Dad seemed angry that she was doing so well. He drank more than usual and began a slow, steady descent into despair. Alcohol does not cheer dad up.

Sunday night was always his night to tie one on. It would start with beers in the sunny afternoon. He would be quite happy, playful. We'd even toss a baseball or a football. But by evening, he was into the wine and his spirits would spiral. He looked so large during the day. But he seemed to shrink after the sun went down. Especially his head. I could actually see it get smaller. The night would always end with him in the living room, completely blitzed, listening to Johnny Cash, with his little, round head tilted slightly to the side.

Dad didn't say a kind word all through dinner tonight. He repeatedly smothered any gesture of enthusiasm on mom's part. She said she was really looking forward to tomorrow when we were scheduled to go to a new camp. Dad just looked at her with a patronizing smile and said, "No, you're not."

I sat there and simmered. *What about the patience you preached? She's trying her fucking best and you're chopping her down.*

I was so glad when dad said he was tired and was going to bed. *Good. Get the fuck out of here.*

Mom suggested we go into the lounge for coffees. I was a little nervous, thinking the fat man might be there but he wasn't.

"I don't know why he does that to you," I said. "You're making a real effort tonight and he just pissed all over it."

"Don't talk like that. I'm not one of your oil-rig friends."

"Sorry. I hate him sometimes. Tonight should have been really great. You're doing better, you seem excited about tomorrow."

"Why wouldn't I be?"

"No, you should be. I'm glad that you are."

"You're such a funny boy."

Okay. Of course. She was fine. And I was odd for suggesting there might have been anything the matter. Mom smiled and lit a cigarette. They didn't have a fire tonight in the lounge. Did they run out of wood? Did someone complain about the smoke?

I watched mom's face. The last year had aged her. But maybe that smile was real. Maybe she had decided to make the most of this trip. Maybe her little outburst at Hell's Gate was going to be it.

Maybe we'd all end up back in Paris and we'd chuckle, *You had us worried there, mom. But you really turned it around after Hell's Gate. That was the best trip we've ever had. C'mon, let's order some Chink food.* If she needed to deny what had been happening in order to put it behind her then who was I to judge?

While mom watched the smoke from her cigarette turn lazy circles I glanced around the lounge. I saw the legs first. Black nylons and black shoes. I followed up the gentle curve of the calf and up past the crossed thigh to a very short black skirt. I finally looked at her face. Real casual-like. It was the German woman from the Norfolk Hotel garden. And she was smiling. Her husband had his back to me. She bounced her foot provocatively and it could have been interpreted in no other way than a rhythm of fucking. Or at least that's how it seemed to my muddled mind. Because I can see a woman scratch her ear and I'll think it's a signal that she wants me.

Without warning, and there should have been a warning, or a sleazy slice from a saxophone at the very least, she uncrossed and recrossed her legs and in doing so, spread them slightly. Check that. She spread them a lot. Enough that I got a good look at her little black mound. She wasn't wearing panties. And she was exposing herself right in front of her husband. I looked at her face. She was quite flushed. She shot another look in my direction. Mom tapped my arm. "Are you listening to me?" she asked.

I pulled my attention away from the German woman.

"Sorry, mom."

"Do you remember how Barnaby's ears used to get in her food?"

"The big wiener dog."

"She wasn't a wiener dog. She was a basset."

"I know. Her poops glowed when I took her for walks after she got cancer."

I looked back to the German woman. She was preparing to leave. I knew she'd have to uncross her legs in order to stand up. Mom could have broken the news right then that she was a lesbian and I wouldn't have heard. The German woman did uncross her legs to get up but she managed to keep her thighs together. And she didn't look at me. Alright, so the pussy reveal was an accident. She wasn't flirting with me after all. But then again, she wasn't wearing panties. That had to count for something.

I glanced up quickly as she passed beside me, following her husband out of the lounge. Didn't even glance at me. About three seconds after she passed, a most wonderful scent arrived like a breeze. I breathed in her fragrance deeply. It was a soft scent of peaches but there was also the unmistakable musky scent of arousal. Peaches and cream. Mmmm, she must have been super horny. Oh lord. She was on her way back to her room and within minutes she would be parting those thighs for her husband and they'd be fucking. Within minutes! I was back beside Mrs. Turner's flower bed with Mr. Happy outside my shorts and the seashells over my ears.

I hadn't noticed that mom had tears in her eyes.

"What's the matter?" I asked.

"I was just remembering when we had to put Barnaby down. Your father wouldn't help. Your sister was at a piano lesson. Do you remember? You came to the vet with me?"

"I didn't go in though. I waited in the car."

"I know. But it was enough to have you drive over there with me. I'll never forget that, Richard. Poor Barnaby."

"She was a good dog. Why don't you get another one?"

"I don't really want another dog. I just miss Barnaby."

Her face started to lose some colour. Her mouth started to sink.

"Don't get all sad about Barnaby, mom."

"I won't."

She got up and kissed me on the forehead.

"Good night."

She walked away. I reached for my coffee and saw I had one good gulp left. I lifted the cup and felt a hand drop lightly on my shoulder.

"Excuse me? Do you have a cigarette?"

The accent was German. The peaches were back.

"Sure," I said and tried to place my trembling cup back on the table without spilling.

The Frau moved around in front of me and sat down. I opened my pack and she pulled a cigarette out.

"Do you have a light?" she asked.

"Yes," I said and tried to get her cigarette lit without shaking. Not successful.

The Frau closed her fingers around my trembling hand to prevent me from burning her eyebrows.

"Are you cold?" she asked.

"No."

"Nervous?"

"A bit."

"Did you see my pussy?"

"Yes."

"Did you like seeing it?"

"Yes."

"Would you like to see it again?"

Finally a breathless pause for reflection.

"But you're married."

"My husband will be there."

I don't know why this didn't upset me. But it didn't.

"So he'll watch us."

"Yes."

"Do what?"

"Whatever we want."

I was smiling like a fool at this point. This was real. She wasn't fooling around.

"Is this something you like? Or is it something he wants you to do?"

"It's something we've talked about."

"That's not what I'm asking. Are you doing this for him? Because if you don't enjoy it then I don't want to do it."

"Do you always know if a woman will give you pleasure before you make love to her? How can I answer that question? Perhaps you are awkward and difficult in bed. Perhaps you are too nervous to perform. Who knows? You are taking the mystery away with all your questions."

She got up.

"We are in room nine. If you are not there in five minutes we will assume you are not coming and would ask that you not change your mind half an hour from now because we will be asleep."

She brushed by my elbow on her way past. Room nine. That was the room right beside mine. She was the one I heard last night calling for "Christus." The scent. Her sound. I was beyond thinking rationally.

I knew if I thought too much I would convince myself the whole thing was crazy, so as I walked down the hallway I kept my mind empty. I also knew if I paused at the door I might chicken out. This was not going to be a replay of Mrs. Turner. I tapped lightly. Then I panicked and almost bolted. But the door opened quickly. It was her husband. He smiled warmly and ushered me inside.

We stood awkwardly for a moment. He looked at me and nodded. "Outstanding," he said. Then he offered his hand. I offered mine. He shook it vigorously.

"Can I get you a drink?"

"Sure," I exclaimed, my voice way too high for my own liking. I made a conscious effort to lower it, to sound relaxed.

There were two brandies on a little table. I looked around for his wife. I noticed the door to the bedroom was closed. We sat down.

"How has your safari been so far?"

"Good. Yup. We went to Hell's Gate today. Saw some zebras. We're off to Lake Baringo tomorrow."

I was going with "yup." I didn't want to get too familiar. "Yes" was too familiar. "Yeah" was halfway. But "yup" was a safe distance.

"We stayed there last year. Outstanding. You'll have a wonderful time. You're travelling with your parents?"

"Yup."

"Your mother seems a little anxious."

Was it that noticeable? Christ almighty.

"She's been a bit nervous," I acknowledged.

"We saw you in the garden at the Norfolk. You were writing in a journal. Are you keeping a travel diary?"

"Just bits and pieces."

"Outstanding. Will you write about this?"

"Maybe."

"Well, if you do, perhaps I could give you our address in Hamburg and you could photocopy the portion that pertains to tonight and mail it to us. Hmmm?"

"No way. Can't do that. Nobody reads my journals." I was starting to get irritable. Too many goddamn questions. "Listen," I said. "I don't really want to get to know you guys. I mean, if this is going to happen, the less I know about you two the better."

"You wish to dispense with the small talk?"

"And the big talk. I just don't want to talk much."

"I understand. But I do want to put your mind at ease about one concern. My wife mentioned you were worried that she was merely a whore to my fantasies."

"I didn't say it like that."

"No. But the meaning was clear. Your concerns are commendable. But I assure you, the pleasures obtained from this unusual rendezvous are mutually shared."

"So, you've done this before?"

"Of course. Many times."

I nodded. I felt even more pressure. They'd probably had some real stallions. Aryan stallions with monster dongs. The German sipped his brandy and studied me. He was making me nervous.

"So what happens? Do you join in or how does that work?"

"I don't participate."

"So you just sit there and watch us . . . and jerk off?"

The German started to laugh.

"Greta told me you liked everything planned in advance. She was right."

"No. I just want to make sure when I'm on top of your wife you don't sneak in behind and start poking around my butt."

The German laughed again.

"I won't come near."

I drained the last of my brandy.

"I'm ready," I said, sounding like a soldier about to have a bullet removed from his knee.

I got up and walked over to the bedroom door, half expecting to hear his footsteps behind me and a knife plunging into my back. *So, you've done this before? Of course, many times.* Goddamn serial-killing Germans.

I swung the door to the bedroom open. It was dark inside but there were two or three candles burning. My eyes slowly adjusted. I saw the Frau sitting in a chair in the corner of the room. She was still dressed. Her foot was bouncing as before. I stood there a moment.

"So how are you doing?" I asked too loudly.

"Shhh," she whispered.

I went and sat down on the bed. My mouth was dry. I was hoping I wasn't going to have a replay of the time I tried to lose my virginity with a prostitute. I was sixteen and decided if I was going to do it, I might as well do it with a professional. I sold my record collection, worth about two hundred dollars, and set off for downtown where I knew the girls were on the street. On the way, I stopped and bought a basket of strawberries.

I picked up a cute brunette. She took me to a trashy hotel where she proceeded to wash my penis and testicles in a sink with soap and water. "Proper hygiene," she said. I felt like a patient getting washed by a nurse who didn't like patients too much. She led me to the bed, whipped her clothes off, rolled onto her back and spread her legs. There was some awful afternoon game show on the TV.

I had thought we might go back to my place, listen to some music, talk, maybe take a bath, feed strawberries to one another, and then we'd do it. No way. She didn't have time for strawberries. She was a third-act girl all the way. She tried for twelve minutes to charm my worm into a snake but I was just not happening. It was too fast. Too cold. And the crowd on the TV was yelling too loudly to take door number two. She got dressed quickly and had me drop her back downtown.

That was it. Two hundred dollars. For nothing. I sat on my bed in the dark that night and stuffed those strawberries into my mouth as fast as I could to keep from crying.

I could hear the Frau breathing. The waiting was agony. I could barely make out her face. Her legs were crossed like they'd been in the lounge.

"Do you want to see it?" she asked.

"Yes," I said.

She uncrossed her legs, leaving them parted.

"I can't see. It's too dark."

She paused, got up and walked over to me. The peach fragrance enveloped me like warm water in a bath. I was still sitting down. She stood, inches from my face. Slowly she started to lift up her skirt.

"Do you want to see it?" she asked again, this time a little more breathlessly.

"Yes."

It wasn't long before the curtain rose and I had the star of our conversation right there in my face. She kept it nice and trim. I could've roasted a marshmallow in front of her small furnace.

God, she was patient. I guess because she was older. I was completely at her mercy. No girl had ever asked me if I wanted to see her vagina. I've only been with that rich, English girl and three young cooks from the oil patch and they were so damn drunk and nervous they made me nervous. Not the Frau. She was calm and slow. Breathtakingly slow.

"Would you like to kiss it?"

"Yes."

"Help yourself," she whispered.

I started to lean forward. Her husband walked into the room. He went and sat in the chair his wife had just vacated. I couldn't see whether he was dressed or not. I started to lose my nerve. She sensed this.

"Kiss it," she demanded.

I leaned forward and kissed it. She started to breathe more heavily. She stepped back and undid her zipper. Her skirt shimmied down to the floor. She slowly turned in a circle letting me look at the crotch-less nylons she was wearing. Trashy on some women. But they looked damn good on her. I reached out but she backed away. She undid her shirt and this too fell to the floor. She took my fingers inside her mouth and soaked them. Next she took my wet fingers and slid them underneath her black lace bra so I could touch her hardened nipple. She undid her bra and freed her breasts, which sagged a bit from middle age, but her nipples were wunderbar. You could've hung a heavy jacket on a coat hanger from either one of them. She came forward and offered a nipple to my mouth. I suckled it greedily like a newborn.

"There's my baby," she cooed.

I was lost. Completely and utterly gone. Eventually she tugged me off the bed. Her disrobing had been slow and sensual. Mine was fast and frantic. She pulled my shirt over my head and went straight to my jeans. Zzzzzp. Pop. Slide. She got down on her knees and tickled the outside of my underwear. Her fingers tucked inside the elastic and she yanked them down. I popped out.

"Outstanding," said the German.

His voice interrupted my rapture. My eyes had now completely adjusted to the light. He was in the chair with his bathrobe undone. And he was jerking off. I knew he would. But there was something terribly wrong about what I saw. Most men masturbate with their fist. He made do with his thumb and forefinger. That's all he needed. It was as small as a pen cap or half a cigarette. Boy did I feel huge. It all made sense to me. She must have really loved this man to stay with him, having a wiener as small as that. And he must have really loved this woman to allow her to get plowed by normal men from time to time. I felt a real kinship. He had his pen cap. And I had my harelip. This was alright. Somewhere in the universe, god was smiling.

The Frau and I fucked for twenty-five minutes. A record for me. I have never been as connected as I was with her. I didn't want it to end. And finally, when I could no longer control the surge from my constricted balls, she looked right at me and told me how beautiful I was. I started to cry. I couldn't help myself. I didn't sob or make blubbering noises. That would have been lame. But tears spilled from my eyes as my sap spurted inside her. She kissed the tears from my eyes.

When it was over, it was really over. I could sense that they wanted me out of the room so they could go to sleep. She helped me get dressed, pecked me on the cheek and turned away.

The German saw me to the door and shook my hand, "Outstanding," he said. Don't know if he shot his load or not. Don't care.

My legs barely supported me as I walked to my room. I am too sensitive. They had fun. I had fun. And yet I felt lousy. I wanted to stay with her. I wanted to spend the night with her and wake up in the morning and do it again. But she loved her husband. And he loved her. I was just a visitor. An alien. I'd just experienced the best sex I'd ever had but I couldn't shake the dark cloud that had surrounded me.

From my window I could see a corner of the lake. It was dead calm. There was a canoe down by the hotel's boat launch. Right then I knew what I had to do.

I got lucky. Someone had left an oar in the canoe. I pushed off and began paddling out into the lake toward the little island I had seen when I was with Gabriel. I don't know why but I felt like I was stealing. The boats are there for the guests. So what if it was late at night?

What an experience getting here. The water was a little choppy but I love canoes. Just that simple action of dropping a paddle into the water, drawing it gently back and silently moving forward. Glop. Swish. Glide. Cause. Effect. Marvellous.

I felt like a voyageur.

It didn't take long before the nose of my canoe bumped up onto the sand of the little island. I climbed out onto the beach. My depression had passed.

The appeal of the danger silenced any fears I may have had. And the dangers in paddling out here to the island were real. Remain real. The hippos tried to capsize our power boat yesterday. Be a hell of a lot easier to tip a canoe. I shouldn't be thinking about this now. I still have to paddle back.

1:38 a.m.

I thought about poking around the island. I got as far as the tree line and had to stop. The moon provided adequate light on the beach. But it did squat once the trees took over. It was awfully dark in there. I almost forced myself to walk into the darkness. To wander around in those black groves. Perhaps to find a special meaning or something. But I didn't. I chickened out.

I told myself I hadn't come out to the island to explore it. I'd come out to the island to come out to the island. Period. I had to silence that voice that was daring me to go into the trees. So, I took a dump. Right there on the beach. It was the first time I've ever moved my bowels outside. Cue trumpets. I covered the turd in sand and stuck a stone on top — a ceremonial marker. Not quite the same as conquering the black forest. But something.

It was shortly after this that I made my shocking discovery. My canoe was gone. I could see the ridge in the sand where it had been resting. Something had dragged it out into the water.

Either that or I didn't pull it up far enough onto the beach and it drifted away.

And so here I sit writing by moonlight. On a rock. I am tired. I want to return to my room and climb into some clean sheets. But now that I have kicked the crap out of my blues I do not have a clue what to do. Do I try and swim back? Christ, I don't even want that idea in my head. Do I wait until they come for me in the morning? Dad will go to my room and find it empty. He will freak. Mom will freak. I probably alerted the hippos on my way over and now they are just waiting for me to try and swim back. I keep forgetting I am in Africa and there are animals here who will hurt me. How could I lose a fucking canoe?!

2:20 a.m.

Just after I finished writing, I started walking up and down the beach. And that's when I saw it. It was sitting out in the water about seventy yards from the island. It looked tantalizingly close. Then I remembered I wasn't a very good swimmer and suddenly it looked really far away. Screw it, I thought, in thirty seconds I'd have my canoe back and a story to tell the boys at work.

I stripped down to my underwear and stepped into the water. It was damn cold. The worst part about cold water is when it hits the sensitive area of your skin just below the underarms.

I gasped and began to thrash through the water wildly. Images of horrible, prehistoric creatures rising up from below suddenly filled my mind. Funny. I should have been thinking about hippos, maybe snakes or even that goddamn beaver. But I wasn't. It was the other creatures, the grotesque ones never seen, the ones who hide in the mud, snickering and scheming in the darkened depths. These were the ones that forced me back to the beach.

I didn't have long to mourn my failed attempt to rescue my canoe. I heard somebody laugh. I saw a small boat getting closer. I thought about running and hiding, thinking it might be someone from the hotel. And then I heard a voice call my name. I peered out. The smile was unmistakable.

Gabriel started rowing us away from the shore.

"How did you know where I was?" I asked suspiciously.

"I saw you taking the canoe."

"Why didn't you stop me?"

Gabriel shrugged. I looked at my watch. Damn thing was fogged up but still ticking. "That was over four hours ago. What the hell took you so long? I could have been killed."

Gabriel thought I was serious in spite of my smile.

"Is that what you wanted?" he asked, and pointed to a group of crocodiles lying barely submerged not thirty feet from my canoe.

"You are very lucky," said Gabriel, as he tied a line to the canoe and dragged it along behind us.

I have to admit, the sight of those crocs put a chill down my spine. I'm still not sure what I would have done if Gabriel hadn't come along. I wonder if I would have tried a second time for the canoe?

"So who am I to worry about more? You, your father or your mother?"

"Gabriel, I wasn't trying to kill myself. I got it in my head to canoe out to the island. I didn't plan on losing the damn thing."

Is that what you wanted? Just row the boat, fool. Still, I don't know if I was more rattled by the sight of the crocodiles or having been "rescued" by Gabriel. It made the whole excursion seem a little lame. I would rather have had my trip to the island go undetected.

I'm always doing dangerous things. I remember once in the oil patch I climbed out of a pickup truck doing sixty mph down a gravel road. I crawled across the hood of the truck and climbed back in the other window. The guys laughed and thought I was crazy. Perhaps I've got a subconscious desire to die young and have a dashing corpse.

I was so elated on the island. What happened? Gabriel happened. Fucker.

We coasted back to the dock. Gabriel tied up the boat and the canoe. He also took both paddles as if I was going to go back out there again.

"I'll see you tomorrow morning, Richard," he said.

"Yeah, good night." *Good riddance.*

I should have thanked him for coming to get me but I didn't feel like it.

I got back to my room expecting to find a note on the door from dad saying, "Where are you? Come to our room." But there was no note. He used to leave me notes on the fridge when I was a kid. They'd say, "Shovel the walk." They were signed, "The Führer." And he always put a swastika at the bottom. That still makes me laugh.

I've settled under my mosquito net. It is almost three o'clock in the morning. I have chased away the dark clouds. My boat ride with Gabriel has not ruined my mood. I paddled a canoe to the island! In the middle of the night! So what if I got a ride back. So what if Gabriel's got his head up his ass. I am so fucking tired. I won't even wank tonight. Sweet dreams.

Monday, August 15
10:17 a.m.
En Route — Lake Naivasha to Lake Baringo Camp
Kenya, Africa

I am sitting in the back of the van. It's very hard to write with all this goddamn bouncing around. Gabriel just caught my eye in the rearview mirror. He pretended he was scribbling in the air and then he held his thumb up. *You are putting your thoughts and feelings down on paper and that is good.* I guess that's what he meant. Dad didn't see the scribbling part of Gabriel's pantomime. Just the thumb. So dad just gave him a thumbs-up. *Back at ya, brother.*

I woke up at seven and had a bath. Dad and I walked down to Lake Naivasha before breakfast and encountered a mad crab. The crab blocked our path to the lake and reared back on its hind legs in an attack position. The damn thing scared us off. We turned around and came back to the hotel. I'm glad no one saw.

Dad was in great spirits. I was feeling good myself. Still buzzing from my little excursion last night. I heard the German couple going at it this morning but I didn't stick around to listen. Her sounds made me angry. How the hell could he make her moan like that with that dick of his? Maybe he sticks it up her bum. Who knows.

Mom didn't show up for breakfast, which should have been an indication that this morning was not going to go well.

We packed up our stuff and left Naivasha in the van a little after eight. We saw some gazelles and made our first sighting of baboons. Dad got out his checklist and stroked them off with a pencil. Hee hee. What a wiener.

At one point dad belched so loud that Gabriel's shoulders jumped. I hope he doesn't think that dad's a pig. It was just dad's way of letting Gabriel know he was comfortable with him, like he was almost part of the family.

We cruised along, passing more native Africans, who continued to stare with hatred. Dad doesn't reach for his video camera anymore. We've given up trying to wave.

I was standing in the back with my head sticking up through the observation hole, enjoying a smoke, when Gabriel suddenly slammed on his brakes, sending a huge cloud of dust into the air and almost decapitating me. I thought we had hit something.

We all got out. A huge turtle was crossing the road. It was so enormous I could have ridden on its back. I was pretty amazed. Dad got upset because there were no giant turtles on his animal list. He fixed that by writing one in and then checking it off.

I turned to mom. "What do you think?" I asked excitedly.

"It's a big turtle crossing the road," she said.

"Yes, it's really nothing. We shouldn't have stopped. You can see this kind of thing anywhere," I said.

I was so pissed off. How dare she spike my enthusiasm like that? I made a vow never to get excited about anything around her again. We all piled back in the van. I was suddenly in a rotten mood. I cursed her from behind.

What the hell had happened to her? She was a stranger in the van. What a contrast to the woman who used to make silly faces behind dad to get Maggie and me to smile for Christmas pictures.

Dad's pictures were the same every year. Maggie and I would stare off at a crack in the ceiling with fraudulent expressions of wonder on our faces. He hardly ever photographed us looking at the camera. We always had to be looking off at something and contemplating . . . something. The best picture dad ever took of Maggie and me was when mom gave him the finger behind his back. No one ever gave him the finger. We were shocked. And thrilled. And the picture captured that. Mom? Where have you gone?

We bounced along in the van. I saw that mom was craning her neck to look at the instrument panel.

"We're almost out of gas," she said.

Gabriel glanced down at the gas gauge. "Oh, we've got plenty. Three-quarters of a tank."

Mom sat back and thought for a moment. "We're going to run out of gas and we're all going to die," she announced.

"Nobody's going to die, Janet," said Gabriel. "We have plenty of gas."

Janet? That's a little familiar isn't it, Gabriel?

"We're going to run out of gas," she confirmed again.

Dad was so busy trying to enjoy the passing terrain, the rolling hills, the splendour that is Africa, he didn't even notice the ease with which Gabriel used her first name. I could see dad trying to shut mom's voice out.

"We're all going to die," she said again.

Dad blew. "Goddamn it!" he bellowed. "Will you look at the gas gauge! It says there's three-quarters of a tank! Not almost empty! Three-quarters of a tank!"

Dad slapped the gas gauge for good measure and settled back in his seat, confident that reason had prevailed. But mom looked at dad like he had a screw loose.

"The gas gauge is broken," she said quietly. "And we're all going to die."

I watched Gabriel's eyes in the rearview mirror. He kept glancing nervously back at mom. I smiled. Poor Gabriel. He created false histories to give his tours some spice. No need for that nonsense here. This tour had pepper flying everywhere. And I had a feeling Team Clark was just doing warm-up stretches. We hadn't even started the game.

"Mr. Clark, there's a gas station just up the road. It wouldn't be a problem to stop and fill it up the rest of the way."

Dad struggled with what to do. Should he give in to mom's insanity and appease her fears or stand firm and tell Gabriel to drive on? He got soft.

"Whatever," said dad.

The gas station was in a town that would never have been on any tourist map. This wasn't the Africa that Wimpole Tours wanted you to see. We're supposed to see exotic animals not human suffering. There's poverty and then there's African poverty. This gloomy town consisted of dirt and shacks. And the people. The people were numb. Their faces were hopeless/helpless. Take your pick. I'm sure we looked like George, Jane and Elroy Jetson descending on this desolate dust bowl in our shiny white craft with its glistening hubcaps.

Gabriel got out to pump gas. Mom squinted at all the townspeople milling around the van.

"There's blacks everywhere," she exclaimed.

"We're in Africa, Janet," said dad. "There are supposed to be blacks everywhere."

The children started tapping on the windows.

"Jesus!" mom shouted. "They're going to kill us."

"They're just children!" yelled dad.

They were just children, but there were a lot of them. And more were coming. Before long we were surrounded. Mom's anxiety spread like a gasoline fire through the van.

"Where the hell is Gabriel?" asked dad.

Even I started to get wound up. Mom's eyes darted nervously around the sea of tiny black faces. They were all talking and shouting but their voices were muffled behind the closed windows and we couldn't understand a word they were saying. If we had been a normal family, all these children would have been unusual but not threatening. As it was, mom's fear had poisoned us all. The group of children had become an angry, seething horde bent on destroying us.

"We're all going to die," mom said again.

Dad and I said nothing. We were surrounded. And it suddenly felt dangerous. I decided to take action.

"Dad! Give me your mints!"

He looked at me like I had asked him to fall on a grenade.

"Just give them to me."

He fished in his pocket and pulled out his mints. He inspected them before handing them to mom, who in turn handed them to me. We had formed a chain just like prairie settlers had done, handing pails of water from one person to the next to put out a fire in the barn. I looked at the two mints.

"That's it? Where are the rest?"

"In my luggage," he said. "But you leave my goddamn suitcase alone!"

I rolled my window down a few inches. The shouting of the children invaded the van. I tossed the first mint. There was an explosion of activity as the children scrambled to find it. Tiny hands began reaching inside. I couldn't toss the other mint. Their hands were blocking the opening. The sound of the children's voices was deafening.

"Shut the window!" yelled dad.

Mom buried her face in her hands and began to weep. In a panic, I poked the remaining mint through the opening. It fell to the ground. There was another explosion of shouting and wrestling as the children scrambled to get the mint. I thought about what else I had. I flung my pack of cigarettes outside and managed to get my window rolled up without severing any small fingers.

A small riot began. The children began rocking the van back and forth. We were actually being lifted from one set of tires to the other. It felt like we might tip over. The kids were having fun. They were all laughing. But we were the Clarks. Hysterical and insane. Dad was waving at the children with his hands, hoping his frantic gestures would get them to stop. I think he inadvertently got them rocking faster. The kids probably thought we were having the time of our lives. Mom slid down to the floor of the van, moaning. Finally, Gabriel pushed his way through the children. He climbed in and shut the door. He calmly started the engine and we roared off. I looked back to see if we had run anyone over.

Dad was angry with Gabriel.

"Where were you?" he demanded.

"I was getting aspirin," said Gabriel. "I've got a headache."

I could see that dad wanted to criticize him for his bad timing, for both the headache and the aspirin purchase but he kept his mouth shut. Mom crawled back into her seat. The noise of the children was now replaced with the soothing sound of the engine and the squeak of the shock absorbers as we pounded down another dirt road. I felt responsible for the riot.

"Sorry, Gabriel," I said. "I shouldn't have tossed the mint."

"I'm the one who should be sorry. We should never have stopped there," replied Gabriel.

"It's all my fault," said mom.

There was silence for a moment.

"Am I supposed to chime in here at some point?" asked dad.

"If you like," said Gabriel.

"I'm sorry that I didn't tell you to just keep driving. It's all my fault. Anything else that anyone needs to apologize for?"

There were no takers. Mom cocked her ear in the direction of the left front wheel. "What's that noise?"

"What noise?" asked Gabriel.

I could hear something as well, a clicking sound.

"It's just the wheel, it's okay," said Gabriel.

"You're sure it's bolted on tight enough?" asked mom.

"No, Janet, it's not," declared dad.

He looked at his watch and held it up for mom.

"In fact, in about four minutes that wheel is going to fly off and we're going to somersault off the road. And that mob of children is going to catch up to us. Except this time they will carry machetes. And one by one they will hack us to pieces, leaving you, Janet, for last."

We rode along, nobody saying anything. After a few minutes mom piped up again. She'd been thinking.

"Why would they leave me for last?" she asked.

"I don't know," said dad. "Because you're out of your fucking mind and that just seems to be the way it should happen."

At one point we passed a military truck carrying Kenyan soldiers with guns.

"This is it," mom announced.

None of us were interested in reassuring her. So she was left alone to ponder what a group of twenty-five black adults with automatic weapons might do to us.

12:25 p.m.
Lake Baringo Camp
Tent 7
Kenya, Africa

We arrived at the dock on Lake Baringo and waited for the boat that would take us to our island camp.

Me, dad and Gabriel got out of the van and stretched our legs. Mom stayed inside. Dad went back to talk to her. He was trying to be nice.

"Why don't you get out and get some fresh air?" he asked.

She was trembling uncontrollably. Dad stood there beside the open door. He started trembling as well. But the father of his tremors was not fear. *We're going to have to be as patient with her as we can, Richard.* He grabbed her by the arms and began shaking her.

"When did your mind snap!?" he yelled.

"You're hurting me," she cried.

I moved away from the van to the water's edge. I fumbled for my cassette player and earphones and drowned out the shouting with music. I wondered if dad might call off the safari right then and there. I glanced back at the van a couple of times. He had let go of her arms and was no longer yelling, but his new voice — steady, measured and lethal — was more intimidating.

That voice scared me. It was the voice I associated with the time he whipped me. It happened when I was ten. I had stolen a twenty-dollar bill from his wallet. I figured he'd never notice. He asked mom, Maggie and me if one of us had "borrowed" money from his wallet. I lied. Told him I didn't touch it.

I took the money and went with Alex Cooper to Woolco. I felt like a rich kid. We rode bumper cars and I bought two Elvis Presley albums. The crime would never have been solved except I made a stupid mistake.

After I got back from Woolco I took a bath. I was soaking in the tub when mom came in to take my clothes down for a wash. (Just like the hash oil before she left for Paris. You'd think by then I would have learned.) She emptied the pockets of my jeans.

Mom has had a tough history with my pockets. I remember I had Alex and Kurt over one lunch hour. They looked out and saw mom picking at my jeans in the backyard. They asked me what she was doing. I told them she was getting my boogers out of my pockets before she washed them. I thought all little boys put boogers in their pockets and all mothers picked them out before washing. I thought wrong. They were made nauseous and could not finish their grilled cheese sandwiches.

Mom didn't find any boogers in my pockets but she did find twelve dollars and sixty-two cents, my change from the Woolco spree. I lived on a fifty-cent allowance so, naturally, she asked where I got such a princely sum. I was caught completely off guard. Plus I was naked. I had no answer. She knew that I had stolen dad's twenty-dollar bill. I begged and sobbed much like I had done when I won my acquittal for the bookmobile break-in. But mom wasn't hearing any of it. That was the longest afternoon of my life, waiting for dad to come home from work. He wasn't upset that I'd stolen the money. He was furious that I had lied. The voice that was trying to get mom out of the van was the voice that I heard that night.

"Get upstairs and get naked," he demanded.

I knew what this meant. He had this thin, black leather belt. And he had threatened me with it before but he'd never used it. I don't think mom wanted me whipped. I could see that much in her expression.

I walked up those stairs crying, pleading with him not to whip me. And to think there were men like Gary Gilmore who faced their punishment without so much as a whimper. And he was being executed. With guns no less. Jesus. He didn't even want a hood for the shooting. He wanted to look his executioners in the eye.

I stripped down in my bedroom and waited for dad. That was the worst part. Being naked. Vulnerable. Waiting. It was humiliating.

I stood by the bed and pinched my ass. I pinched it as hard as I could, trying to prepare myself for the sting of the belt. At last I heard dad's shoes on the stairs. He was coming up. He went into his closet and I heard the clink of the hangers as he took the belt down. Did Gilmore hear a similar sound? The click of the rifles as the safeties were released?

Dad appeared in my room.

"Get on the bed," he ordered.

I was sniffling. I lay down and buried my face in the pillow. I waited. The first lash arrived with a smack of hot, searing pain. I reacted immediately by trying to cover my ass with my hands. He pushed them aside and continued lashing, emphasizing each lash with a word.

"Don't . . ." *Tschh!* "you . . ." *Tschh!* "ever . . ." *Tschh!* "lie . . ." *Tschh!* "to . . ." *Tschh!* "me . . ." *Tschh!* "again." *Tschh!*

He turned and left my room, slamming the door as he left. I lay on the bed for an hour. I finally got up and gingerly inspected my ass in the mirror. It was streaked with red swollen marks. I touched the marks. They burned.

I never hated dad for that. I had lied and he had punished me. Honesty became a high priority for me afterward; a priority that sometimes rubs people the wrong way. They can blame dad.

It's funny. He looked so angry the night be whipped me and yet he seemed to be in control of himself. He seems way more out of control here in Africa. I think the stress of mom's situation has really messed him up.

I remember how we used to hold hands when we watched television together. I can't remember how old I was when that stopped. I usually think of him as such a bastard but he used to have his tender moments.

Dad went for a long walk down the road, leaving mom shivering inside the van, Gabriel sitting on a boulder retying his boot laces and me humming to music that I really wasn't paying attention to.

The boat finally arrived. I was surprised to find out that Gabriel wasn't coming with us.

Gabriel patted me on the back. "Good luck out there," he said.

"Why aren't you coming?" I asked.

"My job is to drive the van."

"Who's going to save me if I try and kill myself again?"

Gabriel looked at me like I was serious. *Prick.* He nodded at my journal under my arm. "Don't lose that," he said.

Gabriel got back in the van and drove off. I forgot to ask him where he was going. Perhaps he would return to Nairobi for a few days before coming back to collect us. Perhaps he wouldn't come back. Maybe he would ask to be reassigned. I wouldn't blame him if he didn't come back. I felt a real loss as the van turned a corner and disappeared. I clutched my journal tightly and watched the arriving boat with a dark foreboding. Gabriel's presence had somehow kept a lid on things. Would that lid now pop off?

The boat ride to the island was long. Mom stayed inside the covered cabin with her fists clenched and fingers curled. I ended up getting seasick. And dad paced the deck like Captain Queeg, wondering what the hell had gone wrong with his family. I was a puking wimp and mom was a lunatic.

We arrived at the island and were met by Beverly, the Baringo Camp manager. Beverly is very plump, very white and very Scottish. She welcomed us warmly and told us to holler if we needed anything. I almost hollered that I wanted to bury my face in her huge breasts but I didn't. She has massive honeydews. Wow.

The island is pretty sweet. There are only about twenty tents here. There are stand-up showers behind each tent. But there's no running water so you have to tell the camp when you want to have a shower and they send a little guy around to fill the water drum. Not a big guy. A little guy. Even if he's six feet he's a little guy. He's here to serve the rich. Other than the shower and the outhouse, things are the same as any hotel. There's a great restaurant and an outdoor bar.

Right now I am outside my tent looking out at the lake. It's more like an ocean. It's huge. I can't see land across the water. My tent is the size of a small house. When dad said we were going to be staying in tents at Baringo I thought we would finally start roughing it. But who wants to rough it when you can live like royalty? I have a little balcony in front of my tent and this is where I am sitting. I'm going to like Baringo.

I barely ate anything at lunch. Mom seemed to find a little peace of mind. She was just grateful we made it to the island without sinking. She ate more than me. I was wiped after lunch so I told dad I was going to take a nap. And that's just what I'm going to do.

1:20 p.m.

I was in a deep, meaningful sleep when I heard a voice.

"Richard, wake up."

My eyelids fluttered open. I looked toward the front of the tent, where the balcony was, where anybody who was calling me should have been. There was nobody there.

I thought for a moment that maybe I had called out in my sleep. Eventually I noticed the back of someone's head right outside one of the side-window flaps beside my bed. I couldn't tell who it was. I pulled the sheets up to my chin.

"You're going on an island tour by yourself. Your mother's not up to it."

Dad never once turned around. He just marched off. Strange man. He used to pay me a quarter to cut his toenails.

3:05 p.m.

My guide's name is Sedekia. He brought along two of his friends, Tom and William. Sedekia is the son of the tribal chief or elder or whatever they're called. I followed him through underbrush and up mountains (well, big hills anyway). Sedekia is fucking brilliant. He is all of eight years old.

I can't begin to describe the thrill of walking behind these three boys as we cut our way through the trees. They were all dressed in native clothing. I was cynical enough to think for a moment that they did this for the benefit of the tourists. I felt like I had stepped into a time machine.

Sedekia is the leader of our little expedition. He had a walking stick that he used to prod leaves and twigs in our path. That's what island expedition leaders did, I suppose. Nothing was said at the outset of our journey. We all walked in silence. If I ever wanted to experience Africa then those initial moments with the three boys may prove to be the highlight of the trip.

For about thirty minutes the only sounds were the cracking of twigs under our feet and the occasional cry of a bird or some other creature. I was the last in line as we wound our way through the brush. I took advantage of being the caboose and discreetly smoked four bowls. My mind grappled with the beauty that surrounded us. I struggled to find some means of expressing it.

I realized, as I walked, that words had a way of destroying beauty by trying to capture it. It was kind of like trying to keep a great white shark in captivity. The shark always died.

I was trying to think of something profound to say to my young guides, something to express my rapture, but I eventually chose silence. And I'm glad I did. These kids don't need some arrogant interpretation of beauty from a drug addict. They live here. They don't need it defined.

We walked for a long time and I thought of many things. I was high as a kite and my mind was feeling very frisky.

I pictured that great white shark turning belly up in a tank and I thought about how much I hate experts who have an opinion and try to sell it as gospel: experts that news shows roll out to tell us "how it really is" — military experts, hunger experts, brain experts, whatever. What qualifies these people to get an appearance fee and a graphic at the bottom of the screen that says "expert"? Were they know-it-all assholes when they were kids? Are they friends with the show's producer? Did they go to Dartmouth?

The fact is this, we don't need experts on anything. But if you need one for the six o'clock news you should know where to look. The Vietnam vet in a wheelchair should be your military expert. The starving kid in Africa is your hunger expert. And we're all brain experts because we've all got one. But we don't use it. It's too much hard work. We are lazy and dumb.

I thought about where you could turn to find freedom from laziness and stupidity. Well, you could always take an island tour with three African boys. But if your parents couldn't afford that where would you look? Church? What does religion give you? Badges for ignorance and hypocrisy, that's what — a righteous Christian life filled with disclaimers, like a brochure handed over by some smooth salesman at a nifty car dealership.

After all, what's a brochure without disclaimers? And what good's a commandment if it can't be rechiselled a little bit?

Thou Shalt Not Kill*

*Does not apply to minorities on death row or when your government sanctions the killing of other human beings during times of economic opportunity or political distraction. Then you can get the bastards. And if their skin is a different colour or their eyes are not round then all the better.

Of course, a crafty Christian will always find another quote that justifies killing. But that's the beauty of the bible. It's a book for everyone because everyone can interpret it the way they want. Including me.

Judge Not and Ye Shall Not Be Judged*

*Applies only to those who share your views and morals. Does not apply to drug addicts, gypsies, pagans, communists, homosexuals, lesbians, sexual deviants and anyone else you see as different. Judge them mercilessly. And if you get the chance, shoot 'em with a nasty look, or a bullet.

When was the last time anyone heard a bible thumper who wasn't judging somebody? These are the most judgmental people on the planet. They obviously never heard Jesus telling them to back off and leave the hooker alone. It wouldn't be so bad if there weren't so many of them and if they weren't so goddamn sanctimonious.

My mind turned quickly to the Garden of Eden. It was a corny turn in the dirt path but the flora and the fauna of my surroundings were kind of what I imagined the Garden of Eden looking like. A beautiful place. Adam and Eve. Walking around naked. Everything in harmony. There's nothing I've read that says they were stupid so I can speculate that they were smart, happy and probably horny. They were living in a state of grace. And then what happened? The snake came along and offered them the forbidden fruit.

Now what was the fruit? An apple? No. A symbol of knowledge. Of all knowledge? No. Adam and Eve already had some knowledge. Adam knew how soft and tight Eve's snatch felt when he slowly slid inside her and confessed his love. Adam knew that water ran down a hill and not up it. Eve knew which berries were poisonous. She knew when Adam ate meat he sometimes got a stomach ache.

These were knowledgeable people. But they didn't know one thing. They didn't know good and evil. As soon as they ate the fruit they became aware of both. Which meant *neither* existed. Not good. Not evil. It wasn't in their minds. As soon as they became aware of good and evil they fell from grace. Thump!

I followed the six heels of the boys. They were moving more slowly than before. Sedekia turned and smiled. I didn't smile back. I was too busy thinking. Figuring stuff out.

If Adam and Eve were in a state of grace, without good and evil, then it followed that in order to find a similar state of grace I also have to live a life inside my head without good and evil.

I tried to imagine that world as I wound my way through the trees, letting leaves caress my face. Sounds simple. It's not. I challenge anyone, except perhaps a skinhead, to call what was done to the Jews, Poles, Gypsies, Cambodians or the North American Indians anything but evil. I challenge anyone, even the most mean-spirited son of a bitch, to call helping a blind man across a street anything but good. But Adam wouldn't have called it good. So how can we? As soon as our eyes see good or evil we have fallen from grace again. We're snorting around on all fours, digging for worms under a tree.

Just try it. Try to go a day without splitting the world into good and evil. *But Richard, isn't that what defines a psychopath? An inability to differentiate between good and evil or right and wrong?* Good point. But I'll say this. If somebody has truly abandoned the world of good and evil and turns violent then they are a psychopath. If they don't become violent, then they end up a saint. Madmen and saints. Not as far removed from one another as we might think.

Christians think they'll find god by attending a church once a week, saving a few souls and whispering prayers before dinner. They delight in avoiding the spirit-rescuing labours, the kind of thunder that separates the men from the boys, the women from the girls — they never stop talking about good and evil, especially evil. They munch on this spoiled fruit all day long. Don't they know it's bad for them?

I started thinking, if there was no good and evil then what *was* there? I didn't have a clue. But for some reason I thought of the Frau. Which made me think of my tears, her kisses, her tenderness, which made me think of love. And I remembered a German philosopher I had read. He said that when something takes place out of love it takes place beyond good and evil. Could love subdue this ageless, human conflict of opposites? Could love kill the snake?

The theory wasn't perfect but it was a damn sight better than Adam and Eve eating some fruit and getting yelled at by god. I started to wonder what kind of love was beyond good and evil. Romantic love? Cosmic love? Love love? I decided to stop. I felt like I had untangled a big knot in my head and I was just going to get it all tangled up again.

I walked behind my three young guides and dreamed of a world where Christians didn't kill or judge. Neither did Jews or Muslims or Hindus or Buddhists for that matter. Africa, silence, four bowls of a sweet bud and a long walk had a way of making mental masturbation feel about as good as the real thing. I also dreamed that mom would get better.

We arrived at some hot springs that poured out into the lake. Mountains of steam cascaded over the rocks. Sedekia asked if I wanted to go swimming. I told him I hadn't brought my swim trunks. The three boys just laughed, tore off their clothes and charged into the water bare-ass naked.

For all my profound thinking on the walk I was suddenly struck dumb with embarrassment. I shouldn't have hesitated. I should have stripped off my clothes when they did and ran in the water with them. Instead I stood there like a moron, with a pasted smile on my face and watched the boys splash and play in the warm water. They were laughing and talking in their native tongue. I became convinced they were saying I was a suck.

After much circular hand waving on their part (come in the

water) and back-and-forth waving from me (no, that's okay) I finally managed to get my clothes off and run in. The water was warm. I immediately took a nice, long pee. Our swimming and splashing should have been accompanied by some corny and exuberant piano music. I kept trying to be cynical about it, to try and mutilate the moment but the faces of Sedekia, William and Tom were too animated, too alive, too real. I was drawn into their happiness and it took as much coaxing to get me out of the water as it had to get me in.

The four of us have settled on the rocks and we're lying in the sun. They remain naked. I have put on my underwear. I look at the boys and realize they know of no other existance than the island. They have no idea how good they have it.

4:40 p.m.

It didn't take long for me to sniff out trouble. I looked up an incline and spotted a cave that was spewing hot plumes of steam. It looked like the mouth of a dragon. Or an old, battered kettle.

"Can we climb up there?" I asked, pointing to it.

Sedekia looked where I was pointing and shook his head, his smile disappearing.

"Bad place," he said.

"Why?" I asked.

Sedekia said nothing. He wouldn't even look at the damn cave. Of course I was drawn to it. I began to feel that same pull I experienced with the tree line on the island at Naivasha.

"Do you live in a city?" asked Sedekia.

"Yes," I said.

"I want to move to the city one day."

"No you don't. The city is full of bad people."

"Are those the people that hurt your face?"

My illusion was ripped away. There I was enjoying a blissful time with three local Africans. Believing I was someone else in a time long, long ago. Feeding Christians to the lions. Sorting things out with the help of California agriculture and German philosophy. And that little runt had to remind me I was still Richard Clark, with the ugly scar of a harelip. It was not going to make any difference what I did in life. I was always going to have the harelip and people were always going to remind me of it. I could murder twenty-four nuns and all that people would say was, "Oh yeah, that's the guy with the harelip." I could save twenty-four children from a burning bus and all that people would say was . . . well, you get the picture.

"Nobody hurt my face," I said. "I was born like this."

Sedekia lifted up the back of his leg and proudly showed me a jagged scar.

"I got this when I was five," he said.

Well good for you ya little shit. It's not on your fucking face. William and Tom were also showing me little scars they had on their bodies. I suppose a healthy person would have appreciated these gestures. Thinking them thoughtful and kind. Or an egotistical person would have believed the boys thought the harelip was cool. *Heyyyy, it's not so bad. These African kids have scars, too. I'm not ashamed of the damn harelip. I'm proud, real proud.* But I am Richard Clark. So I hated the gestures. Pathetic. Both me and the gestures. But I smiled sweetly.

I got up and started climbing up to the cave where all the steam was pouring out.

"No!" yelled Sedekia.

"I'm going in," I said with mock bravado. "If you want to be my guide then you better come with me."

I reached the mouth of the cave. I didn't know what the little guy was so worried about. It wasn't like North America where you might be worried that a bear was inside. What the hell could have been in a cave in Africa? Bats? I wasn't afraid of bats.

I couldn't see a thing because of the steam. It was also very hot so I covered my face with my hands. Once I was past the steam and inside the cave, I stood for a moment and let my eyes adjust. I felt really far away from the three boys. The steam provided a comforting barrier to the outside world. It was also very loud so I heard nothing but hissing. It was kind of like doing jude. That feeling of being in the womb.

I made my way to the centre of the cave. There was a small stream of crystal-clear water running down the middle. I dunked my hand in. It was hot. I followed the stream to the other end of the cave. Water was dripping from above. I followed the drips up the wall. It was then that I noticed the drawings. Some of them looked like they had been carved by sharp stones. And some of them might have been drawn with charcoal or painted by fingers dipped into some kind of dye.

It was too dark to make out every last detail but I did see animal figures. Some I recognized. Some I didn't. And there were human depictions as well. They were pretty crude. In fact they looked bad. As bad as anything I ever brought home from art class in elementary school. And yet they left me spellbound.

How long ago had they been created? Ten thousand years? Thirty thousand? I felt like I had made a great discovery. Perhaps no one had ever seen this ancient art. Maybe everyone but me had been scared off by fear and superstition.

My mind raced as I looked upon the images. I studied one in particular. It might have been an elephant. Just an outline. But there in the middle of the body was a tiny spiral that looked like the shell of a snail, a coiled snake or a hurricane in the Gulf of Mexico seen from outer space. What the fuck was it? The intestines? The heart? The soul? Why a spiral? And when I looked at some of the other animals and people on the wall I saw the same spiral.

Someone had done this. Someone had stood right where I was standing a long, long time ago and made these pictures. I tried to imagine them, all hairy and savage, dipping a finger into some coloured vegetable dye. How powerful were their arms? How nimble were their hands? Did their eyes sparkle when they painted? What the hell did they see in that goddamn spiral? I knew one thing. They would have kicked my ass if they found me sneaking around their cave. *What if they were still here?* Lurking in the shadows, reaching for a club.

The sound of the hissing steam was broken by a voice. It scared the shit out of me. I immediately regretted going into the cave in my underwear. It was a male voice, menacing and post-puberty. It wasn't Sedekia. The language was foreign. My eyes darted around. I finally made out a pair of sandals sticking out from a corner. They were decorated with what looked like black and red ribbon. Jesus. Somebody or some *thing* had been there the whole time, watching me. It was sitting in darkness so I couldn't see anything but sandals and dark legs. I stood there a moment, terrified and disoriented. I didn't know what the hell to do.

I started backing up to the entrance of the cave. The voice in the corner spoke again. And again it was a foreign language but it was different than the first time. It sounded like Italian but I didn't understand Italian. And then in Russian. And then French. I recognized two of the French words, *liberté* and *la mort*. Freedom and death. I decided to try and say something.

"Je m'appelle Richard, non parle francais."

There was no response.

It was frightening. But it was also very frustrating. I felt like I was being toyed with. *Speak fucking English, you goddamn cave dweller.*

Finally, after something that might have been Spanish, the voice spoke in broken English.

"You seek truth here. You seek freedom. But you stink of death and lies. Leave Africa. Your lives are in danger."

I took a few steps forward. It was too intense to leave. Whatever was in that cave had to be really wise. And really powerful. The cave was glowing. *Is this what Moses felt?* I had goose bumps up and down my arms and my scalp was tingling.

"Who are you?" I asked.

There was no response. The legs belonging to the sandals remained completely still. I tried to see what was above the waist but that part was hidden by shadows. I thought I saw the outline of a head that looked too big, and too long, to be human. I didn't know what to do, so I did what I thought should be done in the presence of something so mighty. I dropped to my knees.

"What is the meaning?" I asked.

It was all I could think of. I felt like a fool. The voice with the sandals liked the question even less than I did.

"Get out!!" it bellowed.

The volume almost broke my bones. I had visions of my hair standing straight up, my teeth falling out and my skin splitting apart. I stumbled backward and splashed through the little stream in the middle of the cave. The stream had turned blood red. The water dripping from the roof had achieved a similar metamorphosis. But it was no longer just dripping. It was pouring. It was sticky and warm. It was raining blood. I could smell the pungent copper scent of blood everywhere. It almost made me vomit. I was drenched in the downpour. Something on all fours moved quickly along the periphery of the cave. That's when I bolted.

On my way out, I saw something I hadn't seen coming in. There was a pile of human skulls stacked in a corner. I passed through the steam again and groped my way out of the cave. I started rubbing my arms and face to get the blood off. But there was nothing there.

Sedekia was waiting up near the entrance. William and Tom were further down below. All wore very worried expressions. I must have looked pretty wild-eyed.

"Are you okay?" asked Sedekia.

I stumbled back down through the shale of the rock face on wobbly legs.

"He warned me to get out of Africa," I whispered, just in case the thing in the cave had really good ears.

"Then you must leave right now," said Sedekia.

"Who's in there?"

"Crocodile Man. He's half-man, half-crocodile."

I didn't want to ask . . .

Which half is crocodile?

The upper half. The half you didn't see.

Oh.

"What the hell's he doing in there?"

"He guards the dead," said Sedekia. "Our fathers have told us never to go inside. I tried to warn you. You can't tell anyone at the camp. I will get in big trouble."

"Don't worry I won't. But I wouldn't believe all that crap about him being part crocodile. It's just superstition," I said, in a gallant attempt to sound like a rational, white, middle-class, regular guy. I might have sounded more persuasive if my voice hadn't been cracking.

We rejoined William and Tom. They looked at me fearfully and kept their distance. It was like I had suddenly become contaminated. I had thought they might look at me like a hero for having braved a journey into the cave, but they looked at me like I was a fool.

"We better go back," said Sedekia. "It's getting late."

After I threw my clothes on, the four of us started walking. I settled in behind the three boys. They talked amongst themselves in their native tongue. Occasionally one of them would shoot a quick, nervous glance back at me.

I tried to convince myself that the voice in the cave belonged to a man. A weird tribal man who spoke in many languages with a really deep voice, but a man nonetheless. Not somebody with magic powers. Certainly not the power to see into the future. And certainly not some half-man, half-crocodile island god. No way. The boys are young and superstitious.

But I never got a good look at the guy's face, so I guess I'll never know.

The experience in the cave didn't scare me half as much as the boys' reactions. They were afraid for me. And that warning to get out of Africa — it hung in the air like gunpowder. The warning was not just for me. Crocodile Man said, "lives." I tried to convince myself that it was nothing. But I was creeped out.

We left the hot springs and went to see a python that the boys had killed four days earlier. This snake was huge. At least eighteen feet long and two feet wide. How these boys killed the snake with small spears, I shall never know. I suppose I could've asked. The snake was being consumed by maggots and flies. I thought about telling the boys about the frogs that my squealing friends and I used to catch in a pond near my house, but I realized it would have been cruel of me to show them up. They were only kids after all.

After we left the python we encountered all sorts of natives just living off the land. Actually, they weren't living off the land when we passed them. They were just walking around.

Everyone was very friendly, offering the customary greeting of "Jambo." They all knew Sedekia and the boys. Sedekia looked nervous. Like he was worried they already knew I went in the cave. It was probably, like Sedekia said, some sacred burial ground. They might have gotten pissed off and shot a poison dart into my neck. Or just beaten the shit out of me.

We passed several gorgeous native girls with their bare tits hanging out and everything. I would have loved to have fucked one of them but the risk of a vengeful husband with a machete cooled my jets.

Like those girls would have even considered having sex with me. Their husbands were probably world-class lovers.

The four of us have stopped to rest on a rock and I'm working on my third cigarette. *Nerves a little fried, Richard?*

"Are you going to leave?" asked Sedekia.

I was annoyed that he was putting so much stock in what Crocodile Man had said.

"Do you think we should?" I asked.

Sedekia nodded.

"Well, we've got people in the West who make predictions all the time and they're hardly ever right."

Sedekia just looked at me with sad eyes. I knew what he was thinking. *Those people in the West are not Crocodile Man. He's never been wrong before.* I told myself he was eight years old and when I was eight years old I still believed in Santa Claus, the Easter bunny and the tooth fairy. But then again, I was catching frogs and Sedekia's killing pythons.

6:10 p.m.

The boys were starting to get antsy that we were sitting for so long but I needed to clear my head a bit before returning to camp. It's not every day you get cursed by a Crocodile Man.

We had walked for about ten minutes when a messenger from the camp ran up. He was out of breath and handed me a piece of paper. I unfolded the handwritten note.

> Your mother is
> worried you have got
> lost, so she has asked
> me to send a search
> party out. Please could
> you come back to
> save the situation.
> Beverly — The manager

I looked at my watch. It was 5:30 and we still had a few hours of daylight. *What the hell was she so worried about?* I told the boys we had better hurry back. Mom must have been freaking out again. Poor dad.

We reached the camp perimeter and Sedekia, William and Tom waved good-bye. I watched as they walked back to their world. Part of me wanted to run and join them. As Sedekia walked away he turned once and offered me one final worried look. *Thanks, Sedekia.*

When I got back to the camp I immediately came to mom and dad's tent and found mom lying on the bed shaking. She looked like an electrocuted corpse. Her face was swollen from crying. Dad was sitting, deflated, in the corner. I sat on her bed and she clasped my hands tightly.

"Thank god you're alive," she said.

"I'm fine, mom. I just had a tour of the island. That's all."

Dad's raspy voice rolled out from his corner of the tent in a monotone. He must have been telling her for three hours that I was fine. "She thought you'd passed out from the heat, got abandoned by your guide and been left behind."

"I thought you were dead, Richard," she blurted out. "I don't know what I would have done."

"Mom, I'm fine. I'm not dead."

I was parched from my walk. I spied a bucket of melted ice cubes. I was so goddamn thirsty I drank the water straight from the bucket. Nobody said anything.

Dad must have had a pretty rough afternoon. And mom as well. I felt tired, but they looked exhausted. Wrecked.

"Sorry," I said.

"It's not your fault," said dad.

I knew it wasn't my fault. I was trying to tell him I was sorry that he'd had such a rotten time but I was too tired to explain.

"Your mother's had another anxiety attack. But this one was bad."

Dad was talking like she wasn't there. When I looked at her I realized that, in fact, she wasn't. I tried again to reassure her about how safe I had been with my three guides. But her eyes looked through me with an almost incomprehensible despair.

Mom is at this moment quite literally insane. Whatever caused her to take that overdose of pills has returned.

Her eyes! My god they are scary to look at. I'm sitting on the other bed looking at them right now. I am ashamed to admit I'm not that concerned for her. I'm concerned for me. Her eyes are like frenzied, black whirlpools. How long can I stand safely on the perimeter before I get sucked in? I can't watch her and write this shit. It's sick. I'm sick.

Dad just went over to the bed and bent down. "Do you want to go home?" he asked gently.

Mom's staring at him with clenched fingers. He just asked her again but got no response. Dad just nodded at me to come outside with him.

6:35 p.m.

I was convinced we were going outside so he could tell me that we were heading back to Nairobi.

"What do you think?" he asked.

I didn't know what to think. I had a chill. Her madness had crept inside my bones. And I was still light-headed from my encounter with Crocodile Man.

I said what a coward says when they want to push responsibility onto someone else. Someone older and more mature. "I don't know."

"I think we'll push on for one more day and see how she does."

I didn't say anything but I must have given him a look that told him I thought he was making a mistake.

"I don't want this safari cancelled unless it has to be," he growled. "This isn't a drive to the mountains for Christ's sake. It's a once-in-a-lifetime trip. You'll never be back and neither will I."

I just nodded. I wanted no part of the decision. I am just along for the ride. He searched my face for approval. I gave him nothing. I felt bad. He wanted me to pat him on the back or at least nod and tell him I was with him all the way. But I wasn't with him. And I don't feel I'm with mom anymore either. I can feel myself pulling away. No longer a son. Just a traveller. An outsider. A sleazy reporter. Watching and scribbling about this family as it comes apart at the seams.

Beverly arrived at the conclusion of our conversation. Her giant rack swayed underneath her sweater and I swear to god I could see two hard nipples poking through the yarn.

"Everything alright then?" she asked.

"We're all fine," confirmed dad.

What a good liar he was. Beverly caught me staring at her breasts. She smiled. She had a big gap between two of her front teeth. I wanted to tell her not to smile. It ruined everything.

"You didn't get eaten out there?" she asked me.

Beverly obviously had no clue about mental illness. It was all kind of funny to her. Mom was a hoot . . . her overreaction and all . . . hee-haw. But I couldn't hate her for that. She didn't understand. And besides I don't think I could have hated her for anything right then. I was too dazzled by her boobs. She could have asked me to shoot a presidential candidate and I would have obeyed.

"I had a great time. Sedekia's a fantastic guide."

She seemed pleased to hear this. I'm glad I put in a good word for Sedekia. I'm always so damn selfish. I never think of others. Beverly told us she'd be in the office if we needed anything.

Dad apologized for any inconvenience. She brushed off his apology with a jolly laugh and a reminder, again, that if we needed anything she was in the office. *Was she coming on to me?* Why would she mention our needs twice and look at me both times? She didn't need to do that. *She wants me.* Or was she just doing what managers did?

I am back in my tent and I just smoked a bowl. I am glad that dad has made the decision to push on. I am ashamed to admit it but I am more than a little curious to see what will happen to mom as the trip unfolds. And the fact remains, we're not actually supposed to push on to anywhere right now anyway. The trip itinerary says we stay on Baringo for a few days so we might as well sit tight. I have already started to imagine her dead and wonder what I will feel like. It can't help but add to the tragedy of my life. *Yes, Richard, it's only a performance for your amusement. Asshole.*

9:42 p.m.

I notified the staff that I wished to take a shower before dinner. I felt like an English nobleman. *You there . . . yes you, the little man with nothing to do . . . run some water, if you please, I wish to take a bawth.* Instead of one of the little guys it was the big girl who came by. I was in a bathrobe when I heard Beverly call out that she was there with the hot water.

I could have stayed inside and let her fill the drum but that was too damn boring. I was really horny for her. I went outside and walked behind my tent. She was just finishing when I appeared around the corner. She smiled again. *Don't smile for Christ's sake! Or get your teeth fixed!*

"I'll bet you're looking forward to a hot shower after that long walk," she said.

When I get really horny I lose the ability to string more than two words together. "Oh yeah," I said.

"Your muscles must be really tired. There. All filled up. Enjoy."

"Oh yeah."

She turned to go. I waited until she passed me, counted to three and dropped my bathrobe. It wasn't really enough time for her to have disappeared around the tent. I was so hoping she had peeked over her shoulder to see me naked. But I didn't look in her direction because that would have made it seem like I had done it on purpose.

I didn't look around until I turned on the water. Beverly was nowhere to be seen. Sigh. I half-expected her to be standing there, breasts heaving, and hopefully smiling with her mouth closed.

The hot water sprayed across my shoulders and made me sleepy. I started to feel really stupid about dropping my bathrobe. Most guys court women with a joke, an easy smile, some winning conversation. I expose myself.

I didn't think mom would come for dinner tonight but she did. And she seemed somewhat better. Quite talkative. I can tell this is going to drive me crazy. I get all ready to treat her special, and she shows up for dinner as though nothing's wrong. I wish she'd be one way or the other. *If you're going to be crazy, be fucking crazy.* But she wasn't crazy tonight.

Dad looked like he was thinking the same thing. But he wasn't hiding his mood and he tumbled into a sulk.

It's a frustrating dynamic for me. When mom is down, dad is up. When mom is up, dad is down. What would happen if they were both up at the same time? Like most parents. Or better yet, what would happen if they were both down at the same time? Now, that I'd like to see. Two low pressure zones colliding over the table.

Dad said very little during dinner. He was in a snit when he arrived and left as soon as he'd finished eating. He's such a child sometimes. I hate his guts when he's like that. It's so fucking selfish!

"Do you remember when you broke your arm?" mom asked.

I nodded. I was about seven.

"I was trying to jump from the trash incinerator to the laundry pole," I said.

"And you came into the house crying. I should have known something was wrong because you hardly ever cried. Even as a baby. You were such a brave little boy."

"And you kissed it better."

Mom laughed. It was a real laugh. It washed a lot of the anxiety from her face. She looked really beautiful.

"You didn't think anything was wrong until I brought home a picture I tried to draw in class."

"And you were always good at drawing."

"No, I wasn't, but the picture was even worse than usual because I couldn't hold the paper down with my left hand."

"That's when it twigged."

"You finally took me to the doctor. Two days after I broke my arm."

"And that doctor didn't believe me. He thought I'd beaten you. He asked you what happened and I immediately jumped in to explain and he shut me right up. He wanted you to tell him."

"I don't remember that."

"That's what happened."

I sipped my coffee.

"I'm sorry you got so upset this afternoon."

I thought she might look at me surprised, like she had last night. *Upset? Oh, Richard, you're a silly boy.* She didn't do that. What she did was worse. The smile disappeared. The tapping foot reappeared.

I felt like an assassin. She had enjoyed about five minutes of pleasant reminiscing and I had to go and drag out this afternoon's ugly carcass and throw it on the table.

I desperately tried to find something positive. The forest had burned down but I wanted to show her that something was still alive. It didn't have to be a wild rose. A dandelion would be fine.

"It's okay, you know," I said. "I was . . . happy in a way . . . to hear how much you cared."

"You didn't think I cared?"

"That's not what I'm saying."

"You were surprised."

"Don't do this."

"Do what?"

She was looking at me very oddly. The connection between us was lost. Her eyes had gone vacant. She was back with the birds in the garden of the Norfolk.

"I've let you down, Richard. I've been a lousy mother."

"No, you haven't," I said with less conviction than I felt.

She tumbled backward. I wasn't a good hiking partner. I didn't reach out my hand. She sat there waiting for me to support her and tell her she was a wonderful mother. But I was strangled. Why the fuck can't I just tell her I love her, and . . . just do that? She looked like a dog I had just promised to walk, teased with the leash and then walked away from. Mom got up and left. I'm crying right now.

I was told they are turning off the electricity at eleven so I better sign off. There are two or three mosquitoes in the tent making a racket. God, they are loud. Maybe I won't be sleeping after all.

I woke up this morning at seven. Or perhaps it should be said that dad came by at seven with a cup of coffee. He brought a whole stack of suicide tools from mom's bag — Bic razor, nail clippers, nail file, compact mirror, even a pen — anything that mom might use to poke or slice open a vein. He also brought her anxiety pills. Dad said he wasn't taking any chances.

No shit. *Then why the hell aren't we heading back to Nairobi?* But of course I kept my mouth shut. This all needs to play itself out. Maybe he wants her to die. Maybe if my drugs run out I can gobble some of those anxiety pills.

I just had two hits of hash oil. I'm really buzzing. I'm also really horny but I will wait until I finish writing.

The night was frightening. As promised, they shut off the electricity at eleven and I was left in darkness. I convinced myself that the natives had cut the electricity cables and were closing in for the massacre. Thank god I didn't make any lecherous advances on any of the native women I passed on my walk with Sedekia. Then I would have had even more inspiration for images of machetes and chopped limbs.

I couldn't sleep. I had a recurring image I couldn't shake. It was a nightmare that mom had told me about many years ago. She was in a high-rise apartment and heard these moans. She went out to the balcony. There, standing on the ground below was Jesus Christ, bound in chains and howling for help. His face was grotesquely distorted with anguish and he was motioning for mom to come down. I kept picturing mom's Jesus staggering across the surface of the lake, making his way to my tent. My fears were intensified by the fact that I couldn't turn on any lights.

The worst part of last night was when I needed to take a piss. I lay there for thirty minutes before I got up the courage. No way was I going outside to the toilet behind the tent. So I opened the flap, hung my pecker out and pissed on the little front balcony. With alternating visions of a machete slicing off my member and Jesus standing there rattling his chains it took me forever to start peeing. The other night I paddled a canoe in crocodile-infested waters and last night I couldn't even get out of bed to go to the bathroom.

Oh man, I just remembered my dream. I was half-asleep and I felt hot, putrid breath on my face. I knew that some horrible beast was breathing on me. Then something wet dripped on my chest. I think it was saliva but I didn't dare look. The breathing finally stopped and I could hear it crawling away from my cot. I waited until I couldn't hear anything and then I counted to twenty. When I finally opened my eyes I saw a shadow moving outside my tent. The silhouette of the head had the unmistakable shape of a crocodile.

That freak in the cave has crawled inside my skull I don't like that. But then again, maybe it wasn't a dream. Am I sure I saw the shadow before waking up? Fuck that. It was a dream. There was no Crocodile Man in my tent.

Dad just called me. I better go see what he wants.

8:20 a.m.

Dad had me come out to my balcony to watch a pair of native fishermen paddling their boat across the still waters. They were singing. Dad had that sloppy smile on his face that he usually gets when he's been drinking.

"That's what this trip is all about," he said. "Right there."

Dad sipped his coffee and lost himself completely. It was nice but it wasn't worth the face he was making. It's so hard to appreciate something when the other person is making way too much of it.

"Nothing's changed for them," he said. "They've been fishing since the dawn of man."

"They must be tired," I said.

Father and son enjoy quiet moment. Father shares insight into moment. Son spikes moment. Father beats son into a coma.

Dad obviously didn't hear me or was ignoring me because he still smiled like a fool. He drained his coffee and walked away.

"Get dressed, we're going soon."

"Nairobi?"

"Not today."

We are off to visit a native tribe this morning. They live on one of the nearby islands. Perhaps they will cook us in big black pots and then eat us. I'm such a fucking redneck. Too much time in the oil patch. Got to do something with my life.

1:51 p.m.

Sitting on my balcony, listening to some music and watching the kingfisher birds dive for fish in the dark green waters. Ahhhh! Too bad dad isn't here to see my face so he could spike my enchantment.

We took a power boat to see the native tribe. On the way we saw baby crocodiles and a monkey in a tree. The boat was really fast. Mom was terrified. Dad probably could have asked the driver to slow down a bit but I think he got a perverse pleasure from seeing her grip the sides of the boat so tightly. She was muttering about drowning and disease. Mostly though we didn't hear her because the engine was really loud.

Just before we arrived at the tribe's island we went through a marsh filled with exotic birds and lily pads. It occurred to me, as I rode in the boat, naked, sitting on a rock, head bent forward, chin resting in my fist, that the lily pad was quite a good symbol of enlightenment. The flower (heaven) floats on the surface of the water, in the sun. The stalk that supports and sustains the flower, extends down through the water and has its roots in the mud (hell) on the lake floor. Conclusion: You cannot experience heaven until you've been to hell. I have a pretty good handle on mud. I know nothing about flowers.

Journal note: I'm going to stop philosophizing about everything I see. I'm making myself nauseous.

Mom was in good spirits when we arrived at the island. She seemed relieved to be out of the boat. I watched as she took a big gulp of fresh air. She seemed to lose ten years with that single breath.

A friend was waiting when we stepped onto the beach.

"I thought we weren't supposed to see you until we got back to the mainland?" asked dad.

"I have friends on the island," said Gabriel. "Thought it might be more interesting if I am around."

Dad has a way of making people feel like shit. He could have told Gabriel it was a nice surprise to see him there. But he let him know with the tone of his question that he wasn't pleased. I wanted to explain to Gabriel that it wasn't that dad didn't like him. It was just that Gabriel's appearance wasn't included in today's itinerary.

We all followed Gabriel away from the boat. I could tell he was on edge — his familiar, bouncy walk was replaced by that of a stiff and awkward impostor. I imagined this was how he looked when he was rushing to medical classes in London.

Gabriel led us into the village, identified as such by a collection of primitive huts. Gabriel seemed to know everyone. A small girl about four years old came straight to mom and held out her hand. The little girl had big eyes, a runny nose and a dirty face. Mom accepted her hand willingly, almost desperately. I just about burst into tears. Why couldn't her husband or son manage such a gesture? Cold-blooded bastards.

I recognized another familiar face. It was Sedekia. He smiled and waved.

"Sedekia would like to take the men fishing," said Gabriel.

"That sounds great," said dad as he watched the little girl lead mom away. "What about Janet?"

"I'll keep an eye on her," offered Gabriel.

Dad shook his head and waved his hands like this was the most ridiculous idea he had heard in a long time. "No way."

"Well, maybe Richard could stay with her."

"That's not fair to him. Janet should come with us."

"It would not be allowed. Only the men can fish."

"Richard, I'll stay with Janet and you can go fishing."

Gabriel caught my eye and shook his head discreetly. I had no idea what the fuck was going on but I went along anyway. "I've done the fishing thing. I hated it."

"I thought you said you had a good time."

"I liked being out on the lake but I don't like killing things."

Dad snorted, "What a baby."

Sedekia nodded to dad and led him away.

I turned around and saw mom disappearing into one of the huts with the little girl. I followed Gabriel over. We entered. I was almost knocked over by the smell of something burning. It was very potent. So potent it made my ears ring. I saw leaves, or something, burning in a small pit. Whatever it was, it smelled good. Not just good. Intoxicating. Mom was standing just inside the entrance, still holding the little girl's hand. Gabriel walked up to mom and gently touched her shoulder.

"This is the man I was telling you about," he said, pointing to a dark figure sitting motionless at the other end of the hut.

Mom hesitated briefly and then moved in that direction. I was so dizzy I touched the wall to steady myself. Gabriel signalled for me to sit down where I was.

"What are we doing here?" I whispered angrily.

Gabriel smiled and patted my back. "It's okay," he said and walked over to join mom.

As my eyes adjusted I began to see the figure in the corner more clearly. My skin started to quiver. It was Crocodile Man. My first instinct was to rush forward and save mom from this man/creature. I lie. My first instinct was to get the hell out of there. My second instinct was to save mom.

I saw that Crocodile Man was in fact part man, part crocodile but the top half, the head, was a mask made from the head of a real crocodile. This realization restored a modicum of normalcy. At least he wasn't a real "crocodile man."

I couldn't see mom's face. What in Christ was she doing? Sitting across from some weirdo in a crocodile mask. And when had she and Gabriel hatched this plot? Why hadn't Gabriel told me? I was in a position to take charge and get mom out of there but I was too intimidated by everything. I was hoping dad would come back and beat the shit out of everyone.

Crocodile Man sat and stared at mom for quite some time. Finally, he spoke. Gabriel translated. I almost shouted from the back. *Hey Crocodile Man! How come you're using a translator? You spoke English to me, you fucking fraud. You man of many tongues.* I guess it was supposed to seem more authentic with a translator. But then again maybe he didn't know all the languages he used in the cave. He probably had a few phrases memorized in French and Italian, etc. Perhaps he warned everyone that came into his cave that they stunk of death and should leave Africa.

"You have the eyes of the mystic," said Gabriel. "And have entered the shadow land. He says his eyes were like yours. You have been chosen to bring medicine to your tribe."

Gabriel looked back at Crocodile Man who spoke again. Gabriel turned back to mom.

"He says you are on the verge of the great discovery. You must believe it will happen. You must be strong because things will get much worse before they get better."

I thought the guy sounded like a phony maharishi having an uninspired advice day. *Things will get worse before they get better.* Give me a break.

Gabriel continued to translate.

"You must not let anyone interfere. You will be strange to those whose blood you share but you must not let them stop you. Nor can you wait for messengers to come across the water. Unchain yourself. Let yourself fall. Breathe in the mist. The roar of the lion awaits."

I was struck dumb. His words. Images. My mind. Mom. Jesus. Chains. Water. Saliva. Tent. Crocodile head. Dreams and thoughts and reality started fucking furiously, spilling hot liquid into and all over one another.

Crocodile Man began chanting and beating on a drum. The sounds became hypnotic.

"Get ready," said Gabriel. "He wants to show you the other side."

Mom slowly dropped her head. I pulled a bowl and some hash out of my pocket. The drums were intense. I got off one big haul before Gabriel tapped me on the shoulder. I hadn't seen him come over. "This isn't a Pink Floyd concert, Richard," he said.

I put my bowl away. Gabriel sat down beside me. He began rocking back and forth. I felt like I was tripping on LSD. The chanting. The drums. I moved my hand across in front of me. I saw tracers — several transparent hands followed my real hand and caught up to it when it stopped. I closed my eyes.

Suddenly I was three years old again, running in circles on the freshly cut grass of our front yard with a balloon from my birthday party. But I didn't keep a tight enough grip on the string. It slipped from my hand and floated away. I relived the panic as I chased after it, watching it float higher and higher and farther away until it was just a speck in the sky. I started to cry. It needed to be looked after. It wouldn't know what to do. I became so distraught I didn't want to ride my brand-new Big Wheel or wear my Batman cape. I eventually convinced myself that the balloon came to rest in a faraway country and was found by a pretty little girl about my age with an Irish lilt and black hair and dark eyes. I imagined her walking along a beach with my balloon. I knew one day I would marry that girl.

The images of the girl suddenly slowed down and burned like film stuck in a projector. Everything turned black. I felt myself immersed in warm, salty water. I was folded in on myself. I couldn't open my eyes. And yet I was calm. Warm. Safe. Then something went horribly wrong. The reassuring beat that was pulsing in my ears became chaotic and deafening. My warm world was invaded. I tried to move but could not. I was stabbed, pushed, squeezed. I started to suffocate. I tried to flip forward. To escape. To breathe.

A booming voice brought me back to the hut, back to the swirling, sweet smoke and the beating drum.

"What in the hell is going on in here?!"

My eyes fluttered open to see dad standing over mom. She was rolling around on the dirt, groaning, her hands rubbing up and down over her body. Crocodile Man kept beating his drum and chanting. Dad scooped mom up off the ground, threw her over his shoulder and stormed out. I don't even know if he saw me.

It took me a few seconds to get to my feet and stumble from the hut to the beach. Dad had put mom down and was leaning over her. Though she still appeared unconscious, she was mumbling.

"Janet?" asked dad. "Are you okay?"

Her head began rolling back and forth. Dad was starting to panic.

"Janet!"

Dad slapped her lightly. Mom slowly opened her eyes. It took her a moment to make out dad's face but when she finally did she started screaming and pushing him away. Wherever she had been, it was a hell of a lot better than what she was waking up to. Dad tried to hold her down.

"Richard! Grab an arm!"

I just watched.

"Damn it! Help me!"

I didn't move. I didn't want to restrain her. Dad finally got her arms pinned. But it was like scrubbing fleas off a feral cat in a sink full of water. Mom got a hand free and raked her fingernails across dad's cheek. He let her go. Mom crawled away on her hands and knees. Dad touched his face. There was blood. Gabriel arrived on the beach. *Bad timing, Gabe.* Dad saw him, sprang to his feet and barrelled over. I thought for sure he was going to deck him. But he didn't. He wagged a finger.

"You've just guided your last safari, chief."

Gabriel said nothing. He stood there, like a child who had run out into the street and was now getting scolded. I didn't like Gabriel looking like that. He was supposed to look strong.

"Dad, it's not his fault," I said.

"Bullshit. Help me get your mom in the boat."

We beat a hasty retreat from the island. It wasn't quite the Bay of Pigs but the stench of failure and betrayal lingered in the stiff breeze. I watched Gabriel, hands on his hips, staring down at the sand as we bounced away through the water. Poor guy. He was just trying to help. I'll bet that's the first time that mom had her madness honoured. I would love to know if she found the other side. And if she did, what it looked like.

Nobody said a word all the way back to Baringo. Mom was much calmer by the time we got there and said she didn't need any help getting to their tent. Dad followed close behind. Fucking guy. Probably thought he was a hero for saving her like that.

The expensive shrinks and pills in Paris didn't work. Why not try a shaman? It couldn't hurt. I suppose dad's got good reason to be angry — it was all planned behind his back. I'll bet he thinks that Gabriel and I were trying to pull one over on him. I had fuck-all to do with it.

Dad didn't mention lunch so I went to the restaurant by myself. I ordered some food to take back to my tent. I prefer eating alone in the privacy of my own room. I don't really enjoy watching others eat. I'm always thinking ahead — eight to twelve hours later when their food is coming out the other end.

Leaving the restaurant I passed a beautiful girl with a mole on her cheek. She was with her family. She looked to be in her early twenties. She smiled at me. I wasn't able to smile back. Just a grimace. Must have been real attractive for her. A harelip and a grimace. Jesus Christ.

I decided to lay low this afternoon so I grabbed two beers to bring back to my tent. I ran into dad on my way back. His face was streaked with red scratch marks from mom's fingernails. It looked like he was wearing war paint. He saw the two beers and got surly. "You're drinking them two at a time now?"

"No, I was bringing one to you."

Quick thinking on my part. That line wouldn't have worked if I was just arriving at my tent when I saw him. He would have asked me why I was going to my tent first. I would have told him I was dropping my beer off and then was going to bring him his. No way. His tent was on the way to mine after all. That would have made no sense and he would have told me so. It was good timing he caught me when he did. He sized up my response. He never believes a fucking word I say.

I remember when he tried to bust me in high school. Kurt and I were driving around in dad's Dodge Dart smoking some wicked black hash. I was always terrified of the small blow torch we used. I thought it was going to explode and I'd end up bald and blind. It was up to Kurt to heat the knives in the blue flame, flick the hash and make the smoke. He was like an expert meat carver the way he worked those knives.

We got to an intersection and stopped at a red light. Suddenly, metal crunched. The car lurched forward and the cassette player flew out of the console. *What the fuck?* I looked behind and saw that we'd been rear-ended. The driver was totally blitzed. My first thought was cops. We had paraphernalia in the car. I told the drunk idiot to follow us into a parking lot so we wouldn't block the road. This was supposed to give Kurt time to hide the drug stuff. Well, we went straight, and the bastard turned right and took off. I was left with a smashed back end and no evidence of another car.

I got home and told mom and dad what happened. Dad, half asleep, took one look at his precious Dodge Dart, called me a dumb shit and went back to bed. Mom telephoned the police because an accident report needed to be made. The cops came over, stuck me in the back of their car and for ten minutes drove me up and down our short driveway. Forward. Reverse. Forward. Reverse. I suppose it was an interrogation tactic. They were convinced I was stoned. They were right. They were convinced I had lost control of the car on the icy roads, had spun and run the rear of the car into a pole. They were wrong.

Two nights later, I was over at Kurt's. Dad called and told me to come home immediately. Kurt came along.

"The police just called," he said. "The lab results are in. Pole paint."

Kurt and I cried out that the lab results were impossible. We had been rear-ended. The conversation got murky for the next few minutes but it finally emerged that, in fact, the police hadn't called.

"I never said that," explained dad. "I was just asking what you would do *if they did call* to say it was pole paint."

Dad scurried off to bed. He knew the score. He had tried to smoke out a lie, but when he saw I wasn't going to confess he doubled back and changed his story. What a dink. Kurt and I thought it was the funniest goddamn thing. We spit laughter all the way back to Kurt's house.

That was the night Kurt started calling dad Dick Tracy. That was also the night I realized dad would never forget the twenty dollars I stole.

Dad finally took the beer. But only after he had satisfied himself that I might have been telling the truth. Just like Dick Tracy would.

"How's mom?" I asked.

He didn't say anything. He turned, beer in hand, and marched away. He was still pissed off about Crocodile Man.

I got back to my tent and sat on my little balcony. I was working on my third beer when I heard a whistle from below. I thought it was a bird. It was Gabriel.

"C'mon up," I said.

He shook his head and stayed hidden in the bushes. I went down to him. He looked a little crazy. His eyes were bugging out and he was having trouble swallowing.

Perhaps madness is a flapping beastie that moves from one person to the next, settling on the victim's shoulder to whisper terrible stories in their ear. If this is the case then, for the moment, that beastie was off mom's shoulder and was nibbling on Gabriel's ear.

"How is she?" he asked.

"I don't know."

I thought he was going to start choking. I could have reassured him about mom but then I remembered that he hadn't told me about his secret healing in the hut. It pissed me off. I decided to let him dangle a bit. He had tears in his eyes.

"Your mother wanted to try something, anything."

I was trying to remember back, trying to figure out when Gabriel and mom had time to spend alone. I always think I notice everything and it really sucked to see that I had been duped. Just like dad.

"So what's next, Gabriel? Are you and mom going to fall in love, kill dad and have little mulatto babies?" I asked.

Gabriel could see that underneath my anger I was hurt. Well, it's possible he didn't see any of this but he did come over and take hold of my shoulders.

"She wanted to do this on her own. She made me swear I wouldn't tell you."

"What did you guys talk about?"

"I want you to go check on her for me."

I didn't want to go but I went anyway. All the flaps were down. I tapped on the canvas. "Hello in there," I called. "It's Richard."

I heard movement from inside the tent and dad came out.

"I came to see how she was doing."

"She's sleeping," he said coldly.

"I'll be quiet."

He didn't stand aside. This pissed me off. I moved forward. His arm shot across to block me. I stood there, refusing to go away.

I didn't make eye contact. That's what you're supposed to do with an aggressive, unpredictable dog. And that's what he is now. I don't trust his reactions anymore. Eye contact might have escalated the confrontation into a fistfight and I didn't have the will for that. There are times that I do though — when I really feel like hitting someone. Finally, I think he felt stupid. I know I did. He dropped his arm. I went inside. He stayed where he was.

Mom was curled up on her side. She wasn't sleeping. Her eyes were wide open, staring straight ahead. I sat down beside her. "Mom, are you okay?"

Nothing.

"Can I get you anything?"

No response.

I wanted to hug her. But instead I patted her hand like you pet a dog when you don't want to get hair on yourself. "I'll come check on you later."

I went back outside. Dad was waiting. "He's finished, Richard."

"I think he's just getting started," I said sharply.

"You guys thought you were pretty clever. Getting me to go off fishing like that. What did you think? That a drummer in an alligator mask was going to fix her?"

It would have been the wrong time for me to explain the difference between the alligator (see Florida) and the crocodile (see Africa).

Mom appeared through the flap in the tent. She looked almost fierce. "Don't do it, Ted," she commanded. "Don't get him fired."

Her eyes burned two holes through dad before she turned and went back inside. I turned away as well and started walking. "It was my idea," I said with a not-so-subtle tone of feigned guilt and resignation.

I don't know why I lied. I guess I knew that dad couldn't fire me. But more important, I think I need to have Gabriel here. Even though I feel like he has betrayed me, he is my only ally.

I returned to the bushes below my balcony. Gabriel wasn't there. I went back inside my tent and found him sitting on the floor. He looked up expectantly.

"She's pretty out of it. I'd be surprised if we didn't head back tomorrow."

"But she's alert?"

"She was when your name came up. So are you going to tell me what the fuck's going on?"

Gabriel looked at me softly. "Your mother's obviously not herself right now but she doesn't see herself as crazy and she won't take any of those panic pills. She doesn't want to be controlled."

"She was never like this when I was growing up."

"Your mother had you and your sister to look after. But when she landed in Paris she had nothing. She needs somebody to need her. All good mothers do. She knows the marriage is finished but she can't bring herself to break free. She wanted to leave your father a long time ago but she stayed until you kids were out of the house."

"And we've been out of the house for over a year so why hasn't she divorced him?"

"She doesn't know. Perhaps she doesn't have the strength. Your father has a powerful grip, financial and otherwise."

"This is ridiculous! Why am I asking our driver about my own mother?"

"I've had lots of people confess secrets to me on these trips, Richard. It's safe for them."

"And what secrets did she confess?" I asked sarcastically.

"Something is bothering her but I couldn't get her to talk about it. I think it had to do with you."

This made me uneasy. I'm supposed to be the observer of the mess. Not the cause. "Don't be so fucking mysterious, Gabriel."

"It's nothing specific. It's what I saw when she spoke of you. A very great sadness."

"Because I'm a fuckup."

"I don't think so. She's worried that you might be a drug addict. But it was something else. Can you think of what it might be?"

I thought about it. *What the hell could be so bad?* One bad thing that immediately came to mind had plenty of shelf life, having been a bad thing since the dawn of depravity (Ancient Greece?), and yet was still fresh enough that it made many popular appearances every year on shameless afternoon talk shows.

"Did she say she molested me?"

"Is that something you remember?"

"No. But they say you can suppress those memories."

My mind raced back over my life, sniffing garbage cans, trying to find anything awful that connected mom and me. It was foolish. If there was something that bad, I'd remember. And if it was something that was awful for her, but not for me then I'd never find it because it wasn't awful for me. She'd have to tell me. If she couldn't, well that was her problem.

"I can't think of anything."

"This isn't a test. You don't have to think of it while we're standing here."

"It may not even be about me."

Gabriel looked at me sympathetically. Just like Sedekia did when I tried to dismiss the validity of Crocodile Man. Bastards.

I really didn't want to be linked to mom's madness and I resented him like hell for implying that I was.

"I have to go now," he said.

"Wait. What else did she tell you?"

"That was all. We talked about me and about Africa. And about elephants. She loves the elephants."

Gabriel turned before he left. "Your mother did mention one special memory. She said that the two of you pulled mattresses and sleeping bags into the backyard and slept under the stars because you didn't have a tent and you'd always wanted to go camping."

He shrugged and disappeared. I walked back to the bed and sat down. I remember that night. But I remember it because I went into her room before we went outside and she was just pulling a sweater over her head and her bare breasts were exposed. She didn't see me but she heard me squeal. I rushed from the room like Lincoln's assassin. It's funny. She remembers the stars. And I remember her breasts. *Could that have been the . . . ?* I've got to stop this. Fuck you, Gabriel. He's put all this garbage in my head. Now I'm cursed. I'll analyze and torture myself over every memory connected to mom.

8:20 p.m.

I am at the bar getting quietly drunk. I'm not actually at the bar. I'm at a small table in the bar. It's just me and the bartender. Nobody drinks at this camp. And they all go to bed at eight o'clock.

I knew I needed to calm myself down before we ate. I smoked two lines of jude. It hit me fast. I was back in the quiet, warm waters again, ready for anything. Even dinner with dad. The restaurant is outside under a large canopy. I hate eating outside. Too many bugs and things flying around.

I was surprised when I got there. Mom was with him. She smiled when I sat down, sipped some water and looked dreamily around at the other tables. I looked at dad. He shot me one of his manufactured two-second smiles and joined mom in her surveillance of the restaurant.

Dad was quick to order, which is rare for him. He usually likes to take his time and slam back a few cocktails before eating. He was obviously in a hurry to get dinner over with.

"So what's on tap for tomorrow?" I asked.

"I don't know," he said, sounding irritated.

"I think we're going to see flamingoes," said mom.

"How would you know what we're doing?" asked dad.

"It's in the itinerary."

Dad looked at mom for the first time since they'd sat down. "So you're all better now?" he asked.

"I feel good tonight," she said buoyantly.

"How long do you think that's going to last? What do you think, Richard? Five dollars says she's back in the bughouse by morning."

Life throws you moments where you have a chance to stand up for yourself or for someone else. You don't always realize it until later just how significant those moments are. By seizing them you restore a crumb of dignity and have a shot at a decent life. By ignoring them you slide deeper and deeper into your own shit until you've slid so far that you can't breathe. I, of course, have no crumbs in my hand tonight.

We waited in silence for the food to arrive. As soon as dad had finished clubbing mom over the head his mood improved and he became quite conversational. I would even go so far as to describe him as . . . chipper. So, then it was mom and me who were sullen and depressed. He even had the nerve to comment on it, saying that neither of us were much fun. I looked at him and couldn't believe that she had put up with this asshole for all these years.

Dad talked enthusiastically about the rest of the trip. He said the best part of the safari was to come. We were going to start seeing the large animals: the lions, cheetahs, elephants and rhinos. It was clear that we were not returning to Nairobi the next day.

"Do you know what I'm going to miss the most about this place?" he asked dreamily. "The sound of the singing fishermen in the morning."

Dad looked at mom. It was her turn to reflect. "How about you, Janet? What are you going to miss?"

"I miss the robins."

Silence descended on the table. Dad had tried, and failed, to rally his troops into a cozy circle of reflection. But I didn't feel bad for him. On the contrary. I was delighted. He stuffed the last of his food into his mouth, pushed his chair back and left.

Mom smiled at me. She looked real cocky.

"You did that on purpose," I said. "You don't miss the robins."

"How do you know?"

"Alright, I think you do miss your robins but I also think you were acting right then."

"Do you think this is all an act?"

"Not all the time. But that was."

"So you don't think I'm crazy? You think I'm acting?"

"You tell me."

She wasn't talking. But then again, what the hell was she supposed to say?

"I talked to Gabriel you know," I said. "He said that you were hiding something. Something about me. Something that made you very, very sad."

Mom's cockiness disappeared. "Gabriel is not a psychiatrist," she said scowling at me. "He's a safari driver."

"So what is it? What is this terrible thing I've done to you?"

"He doesn't know me."

"I don't think I know you either. Why won't you talk to me?"

"I can't." Mom reached out and snatched up my hand. She was desperate again. Her desperation made me nauseous.

"I have failed you, Richard."

I kept my free hand stiffly at my side. The hand that mom was holding wasn't really a hand at all. It was a clenched fist.

I did manage to speak. What a hero. "Why do you keep saying that?"

Her face flooded with pain. She squeezed my fist even tighter. She looked like she was ready to talk.

"How have you failed me?" I asked.

Her eyes turned cold. She let go of my hand and got up to leave.

"You're just having some troubles right now," I said. "You'll get through this, I know you will."

Mom walked over and put a hand on my shoulder.

"I love you, Richard."

"I love you, too."

At least I told her that. But there was no emotion in my voice. It was all in my gut. And I didn't want her to see it. For shame, Richard. Fucking pride. I wanted to turn and watch her leave but I couldn't. The fucking drugs were not doing what they were supposed to do. My feelings were bubbling up my throat and threatened to spill out of my eyes. I ordered a whiskey and came to sit in the bar.

I can't decide how much of mom's madness is the result of a chemical fire and how much is the shit flying around her. It's a tricky area. Part of me is tempted to tuck it away inside the wrinkled folds of the brain and absolve dad of any responsibility. And part of me thinks that if dad treated her better then she wouldn't be so messed up.

Dad is not the only one to blame though. Sure, he gets cruel and mean but I know that I factor in somehow. Even if it is only my drugs. And if Gabriel is right then I factor in more than I think. And dad is not the only one on this trip who can't love her. I've stepped back. Stepped back? I've never been close enough to step back.

The pretty brunette with the mole has just arrived. She is at the bar asking for matches. I better act now or forever hold my dick. More later.

11:57 p.m.

I am back in my tent writing by the light of a lantern. The electricity has been shut off again but this time I was prepared. I am quite drunk. Fuck them all. If mom wants to kill herself then she should get on with it. And dad, well, he can drink himself to death. I want nothing more to do with them. How's that for detachment?

I keep forgetting that my job is to narrate this journey, not become a part of it. I must take more drugs and spend more time listening to music.

I had quite a splendid time with Nicole. That's her name. The pretty girl with the mole. Like me, she's on safari with her parents. I asked if I could join her for a drink at the bar. I was drunk enough that I didn't care if she told me to go to hell. She hesitated at first but then agreed. Yes!

When I get drunk I forget about my harelip and I think that girls actually talk to me because they're attracted.

We endured small talk for starters. I found out she is from New Hampshire. She's of Irish descent. I told her she was the first quiet American I had met on this trip. She had no idea what I was talking about. She was subdued and soft, a little shy and very tasty. She didn't like talking about herself but I did find out she had a boyfriend. *Who gives a shit about that when you're thousands of miles away?* I said it was nice she had a boyfriend. Nice, nice, nice. She said she missed him.

She had tiny scars on the side of her wrist, about seven or eight short lines. "Did you cut yourself with a razor?" I asked.

She quickly pulled her sleeve down. "That couldn't have been a suicide attempt," I said. "Not little cuts like that."

"It wasn't."

"You just decided one day to cut yourself?"

"Something like that."

I could tell she was a tortured soul. I felt like inviting her along for the rest of our safari. She would fit right in.

Nicole hates a lot of the things I hate. It's nice when you can meet someone and find out that their hate list is just as packed as yours. And not only that but we cross-referenced lots of hates. For example: She hates vegetarians who still eat fish because they don't think it's meat. It was unnatural to watch love blossom amidst so much hate. Like an evergreen tree erupting up through the dry sand of a desert.

I could see Nicole catching herself at times. Telling herself she was laughing too loud, smiling too much. Reminding herself that she had a relationship waiting in New Hampshire. But, much to my relief, she did not allow the shadow of her boyfriend to ruin the night.

Nicole collects bizarre *Associated Press* news clippings. She keeps them in an old scrapbook beside her bed. She told me about a girl who was planning to commit suicide but wanted her friend there to give her strength. Her friend stood beside her when she pulled the trigger. The bullet passed through the head of the girl who was committing suicide and hit the friend who was standing on the other side. The wrong side as it turned out. Both died instantly. Nicole said she felt bad for the friend but giggled uncontrollably at her lack of foresight.

I almost mentioned to Nicole that perhaps it was a planned double suicide but I didn't want to rain on her parade.

She twirled her baton, lifted her knees high and marched straight into another *AP* story, this one about an overweight aunt and a missing toddler.

Apparently this aunt got really drunk at a family party and plopped herself down in a big, comfy chair. Time passed, games of rummy dealt, potato salad eaten. Finally, someone asked where the toddler was. Everyone started looking. Panic set in. They eventually found him, suffocated under the fat ass of the aunt. No joke. All true. God bless *AP* and sick newspaper editors.

Nicole acknowledged she thought the accident was horrible but she couldn't hide the gleam in her eye. "The worst part wasn't the death of the toddler. That was bad enough," she said. "No, the worst part would wait patiently, until years later when others would innocently ask how the toddler had died.

"Imagine if you were the parents?" she asked. "You couldn't answer. How could you? 'Our aunt sat on him and he suffocated.' What would you do if they smirked? Would you kill them with your bare hands right there on the spot? You'd have to say it was crib death."

I loved Nicole for thinking into the future like that, taking a horrible story and saying, no, it gets worse, much worse.

I probed for stories that involved her personally but she wasn't biting. She said she didn't like talking about herself. I did find out she lost her virginity at thirteen. Wow. But she wouldn't tell me the details. I was going to tell her about the prostitute, the strawberries and my record collection but I was interrupted by a very satisfying "I think I dig you" moment, where we both stopped talking. And our eyes met. I almost asked her if she'd ever found a balloon on a beach when she was a little girl but I didn't want to hear she hadn't.

I cleared my throat even though I didn't have to. It seemed like a cool way to get her undivided attention before I started my own story.

"We had this little Englishman in grade seven. Trevor Finch was his name. Always dressed in a suit. Funny accent. You know, the kind of guy you throw snowballs at. Trevor sat in front of Dean Devlin. And Dean was giving him some wicked rubber fingers to the back of his head."

"What are rubber fingers?"

I was thrilled that I could teach her something, and maybe even touch her at the same time.

"First you loosen the finger beside your pinkie and get it wobbling back and forth and then, thwack!"

I demonstrated lightly on Nicole's arm.

"Ouch!"

"And that was a soft one. Dean was awesome. His really hurt. Anyway, Dean was giving it to the back of Trevor's head. And finally, Trevor couldn't take it anymore. He spun around and punched Dean in the jaw. You should have seen Dean's face. Utter and complete shock. The little Englishman had stood up for himself."

"Good for him. And that was it? I'll bet Dean stopped teasing him. Bullies hate being stood up to."

"He did. But first he beat the shit out of him. Right there in the classroom. After that he never teased Trevor again."

"Did you ever have to stand up for yourself?"

My momentum screeched to a halt. Burned rubber swirled around my head.

"Why would I have had to do that?"

Nicole sipped her beer and innocently shrugged her shoulders.

"Oh, you mean my face," I said coldly.

"I don't know what you're talking about," she said cautiously.

I stood up and looked at myself in the mirror behind the bar. "You don't know what I'm talking about? Tell me that you can sit there and say there's nothing wrong with my face."

Nicole was studying my face in the reflection of the mirror. "You've got a little, tiny scar on your top lip and it looks like you broke your nose once. So what's your problem?"

"Don't be kind because it's worse than being cruel."

"I should be getting back," she said and started to get up. I dropped my hand gently on her arm.

"There are times when I'm walking down the street, feeling pretty good about things, got a bit of a swagger going, thinking I'm quite the lad, and then suddenly, from a shop window, I catch a reflection of myself. Poof! You see? That's you. Not that guy in your head."

I took my hand off Nicole's arm after she sat back down but I couldn't look at her. My ass found the bar stool again and I pretended to be interested in the gouged wood that surrounded my beer coaster. "I was born with a cleft lip and palate. Do you know what that is?"

"I've heard about it but I've never seen one."

"Well, guess what? You're looking at a surgically repaired harelip as we speak."

"I don't get it. Your face looks fine."

I knew she was lying. But even if she wasn't I felt like a paranoid idiot for making the connection between her question about standing up for myself and my face.

She could sense I was nose-diving. And I suppose she could have gotten up again and ran. But, to her credit, she didn't. She asked me if I knew what caused my harelip.

I had to work really, really hard to crawl out from the debris I had accidentally exploded on top of myself. I drained the last of my beer in three big swallows and the stinging in my throat brought words to my mouth.

"I have heard from reliable sources who have studied these things," I said with a scholarly tone. "That women who look upon gypsies whilst pregnant are doomed to have a baby with a harelip." I lit a smoke and exhaled through my nose because I thought it would look good. "So when we start having kids don't you be sneaking a peek at any goddamn gypsies."

Nicole was giggling. I turned to face her triumphantly. My elation did not last long.

"It's not too late you know," she said. "If Trevor Finch could do it. You can too."

Nicole was too fucking smart. I should have asked her to marry me right there and then. Instead, my mood grew sullen and distant. I knew she was right but I couldn't bring myself to tell her so. It all seemed so condescending. Like I was a fucking cripple. Like that man with no arms or legs outside the Norfolk.

I think Nicole thought my silence meant I was thinking about Trevor and seeing him as my big inspiration. I was thinking about him alright but I was thinking I'd tie a plastic bag around my neck and asphyxiate myself if Trevor Finch was going to be the catalyst for turning my life around. I mean, c'mon.

We were the only two left at the bar and the bartender was giving us looks to get the hell out of there. Nicole decided it was time to call it a night. I offered to walk her back to her tent. I purposely led her back to mine. I was feeling intensely sorry for myself and I figured that if I could fuck her I would feel better. I was hoping she was as drunk as she seemed.

"This isn't my tent," she said.

"Oops. Wrong turn."

I opened the flap. "You want to come in?"

"No," she said firmly.

"What's the matter? Am I not pretty enough?"

"Sorry, Richard, I don't meet a guy and fuck him three hours later."

I was only joking about not being pretty enough. Kind of. Not really. I stood there hating her. Hating myself. She took two steps forward and kissed me tenderly on my lips. "I was a freak in high school, too," she said. "And I didn't stand up for myself either." Then she turned and walked away. My hatred was gone. At least for her.

I've been crying since I got back to my tent. Nicole told me something about herself to make me feel better. But I don't deserve her. I feel like a monster. I am a monster. I deserve my harelip. I deserve to die.

I've been pretty good about getting up at seven o'clock on this trip. Not this morning. Dad woke me up around eight-thirty. I must have been out of it because he said he yelled at me several times from outside the tent. He eventually came in and shook me awake. He assumed I got drunk last night. He assumed correctly. Surprisingly, I do not have a headache. That's because love came a callin'. As dad was leaving he said, "Where did you get the rose?"

I lay there not having a clue what the fuck he was talking about. It wasn't until I rolled over and felt a sharp sting on my ankle that I saw it.

There was a red rose at the end of my bed. I had squished it slightly but it was undamaged. The fragrance was luscious. I breathed the mistress scent deep into my lungs with an enthusiasm that had previously been stubbornly faithful to jude. I held the flower in my hand like an ape. *Rose . . . pretty.* I was so blunted from alcohol that it took me about five minutes to make the connection. This delay would prove costly.

Like trying to light a match in the wind I tried to figure out who the covert admirer might have been. For no good reason I thought that perhaps the camp staff came in at night to leave roses for those guests who were leaving the next day. But we weren't leaving today. And then I thought that perhaps Beverly, the manager, had left it. Maybe she *had* seen me naked and was thanking me.

By the time I considered the possibility that Nicole had snuck into my tent and left the rose while I slept, I remembered something she had said last night — she was leaving today.

I rushed to the camp office. Still feeling the disorienting effects of too much booze from last night and too sudden a catapult from my bed this morning I had to look down to make sure I had put clothes on. Beverly was there. I was so frantic she thought something was terribly wrong. I told her everything was fine, I was looking for Nicole. She didn't know anyone by that name. As soon as I mentioned the mole she knew who I was looking for. Then she got a little frosty. I was right. Beverly does like me. She was jealous. But I had no time for her possessiveness. I needed to find Nicole. Beverly seemed a little too pleased to inform me that Nicole and her family might be down at the dock but had probably already left.

I ran as fast as I could. I had not sprinted in a long time. I was terribly out of shape and I was also possibly in love. I barely made it to the dock without puking.

My timing could not have been worse. The boat was a hundred yards out. I would have preferred that the boat been out of sight completely. That way I wouldn't have known that I'd just missed her by a minute.

I could see Nicole with her mom and dad. They were all facing the other way. There was no point in shouting. She would never have heard me above the noise of the engine. I'm also not into making a spectacle of myself, no matter how madly in love. (Unless, of course, I'm giving my best friend's mother a peek at Mr. Happy.)

So I stood on the dock and I prayed. I had nothing to pray to so I prayed to Crocodile Man. I prayed for him to make Nicole turn around and see me there. I prayed that it meant more to me than anything in my life. And guess what? Cue the fucking music. She did turn around. And she kind of squinted. And I jumped up and down and flapped my arms like an idiot. She saw who it was and she waved.

I stood and watched her until her boat disappeared. I haven't felt such exhilaration in all my life. Well, I'm being overly dramatic. I've had several drug rushes that beat this one easily but I've never had a clean rush like that.

It's amazing. One simple moment has changed everything for me. I have hope in my life. I feel like all things are suddenly possible. I would do anything for Nicole. I would get clean and sober for her. I'm going to love my parents and make sure they get home safely. And once I get them home I'm going searching for Nicole. And when I find her I'm going to ask her to marry me.

12:04 p.m.

I am sitting on a rock, concealed in steam, surrounded by thousands of flamingoes. I am watching dad follow mom around. It looks like he is trying to talk to her but I can't hear them because of the roar of the hot springs. Yes, more hot springs. But no caves. And hopefully no Crocodile Man.

After I fell in love this morning I went to have a quick breakfast with mom and dad. We were running late. The boat that was to take us to the flamingoes was already waiting. Dad was in a state. He kept checking his watch. Being late for anything is a rare and disturbing experience for him.

I think he was also self-conscious because mom's scratch marks on his face were still red and angry and he couldn't hide them. I could see he had tried. There was a shine of cream on his face.

I was also showing a bit of a shine.

"What's the matter with you?" asked mom.

"Nothing," I said.

"You're smiling."

"So?"

Mom was really checking me out. "Tell me," she said.

"There's nothing to tell. I'm happy."

"You've met a girl."

I must have had that "aw shucks" look that us guys get because she wagged a finger at me.

"You did meet a girl."

My smile told her she was correct. And right there and then her mood began to nosedive.

"I hope you didn't get into trouble last night," said dad.

I shook my head and kept stealing glances back at mom. She wouldn't look at me. Was she fucking jealous? I started thinking that maybe she did molest me. Maybe this was why she was so damn upset. Thinking about the possibility that she might have molested me stirred up some righteous anger so I decided to provoke her.

"She left me a rose this morning."

Neither mom nor dad asked me anything about this girl who had just changed my life.

"Her name's Nicole. She's from New Hampshire."

Mom looked the other way and dad called the waiter over.

"It's the most beautiful rose you've ever seen. I think I'm going to marry this girl."

"What's her last name?" dad finally asked.

"I don't know."

"You're going to marry her but you don't know her last name?"

"That's the best part. I hardly know anything about her."

"Hmmm," said dad.

"What kind of girl leaves a rose for a boy she doesn't know?" asked mom.

"The kind of girl I'm going to marry."

"You're talking crazy," said dad.

"No, he's not," said mom. "He's serious. I'll be back at the tent."

Mom got up and left. Our food arrived. Dad scooped two spoonfuls of brown sugar into his oatmeal. I watched it melt.

"I wish you wouldn't do that."

"Do what?"

"Play games."

"I'm not playing games. I love this girl. Why should that upset her? That should make her happy."

Dad slurped away at his oatmeal.

"Do you know if she ever molested me?"

Now if this had been a scene from a badly directed movie, dad would have spit his oatmeal all over the table. As it was, he calmly took a napkin and wiped his mouth.

"I beg your pardon?" he asked.

"Do you know if she ever molested me?"

Dad couldn't tell if I was joking or not. I can be pretty deadpan.

"That's not even funny," he said.

"That's not a joke."

He got flustered. Looked around at the tables to make sure no one was listening. Looked back at me. Then he got angry.

"Why the hell would you ask a question like that?"

"I've got two really good reasons."

"I just need one."

"No, I've got two. First, she's always been very strange about women in my life."

"I don't recall you having a lot of women in your life."

"I had that girlfriend in high school."

"Who?"

"Tiffany. Mom called her a tart."

We only went around for three weeks before she dumped me like a penny stock in a free fall but dad didn't need to know that.

"And you saw her just now. She couldn't handle it. It's like she's got some weird jealous attachment to me."

"Your mother's out of her mind right now. You come to breakfast and announce that you're getting married to some girl you met last night when you were drunk. And not only are you surprised that she gets upset, as even a stable mother might, but you follow this ridiculous reaction with the conclusion that she must have molested you as a child."

He was right of course. He had dismantled my first reason. Dad is very smart sometimes. I love his logic. No sarcasm. I really do.

"And what was the second thing?" he asked.

I was just about to launch into what Gabriel had told me but the waiter came over with coffee refills. Thank god he did. As the waiter poured the coffee, I realized that to drag Gabriel into all of this would just make matters worse. The waiter left. I decided I could say what I needed to say. I'd just change the circumstances.

"I've been talking to mom a lot on this trip you know," I said. "And she's told me things about herself."

Dad bit down on a slice of apple. *Crunch.*

"Like what?"

"Like how she feels that her life stopped having any purpose once you guys arrived in Paris. She didn't have Maggie and me to raise anymore."

"How do you get from there to molestation?"

"She's always saying that she's failed me as a mother."

"She's depressed."

"And she hinted that it's something to do with me."

"She's got a chemical imbalance, Richard. You'll drive yourself crazy analyzing everything she says to you. I know. I've tried."

"No, I don't agree. I think there is something. Something she's too afraid to tell me."

"There's nothing there."

His voice was cold and menacing. At first, I thought he had grown irritated because we were talking about something he thought was really beyond stupid and was therefore not worthy of further discussion. But his reaction was too intense. It didn't take much conjecturing on my part to see that there was a whole lot there and he knew what it was. I also saw that there would be little point in pursuing any of it with him.

Mom holds the key for both of us. My time is running short. We will be back in Paris soon and she will be doped out on drugs in a mental home. No, the time to act is now. Out here in the wilderness.

I wasn't sure if mom was going to be joining us for our morning game drive but she came along. Why the hell we came to see some goddamn flamingoes I'll never know. We took the boat to another island where we were met by a different driver and a van. Dad was probably wishing Gabriel was with us because Gabriel wouldn't have made the mistake that this other meathead did.

"Richard, can I have a cigarette?" asked mom as we bumped along a choppy dirt road. I gave her one. Dad was studying his map even though he probably had no idea where we were or where we were going. And then the driver chimed in with the news that would ruin the morning.

"One of our vans went missing last night," he said.

Dad and I shrunk like pierced balloons. We didn't have time to imagine what her anxiety would do with a missing van. She was on it like a shot.

"No, no, no," she said. "That's it."

"They'll find the van," said the driver.

"But the passengers will be slaughtered."

The driver turned his head and glanced back at mom. I think he was making sure he heard what he thought he heard from the person he thought he heard it from. He looked back a few more times as mom stared, panic-stricken, out her window, shaking her head, clutching her fingers.

He seemed amused. "Don't do that," he said. "Now you make me nervous." He chuckled and looked at dad expecting to get a manly confirmation nod. Dad's nod was supposed to confirm that the little woman was afraid, *silly woman*, but that the men knew better. They were, after all, men. But dad didn't nod. He just glared.

"It's my fault," said mom.

Dad tried to ignore her and continued reading his map.

"What's your fault?" I asked.

"This trip was my idea. If anything happens it'll be all my fault."

"Nothing's going to happen to us," muttered dad like his mouth was stuffed with marbles.

"We're all going to die."

Dad threw his map in the air. It blew back and landed in my lap.

"Janet!" he shouted. "You are absolutely correct. We *are* all going to die. It is our natural birthright. But it is not something we need to be reminded of every five goddamn minutes. Are we going to die in this van today? Probably not. But, if we are, then I have one last request. Can you shut the hell up for, say, ten minutes so we can at least die in peace?"

Dad snapped his fingers, well, actually his thumb and middle finger. I passed the map to mom who handed it to dad.

Mom was quiet . . . until we spotted a one-legged boy. He was a native and he was hobbling down the side of the road on a crutch made from a tree limb. Our driver was doing what he was paid to do — offer insights into the local customs and people.

"That boy was bitten by a snake," he said. "An infection set in and his father had to cut off his leg with a machete."

Mom shook her head and began mumbling. Dad's nose was buried in his map. He kept reading but his voice tremored with anger.

"Do you have any stories that don't involve missing vans or amputations?" asked dad. "How about the weather? Can we talk about the weather?"

The driver decided he didn't like dad very much. He shut up. *Good.*

I watched as the one-legged boy faded in the distance. When I knew he couldn't see me I waved. *Hello, crippled brother. I am your friend.* I saw myself in him, amputated, fucked-over, hobbling through life on a dusty road. I didn't continue this pathetic comparison for long because dad yelled at mom to stop mumbling and I forgot everything and went numb.

The morning was ruined. We rode in silence to the flamingoes. Silence made sense. All of us had much to think about. Mom's mind was filled with images of the three of us being butchered by a gang of blacks. Dad's mind was carefully rehearsing the phone call to Wimpole Tours asking them to get us on the next flight to Paris. And me? Well, I had my front claws frantically digging in the dirt, trying to unearth that ugly blind worm that connected mom and me.

If mom had molested me why the fuck couldn't I remember? Therapy geeks say that we suppress stuff like this. I think that's bullshit. I'd remember. Unless I was too young. But too young would be five and under. What can a grown woman do with a four-year-old boy? *Probably stuff I wouldn't want to remember.*

No, if she had molested me, it would have happened later.

Maybe she had had a bout of madness back then as well. Maybe she was sick when she did it. But that doesn't change the fact that I don't remember a thing. I started thinking about getting hypnotized when I got back home. But I don't believe in that crap either.

I had enjoyed a short interlude of relief from Nicole's rose. But I ended up right back in the meat grinder. I sat in the back of the van and slung hate in mom's direction. She was keeping something big from me. I wished that Gabriel had never said anything. I was getting obsessed. I hated her guts. I hoped that she'd kill herself. Actually, I hoped that she'd tell me her secret first and then kill herself.

But then I thought of Gabriel. Who the fuck was he? A doctor? A shaman? No. He never said mom revealed anything specific. He was just speculating. I started to calm down. I was getting all worked up over Gabriel's hunch. The guy drives vans for a living. Just like mom said. What the hell was I doing placing so much importance on what he thought? It was stupid. Once I had torn Gabriel limb from limb and set him on fire I started to feel better.

I sat and watched the back of dad's head bounce up and down just like it did during our family car trips in our station wagon. We took it all the way to California one summer. The combination of winding roads and mom's cigarettes sometimes made me carsick. We'd pull over so I could get some fresh air from Mother Nature and some stale insults from dad. It drove him nuts. If we were meant to arrive at the Motel 6 in Butte, Montana at four o'clock then this meant four o'clock, not 4:20.

I still remember dad taking his hand off the steering wheel and stretching his fingers. I thought it looked like he was saying "wow" with his hand. I'd actually mouth "wow" to myself when he did it. It wasn't until I started driving that I realized he was drying the sweat off his hand. Wow.

Farting was always a big highlight on these trips. I've got to hand it to dad. Like me, he never quite grew up. All of it was funny — farting, boogers, stuff between your toes. Not menstrual stuff though. He didn't think that was funny at all. Neither did I. I still don't.

Nothing would get us laughing harder than a well-timed fart during a car trip. Maggie always got more upset than mom. I mean she got crazy. She'd scream at dad and me about how immature we were and then try and hold her breath. But our farts were like boa constrictors. They sensed when she was ready to exhale and waited . . . patiently . . . for her to inhale again. Dad would adopt the calm, authoritative tone of an anesthesiologist and tell her not to fight it.

Dad also claimed that farts you could hear were farts that didn't smell. A shivering family with the windows rolled down in twenty-below weather was proof that his theory was dead wrong.

Most young men leave home with a few words of advice from the old man. *The stick slung over the shoulder. The sack of clothes hanging from the stick. The sound of chickens. The country road stretching out as far as the eye can see. The bus pulling up. The father saying, "It's not the size of the dog in the fight, son. It's the size of the fight in the dog."* Or something else just as corny and appropriate. But not me. I left home with "If you can hear 'em, you can't smell 'em."

Maggie's hysteria, provoked by our flatulence, would only cause us to laugh harder. She never did figure out that if she never reacted then dad and I probably wouldn't have farted.

Poor Maggie. She had to go and get pregnant and miss out on all this fun. She didn't seem resentful at all about not coming to Africa. Not that she could have. She's due any day now. Still, I would have been pissed. But I don't think Maggie gives a shit. She loves the idea of becoming a mother. She never really wanted to explore or take chances. Not that it matters much. I've done both and I'm still lost.

I have Maggie to thank for helping me realize that women have bowel movements. It's not the type of epiphany that comes up very often among men when they gather to discuss women.

I must have been twelve or thirteen at the time and I went into the bathroom I shared with Maggie. I flipped up the lid to take a pee before I got dressed for school and I saw it. It was the biggest dump I had ever seen in my life. It was Maggie's. She did this. *Holy cow. Girls crap.*

I love Maggie but I cannot say that we are very close. She has found her life's purpose but I haven't found mine. She seems so far away from all this right now with her baby in her belly and her future mapped out. Part of me is jealous. Part of me craves the comfort of monotony that she has found.

Maggie likes her windows spotless and her driveway cleared of snow before breakfast. I guess she's more like dad and I am more like mom. I wonder if this means I'm destined for a life of insanity. I hope not.

Dad will have to call Maggie when we get back to Paris and tell her about mom. She's in for quite a shock. Maybe dad should wait until after she's had her baby. Funny, mom mentioned the pregnancy once in Paris before we left but not a word since we got here.

I don't think Maggie likes us much. I pushed her away by being so drunk and stoned that she gave me an ultimatum before I left for Paris — shape up or she's telling dad I need to get my ass out of the condominium and find my own digs.

Mom and dad pushed her away when they didn't come home for her wedding in March. She has found new in-laws, a new family. That's probably a smart choice. Mom and dad and I are crazy. Maggie doesn't belong on this trip. She's okay. This trip is for the loons, the addicts, the drunks, the desperate. This is no place for pregnant mothers.

I'm still surrounded by thousands of flamingoes. Big fucking deal. There could be a million of them and I wouldn't give a shit. They remind me of suburbia. They look plastic. When the hell are we going to see some real animals?

I'm watching mom stumble forward, literally crippled by fear. She's disappearing and reappearing in the steam. What an apocalyptic image. It looks like hell on earth.

I've never really worried about hell after death. I'll worry even less about it after seeing mom in the steam. Hell is here. Not down there (wherever that is). It's now. Not later. The dumb-dumbs don't get it. They think the worst is yet to come. Sorry. It's already here, every fucking day, for every single one of us. You don't believe me? Look around. If you can't see demons dancing and fires burning in Treblinka, Hiroshima or Wounded Knee then you need to pull your head out of your ass and smell some burning flesh.

Anyway, all I'm trying to say is that mom is walking around in her own personal hell right now and her predicament is made more visually dramatic with all the steam. Dad just whistled at me. Woof, woof. I guess he wants me to come over.

Minutes Later

Dad had forgotten the trouble with Gabriel and my questions about incest. I think he even forgot to check the flamingoes off his animal list. His focus was completely on mom. We walked about ten yards behind her. Dad pulled out a mint, looked at it and his shoulders sagged. He unwrapped it and popped it in his mouth.

"I've seen enough," he said. "I think we've hit rock bottom."

"She's pretty out of it," I said, stating the obvious.

"I'm going to call Wimpole this afternoon. We should be able to get to Nairobi by Thursday and we'll be back in Paris by Friday night. I'm sorry, Richard."

"We've seen a lot. I don't care."

"It's so pitiful. Look at her."

Mom looked like she was drunk or wearing a blindfold. Or, was drunk, with a blindfold . . . on a creaky ship . . . in choppy water. Nah. Too much. Just drunk with a blindfold. I don't know what was worse. Her stumbling around like that or dad and me watching her, shaking our heads. Pity is a horrible feeling to have for someone. It's poison.

"No," he said, as if I was disagreeing with him. "This has got to stop. She's completely out of her mind."

Dad moved on ahead and joined mom. She's been out of her mind since we got off the plane. None of this is new. It's seeing mom in this setting that's chilled dad to the bone. He's afraid something will happen now and he'll feel responsible and rotten for the rest of his life. I, on the other hand, feel right at home in the steam. I don't want to leave it.

Dad's right. Any further delay in getting her back could prove disastrous. He's waving to tell me it's time to return to the van. I don't want to. I am quite happy sitting here in hell.

2:52 p.m.

I have been back in my tent for half an hour. I have all these goodies and the trip is now being cut short. What do I do? Should I attempt to smoke everything before we leave for Paris on Friday? Should I throw it all out? That would be such a waste. What to do? Perhaps I could try and sell the stuff to a few of the drivers.

There is nothing planned for this afternoon. I will lay low. I just lit a joint. I don't feel like being outside. I think I will try and finish my stash before we leave. I don't want to see it go to waste. It will be a great challenge.

3:20 p.m.

Jesus murphy. I was exhaling a huge plume of smoke and dad poked his head in my tent.

"Can I see you for a second?" he asked before pulling his head back outside.

I just about had a heart attack. The tent reeked of pot. How could he not smell it? I snuffed out my joint and blitzed the incriminating air with several healthy squirts of fresh orange fragrance before going outside. He's always claimed to be naive about drugs. Is proud of the fact that he's never been around anyone smoking marijuana. He says he doesn't even know what it smells like. Thank god.

He was waiting out on my balcony. I tried to stay far enough away so he couldn't smell my clothes. I wasn't in the mood to test Dick Tracy and see how naive he really was. I knew my eyes must have been burning red.

"We may have a change of plans," he said.

"Again?"

"No, not again," he said with irritation. "I just had a long talk with your mother. I told her I was on my way to call Wimpole Tours. She begged me not to do it. She wants to see the safari through until the end. She's promised to make more of an effort."

"I don't think it's a question of making more of an effort. She doesn't seem to have any control over herself."

He crossed his arms and shook his head. "I'm not too sure about that."

"You think she's putting this on?"

"Not at all. But I think she's got more control than we think. And she admitted she hasn't been taking her medication. She's promised to do that now. So what do you think?"

My head was spinning. I was wishing I hadn't smoked that bone. "We should head back."

His voice flared with exasperation. "Why?"

"You asked me for my opinion. What are you getting so angry for?"

He pasted a surprised look on his face.

"I'm not angry. I just want to know why you think we should leave. That's all."

Mom came around the corner. "I don't want to go back. We haven't seen the big animals yet."

Mom was getting closer to me. I got nervous. Unlike dad, she knows what marijuana smells like.

"We're having tea and cakes at four o'clock," announced dad. "We can have a family conference."

Dad left. Mom smiled. I made a move for my tent.

"Your eyes are red."

"No they're not."

"And you stink of pot."

"I do not."

"You're so messed up, Richard. I don't hate you for being a drug addict. I hate you for destroying me like this."

"I'm not a drug addict."

I hated having to say that. I felt like I was in one of those stupid after-school specials.

She opened her mouth to say something. I stopped her.

"I already know what you're going to say. It's all my fault. You can apologize later."

I came inside. I didn't have to make such a cold departure, but I'm tired of her. I've been in here for at least fifteen minutes and I think she's still standing out there. What the hell is she doing? I'm going to peek through the tent to see if she's still there.

She's there. Standing on the balcony. Looking out at the lake. And she's crying. Not loud. But I could hear her sniffling and I saw her shoulders moving up and down. Damn it! I am totally fucked right now. I know what I should do. I should go out and let her know she was always there for me. Tell her I don't take drugs because of her. Admit that I'm an addict. Tell her I'm going to stop.

Stop talking to yourself, hero boy. Get the fuck out there.

I just went outside. She was gone. I could have run after her but I'm back here in my tent. I had my chance. She was waiting for me.

4:02 p.m.

I'm on my way to the canopied restaurant for tea and cakes. I did it. I just threw away all my goodies. I took everything down to the lake and tossed it all. I feel a tremendous sense of accomplishment. That stuff was worth a lot of money. But I had to. I don't want mom to smell anything on me again. I'd be forever haunted if I felt like my smoky clothes were the final nudge that drove her to suicide.

I did save my jude though. I'm going to quit everything once I get back to Canada, I just need a little something to get me through Africa. And jude doesn't smell. I'll try to abstain from alcohol as well. Mom doesn't need to see her husband and her son in drunken stupors. It's not a perfect solution but I'm too raw to toss everything away. I'll have tea now. And cakes.

5:08 p.m.

Got myself cleaned up before I joined mom and dad for the family conference. Got some drops in my eyes and splashed a little cologne on my neck. I didn't want mom freaking out on me. And I didn't want to be freaking out, so I smoked a few lines of jude.

Dad was in good spirits. It was a conference after all — something he was familiar with. He was in a mood to get things resolved. He was a true diplomat, emphasizing that we would be making the decision about continuing the trip as a family.

"I think the person whose opinion matters the most is Janet," he said. "If she really believes that she would like to carry on then we'll have to consider that option carefully. On the other hand, if she feels strongly that she would like to go back, then we will leave for Nairobi first thing in the morning."

Dad turned to mom and raised his eyebrows in a most sincere manner. He looked like Paul McCartney singing "Let it Be." "Janet, what do you want to do?"

Mom was staring at me. She didn't seem to hear him.

"Janet?" asked dad.

Mom continued to stare. What the hell was she staring at? My eyes weren't red anymore.

"Mom," I said. "Do you want to go back?"

My question succeeded in pulling her out of her trance.

"I want to see the elephants. And then we can go."

"Well how about this," said dad. "Why don't we agree to carry on until we see an elephant and then we'll get together again and see how things are. Agreed?"

Dad looked back and forth between mom and me. I finished off my third tiny cake and rubbed my sticky fingers on my jeans. Mom began to nod her head and she smiled. There was something weird in her smile.

"Agreed," she said.

"Richard?" asked dad.

The whole thing was completely insane. I felt like we were witches making some kind of evil pact over a bubbling cauldron. "Agreed," I said.

"The ayes have it," said dad without the aid of a gavel. "Now let's try and make the most out of the rest of the safari."

"What about Gabriel?" I asked.

"I called Wimpole Tours this morning. They're going to have a new driver meet us on the mainland tomorrow morning."

"What?!" exclaimed mom. I hissed air through my teeth to express my own disapproval.

"Why did we vote on continuing the safari but let you decide what happens to Gabriel on your own?" asked mom.

"Because I'm paying for the trip."

The great diplomat had left without saying good-bye. The dictator had returned without saying hello. Mom's eyes welled up with tears.

"That's the shits," she said.

"He almost killed you, Janet," said dad. "It's not just about us. It's for the protection of other families as well. I don't see how he can act as a guide with that kind of behaviour. His supervisors had to be told."

"If he goes then I want to go home," announced mom.

She got up from the table and marched away.

"So, how long did we have harmony and agreement?" I asked as I looked at my watch. "I got thirty-seven seconds. What did you get?"

I was expecting him to tell me to shut up but he wasn't even paying attention. The whole situation is so futile. Having tea and cakes and a conference. Trying to restore order. It was like sweeping the concrete porch after the house has burned to the ground.

He looked defeated, like he did on Sunday nights when he was drunk on wine and cowboy music. The difference this time was that he wasn't drunk. His wrinkled head looked heavy, like it was going to snap from his neck and roll off the table onto the floor.

I felt very awkward. He wasn't saying anything. So I decided to make a quick exit.

"I'll go check on mom."

With that I bolted the table and left him to his woes. It was for the best. He didn't want to be seen like that and I certainly didn't want to sit around watching him. I knew that an order of scotch would quickly follow.

The wind started to kick up as I left the restaurant. I passed Beverly on one of the paths. She had a big jacket on so I couldn't see her breasts. She breezed by.

"Jambo," she said.

"Jambo."

"Good night to stay inside," she said. "Big storm coming in."

Finally some good news. I love storms. I came to a clearing in the path and saw that, sure enough, the waves on the lake were starting to rise, their white tips getting blown to the wind. But what really got me excited was what I saw on the horizon. A giant, swirling, black mass of clouds. Birds were flying in from the lake, seeking refuge in the trees of the island. Tonight would be the perfect night for a murder or a suicide.

I arrived at mom and dad's tent. The wind was really starting to howl. The flaps were fluttering wildly and the poles were beginning to groan.

She wasn't there. I tried not to panic but this is not a camp with a lot of options of where to spend your time. I went around to the outdoor bathroom beside their tent and tapped on the door.

"Mom? Are you in there?"

I knocked again. No response. I slowly opened the door, expecting to see a big oblong-shaped pool of dark blood, a gleaming razor blade and mom at peace. The bathroom was empty.

The wind knocked something down, near where I was standing. I didn't see what it was but it got me running.

I ran wildly down the path leading back to the restaurant. I had to tell dad. We'd have to send out a search party. As I neared the flapping canopy of the restaurant, I had one more thought as to where she might be.

I doubled back and raced to my tent. I opened the flap and there she was, sitting on my bed with a cigarette. One of her bags was beside the bed. She looked at me calmly.

"I don't want to be with him tonight," she said. "Do you have a light?"

I was relieved to have found her alive. But I also felt like my fortress had been invaded. What was I supposed to do? Turn her out? I lit her cigarette. She held my hand with both her hands as I did so. Her skin was burning up.

I am sitting on my balcony and she is still inside. I am uneasy with the coming night. She probably won't end up staying in the tent but I am scared. Of her madness? I suppose. The wind is snapping at the pages of my journal making it very difficult to write. And it has started to rain. More later.

6:02 p.m.

A quick note. Dad just burst into my tent, out of breath, soaked from the rain.

"Your mother's gone," he exclaimed.

He saw her curled up on my bed before I had a chance to respond. At first he looked relieved but confusion set in quickly.

"What's going on?"

"She wants to stay here tonight."

"Why didn't you tell me? I just told the front desk she'd gone missing."

"You should have checked here first."

"How the hell was I supposed to guess she'd be sleeping on your goddamn bed?!"

He was livid and he was drunk. No need to argue.

"Sorry, I should have come back and said something."

He stood there shaking, with both his fists clenched over his groin like someone had just tried to knee him in the nuts.

"I'll go tell the front desk she's okay," he sputtered.

"What time are we meeting for dinner?"

"I'm not hungry."

He punched his way through the tent flap and was gone. What a prick. How the fuck was this my fault? Why didn't he check here before running like a lunatic to the front desk? Screw it. I'm glad she's spending the night now.

7:30 p.m.

I'm at the restaurant waiting for some food to take back to my tent. They were right about the storm. It's not quite a hurricane but the weather is furious. The gods are angry. The water feels good dripping from my bangs.

Mom rolled over on the bed after dad left.

"He's probably jealous because I'm staying with you tonight," she said.

I left that comment completely alone. Wouldn't touch it.

"I'll go get us some food."

Mom could tell I was uncomfortable. Perhaps my lip was twitching. I don't know.

"I didn't say he was jealous because of anything sexual."

"I didn't say that. I wasn't thinking that. I'll go get the food."

I was finished with the jealousy issue. Didn't want to discuss it. But mom felt obliged to explain herself lest I "got the wrong idea."

"He doesn't like the fact that I have somewhere else to go tonight. But he better get used to it. Because I'm leaving. I won't let him control my life anymore."

She got off the bed, came over and gave me a hug.

"He gets quite upset about how close we are. He sometimes asks me about it."

I patted her on the back and tried to pull away without hurting her feelings. That was news to me. I didn't know we were that close. It felt like she was playing head games with me. Stirring the pot. Playing dad and me off one another. My voice splintered as I tried to speak.

"I'll get the food."

I fumbled with the tent flap and pushed my way outside. The rain stung my face. Big drops. Harsh wind. I started up the path to the restaurant. I slowly became aware that I was walking awkwardly, like I used to back in the hallways in grade seven, like I needed my big, black binder to cover myself, to cover my erection.

I passed dad's tent and saw him through one of the open flaps. He was sitting on the bed with his back to me. He raised a glass to his mouth. A half-empty bottle of scotch sat tilting on the mattress.

All hell is breaking loose. I'm waiting for two chicken dishes with noodles. I have zero interest in eating anything right now. I might as well be waiting for a dead rat.

9:25 p.m.

I slugged back a beer while I was waiting for the food. I also did something that eased my mind considerably. I went to Beverly and asked that a cot be delivered to my tent. I always feel the need to explain things to people when no explanations are necessary, so I told her that mom was going to be staying in my tent. None of her goddamn business but I said it anyway. I always think that people are suspicious of me. That I'm up to something. I'm up to nothing. I'm just doing normal stuff.

Beverly asked if everything was okay. I must have looked pretty scary. The rain. The wind. My hair. My mind. My eyes. I told her things were good. She asked about mom. I said that mom was fine. *Then why isn't she staying with your father tonight, young man?*

I was so preoccupied with getting the cot that I hadn't noticed Beverly's tits. She was leaning forward on the counter in a baby-blue dress shirt. No bra. The shirt was undone to the fourth button. A serious plunge. And her breasts were almost completely exposed. I could actually see the beginning of her nipples. Her breasts were huge, swelling, threatening to snap the tiny thread on that fourth button. The tension was unbearable.

I don't know how long I stared at her breasts. I didn't care and she clearly didn't mind. She came out from behind the counter to find someone to bring me the cot. Her breasts brushed across my back. I turned around after she went by. There was more than enough room to pass without rubbing her breasts on me.

Beverly talked to someone in the adjoining room about getting me a cot and came back. Her blue shirt fluttered down over a pair of black leggings. I knew I would start with the leggings. Get those pulled down right away. She'd look bloated if I took the shirt off first, her belly sticking up over the elastic and everything. I'd avoid that. Get those leggings off lickety-split, slide my hands up under that shirt. She returned to the counter. I was facing her this time so she wasn't as bold. She didn't brush me.

I imagined her whispering it was too bad I had a guest that night. That she had planned to drop by later and check on me, make sure I wasn't frightened by the storm. I stood there like a mute and fantasized some more. *You were a bad boy, Richard Clark, dropping your bathrobe and letting me see your young, naked body like that.* Beverly smiled and disappeared into another office.

I don't know how long I stood there, perhaps ten minutes, waiting for her to come back. I cursed mom's name. Why the hell did she have to stay with me tonight? Of all nights.

Beverly had seen me naked! She had liked it. Maybe. She had shown me most of her breasts. Yes. She tickled my back with them. Yes. She knew this was my last night. Yes. I tried to think of something to say when she got back. *Hey, you look really nice . . .* no . . . *you look really hot . . .* too bold . . . *Hey, how about you and me getting together later? . . .* boring . . . *I'd love to hear about Scotland . . . .*

Beverly returned but there were two camp staffers with her. The three were talking about an order of lightbulbs. Beverly was the manager again. Not the sultry seductress. She asked me in a professional voice if I needed anything else. I mumbled an apology and left quickly. I was crazed. Furious. Horny. I stumbled my way back to pick up dinner.

The restaurant folks put the food in plastic bags and I raced back to my tent. Mom was wiping down my little writing table for dinner. She looked completely different. Her eyes were shimmering with exuberance, like she'd had a few, but I don't think she had. She'd changed out of the dirty clothes she'd been wearing for the past two days. She'd put on a dress. It was crisp and clean and short. And there was something else about her that took me until we were sitting down to notice. She had put makeup on. A little eyeliner and red lipstick. And even though the tent was filled with the smell of insect repellent and garlic chicken, I caught a whiff of perfume. A soft and pleasant perfume.

Mom wanted to turn off the light and eat beside the glow of the lantern lamp. I was so irritated by her. I was thinking of Beverly's breasts. And how mom was standing between me and that nice rack. I told mom I wanted to see what the hell I was eating so we left the light on. She was unconcerned with my mood. She guided a forkful of chicken into her mouth.

"This is delicious," she said.

Mom was devouring her meal. She wasn't picking at her plate like she'd been doing since we landed. Tonight was different. Tonight she was hungry.

"Did I ever tell you what a handsome boy you are. I've never told you that before. And I should have."

Her compliment made me queasy. The rain pelted the canvas of the tent. It sounded like corks being dropped on a bass drum. I was blushing. I lifted my beer to my mouth and took three big swallows. I set the bottle down too hard and watched as the foam lifted up the neck and spilled slowly over the top and down the side.

Mom reached into her pocket and put two tiny pills on the table beside her bottle of beer. She put one in her mouth and chased it down with a sip of beer.

"My anxiety pills," she said without me asking. She took the second one. "I haven't been taking them. But I want to now. I want to finish the safari." She swallowed the second pill and smiled at me. "All better," she said.

I had barely touched my food. My stomach was twisted up in knots. I hadn't been able to get Beverly's breasts off my mind. I've never understood guys that could go to a peeler palace on their lunch hour, dive into a big steak and watch women strip naked with loud music playing. I went once and I'll never go again. I got way too horny. I wanted the girl right there and then. And if I couldn't have her, which of course I couldn't, I wanted to masturbate. And eat? Forget it. When I get horny it's like I have the flu.

The combination of being horny and smelling mom's perfume was too much. I pushed my plate away and lit a cigarette.

"What's the matter?" she asked.

"Nothing."

"You've hardly touched your pasta."

"I'm just not hungry right now."

"You're not being honest with me."

"You're right. I've got a ravenous appetite. I just don't want to admit it."

"One of the reasons I came to your tent was to get away from your father's foul humour."

"Mom, this trip has been a rolling nightmare. I think I'm entitled to a little sarcasm."

"I just want to know what's bothering you."

"It's you. Right now at this moment, it's you."

"What about me?"

"You're all fine now. You got makeup on, clean clothes, you got your appetite back."

"Is that a bad thing?"

"Don't do that. I'm not saying that. It just knocks me sideways that's all. One hour you're up, the next hour you're down and the next hour you're up again."

"How would you prefer me?"

"That's not what I'm saying."

"Did you know that your father and I have not slept together in ten years?"

"I don't need to know this."

"Ten years, Richard."

"I don't know what to tell you."

My mouth was shut to any further discussion. But my mind did acknowledge that ten years was an awfully long time. If it was true. It might not have been. Surely they couldn't have gone ten years.

"I tell you that only because I hope that you don't let the same thing happen with you and Nicole."

She was pretty smart. Dropping in Nicole's name like that. I hadn't been thinking about Nicole much. But all of a sudden my mind sparkled and popped with pretty pictures. Pictures of us exchanging letters. My letters would be longer because I love to burden others with my dumb opinions. Hearing her tease me at the movies because I eat my popcorn one piece at a time. Deciding where we wanted to live. Vancouver Island. Prague. New York. Buying her peach perfume. Watching her shivering thighs slide past my ears.

"I'm not talking about sex," she said. "I'm talking about friendship, putting an arm around her, letting her know you still care about her."

"You sound like a five-dollar self-help book."

"And you sound like a pretentious, full-of-shit nineteen-year-old," she spat.

"If I have any problems with getting close to someone they have nothing to do with sex," I said, as I pinched my top lip with my thumb and forefinger. "They have to do with this."

I tucked my finger underneath my upper lip and pushed it out, achieving, I hoped, a very grotesque effect.

"That's such a cop-out. You can barely notice it. You'd think you'd have that figured out by now."

"I don't have anything figured out and I don't want to sit here and talk about shame and this deep freeze for a heart that dad's passed onto me."

"I didn't say anything about shame."

Oops. Deny. Accuse. "Sure you did."

"I did not. That's in your mind."

"What's in my mind is private! It's none of your business!"

"You're obviously not ready to talk about this. But when you've been with Nicole for three years and your fire starts to die and you two start fighting and drifting apart then . . ."

"Then I'll know that it was not meant to be."

"No! Not if you love her."

"Mom, I don't even know Nicole. I'll probably never see her again. It's insane talking about her like this."

"You said you were going to marry her."

"She gave me a fucking rose. That's all. I'm such a loser. I turned that one act of kindness into a pipe dream about seeing her again and getting married. It'll never happen. She took pity on me. That's all it was."

I devastated myself by giving voice to the fact that I had built a castle in the sky. A place for me to hug some hope. I'm a cynic with a black heart but deep down I just want a happy ending.

"Nicole did not take pity on you."

"They all take pity on me. And I know what they think. Such

a witty lad. Such strong hands. Such kind eyes. Pause. Shame about the harelip."

"It's a cleft lip and palate, and that's not true."

"It is true."

I became overwhelmed with how useless I felt. My eyes filled with tears. I had not cried in front of mom since I broke my arm.

"Please don't be upset."

"You started it! Telling me about your sex life with dad. That is none of my business!"

"I'm sorry."

"I don't think you brought it up to be helpful. And I don't think you brought it up because of your monumental concerns that I'm going to end up like dad."

"What are you saying?"

"Forget it. I'm going to get a coffee."

"Tell me."

I ignored her and started for the tent flap. She bolted out of her chair and blocked me from leaving. Her mouth was taut. "You tell me what you mean."

"I don't know anything anymore."

She wasn't moving. I was not about to push her aside. And the way she was looking at me I wasn't sure I could have done so without losing an eye to one of her fingernails.

"I think you're keeping stuff from me," I said. "Stuff that makes you depressed."

"Like what?"

"You tell me."

"How can I tell you about something if I don't know what it is?"

"Did you ever touch me when I was a kid?"

There. I had said it. I had finally asked the question. Damn the repercussions. She was pushing. She got it. Right between the eyes. I thought she'd burst into tears. But she started to laugh. And in her laughter I saw many shades. There was a trace of embarrassment. There was also a splash of pity and a hint of relief.

"Is that what Gabriel told you?" she asked warily.

"No."

"What does any of this have to do with me talking about my relationship with your father?"

"I think you were trolling the waters. To see how I'd react. Get us talking about sex. You're all dressed up. You've got makeup and perfume on. You were trying to see where I was at with all this."

"With all what?" she asked bewilderedly.

"You spending the night. Your feelings for me. Telling me how dad gets jealous with how close we are."

She examined me. Looked me up and down. Checked every nook and cranny. And upon the completion of her examination, she delivered her diagnosis.

"You're insane. The drugs have destroyed your brain."

"Whatever. I'm crazy. You're crazy. We're all crazy."

"Why did you get an erection when I hugged you earlier?"

"I did not."

"I felt it."

My legs were getting weak. I just wanted to get the hell out of there.

"I was thinking about Nicole."

She smiled a cruel smile. A mocking smile. A "nice try" smile. And then she spat like a cornered cat, "I never touched you when you were young. Ever! It sickens me to think that you would even consider something like that. And as far as tonight is concerned, I thought it would be nice for me to get a change of clothes to make myself feel better. I know in your own twisted mind it was all an effort to seduce you but that's your problem. And it's a serious, sick problem. It's not me. It's you. You need help, Richard."

She stepped aside, still glaring at me.

"It's not your lip that makes girls run. It's your mind. They can tell. You're not right."

I escaped outside and walked slowly through the rain. I felt like it was all over. Finished. But I couldn't tell myself what "it" was.

I am at the bar drinking coffee. I will not drink any more alcohol tonight. My mind is empty.

I stayed in the bar until it closed at eleven. I figured this would give mom enough time to get her things packed up and return to her own tent. Dad would be asleep. She wouldn't have to worry about him.

The rain continued as I made my way back. I was looking forward to climbing into my bed and resting my mind for awhile. I got back to the tent. It was dark but I could see that mom had not left. She was asleep in my bed. How could she have stayed after saying the things she did? And hearing my accusations?

I was really angry to see her there. My adrenaline was racing. She was not completely under the covers. Sleep had tossed some of them off her body. Her bare leg was sticking out. I could see all the way up to the top of her thigh. I thought I saw the slope of her breast. I wondered whether she was completely naked. I found myself staring at her gentle curves. I was no longer angry. But my heart was still pounding.

I found my cot resting just inside the entrance. They must have delivered it while I was at the bar. Mom hadn't opened it up for me. The least she could have done was to get it ready for me. Unfold it. Pull the sheets down at an angle. Fluff a pillow. Things a mom should do. Was she punishing me? I unfolded the cot as quietly as I could. I am in the cot right now, writing by lantern light. I am naked under the sheets. I have an erection but I will not masturbate with her in the tent. I will wait until she's gone in the morning. I am so tempted because I am so horny. I cannot sleep.

3:32 a.m.

Something has happened. I was asleep on my cot. I became aware of the sweet smell of baby oil. I felt the cool night air on my chest. My sheets were down around my hips. I felt a warm hand riding up and down over my erection. I dared not open my eyes. I felt the gentle tapping of her breasts on my thigh. I could hear my own breathing. But I could also hear her breathing, which was louder than mine. And I heard this soft whisper saying, "I'm sorry, I'm so sorry."

I finally opened my eyes. I sat up and saw that mom was where she was before. In the bed. In exactly the same position. It was a dream. Mom is right though. I need to get some help. Dreams like this aren't healthy. But at least I haven't hurt anyone. I hadn't even been thinking these thoughts until Gabriel put them in my head. It's all going to be okay. It was just a dream. A dream I can never tell anyone. There are worse things. There are grandfathers gassing kittens in burlap sacks and aunts with fat asses suffocating infants.

I was sitting up in the cot when I woke up from my dream. The rain had stopped. Soothing light from the moon had wrapped its arms around the tent. Something warm was dripping down my thigh. My belly and chest were splattered with thick pools of sap. It glistened like mercury in the light from the moon. I still had my erection. I ran my thumb along my length and felt the unmistakable slippery slide of baby oil.

Thursday, August 18
2:34 p.m.
Maralal Safari Lodge
Cabin 12
Kenya, Africa

I thought Baringo was paradise. But Maralal is even better. I have my own cabin. As I write I can see zebras grazing about twenty yards from my window.

I feel like the safari has only just begun. We are finally seeing big game. No more fucking flamingoes. We've entered the best part of the trip. I am so happy here. I am glad we've left the madness of Baringo behind.

Dad woke me up at seven this morning by rattling on my tent flap and yelling my name. I snapped awake and shouted that everything was okay. He yelled back that he wasn't asking if everything was okay. He was just telling me to get moving. He asked what was wrong. I shouted that there was nothing wrong. He grumbled something and walked away.

It took awhile for my dream to resurface. Perhaps I was trying to forget it. I grew anxious about how I'd treat mom this morning. Would she see it in my eyes? Would she sense what I had dreamed? Slap me six times? Three on the left cheek. Three on the right. I didn't need to worry. The bed was empty and neatly made. Her bag was gone. She must have left early. An awful feeling slowly settled in. If she wasn't in my tent then where the hell was she? Dad must have assumed when he woke me up that mom was still with me.

I remembered accusing her of molesting me. Jesus, if that wouldn't drive a person to suicide, what would? I rushed outside and ran like a lunatic to mom and dad's tent. I arrived, out of breath, to find mom quietly packing her stuff into the last of her bags. She turned and smiled sweetly. Dad wasn't there.

"How did you sleep?" she asked.

"Good," I said, relieved. "You must have been up early?"

"I was. But I had the best night's rest I've had in a long time. Your father's gone to the restaurant. We're to meet him for breakfast."

There was a momentary pause where our eyes met. "I'm sorry about the things I said last night."

"What things?" she asked.

"You know."

"I don't know."

"Yes, you do and I'm sorry."

"Richard Clark, I have no recollection of anything being said to me last night by you or any other person that requires an apology. The only bad thing you did was grind your teeth, which you shouldn't do because you'll lose enamel."

I left their tent and walked back to my own. So that was the game plan. Complete denial. She hadn't been drunk so she couldn't have blacked out. No, she was denying the whole thing. Good.

I got back to my tent and a camp staffer was folding up my cot. I grabbed my cigarettes off the table and lit a smoke. The staffer smiled at me as he wheeled the cot away. I could hear the squeak of the tiny wheels as it was scuttled away over the pebbles on the path. After the sound disappeared an overwhelming silence was left behind in the tent. Not a disturbing silence. It was a calm silence. I should have been freaking out right then. But I was surprised at how good I felt. Not good. Just relieved. The perfume. The cot. The evidence. Were gone.

Last night had been wild. The storm. Mom staying over. The accusations. Being naked with her in the room. The weird dream. I should have felt sickened. But I didn't. I was really looking forward to the rest of the safari.

As I walked up the pebble path to the restaurant I finally noticed the clear blue skies. The storm had passed and left a palpable tranquillity. *Are you trying to say it was really calm outside?* Yes I am. *Thank you.*

I had a hungry-man's appetite at breakfast. I ordered it all: scrambled eggs, bacon, sausage, potatoes showered in Tabasco sauce, four slices of toast with strawberry jam, a large orange juice and about two litres of coffee. Mom was the same. She ate like a pig. Dad was the odd man out. He picked at his grapefruit, looking distracted, tense. He also looked nauseous.

"What time does the boat leave?" I asked.

"Nine o'clock," he said.

That was the extent of dad's contribution to our breakfast. He excused himself from the table, presumably to retch.

Mom and I had zero tension between us. Neither of us had any accusations or confessions. It was such a welcome change from last night. I felt closer to her than I had in years.

"He's amazing," she said with a chuckle. "He finished off a bottle of scotch last night. You'd think he'd have been passed out, face down on the floor. But at six o'clock this morning he's up, shaving, humming, drinking coffee. You know, he's never missed a day of work in his life."

"He's told me. A hundred times."

"It's true. That's why it's so hard to talk to him about his drinking."

"Has he ever hit you when he was drunk?"

"Your father's never hit me. Drunk or sober. He threw a cabbage at me once."

I was on the verge of telling her about his forearm to my throat and the attack on the fat man but I didn't. No point in betraying dad or giving her one more thing to worry about. I chose, instead, the safer path of something she was already familiar with.

"He whipped my naked ass once."

"He wasn't drunk."

"You stayed so silent when he did it. You didn't defend me."

"You're my baby. It tore me apart. I hated the fact you were getting punished but I also didn't like that you lied. Your father demands honesty. You could cut off his big toe and he'd forgive you in a week. Lie to him and you'll pay the price for a year."

Or a lifetime.

"Do you think he's always honest?"

"With everyone but himself."

"Have you ever lied to him?"

Mom thought for a moment or wanted me to think that she was seriously looking back on all her years with him and recalling everything. She took forever to answer.

"Our life together is a lie. This safari through Africa is a lie. We're all pretending to be one big, happy family taking the dream vacation of a lifetime."

"I'm not pretending anything like that. This is a fucking disaster."

"Your father pretends it and please stop swearing." She looked at her watch. "It's five after nine. He'll be down at the dock by now."

Mom got up from the table and came over to me. She kissed me on the top of my head. "Thanks for letting me stay last night. I won't have to do that again. I know you like your privacy."

She walked away and left me with butterflies in my belly. What the hell did she mean, *I won't have to do that again?* Masturbate me while I slept? It was a dream.

I returned to my tent and grabbed my bags. I thought about sitting on my balcony, smoking a cigarette and having one final, reflective moment on Baringo. But I didn't have time and I didn't feel safe. I reached down to grab my bags.

"Everything alright then?"

I didn't need to turn around to see who it was. The accent was Scottish.

"So, you're leaving now, then?"

Beverly was wearing a low-cut, six-button, red sweater. I don't usually notice clothes so precisely but Beverly provided quite an inspiration for details. She stood at the entrance to my tent with her hands on her hips. I stole a glance at her breasts.

"Did you enjoy yourself on the island?" she asked.

I didn't respond. I had nothing to say. My heart was pounding, my underwear swelling. I walked slowly toward her. God knows how I looked. Desperate? Crazed? Confident? She backed up a step. I stopped in front of her.

"Beverly," I said. "Can I see your breasts?"

Her face wrinkled up with confusion. "Pardon me?" she asked.

There was still one last chance to be a coward, or seize the day.

"I want to see your breasts."

I could hear her ask, "Right now?"

I could hear myself confirm, "Right now."

I could see her slowly unbuttoning her sweater. One, two, three, four, five, six. I could see her sliding the sweater off her shoulders. I could see her standing there in a blueberry bra with tulip-shaped cups, the tops of her breasts completely exposed. I could hear her say, "Well, here they are." I could see her reach behind to unclasp the bra. I could see her breasts spill out and jiggle. I could see myself lean forward. I could feel my mouth surround her hardened nipple.

I could see and hear and feel all these wonderful things, but what I really heard was Beverly say, "You'll see nothing of the kind." And what I really saw was a terrified woman turn and run from my tent.

I stood there swaying back and forth, caught in the turbulence of her tail engine. Why had she come to my tent? What were these games she was playing? Maybe she was just checking to see if the cot had been collected. Maybe that's why she had come by. Maybe that's all it was. And I had lumbered right at her, looking like the Boston Strangler, asking to see her tits. Jesus. What was happening to me? What had I done? I quickly got my bags and rushed to the dock. Like Gilligan, I just wanted to get the hell off the island.

The velocity of my mood swings is starting to scare me. Whatever mom has, it's contagious. I've got it. And dad too. I have a mental picture of those little felt-covered hammers inside a piano. And we are them. Up and down. Back and forth. And I see a madman sitting at the piano. And he started slowly, deliberately, but now he is speeding up. Playing faster. And the sounds are terrible, out of tune, off-key. And the little felt-covered hammers are becoming a blur.

Mom and dad were already on the boat when I arrived at the dock. Dad was still distracted and tense. I think mom was right. He was probably jealous. *Fuck off.* Or upset that she had somewhere else to go. Probably scared the hell out of him. What would he do if she took off for good?

Our boat skimmed out into the lake and I looked back and saw Beverly standing at the dock. No doubt making sure that the strangler had left the island. I imagined what Nicole was seeing when I was standing there and waving like a fool. *Poor guy*, she must have thought. *He'll find some nice girl with her own disfigurement, a burn on her face, or a beard or buck teeth. Someone will love this creature. But not someone pretty like me.*

I started thinking I would get my harelip fixed for Nicole. Get a nice cupid's bow for an upper lip. I remember when I was young, a neighbour, a nurse, asked mom how come they never got it fixed properly. I was staging an elaborate battle with my little army men in the dining room. I always had the Germans win. They had the cool helmets.

Mom got very testy with the nosy neighbour. Mom told her that I had already had four operations. Three I don't remember, I was too young. The first one was done fresh out of the oven. God, I bet I looked hideous. They must have considered tossing me in the garbage can. Probably explains why there are no baby pictures. The only pictures of me are after the age of three, after my surgeries.

I remember the fourth operation. It scared the hell out of me and it hurt like a mothergrabber. But I don't think it hurt me half as much as it hurt mom. She cried for days before and for days after. I thought I had done something wrong so I told her I didn't want any more stupid operations. And that was it. I was scheduled for a fifth but mom and I called it off. She seemed relieved. I know I was. Until the teasing started, of course. A fifth operation would have helped but I'll always have a little reminder there. I think it's ironic that the nose part of the operation is called a rhinoplasty. *Why is that ironic?* Because we're in Africa. *Okay.*

Some guy at work asked me when I was going to get the damn thing fixed. I told him to mind his own fucking business. The truth is, I've never really wanted to get it fixed. What else could I blame all my troubles on? I hate my face but I have also grown to appreciate its worth. Makes me feel like that French guy with the big nose who knows how to talk to women. Wonder when I'll learn to do the talking part.

I have always told myself that I'd get things fixed when I found a woman who loved me for all of me, including my face. If Nicole proves to be that girl then I will do it for her. And on that day I will surrender and die and become like the rest of the motherfuckers, scarless and normal. And I'll get a job in an office and someone will ask me how I am on a Monday and I will look at them astonished, as if they'd just asked the dumbest question I'd ever heard. *How the heck do you think I am you dodo bird? It's Monday.* And we'll laugh that knowing laugh, comfortable in the fact that we are singing from the same song page. I'll start calling Wednesday hump day. I'll be in a really good mood on Fridays and the person I saw on Monday will ask me how I am on Friday and I'll tell that person that I am feeling fine. Real fine. *It's Friday. How could you not feel fine on a Friday?* And we'll both talk about freedom. Not freedom from laziness or ignorance or greed or lies. No, no. We'll be talking about the weekend.

Just as we rounded the end of the island I saw a small boy crouched in the trees, watching us. I couldn't see for sure but I think it was Sedekia. Getting one final glimpse of the doomed family.

The boat ride was a solitary voyage for all of us. We were staying clear of one another. I saw a family huddled over a checkerboard. The father had a big hand on his son's chubby shoulder. The wife and daughter giggled and teased and pretended to cheat. They were a happy family practising some shenanigans. These were some serious high jinks. Some tomfoolery. This should have been a moment where I looked at them and thought, *now why can't our family be like that?* Instead, I hated that happy family.

I wouldn't trade what I've got for anything. I don't want be out here in Africa teasing and giggling and I don't want dad's hand on my shoulder. I want to be doing exactly what we're doing. Dancing in the fire. Screaming. Crying. Burning. If that don't beat the shit out of cheating at checkers I don't know what does.

We arrived at the dock. Gabriel was there, standing beside our white van. I was thrilled to see him but I never let anyone see that I'm thrilled to see them so I kept it to myself. There was another driver at the wheel of our van. My heart sank. A Mercedes-Benz was parked nearby. Two suits, a man and a woman, were waiting in front of the Mercedes. They had "Wimpole Tours" patches stitched on their lapels.

I walked over to Gabriel. Mom wouldn't follow. She went to the edge of the lake and looked out, hoping, I'm sure, that a rogue wave would rise up and take her away. Dad went over to talk to the suits.

Gabriel took my hand and shook it. There were tears in his eyes. "I think this is the end of the road."

"This is bullshit is what this is."

I was impressed that Gabriel had come out to see us one last time. He didn't have to.

"I want to say good-bye to your mom. I'll be right back."

Gabriel walked away and cautiously joined mom down by the lake. I looked to see if he'd put his arm around her. He didn't. I was just about to go make one final appeal to dad when one of the suits shouted a name. It might have been Ernie. Hell, it could have been Bert. It doesn't matter. The driver in our van, a real corpse of a guy, got out and went over. He was told something by the man in the suit, he nodded and climbed inside their car. Dad shook hands with both the Wimpole reps.

Gabriel went to dad looking very apologetic. He hadn't seen the driver get in the car. "Mr. Clark . . ." he started.

"Forget it," said dad and, spotting mom standing down by the water, he shouted. "Janet! We're leaving."

Mom kept her back to us and shouted back. "Is Gabriel driving?"

"Yes!" hollered dad.

Dad was embarrassed and angry. Embarrassed that he'd done a good deed. And angry because he'd caved in to Janet's wishes. He climbed into the van. Gabriel rushed over to the car and grabbed his duffel bag. He was stopped for a moment by the suits who looked like they had some stern words of warning for him. Mom came up from the lake. "I knew he'd change his mind."

Gabriel started up the engine and we were off. I guess this explains why dad was so distracted at breakfast. He must have been thinking about what to do with Gabriel. Either that or mom put the boots to him. He hates changing his mind about decisions he has made. He thinks it's an indication of weakness.

We drove all the way to Maralal in silence. Gabriel knew better than to try and make conversation. Everyone wanted to be left alone. We saw nothing in the way of animals. But the countryside was soothing — sloping hills and cool air. We passed a few more native folks who glared at us. We may be crazy but we still look like rich, white pigs.

We arrived at Maralal around noon and mom didn't even freak out when Gabriel told us that we had to have an armed escort take us back and forth from our cabins to the lodge (fifty yards). This is big-game country. Survival of the fittest. It isn't an exaggerated tag line here. The strong survive and the weak get eaten.

We had lunch on a large balcony that overlooks some salt pits. There were animals everywhere, licking salt, grooming, swatting flies with their tails. Our waiter told us that the lions come to lick salt once in awhile and when that happens obviously the other animals clear out. All of them except the African buffalo. *They're nasty boogers and mean as all get out, the world-champion bullrider said, kicking the toe of his boot into the dirt and tucking a thumb into his jeans.*

Dad had finally started to loosen up. He commented that Maralal was truly spectacular. Mom seemed to agree. She watched the animals licking salt with the type of animated expression you're supposed to have in Africa. There wasn't a lot of conversation, just a cozy, comfy mood.

A hotel escort led us back to our respective cabins. Mom said she was going to have a nap this afternoon. Dad just called me out of my cabin to show me thousands of army ants, moving in formation. Big ants. Good deal. Whoopee! Gabriel comes at five o'clock to take us to see a leopard.

I'm going to like it here. But we're only staying for one night. What a drag. I am surprised that we have made it this far. I thought we'd be back in Nairobi by now.

At lunch I saw some father kiss his teenage daughter on the lips. Hmmm. It got me thinking about incest and molestation. It occurred to me as I watched the doe-eyed daughter wipe her mouth afterward that incidents are not what cause problems, reactions are. Let's say there's a seven-year-old boy who gets lured behind a fence by an ice-cream man who masturbates in front of him. The parents find out. His mother cries. His father screams that he will kill the ice-cream man. I think the boy will be more damaged by the reactions than by the actual incident. That isn't to say that the parents should tell the boy that what the ice-cream man did is a good thing because it's not. But they must freak out on their own. They shouldn't make the boy feel any worse than he already does. People are always doing that. They do more damage with their hysterical reactions than the actual incident could ever do.

I fucking hate hysterical people. I see them on the news all the time. Usually at disasters, trial verdicts or political rallies. Screaming and yelling. I really think these people should be plucked from society, put on a boat and sent to an island far away. We'd all be better off. They contribute nothing. Some people dream of a world with no hunger or no wars. I dream of a world with quiet people where crisis is met with silent, salty tears and a little sniffling.

Events don't damage people. Hysterical reactions do. I'm going to write a paper on this one day. Not for anyone or anything. Just to write a paper on something. Make myself feel important.

I have become obsessed with the idea that mom molested me when I was young. I seek an easy answer to my problems. Like an idiot, I want a simple explanation but I don't think one exists. We are not defined by a single tragic event from childhood. I have to find something else to think about.

6:13 p.m.

I had some time to kill before the leopard . . . scratch that . . . that's what dad always says. I don't want to start talking like him. He's always talking about killing time. Kill poachers and prophets but don't kill time. It's too precious. I'm talking out my ass. I'm always killing time. Just like him. Beating the shit out of it. When am I going to smarten up and feel that tingle of timelessness, that itch of immortality? I've had moments of this but they are too few and far between to count for anything. I'm still a slave to time.

I'll start again. I had some time before the leopard but there wasn't much I could do. I really wanted to go get a beer at the restaurant but I felt lame having to ask the front desk to send the armed escort so I didn't.

There was a stack of wood beside the fireplace in my room. I didn't have enough time for a fire then but I plan to have one tonight. I love the smell of burning wood. Brings back childhood memories of walking home on cold, winter nights in the old neighbourhood. I always thought something horrible was going to swoop down from the sky and carry me off into the blackness, past the stars, to a place that was even colder, a place where I would be left to shiver and die. But the smell of the smoke kept me calm. And if nobody was having a fire that night I would think of myself in a hot bath. There's something about having hot water slowly slide up around your body, raising goose bumps, that will chase away the beasties that swoop down from the sky.

Trapped in my cabin with nowhere to go I decided to groom my pubic hair. I don't think most men worry about this kind of thing and some women don't either. One of the cooks in the patch had a huge bush. Turned me right off.

My dick always looks smaller when I haven't groomed. So that's what I did. I got a pair of scissors from my shaving kit and stood in the shower. Trimmed pubic hairs look disgusting on a polished white surface. They look like a swarm of spiders. Pubic hair is so stiff and wiry. Why the hell couldn't it be silky? If there were a heaven, things like that would be fixed. Pubic hair would be soft and nice to touch.

I always get turned on from the sight of my junk once the grooming is done. Doesn't look like my own boring dick anymore. It looks like I've replaced it with another, heartier version. But I didn't even get a hint of an erection this time. I wonder if I'm coming down with something?

I got dressed and we were off to see the leopard, *the wonderful leopard of Oz, becuz, becuz, becuz, becuz, becuuuuz, becuz of the wonderful things he duz.* An armed escort led me to the van. I liked being protected like that. Made me feel important, like I was Yasser Arafat or Michael Jackson or someone else people wanted to kill.

The drive to the leopard was short — right around the corner from the lodge but things started to go bad very quickly. At the top of this small hill there was a small observation hut. We were supposed to walk to it but mom wouldn't get out of the van. Gabriel had brought along a park ranger with a rifle. This made mom even more nervous. She wanted to know why he needed the gun. Gabriel explained that it was just a precaution. She wasn't buying any of it. She told us we were all mad — the leopard would sneak up, we wouldn't stand a chance.

I stood off to the side with Gabriel and the escort while dad climbed in the van and tried to reason with her. I couldn't hear anything but I could see from his face that he was trying to be as patient and understanding as he could.

"I'm glad you're back," I said.

"Your father surprised me," said Gabriel with a smile. "But I'm happy he did. I would have felt badly if things had ended that way."

Gabriel and I watched as dad tried to negotiate with mom to get her out of the van.

"Not that it matters," he said. "I have a feeling you will be heading home soon anyway."

"I talked to her about some of the stuff you told me. I probably shouldn't have. But I had to. So, if she's a little cold you'll know why."

Gabriel was silent. But I could tell he was upset. This pissed me off. He wasn't family. These were our secrets. Not his. He didn't have a right to be upset.

"And what was her reaction?"

"She denied any connection between us. I kind of accused her of molestation. Which was a mistake."

"Kind of?" he asked, with an impatient snort. "You either accused her or you didn't. And if you did, you didn't get that idea from me because I never said that. Perhaps your confusion was based on your feelings for her. Not the other way around."

I hated being talked down to like that. I spoke calmly but I wanted to hit him in the nose with my forehead.

"I never said that *you* told me. All I told her was that you kind of felt there was a link between her depression and me. That's it."

He nodded at me like he was a king and I was a beggar. "You should try and find something to say other than, 'kind of.' Western kids love to say that. It's so vague and cautious. Commit to your words, Richard, and maybe your words might mean something."

Gabriel walked away from me and started talking to the park ranger in Swahili. I was stung. He called me a kid. He called me vague. He accused me of having secret feelings for my own mother. The fucker gave me advice.

I hated him right then. He was angry with me for telling mom what he had told me. He felt betrayed. What about how he had *kind of* betrayed mom by talking to me? Fucking hypocrite. *Commit to your words and your words might mean something.* Who the hell did he think he was? The DalaifuckingLama?

Dad finally coaxed mom out of the van. He kept his hand on her back and we made our way up the small hill to the observation hut. Our escort had his rifle slung over his shoulder. Mom asked him three times if it wouldn't be better for him to have the rifle ready in his hands so he could fire quickly. He didn't speak a word of English so he ignored her.

From the inside, the observation hut resembled the gun tower of an old fort. It had narrow slats just wide enough to stick the barrel of a rifle through. Gabriel guided us to a bench behind the slats.

"You see that tree," he said, pointing. "That's where he'll come. Hopefully."

Dad and I peered through the slats. Mom refused. She sat stiffly, staring at her hands and picking at her fingernails. She must have thought that if she got her nose anywhere near that tiny opening a huge claw would swipe up and rip her face from her skull. There was a big tree not far from the hut. A big hunk of meat was hanging from one of the branches.

Gabriel explained how rare it was to see a leopard. He wanted us to know that this was a big deal. Dad had his animal checklist on his lap, pen poised. Gabriel gave us some background on the leopard, which I have forgotten. In spite of my dark mood from Gabriel's regal comments, I found myself getting excited. It seemed like cheating to hang meat to attract the spotted cat but I didn't care.

"What are you doing?" dad asked mom. "Watch for the leopard."

"This is it," said mom.

"Jesus Christ," said dad.

"We're not safe in here."

"We're in a hut. There's no way it can get in. And even if it tried, the man's got a rifle."

"Doesn't matter."

"It can't get us mom," I said, staring at the tree.

"We're all going to be torn to pieces."

Mom got up and stood by the door. I think dad was worried she was going to make a dash for the van.

"Sit down!" he barked.

"I am not putting my family in danger. We shouldn't be here!"

"We're here because you wanted to be! This trip was your idea! You love animals! We're here to see animals! Now sit down!"

"No! We've got to get out of here before it's too late."

Dad got up from the bench. He looked whipped, like a goalie who had given up four goals on six shots and was pulling himself out of the game, skating over to his coach, mumbling, "I just don't have it tonight." He shouldn't have felt bad. You can't fight mom's madness. It's like sending a fifteen-year-old goalie onto the ice to play against the Montreal Canadiens . . . when they had Guy Lafleur.

Dad tapped me on the back to let me know it was time to go.

We drove back to the lodge in silence. I sat behind mom and fantasized about strangling her. I was livid. I'm still furious. And not just with her. With Gabriel too. He's the one who started the whole molestation inquest anyway. Everything's blown to hell right now. I really wanted to see that leopard.

I have one thing that gives me hope and that is Nicole. I think of her and the storm subsides. I wish I had taken a picture of her. I still have the rose. It is right beside me on my desk. It is drying. I will never throw it away. I will find Nicole. I will travel to New Hampshire and find out if it was love or pity.

Dad's outside my door right now, calling me to dinner. Fuck off! I'm building sand castles for me and my girl.

8:52 p.m.

I'm alone on the balcony overlooking the salt pits. There is a bird making a strange sound. A light breeze is blowing. It is dark but diffused lights illuminate the area. There are a few zebras and a lot of gazelles. A big buffalo is standing absolutely still off in the distance. Is he asleep? Wonder if anyone's ever tried to tip one over?

A few other people are here with me. I wish they'd leave. I want the balcony for myself. They look stupid and they irritate me. I judge mercilessly when I am like this. I look at these people and I imagine what is underneath all the bullshit. Bones. I imagine them as skeletons, sitting, drinking, laughing, moving around. It isn't scary. It's a relief. Helps take the edge off things. In a hundred years none of them will be around. All of them will be dead. They'll be ash scattered in the trees. Sour corpses in caskets. None of what they say tonight will matter. The worms and the wind will see to that.

I know when the time comes for me to slip these earthly bonds I want my body to be cremated. I have never understood why people would want to be buried in a casket. The image of my body slowly rotting fills me with disgust. I want nothing left of me but ash. Either that or I will return to Africa and offer my diseased body to a leopard or a pride of lions. Let them kill me and eat me. And then, when they are done with the big pieces, let the hyenas have the smaller ones. And then let the birds swallow the scraps. And let the bugs finish off the rest. Nothing will go to waste. My body will be torn asunder and rest in the bellies of these majestic and scavenging beasts. What a noble death.

I can afford to think these grand ideas. My body is young and healthy. Let's see how brave I am when I'm old and dying. I'll probably be pumped to the gills on morphine, lying in my urine, curled up in a fetal position, whimpering that life is cruel. But that's not tonight. Tonight I am king.

Dinner was difficult. I was still angry with mom for ruining the leopard sighting. I was surprised to see her outside my cabin when dad came to get me. I thought for sure he would have confined her to quarters. But there she was. And in spite of our very capable and armed escort, was nervously on the lookout for a charging buffalo.

The trouble started when I excused myself during dinner to go take a piss. Some guys take forever. I don't mess around. Pee, splash water on my hands, dry them quickly and it's over. I'm in, I'm out. I was gone for all of a minute. Maybe. I returned to the restaurant and mom was standing beside the table clutching a napkin. Dad had a grip on her elbow.

"Sit down," he seethed.

Mom saw me approaching the table and her eyes filled with tears. She gave me a big hug, which I received limply.

"You made it," she said.

"Made what?" I asked, a little confused, a little annoyed.

"Made it back."

She offered the relieved smile of a mother whose son had returned from three years of mustard gas, hand-to-hand combat, lousy rations, rats, mud and trench warfare. She let me know with her smile that she loved me, that she was worried about me, that she almost gave up hope and didn't know if I'd make it back.

The waiter brought dad another scotch. With her son safely home, mom was free to focus her abundant and varied concerns on her husband.

"I think you've had enough," she said.

"Do you? I've only just begun."

I could see trouble brewing. I thought I'd inject something positive, something about the future, something about me, to get our thoughts off missing sons, alcohol and provocation.

"I'm finally looking forward to going to school," I announced. "I've been thinking the University of Victoria might be a sweet place to study."

Dad didn't miss a beat. "Well, you just keep on thinking, sunshine, because nothing's been decided yet."

"What do you mean?" I asked.

"There's a lot that needs to be resolved before I invest that kind of money in you. Okay?"

I could tell he was really pissy because he added 'okay' to the end of his sentence. It was a high-pitched, rising finale. An *I'm done talking, I'm right, you're wrong, case closed, shut your mouth* conclusion to his sentence.

I wasn't going to argue. He already said he was going to pay for university and I knew he'd been drinking. There was no point. But I got irritated anyway.

"What needs to be resolved?"

"I don't want to talk about it right now. You just carry on with your rig work and we'll see what happens."

"You did promise him, Ted," said mom. "I heard you."

"You're out of your mind. What you heard doesn't count anymore."

Mom felt the burn of dad's bullwhip and didn't like it. She grimaced. "I'm not going to sit here and watch you get drunk," she said as she got up from the table.

"Yet you want Richard and me to sit around and watch you go bananas and destroy this family?"

"You're drunk."

"A little louder. I don't think they heard you at the next table."

Dad turned to the family sitting next to us. They nervously fingered menus, forks, anything they could get their hands on. "Did you hear that?" he called out. "She called me a drunk."

Actually, that wasn't true. She had merely stated the obvious. That he *was* drunk. She didn't say he was one. He was embarrassing himself for no reason. I got a kick out of this.

The family had two young kids who looked pretty scared. Strike that. The whole family looked scared. Ma, pa and the two little 'uns.

Dad raised his voice.

"Tell everyone, Janet. Go on. Get up. Shout it out. I'm the reason you're insane. You're crazy because I drink too much."

I don't know why she didn't just leave. She could have. But she just stood there, seemingly transfixed by his public outburst.

"You can't do that can you? And not because you're worried about making a scene in front of everyone. It's because it's just not true. You know why you're crazy. Why don't you tell us? Tell Richard. Tell him."

Mom moved quickly into dad's face. He jerked back. "You're a bastard," she hissed.

"Why don't you just do it?" he whispered to her. "Why don't you get it over with? Do yourself and all of us a favour."

They were inches apart. I thought she might bite his nose off and spit it into the air with a spray of blood. But she didn't. She started to laugh contemptuously. She laughed right in his face, turned and quickly left the restaurant.

"You didn't have to be cruel to her," I said.

"You don't know what you're talking about," he said, looking for our waiter.

I left the table and found mom waiting at the front desk for an escort to take her back to her cabin. "Are you okay?" I asked.

"Don't believe him, Richard. Don't believe anything he tells you. He's a liar."

The escort arrived with his gun.

"Do you want me to come with you?" I asked.

"No."

"You can stay in my cabin tonight if you want."

She made eye contact with me. My adrenaline started to scamper. She seemed to catch her breath. And then she walked away through the door. She looked so vulnerable being led down this narrow path by a man carrying a rifle. But at least she was protected. She had her bodyguard. I wondered how much it would cost to pay that guy to protect her for the rest of her life. Protect her from leopards and wild buffalo. And broken gas gauges. And mobs of black children. And cruel husbands. And cowardly sons.

I retired to the balcony and began ordering coffee. I thought about ordering whiskey but the night was already threatened by scattered fires. It didn't need me slapping down my ten bucks, yanking the nozzle off the gasoline pump and squeezing.

Dad is getting worse as this trip goes along. Tonight he was out of control. I think mom was just as shocked at how loud and grotesque he was. I think it scared her. I know it scared me. He has clearly reached the end of his rope. He has to cancel the rest of the trip. Ah, bullshit. I say that every day and here we are. Still on safari.

I'm not going to accept his money even if he does decide to pay for university. I don't want to owe him anything. I'll apply for student loans.

But I know what will happen. He'll change his mind and offer to pay and I'll accept it. I'm so brave in this journal and such a yellowbelly when the rubber meets the road.

I don't hate him for telling mom to kill herself. I've thought the same thing. But then again I've never been pissed off enough to actually say it to her face. This might turn out to be good for her though. Now there's no way she'll do it. Just to defy him.

Mom and Gabriel have just come out on the balcony. They have spotted me.

11:37 p.m.

I am back in my cabin. I have tried for the last half hour to light a fire in the fireplace. I had my heart set on it. Couldn't do it. I couldn't light a fucking fire. What a loser. I even burned some of the books I brought with me to try and get it started but the damn wood just wouldn't ignite. I should be sitting here writing beside a roaring fire, but I'm not. The fireplace is cold and dark. I started to light my journal on fire and it caught. Thank god I rescued it before it ignited. I burn this paper chapel and I'm toast. I'm freaked out right now. I need to go for a walk but I can't because of the buffaloes. I'm trapped.

1:12 a.m.

I've been lying on my bed for the last hour. I did a couple of lines of jude. I really didn't want to, but I had to. It was either that or light my hair on fire.

It is deathly quiet outside. I think I'm the only one awake for several hundred miles.

Mom and Gabriel came over to my table. Mom looked like she had been crying. Her eyes were red and swollen. I thought when she left me she was going back to her cabin but instead she went to Gabriel.

Mom sat down beside me. Gabriel remained standing. I pulled a chair out for him.

"I better not," he said. "Your father might think I am interfering again."

I turned to mom. "How are you?"

"Not good."

"I'm going to leave you two," said Gabriel.

I caught up with him at the end of the balcony. "What's going on?"

"She just sat in my room. She can't stay there. I took her to the front desk to see if there were any available cabins. There aren't."

"She can stay with me."

"She won't."

"Did she say why? Does it have anything to do with me?"

Gabriel looked terrified. He shook his head. He kept glancing back to where mom was sitting.

"What the hell's the matter with you?" I asked. "What did she say?"

"A bird hit the door of my room while I was talking to your mother. It broke its neck. It died in my hands."

"So?"

Gabriel grabbed me by the shoulders, his expression fierce. "Richard! I don't want you thinking about anything but getting her home. And I don't mean to Paris. To Canada. Promise me. Promise me that you'll get her home."

I was shocked by his emotion.

"Why the hell do you care so much?"

He gave me one final shake. "Get her home."

He released me and walked away. I watched as he glided between the tables in the restaurant. In two days we would probably be gone and his relationship with us would come to an end. Why bother? And why this sudden urgency to get mom home? Goddamn it, I hate that those two talk behind my back.

I returned to the table. Mom was watching the zebras in the salt pits.

"Can I get you something to drink?" I asked.

She thought about it. "A glass of water would be nice."

I ordered her water and another coffee for me. I really felt like a whiskey but decided not to drink in front of her. Her water arrived and she drank it down before the waiter had a chance to hand me my coffee. He asked her if she wanted another. She shook her head.

"Gabriel told me about the bird."

"What bird?"

"The one that hit his door."

"What are you talking about?"

"He just told me."

Mom shook her head sadly. "He's a kind, considerate man but he's crazy."

I didn't know what else to say to her. She seemed so far away. I was worried about pushing her further.

"Do you want to go home?" I asked.

"Don't talk to me like I'm a child."

"I'm not."

"It's your tone."

"What?"

"Do you want to go home?" she said, imitating a parental voice talking to a baby or a master cooing to a dog.

"I was just asking for Christ's sake."

She put her finger up to my lips. "Shhhhhhhh, just sit with me."

It was a perfect night for saying nothing or saying everything. It didn't matter. If I was the reason she was so depressed then this would be the time to reveal it. But I would push for nothing. The waters were absolutely still. I didn't want to toss anything that might make a splash. Neither a pebble nor a stone.

I started to feel really sad for her. She hadn't done any of this on purpose. I regretted all the anger I had spewed at her over the last few days, even though most of it was in my head. *It's not her fault.* I told myself to keep remembering that. *It's not her fault.*

And so the two of us sat. Not so much as mother and son. But as tortured comrades. Our common ground was our pain. We could not speak of this pain. So we sat in silence, comforted, I think, by our physical proximity alone.

We watched the zebras twitch and flick their tails. We listened to the clop of hooves on the dirt. All under the black canopy of the African night. Our yard back home seemed so far away. Lying on mattresses, watching the stars in the same sky, a different time, but the same sky. Our little backyard with its trimmed edges and crab apple tree.

Maybe Gabriel was right. Maybe that's where she needed to go when this safari was over. People were renting the house, they could be given a month's notice. She could move back. She could leave dad. Get herself sorted out. I'd help her. I would get her home.

The other people on the balcony eventually left for their cabins and we were alone. The waiter said the bar was closing but we could stay if we wanted. I signed the bill. The waiter left. Mom finally spoke after everyone had gone.

"Did I ever tell you about the day you were born?" she asked.

"No."

"Liar. I tell you every birthday."

She was right. She did always tell me on my birthday. I always tuned it out though. I didn't give a shit.

"You were very difficult. I was sick through most of the pregnancy. The last week before you were born it rained and rained. It was so gloomy. I just wanted to get it over with. The delivery was easy. I was happy about that. When I was back in my room they brought you to me, all bundled up in a little blanket. And they laid you on my chest."

I tugged my top lip with my finger until it touched my nose, and held it there. "And you took one look at this and you started to scream."

"Don't do that!" she spat.

She was trembling. I put a hand on her shoulder. "I'm sorry."

It took her a moment to recover, then she looked out at the salt pits and started talking again. "I know you might think I'm being melodramatic but as soon as the nurse laid you down on my chest the sun came out and streamed in through the window. That's when I knew you were special. The nurse opened the window and I cuddled you all afternoon, listening to the robins and looking at you. And ever since then the robin has been my favourite bird. And it's not that I miss the robins so much as I miss the feeling of that afternoon."

I thought she'd be close to tears but she wasn't. Her eyes were bold. She turned to me.

"I want you to promise me something."

I waited.

"Promise me that you'll stop destroying yourself with drugs."

The pitch was high and inside, just below my chin. I wasn't expecting it. I didn't have time to think, to lie. "When?"

"Soon. Promise me."

I didn't take the moment lightly. There was something deadly serious about it. I knew if I promised I would have to honour it.

"I promise," I said.

She nodded and turned once again to watch the animals in the salt pits. I decided to take advantage of the peaceful, easy feeling between us. I had asked before but this time I tried not to sound like I was talking to a baby.

"Do you want to go back . . . not to Paris . . . to Canada?"

She did not respond. At first I thought she was thinking it over.

"What do you think?" I asked.

Her attention had become diverted. I followed her gaze. And I saw why she hadn't answered my question. A storm was gathering. Off in the distance several female lions were moving through the grass, bellies low to the ground.

Technically, a female lion is a lioness. Only the males are called lions. Gabriel told me this. But I think that's stupid. It's too hard to say lioness when there are more than one. Let alone write it. Lionesses. What the fuck is that? So, I'll call them lions and I'll know they are females. If I see a male I won't call him a lion. I'll call him a male lion. And maybe I'll describe his mane. Maybe not. But there were no male lions near the salt pits. Only lions (the females).

There were still several zebras and gazelles around. I had seen enough nature shows to know that these lions weren't sneaking in for a lick of salt. I stood up.

"Let's go," I said.

"I see them."

"C'mon, we don't need to see this."

But she wouldn't move. She sat there and watched. And I watched. There was such a stench of danger. It smelled like rubbing alcohol. You can't smell that odour through a television.

My surging adrenaline made my knees shake. Something was going to be killed. Soon. Very soon. I wanted to shout a warning to the animals in the salt pits. I almost did. Like some frightened, suburban kid from Canada, trying to break up a dog fight.

One of the lions suddenly broke into a sprint. The zebras and gazelles scattered. One of the zebras was too slow. The lion jumped on its back and locked her claws into the skin. The zebra tried to shake the lion off but the claws were too long and sunk too deep. The zebra staggered under the weight.

Mom stood up and moved to the edge of the balcony to get a closer look. I stayed where I was. The zebra collapsed. The other lions arrived. The attacking lion gripped its powerful jaws around the zebra's throat and clamped down. They usually try to snap their prey's spinal cord but if unable to do that they will resort to suffocation. The spinal cord snap is quick and deadly. This was going to be long and ugly. The zebra kicked. It was still alive as the other lions started tearing inside. It was still alive as the lions tore out a red and glistening organ and began to feed. It was still kicking. Blood was gushing over the paws of the lions forming pools in the packed dirt. And still the damn thing was alive.

"I can't watch anymore," I said and walked as best I could to the front desk. My legs were jelly.

I waited there for her. She watched it all. Maybe she watched until the eyelids fluttered shut and the kicking ceased. After several minutes she joined me. She looked completely relaxed, as if she'd just watched a robin bathe in a birdbath.

We got an escort and I walked with her to their cabin.

"Are you sure you want to stay here?"

"He'll be asleep. I'll be fine."

She leaned forward and kissed me on my cheek. "You're a beautiful boy and don't you forget it."

She turned and entered the dark cabin. I waited for a moment to make sure everything was okay. I don't know what I was expecting. Gunshots? Screams? Satisfied, I walked with my escort back to my own cabin.

It is so quiet now. I wonder if the vultures have moved in on the dead zebra. Perhaps the lions are still feeding. I will keep my promise to mom about the drugs. Soon.

I have to stop bullshitting myself. This is eating me alive. I don't have to tell anyone but I have to admit the truth, at least in my own mind.

I saw the baby oil last night. I felt it. Was it a dream? I can't say. But to deny it would be a lie. I hate lies.

Now that I've committed it to paper I cannot call her anything but Janet for the duration of this safari.

Who knows why it happened? It doesn't matter. But Gabriel was wrong. It's not me who has feelings for her.

Fuck Gabriel.

And fuck normal families.

Fuck them all.

Friday, August 19
1:14 p.m.
Shaba Camp
Tent 3
Kenya, Africa

Woke up at seven o'clock with a splitting headache. I'm waking up at the same time every morning. Just like dad. This is not good. Next thing I know I'll be hoarding mints in my pocket. I didn't have any aspirin in my cabin so I had to wait until breakfast to get relief. There was a buzz throughout the lodge about the zebra kill.

Everyone was disappointed that they missed it. Trust me, fellow tourists, this was not like watching a house cat trap a moth. Actually, I wish they would have seen it. Most of them would have complained to the management and the Americans might have sued.

I went out on the balcony for a smoke and the zebra was gone. The park rangers had dragged the carcass somewhere far away. I guess the smell of rotting meat wouldn't go well with the grapefruits and scrambled eggs. How the hell did they scare the lions off?

I hated everything as I stood on the balcony smoking my cigarette, which only made my headache worse. Not the hate. The cigarette. I thought about masturbating to relieve some of the tension but my head hurt too much even for that. It started in my left shoulder blade, ran like a fault line through my shoulder, up my neck, swung around my ear and crashed into my left eyeball. There are certain headaches that reduce the fear of death. You would embrace it if it meant the pounding would stop. I had one of those. The animals were being extra cautious around the salt pits. Death was still in the air.

The three of us had breakfast together. These little rituals have become exhausted stabs at normality. I have this image of the three of us sitting at a table on a great ocean liner. It hits a huge wave — head-on. The wave lifts up the bow of the ship until it is almost perpendicular. The great ship doesn't recover. The weight in the stern pulls her down. The bow rises into the black sky and sinks into the freezing waters. The kind of water that is so cold it feels like fire and shoots tiny spears through your body.

There is a deafening roar as water rushes past the portholes. Glasses and chairs are snapping. Everything is falling. But we are quietly eating. The ship is completely submerged, pointed butt-first as it knifes down to the ocean floor. And my ears rupture from the pressure as we continue descending. And then my eyeballs pop out of their sockets and dangle over my cheeks as I turn to dad and ask him to pass me the butter.

Nothing was said about returning to Nairobi. We have settled into an insane but predictable pattern. The mornings are peaceful and provide hope that we will indeed muscle through. As the day progresses, things begin to unravel and by evening all hell is breaking loose. And I think, that's it, surely now the trip will be cancelled. But then morning comes, and we gather again for our breakfast. And the madness of the night is smothered in rivers of maple syrup. (I'm exaggerating. We've actually only had pancakes once.)

Dad said the camp we were going to today was beside a river. He asked Janet how she felt about trying one more day. She nodded and thought that this was a good idea. Nobody asked me. Not that I wanted to be asked. My head hurt too much.

Dad tried calling Maggie this morning. No answer. Maybe she's at the hospital. Janet didn't say a thing. You'd think she'd be interested. Fucking grandchild. First one.

There was a family of fat people sitting beside us. Now I've got nothing against fat people. I really don't. But I go nuts with people that are lazy. And it's been my experience that some, not all, fat people are fucking lazy. I've heard of the pituitary gland. I know what they say. And I know that some people are fat and cannot help it. But there are some that just don't move around enough. Lenny was like that.

Lenny and I worked together in the oil patch for awhile and we'd hang sometimes during our week off. He always broke into a sweat when we finished work and were flying back. But that wasn't because he was fat. It was because he was nervous. He had a bus to catch. Actually, he had two buses to catch to get home. One from the airport and then a connecting bus. We went through this every time; his panic about missing the connecting bus because it stopped running at a certain hour.

The guys from the crew always stayed for a beer at the airport before going home. Not Lenny. He had that bus to catch. If we were late for some reason getting in, which happened quite often, he'd take a cab. Lenny lived far from the airport. The cab ride home would cost him forty bucks. That's an expensive cab ride so I kind of understood his obsession with making the connecting bus. That all ended when I finally questioned him about the specifics of his bus schedule and discovered the truth.

It turned out that the stop for his connecting bus was, by his own admission, two or three minutes by car from his house. This made no sense. Who cares about the connecting bus? So what if it stops running? A two- or three-minute car ride is a ten- or fifteen-minute walk. Give or take. *Stay for a beer. Take the first bus. Relax. You miss the connecting bus? Walk.* I suggested this one time when he knew the connecting bus had stopped running. He just shrugged his shoulders and said he'd "cab it." I was stunned. He'd spend his forty bucks on a cab to avoid that ten-minute walk. I was thinking, *that's a short fucking walk, Lenny, and you sure as hell could use the fucking exercise.* Laziness. I was so angry I stopped talking to him after that. I kept thinking about him plopped down in the back of that cab, gut hanging out, that meter clicking over and over. What a waste of money. What a lazy slob. And I think he expensed the cab fare. What a fucking thief.

If we could rid the world of two things we would live in a utopia. Laziness and ignorance. Get rid of them and we'd have no wars, no black power, no white power, no television, no churches and a lot of skinny people walking home and saving money on cabs.

We went to our cabins to pack up. I returned to see the fireplace filled with wood and was reminded what a failure I had been the night before. There were over a hundred burned matches scattered around inside the fireplace. Something is wrong if you can't light a fire in a hundred tries.

We drove with Gabriel for about four hours today. The roads were very rough. The bouncing got rid of my headache. Shook my shoulder blade up enough to stop that throbbing in my eyeball. The headache was actually a nice respite from the emotional upheaval, which returned as soon as the headache disappeared. I am never happy.

On our way out of Maralal this morning we passed tribesmen walking away from a town. They indicated they wanted a lift by laying their right hand flat and motioning to the ground. Gabriel explained that they were walking because they had spent all their money (earned by selling meat or produce) on beer in the town and could not afford a taxi. The taxis are called "Happy Taxis" and they are always filled with about fourteen people in a car just slightly larger than a Volkswagen. Or, if it's a small bus that should seat thirty, they have sixty, including passengers on the roof. Their motto is, "Always room for one more." Lenny would appreciate that.

I took a piss beside the road. Janet told me to go fast and dad told her to shut up.

No more tunes for the rest of the trip. I ripped the wires out of my earphones on my cassette player. I did this because the sound had gotten a little fuzzy and I had a tantrum. I'll have to start hearing my music in the wind. Or pout for the rest of the safari that my bad temper just exploded a handy tunnel of escape.

Dad mentioned that a park ranger would be joining us for our game drive this afternoon.

"I don't know that we can afford that," Janet said.

"Afford what?" asked dad in a short, quiet breath.

"The park ranger."

"It's part of the package. You know that."

"What about Baringo?"

"I'm not talking to you right now."

"You said our budget was three hundred shillings a day. We spent two thousand shillings a day on booze alone. What happens when we run out of money? We'll be stuck here."

"Two thousand shillings a day? On booze?"

Janet said nothing. Dad started twisting up the map he was looking at.

"What did we drink at Baringo?" he asked.

"How should I know?"

"Beer. How much was a beer?"

"I have no idea."

"Ten shillings. Can you divide two thousand by ten?"

"I don't want to."

Dad started to work himself into a lather. He began waving the map around and his voice got louder and louder.

"I'll do it for you then. Two thousand divided by ten equals two hundred. Two hundred beers, Janet. A day. You're telling me that, as a family, we drank two hundred beers a day? Is that right!?"

He finished by crumpling the map into a tight ball. I thought he was going to toss it out the window.

Janet was completely unaffected by his tirade. In fact, I thought I saw the trace of a smile. I don't think she was as worried about the budget as she made out. These are cruel games we are playing with one another.

I watched dad after he calmed down again. He looked so serious and professional. Like a Secret Service agent. It has been so long since we've hugged. I guess some fathers maintain that with their sons. Hugging and stuff. I got a handshake when I got off the plane in Paris and I'll get another when I leave. Part of me thinks that things would be better between us if he hugged me. What nonsense. We'd both just be really uncomfortable and nothing would change.

I'm grateful we abandoned one form of physical contact we used to share. The toenail trimming. He had his own name for the dirty bits between his toes. As I was cutting his nails he'd say, "Make sure you get the schmeglies." And I would. He used that word for anything that was crumb-sized and sitting where it shouldn't. He was always bending down and picking schmeglies off the floor and flicking them in the garbage. He never let us eat in the car. "Don't!" he'd yell. "You'll leave schmeglies." He hasn't used that word in a really long time. I miss it.

The rest of the drive was uneventful. We saw no animals. It was basically a destination trip to get us from Maralal to Shaba. Gabriel gave us a running commentary of anecdotes and stories. The only thing that caught my ear was hearing that a poacher had been shot the day before. Shot and killed. Good. Poachers are dead meat in Kenya. Why don't they hack the teeth from these scumbags and sell them to some rich asshole and see how they like it? *But they'd already be dead.* How about before they are shot? *Did you know that scumbag is slang for condom?* I didn't know that. *Well now you do so be careful who you use it with.*

We arrived at Shaba and were shown to our respective tents. My tent is right beside theirs. That's too damn close for my liking. There is no electricity. Gabriel told us that they had to get rid of all the camp trucks and the generators because the natives kept coming in and stealing all the wire to make necklaces. Right on.

I got to my tent and tossed my bags on the bed. There was a gas lantern on a little table. Normally I would have closed the blinds and masturbated, especially after not doing so this morning. But I wasn't horny. At all. I'm still not, even though I usually get horny sitting in a car for too long and we travelled for four hours this morning. I touched myself briefly and got no response. Oh well, it'll probably do me good to leave my weenie alone for awhile.

I could hear the sound of rushing water from my tent. The surrounding area is thick with plants and trees. I followed the sound until I found a clearing and saw a big river. Nice and wide. Already I'm thinking what a challenge it would be to swim across to the other side, smoke a cigarette and swim back. But there were crocodiles scattered all over the opposite bank, sunning themselves.

We leave soon on our game drive. Gabriel told us we should probably see some lions this afternoon. Yee-ha.

4:12 p.m.

I am in the van. We drove around for about an hour. We saw vultures and elephants. Strike that. We saw a single elephant cross the dirt road in front of us. It was still pretty impressive. I wondered (as per our family conference) if we'd head back now that Janet had seen an elephant. I decided not to mention it. Dad checked the elephant off his list with gusto. There's no stopping him now.

Janet has been remarkably calm. She does love the elephants. She actually got a little excited when she saw this one. She wasn't scared either.

At the moment we are stopped beside a pride of lions feeding on a dead giraffe. Dad is pissed because I'm not shooting it. He had convinced me to give up my videotaping boycott shortly after lunch. I shot for awhile after we got to the lions. I stopped about five minutes ago.

My problem isn't the lions. The lions are great. The giraffe has been dead for about three days. The smell of the decaying meat is pretty ripe. Gabriel told us that this will probably be the last day that the lions will feed on the giraffe. Lions will eat semi-rotten meat but not totally rotten meat. There are about fifteen lions inside the belly. All females and cubs. Some are eating and some are sleeping, right in the belly. The cubs are covered in blood. You couldn't find an orange or yellow hair on them if you tried.

A large male lion is resting about thirty feet from the dead giraffe. He is truly magnificent. He must have eaten already. He looks pretty content. He has a nasty gash down the side of his face. Gabriel said he probably got kicked by a zebra. How the hell would he know? Was he there?

Anyway, we come upon this classic African scene: the lions feeding, the dead giraffe. Everyone's covered in blood. The stench of rotting meat. There's even a majestic male lion. Perfect.

But there was something even more disgusting than putrid meat that just ruined everything. Twelve safari tour vans, not including ours. I just about puked. Twelve of them! I counted. The tourists in the other vans were wearing goofy safari clothes and "capturing" the lions for their stupid neighbours back home with expensive, high-tech toys that whirred and clicked and hummed. Two of them were even wearing pith helmets. I wanted to open a vein right there and then. Not to kill myself. No, no. I wanted to offer the pith helmets a transfusion. I wanted them to feel the shame I would have felt if I were them. *Here, take some of this. Now, look at yourselves in the vanity mirror. Go on. It's right there under the sunshade. There you go.*

Now, what do you see? It's okay. Don't wince, don't bury your face in your hands. Just take off the goddamn helmets.

It felt like a long line at Disneyland. All this overweight, pasty, white mediocrity circling the lions and snapping and pointing and giggling and gasping and burping. What a lame species we are. We can find a cure for polio but we behave like assholes at a lion kill. Dad can sit there and videotape to his heart's content. What Janet and I witnessed at Maralal was pure — this is a disgrace.

Dad just interrupted my writing.

"Richard, he's looking at you," he said.

I didn't look up.

"Who?" I asked.

"The male lion."

I looked over and sure enough he was. His stare raised the hairs on my arms. "He's just looking around. He's had a big lunch. He's resting."

"No. He's staring at you," said Janet.

"How do you know he's not looking at you?" I asked.

"Because he's not," said Janet pausing. "That's very strange."

I was starting to get irritated. Mostly because I knew the lion was staring at me and it was making me uncomfortable. Gabriel talked to the park ranger in his native tongue. They both laughed.

"It's unanimous," announced Gabriel. "Our friend here has confirmed that the lion is indeed staring at Richard."

The park ranger chuckled and turned and smiled at me, a big, gap-toothed grin.

"Who gives a flying fuck?!" I shouted, louder than I meant to.

There was silence in the van.

"Jesus, Richard," said dad. "Relax. We're just joking around."

I felt like an idiot for overreacting, so I have not spoken since. We're still sitting beside the dead giraffe. Dad wants to *take it all in.* I've looked up a couple of times and the male lion is still staring at me. I just gave him the finger.

We're finally moving. Thank god. I was just about to —

We have now stopped to watch little monkeys running around chasing each other. Chance for a quick update. Just when we started to leave the lions, I glanced up and saw Nicole in one of the other tour vans. I couldn't have been any more excited if I'd been out camping and seen a Sasquatch rambling across a creek. If I hadn't been writing in this damn thing I would have seen her sooner.

"Stop the van!" I yelled. "There's Nicole!"

I scared the hell out of everyone. Gabriel slammed on the brakes. I stuck my head out the window and began yelling her name. *So much for never wanting to make a spectacle of myself.* She had her back to me and the windows of her van were closed.

"Gabriel! Hit your horn!"

"For Christ's sakes, Richard," said dad. "What the hell's wrong with you?"

I shouted her name again and, to my horror, I saw that her van was starting to roll away. "Hit your horn!" I demanded.

"I can't," Gabriel said. "It might . . ."

"Hit your horn!!"

He did. The noise did two things. It caused Nicole and everyone in her van to look back, unfortunately they were already too far away for her to recognize me. The noise also spooked the lions. They immediately abandoned the belly of the giraffe and scattered. Needless to say, the recent van arrivals to the kill were not impressed. Gabriel, trying to apologize, held up his hands to the vanloads of people.

"Way to go, Richard," said dad.

Nicole's van was headed down the road, kicking up dust.

"Gabriel! Can you follow them?"

"Forget it," said dad.

"I just want to get her phone number!"

Dad could see I was desperate. I was practically crying.

"Is that the direction we're headed?" he asked Gabriel.

"Not really," said Gabriel. "But it wouldn't take long to get turned around again."

"No, no," said dad. "Forget it. We're not going chasing around after girls. We're on safari."

Dad wasn't being mean. He was just being dad. There was nothing on today's itinerary about following another safari van so his son could get the phone number of his future wife. It would be a detour. An unnecessary one.

Dad unfolded his map and began studying. Gabriel paused for a moment. We made eye contact in his rearview mirror. He gave me a "what can I do?" look. I shrugged to show him it was no big deal. So he drove us off, heading in the opposite direction that Nicole had gone.

I turned around once and watched her van disappear as we descended down a hill.

"Good-bye," I whispered to myself.

It all made sense. Nicole, ascending like the balloon that escaped my tiny hand so many years ago. The Clark's journey through hell wasn't completed yet so, of course, we descended and continued on our sordid way.

"You'll see her again," offered Janet, giving me one of her patented, cheer-up smiles.

"I hope you're not going to sulk about this," said dad, his nose buried in his map.

I wasn't sulking. I was beyond that. I was devastated. I'm still devastated. What were the odds of seeing her again after Baringo? And yet there she was. An hour ago. She was right there. But I couldn't talk to her. It was so fucking cruel.

The truth is that if I had really wanted to talk to her I could have put up such a fight that Dad would have had no choice. I could have jumped out of the van and chased after her on foot. That would have been the romantic thing to do. But dad's decision was, masochistically, okay with me. It fit.

My shrug to Gabriel in the mirror was not a fair reflection of my feelings for Nicole. An oh-I'm-not-that-interested-anyway reaction. On the contrary. My shrug, and subsequent silence, was the result of my desperate desire to see her being crushed by the realization that it would probably never happen.

Every once in awhile I like to confirm that my life will always be about tripping on the two-yard line. I like to confirm that I will never taste the thrill of victory. I will always be the guy falling off the ski jump.

I'm like that Greek guy who is forever bending down to a receding pool of water or stretching his hand up to that cluster of grapes that pulls just out of reach. For all eternity. I will always come close but I will never quite get there. That will be my legacy. It's what I deserve.

Dad's giving me a hard time for ignoring the monkeys and keeping my nose buried in my journal. Too bad. I'm not interested in monkeys right now. I'll never see Nicole again. Right now, I accept the fact that I am a loser and that I don't deserve anyone like her in my life. But soon I will be in a rage, ripping myself to pieces over the fact that I didn't try harder to get to her. I will be haunted by the image of her van disappearing in a cloud of dust. I will be forty-five years old, alone, lying awake, watching that van drive away.

6:37 p.m.

Got back to my tent a little while ago. I wasn't horny but I tried to masturbate anyway. My damn pecker just wouldn't respond. That's never, ever happened before. I am so fucking depressed right now. I noticed I have sprouted a wart on my left forefinger, right there on the side, near my knuckle. It must be new. I didn't notice it before. Great, now I've got crap growing on me. Something is terribly wrong. I am sitting here naked, looking down at my pathetic dick. I just smacked it. Goddamn worthless thing.

I have been troubled tonight by a horrible thought. What if it wasn't Nicole who left me the rose? I mean, I don't know for a fact that she did. What if it was Janet? How will I ever know? I want to hurt myself. I want to do terrible things. If I had a knife I'd cut my dick off. My head is exploding.

6:53 p.m.

A quick note before I join the parents for dinner. I'm not going to have enough jude to get me through the rest of the trip. (If it goes the distance.) I just smoked two long lines and I don't have much left. Fuck, I wish I hadn't thrown out all the other stuff.

We finished with the monkeys and started back. I don't know why we sat for so long looking at the damn things. Gorillas I could understand. But little monkeys, no more than a foot high? Fuck that.

A weird thing happened on the drive back. Dad and Janet started talking to each other. Not a whole lot, but way more than usual. My silent sulk brought them together. They both completely ignored me and let me stew like a smelly prune in the back of the van. They actually reminisced about their honeymoon. Perhaps this is what they need — for me to be sulking and silent for the rest of the trip. Maybe then things would be hunky-dory.

It wasn't just dad and Janet. Gabriel got into the spirit of things as well. Even the park ranger was laughing. The happier the four of them got, the more inconsolable I became. If I'm pouty and alone with one person I can usually recover. But put me with a group and I become the peculiar outcast, standing off in a corner.

I get teased about this often, especially at parties. I don't care. Yes, I feel isolated but I also feel immune and powerful. It's like I have suddenly emerged from a secret chamber of a pyramid after centuries of sleep. The creatures around me look insignificant and strange. I am superior. I am a god. But I am not a loving god. I watch them the way a tower guard watches prisoners in the yard.

My problem in the van was that I wasn't feeling god-like. Instead, I was frightened that, like Janet, I was destined for a life of madness.

Is my blood contaminated with these awful seeds of insanity? It's one thing to be odd and isolated and a god. It's quite another to be locked up in a little room, packed with so many pills that your eyes water and your fingers tremble. I'm late for dinner.

I am at the bar enjoying a whiskey and a beer. Actually, I've already had the whiskey. Two shots. I am feeling the effects. Buzzing nicely. Like a noisy light. I'm still on my first beer. There is a poster behind the bar that shows two monks carrying signs. One sign says, "Love Thine Enemy." The other sign says, "Drink is the enemy." What a stupid thing to have up in a bar. Reminding alcoholics that drink is the enemy. You're supposed to encourage the bastards, like Budweiser does, not make them feel bad. It's supposed to be funny. I don't get it.

I've been to one A.A. meeting in my life. A do-gooder guy at work thought I had a drinking problem so he took me to one. I went along because, like sticking my dick in a shampoo bottle, I like to try everything at least once. Everyone was too damn nice. They heard I was a "newcomer" and flocked around me like I was Bobby Hull at a trading card show. I enjoyed that part.

They could talk all they wanted about the fact that they weren't a religious group. Bullfuckingshit. They had that expression "higher power" as a clever front for the guy on the cross but they weren't fooling me. You could feel Jesus everywhere in the room. I liked a few of the people but most of them had that glassy-eyed, I'm-in-a-cult-and-I-don't-even-know-it stare. They had found *the way*. I never get along real well with people who have found *the way*. Strike that. I don't like people who have followed someone else's way and called it their own.

I have never said a dirty word about Jesus. Ever. But I can't stand the people who follow him. I can't stand people who follow anything but their favourite team.

We are a society of cowards. How many Christians would go into the desert and survive for forty days and forty nights — with only water from the dew of leaves in the morning to drink, with only bugs and the occasional root of some bitter plant to eat, with no shelter from the scorching sun of the day or the chilling cold of the night, with no toilet paper? How many would do this? Maybe nine. Nine of the millions who call themselves Christians.

It takes hard work to become a captain of eternity. Jesus did really well on his test. On his own! With no cheating. But now there are millions of people looking over his shoulder, stealing answers. Why? Because they don't want to find them on their own. It's not like stealing a peek during a math test either — answers that work for one person don't work for anyone else. You can't steal life answers and pretend they're your own. It's like wearing someone else's underwear.

The captains of eternity knew the secret. You have to find your own way. No matter how scary it gets, or lonely, or baffling or insane, you have to cut your own path. There is no shortcut to salvation. As soon as you butt in line with a bunch of other lazy and ignorant people and start following someone, it's over.

These lines of followers stretch as far as the eye can see and everyone in line is pretty goddamn cocky about it. The Jews tell us they're chosen, Buddhists are enlightened, Christians are saved, Hindus are reincarnated and Muslims are devoted.

And the rest of us? Walking our solitary walk? We don't have a fucking chance. Do we? Balderdash. There are as many roads to paradise as there are people on this planet. Hallelujah. We're all captains of eternity, baby. Fuck the long lines. Keep walking. Stay strong.

I was a little late for dinner and was worried that Janet was going to be in a twister, thinking I had wandered down to the river and been dragged below by the crocodiles.

"We're on holiday for Christ's sake," said dad, shaking his head at Janet, oblivious to the fact that I had just sat down. "Why can't you loosen up and have some fun?"

"Don't push me," she said.

"I'm not pushing, I'm just —"

Janet's voice dropped several octaves. It was strong. Full of bass. It didn't sound like her at all. "You're pushing me. You're always pushing me. I'm sick of it. I'm sick of you."

A camp worker arrived with a tray of beers. Janet almost knocked him over as she bolted from the table. Dad slapped a rattled smile on his face.

"I'm tired of her goddamn accusations," he said. "I've never missed a day's work in my life."

I remained silent. He was steaming. The focus of concern was never supposed to be on him. It had to remain firmly and eternally on Janet. That way he would never have to dance with his demons.

There was a man sitting alone at another table who kept looking over at me. He reminded me of a madman from a recurring dream I have had — the same lifeless face, the same crooked head, the same cruel mouth bent into a hideous smile.

In my dream, the madman, dressed in tattered clothes, paces back and forth on the sidewalk in front of our house. He shoots ferocious glances at the house as I watch him through a slight parting in the window drapes. Janet and dad sit calmly in the living room, Glen Campbell sings about a Wichita lineman. The madman moves quickly up our driveway. I run as fast as I can, catching a distorted glimpse of him through the frosted window beside the front door. I am desperate to reach the door first, to slam, to lock. I always wake up before I get there but I tell myself in the darkness and the sweat of my bed that I would have been able to throw the bolt before the madman got inside.

Dinner was mercifully short. The beef barley soup was really fucking good. Dad didn't bother with coffee afterward. He told me he'd see me in the morning and took off.

I sat for awhile at the table finishing my coffee. The man with the lifeless face was still looking at me. He was by himself. Where the hell was his family? Who goes on a safari alone? Only a fucking psychotic that's who.

I tried to ignore him but his staring was making my neck tremble, which caused my head to shake. I was embarrassed and hoped no one saw. I hated his guts. He was fucking with me. Every time I looked up he was staring at me.

I finally reached a point where I had had enough. I braced myself to look up and return his stare until he looked away. And if he didn't look away I was going to walk over to his table and ask him, in a low, threatening growl, *You got a fucking problem, buddy?* or maybe, *What's the problem?* or *Is there a problem here?* or *What's the deal?* or *You got problems, buddy.*

That was it. That's what I decided to do. I took a deep breath and tensed my neck. I'd stare that fucker down. I looked up and sure enough, he was still staring at me. A warm splash spread down my back. But I held firm. I stared. And I kept staring. And I tried to look mean. This went on for quite some time.

I was just about to get up and go over when I saw it. The frame surrounding him provided the first clue. Then I moved my head. And then I stuck out my tongue. And then I knew. The sudden realization kicked the breath from my lungs. I had been staring at myself in a mirror at the end of the restaurant. *Every time I looked up he was staring at me.* Of course he was. Holy mother of the gods. I was so relieved. It was me. I started to laugh. Not really but I felt like it.

I finished my coffee and came to the bar. I feel like my attic has been swept clean of debris. There are no monsters under the bed, no madmen trying to get in the front door, no vampires or boogies or sick, stinky ghouls. There is just me. Only me.

Somebody said it before. I have met the enemy. And the enemy is me. This sounds corny even as I write it but I am still vibrating from the experience. Something really important happened tonight. I have had a significant experience. Either that or I am just insane and this mirror illusion confirms it.

A quick note before bed. I just took my lantern outside and had a quick shower.

Weird light always gets me hard. Candlelight, morning light through a window. That kind of stuff. Anything that makes my meat look different. But I didn't even get the slightest hint of an erection. Trying not to worry about it.

Normally I would have been creeped out in the shower. Nighttime. Shadows. I could have imagined all kinds of things going wrong. Giant cockroaches crawling down the nozzle. A bat swooping through, getting caught in the water spray, panicking, ripping my scalp to escape. Disgusting, squishy things, crawling all over my bare feet. But I didn't imagine a single one. I'm proud of myself. I brought three beers back from the bar, so I'll drain these, smoke a few cigarettes, take a piss and go to sleep.

I am writing by lantern light. I like it. It makes my writing seem more profound. It makes me seem more profound. I imagine people walking past my tent and seeing me hunched over my journal. "Look at him," they'd say, "He's intense." I would ignore them. Because I'm too busy writing. Too busy being intense.

There are fireflies buzzing inside the tent. They are great to watch. I wonder what makes them glow? I should try and write a postcard to Maggie. I have not sent her anything. She's always so good about writing letters and stuff. I never think of anyone but myself. I guess that's a bad thing. Long pause for reflection. So, why don't I feel bad about it?

Dad and Janet are talking in their tent. Our tents are close but I didn't think I could actually hear them.

"You just can't drop it, can you?"

"You're an alcoholic."

"Bullshit!"

"You think I'm trying to set an example? I'm not. I didn't want a beer tonight. Big deal."

Dad laughed. "How you can focus on my so-called problems with all that's been going on with you is completely beyond my comprehension."

"I'm not saying I don't have problems. But you've got them as well. And so does Richard."

"Not as bad. Not even close."

"I didn't know there was an instrument that measured such a thing."

"There is. It's called common sense."

"I'm so sick of you!"

"Then divorce me."

He's challenging her to a divorce. This is her chance.

Hold on. Someone is crying.

"Janet, I can't handle another suicide attempt."

It's dad! Holy shit. Dad is crying. I'm hearing nothing from her. No soothing words. No promises that she'll never do it again. God, it's a sickening sound to hear him like this. I could hear a femur snapping right beside my ear and it wouldn't be more disturbing.

I've never heard him cry before. This is dangerous. He isn't getting in touch with feelings. He's losing it. And if he loses it then we lose the skipper and the good ship Clark will never make it out of the rocks.

I feel like a greasy voyeur. Doesn't he know how close our tents are? If he did, he wouldn't be doing this. His sobbing is subsiding. Thank god. He just blew his nose.

"Thanks," he said.

She must have handed him a napkin. So I know she's not just sitting there coldly. I wonder if she's as appalled as I am. Maybe she doesn't know what to say. Dad just cleared his throat. "I can't lose you again, the doctor came out when they were trying to revive you and . . . I thought you were gone."

Dad is sobbing again. Enough already!

"I wish they hadn't brought me back."

"You don't mean that. You've got two beautiful children and the rest of your life ahead of you."

I just made a mental note never to allow dad up on the forty-storey hotel when it was my turn to jump. Hearing desk calendar reminders like "You've got the rest of your life ahead of you," don't cut it. Lesson one in suicide prevention: Suicide is a once-in-a-lifetime encounter. You have to be original when trying to talk someone out of it.

"I have a drug addict son who will be dead in five years and a knocked-up daughter who doesn't like this family anymore. And the only life I've got ahead of me is one spent cooking you steaks and living with your abuse."

"What happened to your dreams? There were so many things you wanted to do. Now that the kids are grown up you can do them."

"I wanted to be a ballet dancer. I wanted Maggie to get a university degree. I wanted Richard to turn out okay. I wanted a husband who would hold my hand in public."

"You're just depressed. We'll fix that."

"I'm not going into the hospital again."

"You can't do it on your own. You need help."

"So do you."

"I don't want to lose you."

Boy, is he trying. I have to hand it to him. In spite of his clichés, he was being quite courageous, like a soldier charging a machine-gun nest. Janet had the bullet belt slung over her shoulder and her finger squeezing the trigger. Empty shells were cartwheeling through the air. But dad was under orders to bring the enemy back — alive. So he ran heroically, without his gun.

Maybe they have this conversation all the time. Maybe he's not the cold-blooded bastard he seems to be.

The whole episode has fried my brain. I have never heard intimate talk between them. I want to run naked into their tent and start breaking bottles.

Am I hearing what I think I'm hearing? She has started to moan.

I need my goddamn earphones! It's not just the fact that they're having sex that is revolting me; it's that the sounds don't jibe with the great chasm between them. Like two lost climbers, they're shouting from one edge of the abyss to the other. Of course, added to my visually dramatic description is the fact that most children, no matter how confused, don't like to listen to their parents having sex.

The sounds grow louder as I write. I feel trapped. I can't even go for a walk. It's dark outside. There are animals that will eat me. But I can't take it anymore. I would rather be stalked by a cheetah than listen to another sound. I'm out of here.

11:17 p.m.

I am back and all is quiet again. Praise the lord. I'm going to have a quick smoke and go to bed. I am exhausted.

I left the tent wearing only shorts and a T-shirt and stumbled my way to the bar. I didn't realize how much I'd had to drink. And I didn't take my flashlight. It was late and the last thing I wanted was a report of some jackass wandering around the camp with a flashlight. It was dark enough so I could move around without being noticed but there was just enough light from the moon that I could kind of see where I was going. Gnarled roots on the path kept tripping me up. I fell at one point and cut my elbow. It's still bleeding.

The bar was closed when I got there so I stood outside and tried to figure out where I could go. I thought of the camp office. But I didn't know where it was. I found a bush along the path and I hid behind it. I don't know why I did this but I guess I thought I could pass some time there. It's not like we were in fucking Rome. I mean, I couldn't exactly wander into a busy square and get an espresso in a bright cafe on the corner. So there I was, squatting behind this bush. I wasn't even thinking that I looked a hell of a lot more suspicious crouching behind a bush than I did standing like a fool in front of the bar.

I was reminded of a winter's night in grade eight. Of a snowball thrown by a friend. A window on a passing bus breaking. An enraged bus driver slamming on his brakes. Five young guys, including me, running down an alley. Nipplehead hiding behind a leafless shrub with his shocking helmet of red hair. The wild-eyed driver seeing him easily.

Walking back shortly afterward and finding Nipplehead sprawled out in the snow, recovering from a punch to the jaw. Pissing ourselves laughing. Angry bus driver. Red hair. Leafless shrub. Beacon. Thump! Stupid Nipplehead.

I hid behind the bush for quite some time. But it wasn't thoughts of Nipplehead that got me moving. It was the tickling on my feet and ankles. At first I just scratched myself, thinking it was dry skin. But then I realized that dry skin didn't crawl.

I rushed out from behind the bush and looked at my legs in the moonlight. My skin was alive with movement. Brown, hairy hives. Moving, brown, hairy hives. Spiders. Little, brown, angry, fucking spiders. Baby spiders, tarantulas, something. Swarming up my ankles and calves. The bastards were biting me. Jesus.

I started to run. As much as their bites hurt I didn't want to touch them with my hands. Somehow, in the throes of revulsion, I managed to think ahead. I knew the shower was not an option. They only loaded enough water for one shower and I had had mine. I would have rushed into the stall, pulled the string expecting immediate relief and crashed, in a violent, head-on collision with the empty water drum. Then the screaming would have started. Lantern lights would have lit up throughout the camp. People would have followed the screams to the shower, and found me there, curled up in a corner. The spiders would have been long gone by that point. They'd have blamed it on the drugs. Rushed me back to Canada. Straight to detox. Convinced me I never had spiders on my legs.

I would have attended a Narcotics Anonymous meeting and told the story of that awful night, the night of my rock bottom. There would have been nods of sympathy. Hugs. A newcomer pin.

I knew I really had only one choice. The river. I rushed through the maze of paths. I ran into the river and waded out until the water reached my waist. I started rubbing my hands over my legs and swearing at the spiders.

"You little fucking pricks," I spat.

I hadn't wanted to swear before I got in the water because I didn't want to make them angrier than they already were. Even though I probably got rid of the spiders within ten seconds, I kept rubbing and scrubbing and swearing for at least a minute.

I didn't leave the river right away. I stood in the cool water, motionless. It felt good. I looked at the opposite bank. A familiar, seductive fire started to burn. I could make it. It wasn't that far. But this was a wide river. What if it carried me away? It didn't look to be moving that fast. What about the crocodiles I had seen sunning themselves? They were probably sleeping. Or they'd moved on.

I'd be quiet. I'd swim quickly. I'd touch the other bank. No, I'd get out and stand there. Just for ten seconds. And then I'd come right back. It would all be over in less than two minutes. I told myself that in three minutes I could be walking back to my tent with wet hair and a real sense of achievement. If I got depressed tomorrow, I could think back to tonight and remind myself that I swam the river.

It's not as if I was asking myself to jump twenty-five feet from a standing start or lift a two-hundred-pound oil drum over my head. This could be done. Yes, it was dangerous. But it wasn't that dangerous. There were lots of other things that were more dangerous. Like taking a kayak across Lake Superior when they got those November storms with eighty-mile-an-hour wind gusts and thirty-foot waves. But the river was dangerous enough to make it a challenge. A good challenge. No one would know. It would be my own secret victory. And I needed one of those.

Now that the idea was in my head, I knew that if I didn't do it I would feel like a failure. I cursed myself. Why did I put that idea in there? Now I almost had to do it. Not for tomorrow's depression. But for the one that would come tonight.

I couldn't think about it anymore. It was time to go. The river was moving much faster than I thought. I got swept along.

I tried not to splash too much, didn't want to wake those sleeping crocs — a ridiculous consideration in hindsight because I was on the verge of drowning. By the time I reached the middle of the river I panicked. *This was a stupid idea.* My arms were weak and the current was really, really strong. *Just swim. It's no big fucking deal.* But I was just kidding myself. It was a big deal. I did not have the strength to get across. My ears were ringing. I coughed grimy water from my throat. The opposite bank of the river blurred by in a series of ugly, black shapes. I needed to reach for those shapes. Make them my life's goal. Everything got pushed into my kicking, my flailing arms. Into my survival. I needed that feeling, *This is it. Do it or die.*

I reached the opposite side and scampered up the bank with visions of crocodiles hot on my heels. I stood there and started to count to ten. That's what I had said. Ten seconds on the other side. No time to think about the dangers of swimming back. While I was counting, I grabbed a twig that was lying near my feet. A twig sounds kind of feeble but what the hell was I supposed to do? Fell a tree and drag it back across the river in my teeth? A twig was perfect. I'd take it home as a souvenir. I suppose I could have looked for a stone but I was only counting to ten, not thirty.

When I reached seven I heard whimpering. It sounded like a whiny, greedy kid in a shopping cart at a grocery store. I looked behind me. At first I didn't know what it was. It looked like a pit bull. A skinny pit bull with a really long neck. With spots and a big, ugly mouth hanging open. Smiling. I swear to god, my first reaction was to make that little clicking sound I do with my tongue when I see a cat or a dog. DoctorfuckingDoolittle.

It was a hyena. I had never seen one in person. Not even at the zoo. What ugly, ugly animals they are. No wonder they're the only enemy the lion has out here. It looked exactly like a beast from hell, sent up first to terrify me and then shred me like beef brisket. But it was alone. And I had startled it. It was standing there eyeballing me. And whimpering like I said. I know everyone talks about the laughing hyena. But it didn't sound like a laugh. It was a whimper. A scary whimper. I didn't want to move too quickly. I remembered from my nature shows that they had incredibly powerful jaws. They could snap the bone of a zebra with a single bite. I wished my twig was a branch. No, a sword. No, a gun. An automatic.

I started backing away slowly, rubbing my twig for good luck. I had forgotten something about hyenas — where there is one, there will surely be others.

At first they just looked like tiny flashlights bouncing up and down and getting closer. These little phantom lights finally took form. The pack had arrived, bringing their terrible whimpering sounds with them. These weren't whimpers of fear or injury. These were whimpers of excitement, like hyperactive kids at a birthday party at McDonald's. I didn't wait to see how many there were.

I ran into the water and splashed and kicked as hard as I could. Let the crocodiles take me. I would rather have been drowned by a crocodile than ripped apart by hyenas.

With all the credit going to blind fear I made excellent time getting back. I staggered out of the water and realized I had no idea where I was. But I didn't care. The hyenas couldn't get me. That's all I cared about. I clutched my twig triumphantly. It was my proof that I had been to the other side. Getting to the other side was what Crocodile Man had tried to get Janet to do. Only I think he was talking about something in the spirit world. Not some river. At least not a real river.

I don't want to exaggerate the hyena encounter. They were close but they weren't that close. It's not like I barely escaped. I was right beside the river. I was never really in danger. And besides, hyenas are territorial. They just wanted me off their turf. They were just dogs. Wild dogs. With big teeth. And jaws that could snap steel. What a fucking idiot.

I did one smart thing. I saw which way the river was flowing and I walked in the opposite direction. If I had gone the other way I could have ended up in Tanzania.

As I neared the camp someone came bursting out of the trees and nearly knocked me down. Scared the shit out of me. It was Gabriel.

"Jesus, man," he exclaimed. "What the hell are you doing?"

I just shook my head with as much arrogance as I could muster. He wouldn't have understood. He told me that one of the other guides said there was some crazy kid swimming across the river. Great. Everything had gone so well. Now I was going to return to a panicked camp. Janet would be hysterical. Dad would never forgive me.

Gabriel and I rushed back to his living quarters. It was more like an old shack. He assured the other guide that I was okay. Obviously I was okay. I was standing there wasn't I? Turned out the guy hadn't told anyone at the camp. Thank god.

Someone handed me a towel. I didn't make much of an effort to dry off. I was going to wear my wet clothes like a badge for a little while longer.

I was appalled when I saw the cramped conditions of Gabriel's room. There were three bunk beds packed into the shack. Including Gabriel, there were eight guides sleeping there. Six in the beds and two on the floor. It looked like a slave ship. The guides didn't seem to mind. At least not at that moment. They were too busy smiling at me and saying words I could not understand. A few were laughing at me (not with me). One guy rotated his finger around his temple. A universal sign.

Gabriel walked me back to my tent. I wanted to tell him that I thought it was disgusting that they put all the tour guides in a little room like that. But I thought it might sound condescending. I couldn't think of anything else to talk about so we walked in silence.

We got to my tent and I turned around to say good night. He was looking at me the way dad and I look at Janet. The way I've looked at lunatics on street corners, muttering to themselves. I didn't want him thinking that about me.

"I wasn't trying to do the big ugly you know. I'd explain but you wouldn't understand."

"I never said you were."

But he had. With his eyes. With the tone of his voice. I can smell well-intentioned, charitable concern. It oozes like a stinky sweat. A gust of wind hit the candle I had just lit. It flickered and threatened to blow out, leaving me only the smell of burned wax and a wisp of smoke.

"It's just a river. It was just a swim."

Gabriel nodded. He smiled and gave me a hug. "Go to bed."

Gabriel turned and left. That hug was the worst part of the whole night. I have to remind myself that he doesn't know me. I know me. And I know what I did. And I know why I did it — to feel like I do right now. If he thinks otherwise, that's his problem. Let him add me to his list of worries. He shares a shack with seven other men. Because he's not as smart as he thinks he is. If he knew stuff he wouldn't be there. He's there. And I'm here. I've got my twig. And he's in a room with fourteen smelly feet. He can think what he wants to think.

I did it. I ran the gauntlet. And this time Gabriel didn't have to "rescue" me. I crossed the river, counted to ten and came back again. I have challenged the beasts from hell. They snarled and snapped and belched fire but they could not catch me. Like a Greek hero, I have won my battle. I have stolen the golden branch from the hellhounds. Golden branch sounds a hell of a lot better than golden twig. I have no more tests for myself on this trip. My clothes drip as I write.

I have never felt more alive.

I woke up at six-thirty still buzzing from last night. I'm still buzzing. I hoped all this buzzing would somehow get Mr. Happy excited but alas things were dormant again this morning. I'm starting to get worried. I can swim rivers and steal gold from hyenas but I can't do the five-finger shuffle.

One of the good things about being on safari in Africa is that Saturdays don't feel like Saturday. No sound of mowers. No one washing the car. No yard sales.

I slept in the clothes I wore last night. I wanted those waters to soak right through. These are significant times for me. There is a sense of urgency about all this. The four of us have been flung together for a reason. And — like the rule of the land — only the strong will survive. Actually, dad could cancel the trip today and ruin all my gallant talk.

I won't be wearing shorts today. My legs are a mess of red welts and rashes. Those spiders really did a number on me. I'm going to have to see if Gabriel can sneak me some cream. (Don't want dad or Janet asking questions about last night.) The itching is driving me crazy. My elbow stopped bleeding. It's still throbbing a bit though.

I wonder if it will leave a scar. I hope not. I wouldn't mind a scar from the river swim. Like if one of those hyenas had sunk its teeth into me — that would be something. But I don't want a scar from being drunk and stumbling around in the dark.

Gabriel better not start talking to me soft and slow. Giving me more hugs. That's got to be the worst part of Janet's situation. I'll have to show Gabriel that I'm not unhinged. I know I'm not suicidal and that's all that matters. I do crazy stuff. I've always done crazy stuff.

I am tired of people who try to come up with reasons for doing what they do. Reasons and explanations and justifications and bullshit and double bullshit. Who the hell knows why we do what we do? Not one of us is smart enough to come up with a good answer every time we do something. *I beat my kid because my father beat me.* Fuck off. *I poisoned that dog because my mother was a prostitute.* Eat me.

I could come up with fourteen really solid reasons why I crossed the river last night. But ultimately, if I am honest, I have to say that I did it for no good reason. That guy who climbed Everest should never have said he climbed it *because it was there.* (If in fact he said that at all.) It would have been much better to have said *I climbed it for no good reason.* Or the guy who walks into a fast-food restaurant and takes out twelve people with a semi-automatic. *Why'd you do it?* ask the reporters surrounding him as he's being led from the jail to a police van with a jacket thrown over his head. A simple shrug of the shoulders. *For no good reason.*

I have considered suicide. But I'd only do it if I could be sure it would turn out the way I imagine it should — me, buzzing around like a bluebottle fly watching the grief and the tears of family and friends. Seeing my own memorial service, a room packed with people, standing room only. Hearing nice things, remarkable things, being said about me.

But in my suicide/memorial service fantasy I always hang around too long. I hang around until people stop talking about me and get on with their lives. Until I am just a distant memory, a tiny wellhead for a momentary pause of reflection but nothing more. That's why I won't kill myself. It's not worth two weeks of attention that I might not even see.

I met the folks for breakfast after one more frustrating attempt to raise my hibernating member. No go. I gave it a quick smack with the back of my hand before tucking it away. I also inspected my wart. Damn thing. I wonder if it's going to start spreading across my hands, then up my arms and up my neck, eventually covering my face.

Wouldn't that be something? Wouldn't notice the harelip anymore.

The two of them were already seated when I arrived at the restaurant.

I assumed that because they had sex last night they would be in glorious spirits.

Dad was looking at Janet who was staring at her lap. She was picking at the skin around her fingernails again. The haunt had returned to her eyes. Dad turned to me.

"It's bad," was all he said.

I was immediately released from the fears of my warts and my uncooperative penis. There's nothing like the sight of someone worse off than yourself to brighten your day. But even as I sat there I had to acknowledge that it was unclear which one of us was the most fucked up. It's like the Tour de France. We keep trading the yellow jersey.

Janet only stayed at the table for fifteen minutes. She whispered the same thing over and over, "It's going to get better."

She never even looked up. Her head remained bowed. She looked so old. I tried to remember what her face looked like before they left for Paris but I couldn't. That seems so long ago.

Dad came by after breakfast, carrying more suicide tools. This time he brought his own stuff, mostly things from his toiletry bag. Four retractable razor cartridges. (How the hell she'd cut herself with one of those I don't know.) A bottle of dad's cologne. (I guess he's worried she could smash the bottle and use the broken glass to cut herself. I wanted to tell him she could get a glass from the restaurant. I also wanted to ask him where his glass bottle of scotch was.) A plastic bottle of Tylenol. (Now that made sense. Actually, that was the only thing that did.)

If she really wants to kill herself, Africa provides a multitude of diverse choices, none of which can be found in dad's toiletry bag. It was a noble but stupid effort on his part. He's really rattled. I have to respect his concern though. He was there when she tried to kill herself before. Maybe he is seeing the same signs this morning.

Dad thinks we might head back to Nairobi tomorrow. I won't mind. We have seen what we came to see. Janet will soon be back in Paris, in a clean room with fresh flowers, a TV and a window that only opens four inches.

We were all supposed to go on a game drive this morning but Janet said she wasn't up to it. Dad told me that he couldn't take the chance of leaving her alone so I am to go with Gabriel by myself.

11:26 a.m.

I am back in my tent. Didn't go out for very long. I met Gabriel at the van a little after nine. Dad was there to see us off. He seemed in good spirits. He's a bigger man than me. I would have been sulking if I was the one who had to stay behind.

I was surprised that Janet didn't come rushing out of her tent, begging me to stay. Dad said she was sleeping. Bullshit. Her eyes may have been closed but she wasn't asleep. Unless, of course, her anxiety has evaporated and depression has rolled out over her fields like a big, burning sun, scorching everything. Maybe that's why dad was so concerned this morning. He's already told me he wasn't worried about the anxiety. It's the depression that scares him.

It was sad to drive away and see him standing there waving. I waved back and got quite emotional. He doesn't deserve this. I don't deserve this. And most of all, Janet doesn't deserve this.

Gabriel was quiet for the early part of our drive. We saw families of warthogs and a few gazelles. I was relieved to be away from the turmoil. I was thinking it might work if we finished the safari under these conditions; with dad and me taking turns looking after Janet while the other one went out alone with Gabriel.

Gabriel's silence started to make me nervous though. He was normally talking and guiding and pointing stuff out. I tried a couple of times to ask him dumb questions about the animals. He gave really short answers. He looked as if he had finally had enough of the Clark clan. He was probably hoping we'd end the trip early and return to Nairobi.

We stopped on the side of a dusty road and watched a herd of giraffes. I have to admit, as much as I like seeing all the different animals, I prefer the ones that eat meat. The giraffes are impressive but they don't hold my interest in the way that the lions, or leopards, or even the hyenas do. I've always preferred villains.

Gabriel and I sat without speaking long after the giraffes had disappeared. I finally couldn't take it anymore.

"What the hell are we doing?" I asked.

"Do you think you might be crazy like your mother?"

So that's what he'd been sitting there jacking off to. I started to laugh. I laughed too hard and too long, a mad, nervous laugh.

"Do you like books?" he asked.

I slowly stopped laughing but I kept a pasted smile. "Do I like books? What kind of stupid question is that?"

"How many do you think you've read?"

"Five."

"Your mother said she hardly saw you once you turned thirteen. She said you were holed up in your room like a monk. Reading. Always reading."

"That's horseshit. I was never hiding in my room. I had friends, I played on the football team."

"The books were important though. Weren't they?"

"Not really."

"You needed a tall tree to climb, to escape the thing."

"What thing?"

"The thing that was hunting you down. The same thing that's hunted your mother down."

"Look, I don't know what you're up to but if you think I'm like her, I'm not. I didn't try and kill myself last night."

"I'm not just talking about the river. I'm talking about the poisons you smoke every day."

Gabriel sat patiently. He looked like he still had a belly burst-ing with advice. I could have kept my mouth shut. But he had the keys to the van. He might have sat us out there until sunset.

"Who said I had a drug problem?"

"Your mother."

"She's nuts."

Gabriel turned his eyes on me. They had a powerful effect. I immediately felt humbled and weak.

"You've backed yourself into a dangerous corner, Richard. You think you've read it all and seen it all. You don't want anybody to interfere, to hurt you or touch you or help you. Which means you are left alone to fix your own problems. But you don't seem to care enough."

"And you care way too much about people who won't give a shit about you after they're gone," I said, almost shouting.

"There is not much hope for your mother. But what hope remains, rests with you."

"Wow, strike the piano chord loud and long."

Gabriel sat, unruffled, looking out at the swaying grasses. "You have no idea how much you influence her. You're not just destroying yourself, you're destroying her."

"So you think if you can save me, you can save her?"

"Yes."

I was impressed. Most savvy emancipators would have said something profound about not being able to save anyone, that *you have to save yourself.* I pulled out a cigarette. Gabriel reached over. I didn't know if he wanted a cigarette or if he wanted to hold my hand. I didn't want to hold his hand so I dropped a du Maurier in his palm. He stuck it in his mouth and lit it like he smoked two packs a day, which was odd, because he'd looked so awkward the last time we smoked. I grabbed another cigarette and got it burning.

"Are you on anything right now?" he asked.

"I'm high on life, baby," I said and exhaled a stream of smoke through my nose.

"If you don't stop using drugs to hide the real Richard, then this conversation won't mean shit and you can carry on with the rest of your fucked-up life thinking you know just about everything there is to know and I won't give a damn."

"Jesus, you're swearing. Must be serious."

Gabriel examined the ash at the end of his cigarette. His expression never changed.

"Do you think your mother has a chemical imbalance?"

It took me a moment. I was still back on my own "fucked-up life."

"I think that's part of her problem."

"But not all of it?"

"I don't know."

"You see, your mother is starting to think she does. And that might be the beginning of the end for her. Someone who is moody has negative thoughts from time to time. Your mother has negative thoughts all day, all the time. Do you think she is thinking safe and peaceful thoughts when she gets upset about how much gasoline is left in the tank?"

It was such a dumb question I almost yelled at him. He delicately flicked a half-inch length of ash out the window and carried on.

"We could argue until sunrise about whether the thoughts cause the chemical imbalance or whether the chemical imbalance causes the thoughts."

"I'd like to get back sooner than that if you don't mind."

"We have so little control over our lives. But one of the sacred powers we do have is the control of our perception. We are either jailed or liberated by it. Mental health professionals don't have the ability to change perception. Their solution is to prescribe a pill. Putting someone in a hospital is easier. Then everyone, including the family, can feel that they did their best."

"What if you're wrong? What if the chemical imbalance is causing the negative thoughts? Then what's so bad about medicating someone so you can at least try and help them?"

"Nothing. If you don't want to answer the call."

Dingdong, hello?

"What call?"

"The call to change. Where your father sees mental illness I see a call to change. What is schizophrenia? Manic-depression? They are labels. Labels created in the last hundred years, created and distributed by prescription drug pushers, doctors and academics with small imaginations, who have no awareness about the tapestry that joins the mind, the heart and the soul.

"They come up with a list of symptoms and when your behaviour matches their list they slap a label on you. And once you start believing them the damage is done. The label hangs from your neck like a cowbell.

"For instance, now you see your mother as demented and you start treating her as such. She feels it. She starts believing that she is demented.

"It's very destructive, this labelling business. I see it all the time. People from all over, Swedes, Russians, Americans, Australians, come here to study the animals. Smart, decent people. But they all come here with the same mentality. And they study and observe and tranquilize and collar and tag and label and none of them ends up knowing these animals at all."

"If she doesn't have a chemical imbalance then what the hell's going on?"

"She has a crisis in her soul. As do you by the way. And your father will have one soon enough. But the solution will not be found in hospitals or pills."

"So all she needs to do is harness her thoughts and she'll be right as rain?"

"It's not a solution. It's a step. But it's by no means an easy step. Her soul is in a desperate struggle.

"I asked her to tell me what she saw when she was depressed or anxious. She said she felt as if she was at the edge of a bottomless pit, hanging on by her fingertips. She's there when you see her behave so irrationally. Hanging over the pit. But then she has moments when she manages to pull herself out. But only for a short while. It isn't long before she's back again, hanging by her fingertips.

"She doesn't understand that her solution lies in doing the opposite of what she thinks. She thinks her sanity is restored when she leaves the pit. You and your father pat her on the back, making her believe that she shouldn't be there. She continues to climb out because she's scared. But she has the wrong pictures in her mind, pictures painted by fear.

"It is not a drop into a horrible, bottomless pit. I told her to think of it as falling in love. To think of that exhilaration that feels so good, so scary, both at the same time. It is the drop to freedom.

"Instead of climbing out over and over again or ending the suffering by her own hand or being pulled out by doctors and pills, she needs to let go, to let herself fall. And so do you. You have become separated and split from where you came from and where you need to return, once you have the courage to surrender."

"To what?"

Gabriel sat for a moment. He had taken me this far, which was further than anyone had ever taken me, and I was waiting for the grand finale, waiting to be delivered. I knew he had heard my question so I wasn't going to ask again. We sat in silence for ten minutes. I'm not exaggerating. That's a long time to sit in silence. I wanted to give him time. This was big for me. I felt like he was onto something. Maybe not the whole thing. But part of the thing.

I assumed he was collecting his thoughts, preparing himself. And then he moved. But he didn't open his mouth. He turned the key in the ignition and started the engine. And off we drove. And nary a word was spoken about labels or bottomless pits or plummeting to peace.

Gabriel returned to his role as safari guide. He more than made up for his silence on the first leg of our journey. He was very animated as we made our way back to Shaba. He spotted some monkeys near the side of the road and delivered a rapid-fire summary of their mating habits and diet. We passed a tree and he had plenty to say about that. He even told me about some damn rocks that were lying at the side of the road. I've not seen him so excited about Africa.

I was having a hard time getting my mind back on the game drive. I knew what he was up to. If he could inspire me to face my own crisis then maybe Janet could get better. Two birds. One stone. But this bird is damn skilled at dodging stones.

Gabriel is either the best bullshit artist I have ever met or he is a special person. I haven't decided yet.

I better go eat lunch soon because I think the elephants are coming to raid our camp. We saw them on our way in. Gabriel said they were on their way to the river, which is about fifty yards from my tent. It's like a thunderhead coming through on a hot summer afternoon. The camp manager is concerned that the elephants might get spooked and stampede. He has told us to be extra cautious and not make any loud noises. It has happened before. Camps have been destroyed. People have been hurt. I hope Janet is still sleeping.

Dad is outside my tent calling me. Lunch is being served. I have to go.

1:34 p.m.

Dad and I ate lunch alone. Janet was still sleeping. He was happy to have me back. Happy to have someone to talk to. I told him about the game drive. Told him he didn't miss anything spectacular. Saw some animals but none that he hadn't checked off his list. Except the warthogs. He said he didn't care about missing the warthogs. He said he was really looking forward to going out with Gabriel. He needed a break.

We were both excited about the possibility of an elephant raid. Dad took some food back for Janet and I started back to my tent. On the way, I spotted some baboons on the edge of the camp.

I ran to their tent where dad was quietly leaving a plate of food beside Janet's bed. She was actually sleeping. And by the size of the saliva stain on her pillow, it was a deep sleep. She looked so peaceful. I thought maybe she was dead. I honestly couldn't see her breathing. Maybe she had taken a bottle of pills and dad had spent all morning guarding a corpse. I didn't want to say anything. He would have just gotten angry. Like he was that stupid. Like he wouldn't have noticed she was dead.

I waited for dad outside the tent. "Baboons on the edge of camp," I said. "Let's go."

"I can't. Your mother."

"She's fine. It'll take five minutes. You just left her alone for lunch."

"That's true."

I led him back to the path I had been on. We were like a couple of kids, stealing away for an adventure. He kept telling me to slow down. I got to the place where I had seen the baboons but they were gone. He said it was okay. He had already checked them off his list on our way from Naivasha to Baringo. I moved further down the path.

"We better go back," he said

"The elephants are already at the river. Come on."

I continued leading us down the path.

"Richard, stop right there."

There was something in the tone of his voice that made me stop. Good thing. Not twenty yards in front of me was a bull elephant. Just standing there. He must have been eating leaves. But he wasn't eating anymore. He was staring at us. And he looked really pissed off. His battered white tusks were so long they nearly touched the ground. His ears were spread wide like giant wings. But this was no Dumbo. This was a mean, son-of-a-bitch male. The grooves on his trunk were so deep a child could have used them as hand-holds and climbed it like a tree. And then been killed.

He looked old. Really old. Old and insane. A crazy, old elephant. And big. Jesus, he was big. He could have kicked our asses.

There was no telling what he could have done. A tusk through the gut. A trunk whip. He could have done that, too. Picked one of us up and thrown us against a tree. Tossed us around. Played with our bodies after our skulls were smashed. But he probably would have settled for a good, old-fashioned stomping, pulverizing our bones in about half a minute. They'd have picked us up and tossed us into the back of a truck like we were bags of sand.

"What do we do?" I whispered.

"Let's back away, nice and slow."

I don't think he'd been looking at dad at all. Because the moment I took my small step, his giant ears flapped back. I didn't know it then, but I know it now — this means an elephant is ready to charge. And charge he did. He was no slow, lumbering giant either. He launched at me like a stone out of a slingshot.

Dad and I released ourselves from the weight of our testicles and screamed, shamelessly and loud.

We ran blindly back down the path. Neither of us ever looked back. We ran and ran until finally we arrived at my tent and dared to look behind us. He hadn't followed us. We looked like a pair of pale, shivering albino rats.

Dad started to laugh. Damn, he was pleased. He actually put up his hand for a high five. It was awfully corny but I slapped his hand. I couldn't help it. I got swept up in the excitement. I quickly got self-conscious and hoped that no one had seen. In spite of my shiver of embarrassment, I was actually very happy. It was great to see him so alive.

We found out later that the elephant had veered off the path and destroyed one of the tents. The camp manager said it was a miracle there was nobody in the tent at the time. It could have been worse. The herd could have followed. The whole damn camp could have been demolished.

Dad might have to pay for the tent. And I don't think the tents come cheap. They're not like pup tents. More like cottages. I hope he doesn't have to pay a dime. This is Africa. These things happen. These are wild animals we're dealing with here.

I have found a sunken pit. Not quite a bottomless pit but it'll have to do. It has a waterfall pouring into it. The water circles a trench on the perimeter of the pit and then flows down a channel to the river. I am sitting on a chair in the middle of the pit. I can't hear anything but the sound of the cascading water. It's soothing.

Dad felt really bad about the destroyed tent and offered to pay for a new one. He just about filled his drawers when he found out it would cost three thousand dollars. It all turned out okay though. The camp manager appreciated the fact that dad offered to pay but he said they had insurance to cover the damage. Good man. Big relief for dad. And for me. I didn't want our run from the elephant to be forever tainted by a loss of money for dad. As it is, dad and I will have that story to relive at Christmas for the next forty years. Give or take.

Dad goes out at three o'clock with Gabriel. I will watch Janet. Dad says we will now go back to Nairobi the day after tomorrow. This is the plan.

Dad is standing above me by the top of the waterfall. He doesn't think I know he is there. I feel paranoid with him watching me.

I wonder what he sees, looking down on his raggedy-ass son. Perhaps he is nervous about what I am scribbling in here. Can he see what I'm writing? Nah, he's too far away.

I think he sees a lost cause. A drifter. A dreamless, hopeless rig worker. And I'm not even a real rig worker. They don't put me anywhere near the dangerous equipment. That's for the real men. I scuttle around the rig yard like a crab, picking up garbage and digging drainage ditches.

He must think I have some future. Even a little one. Otherwise, he wouldn't offer to pay for university. It's too important for him that I get a degree and evolve from the primordial mud of rig work.

When dad is away this afternoon I'm going to try some crisis counselling on Janet. I can see why people going through a crisis end up involved in religion and cults. They were probably hanging on by their fingertips. But before they let go they didn't spend much time thinking about what they were surrendering to. I'd have to think about it a lot.

I mean that's a big surrender. It's the whole deal right there. What the fuck would I surrender to? I don't even trust hockey trades I hear about secondhand, let alone words from thousands of years ago, stuff about my soul. I mean, don't you have to hear something like that from the source itself? Don't you have to look that person in the eye? Get a take? Ask yourself, "Is this bullshit or not?" I mean, who are these people who say Jesus is their friend? Have they ever met him? I don't want to let go and drop willy-nilly into the hands of Moses or Jesus or Vishnu or Buddha or Muhammad or whoever. *Thunk.* It's true that millions have done it so at least I'd know that those hands have good reflexes. But I have a fatal fear of ending up glassy-eyed and sure of everything.

So what do you surrender to if you don't want to end up a complete asshole? If you don't want to join some club with a bunch of other brain-dead slobs? Can't you surrender to something that's your own? Not something that some jack-off emissary tells you happened thousands of years ago. That's what I want. I want to surrender to something I can call my own. Something so private and profound that I couldn't tell anyone. That would be the secret rule. As soon as I told someone, I'd lose it.

Dad is still up there staring at me. I've got the creeps. I'm going back to my tent and drink beer.

6:01 p.m.

Dad was not allowed to go on the game drive because Janet said that he shouldn't. She would not give a reason. Dad has spent the entire day watching her. He seemed okay with it.

I could hear them talking in their tent. He asked her very sweetly if he could get her anything. She wanted a glass of water. She asked about me. He said I might go for a swim in the pool. She said I shouldn't go because I would get river blindness. I wanted to yell out that you got river blindness from the river, not the goddamn pool. And she would have yelled back that they had to get the water from somewhere. And she'd have been right. Dad told her I wouldn't go swimming. Her concerns about river blindness were not uttered in the same hysterical voice I have heard before. No, this voice was distant, less interested.

Then things got a little weird.

"Did you tell him?" she asked.

"I've told him nothing," he said.

"You can't tell him."

"I understand that."

"We agreed."

"I know we did."

My imagination started sprinting until I realized that she was probably talking about her suicide attempt. What a liar he was. It was good to hear him lie so smoothly. Made him appear almost human. I was pretty sure I already knew what I was never to know. But then doubt set in. What if she was talking about something other than the suicide attempt? I was back thumbing a ride on the old incest highway. What the hell else would you make a pact about? They sounded like Adolf Hitler and Eva Braun. Or Kennedy's assassins, conspiring, whispering.

I did relieve dad at his post for an hour so he could go have a beer at the bar. I took my place in a chair beside Janet's bed. I looked at her face. Her eyes were closed. She looked so tiny lying there. I wondered at what point I'd have to stop being the child and become the parent. Would she make it to her sixties? I lit a cigarette.

"Can I have one?" she asked.

Her voice startled me. Her eyes were still closed. She slowly opened them and I opened my pack of du Mauriers. She took the pack from my hand and examined it. I don't think she'd seen the new warnings since Health Canada made them big and bold and scary.

The warning on the pack was pretty blunt. It said, "Smoking Can Kill You." I watched Janet study this. I was thinking the warning was a bunch of bologna. They needed to change it. So presumptuous. "Smoking Can Kill You." How dare they assume that I don't have a soul. It should have read, "Smoking Can Kill Your Body." I got pissed off looking at that stupid thing. Making us think that all we are is organic material. Bastards.

I don't suppose Janet would want to think she might survive the death of her body. That the madness might not end when her heart stopped beating. She took one of the cigarettes out ever so slowly and handed back the pack.

"I miss du Mauriers," she said and then lit her cigarette.

I slid the ashtray closer to her.

"You're not going swimming are you?"

"I'm not going near that pool. I'll get river blindness."

"Don't mock me."

She stubbed out the cigarette she had just lit and lay back down. A thought suddenly occurred to her.

"Where did you hear that?"

"Hear what?"

"Me talking about river blindness. Were you eavesdropping?"

"No."

Oh god, busted. Had to think fast.

"What else did you hear?"

"Nothing. I didn't hear anything. Dad told me."

"Told you what?"

"That you thought I'd get river blindness if I swam in the pool."

She seemed to believe my explanation but it didn't matter. She wanted nothing more to do with me.

"You don't have to stay. I'll be fine."

What an idiot. Why the hell had I mentioned the river blindness? It was dumb. I was just trying to lighten the mood a bit. I came to help her and I was screwing up good. I sat there a moment watching her.

"Let go," I whispered.

"What?"

"Let go."

Her eyes opened. "What are you talking about?"

"Do you feel like you're hanging from your fingertips?"

"No."

"Yes you do."

"No I don't."

"You have to."

She looked at me with utter confusion, like I was the one who had snapped. And then her face relaxed and she smiled.

"You've been talking to Gabriel again."

"No, he was talking to me about me. He thinks I need to make some changes in my life."

"If his ideas were that good, he wouldn't be shuttling people around in a van for five dollars an hour. He'd be running a clinic or giving seminars."

"I think the opposite might be true. The ones giving seminars for two hundred and fifty dollars are the phonies."

"I need professional help, Richard. Not bursts of inspirational gossip from Gabriel."

"You've given up."

"I have a medical problem."

"You have a spiritual problem."

"You don't know what I have. I need to be in a safe place and get treated by professionals who know how to deal with this."

Her voice was flat. I didn't believe a word she was saying. She had resigned herself to the idea that she would be institutionalized in Paris.

"You have a chance. These opportunities don't come around very often. Your house is burning down. You have a chance to build a new one."

"I don't want a new one."

"Yes, you do. Deep down you do."

"I'm too tired. And I have no idea what burning houses have to do with anything."

"You need to let go and surrender."

"I have. I've let go of the illusion that I can fight this by myself and I've surrendered to the fact that I need the professional help of doctors and possibly some electroshock therapy to get back to normal."

"Since when are you getting shock treatment?"

"Since nothing else seems to work."

"This is not you talking."

A crack appeared in her armour. Her features softened and then began to tremble. Her eyes welled. "Just leave me alone."

"Don't let him do this to you."

"I've done it to myself." I tried to take her hand but she pulled it away. "It's none of your business anymore."

"We can beat this thing. You and me. We could move back to the house. You could have a chance to start your life again. I could get clean."

She extended her hand to me. I took it. She smiled. "And then you'd finally have your chance to fuck me, wouldn't you?"

I tried to yank my hand back but she held it tight. "It's what you want isn't it?"

I stared at her dumbstruck. She threw my hand away.

"Don't look at me like that," she pleaded. "Don't put ideas in my head. Don't talk to me. And don't come in here like a fucking missionary trying to save me."

She was starting to get hysterical. I wasn't in any hurry to leave. I pulled out my pack of cigarettes.

"Please! Stop torturing me!"

"I'm just leaving you a couple of cigarettes."

I left three cigarettes beside the ashtray. She rolled onto her side and began to sob. I wanted to pat her back but I thought she might scream. So I quietly took my chair and went outside the tent.

What the hell was I doing trying to save her? Gabriel had tried and failed. I had now tried. But I hadn't tried with my own words. I had used Gabriel's. Talking about stuff I didn't really understand. She could hear it in my voice. The sound of a parrot. A parrot missionary. I had failed her. She was being manipulated to return to Paris and do the hospital thing. Dad must have really been working on her.

The news of the electric shock was ringing in my ears. Louder, it seemed, than her angry accusations about my motives for getting her back to Canada, accusations that I quickly set aside like a hot fry pan.

I sat outside the tent for another half hour before dad came weaving up the path, wearing a sloppy, drunken grin.

"How is she?" he asked.

"Sleeping."

He tugged me away from the tent. "Have you ever told her you know about her suicide attempt?" he whispered.

"No."

"Don't!" he said loud enough that I flinched. "Not now. It would only hurt her."

He started walking away.

"She told me she might get electric shock treatment back in Paris." My tone of voice smacked of disapproval.

He stopped and turned around. "It's a possibility. You have a problem with that?"

"I've seen it done on TV and in movies. It seems a bit extreme."

"Extreme?"

He came toward me. I brought my fingers up to my throat. A reflex action.

"Would you rather have her dead?"

"No, I just hope that electric shock is considered a last resort."

"And it will be."

"But it's clearly been discussed."

"And it's something that may happen. But if you think it's a bad idea and have a brilliant alternative I'm all ears."

What the hell was I supposed to say? I believed in what Gabriel had told me. I just couldn't put it in my own words. Even if I could have, dad was the wrong audience for a discussion about surrender. I became a mute, a big dummy standing there.

"I thought so," he said.

He disappeared inside the tent. I don't know why I bothered challenging him like that. He's only trying to do what he thinks is best under the circumstances. I suppose I was pissed off that he had finally broken her spirit.

I returned to my tent and chased two lines. They did nothing to relieve the edge so I smoked two more. And two more after that. I've only got a pinch left. It looks like one final smoke for the flight back to Paris. Until then I will have to make do with beer and whiskey.

The lines had one really positive effect. I got an erection. I was so thrilled I actually smacked it on the table. My balls were ready to burst. They usually get emptied three times a day. And burst they did. I didn't fantasize about anyone although fleeting images of Nicole flashed in and out. The physical rhythms were enough.

It's not drugs that I need. It's masturbation. Take away the goodies. Take away the alcohol. But don't cut off my right hand. Or I will surely get delirium tremens (or at least learn to use my left). I can now write that I honestly thought I would never get another erection. I have conquered this fear. Now I am ready for anything.

I can hear dad trying to convince Janet to come to dinner. She's saying that she's too tired. He sounds like he is losing his patience. It's probably the booze.

I can't worry about Janet and dad anymore. I've got to be selfish. Janet has decided to follow dad along the narrow highway to the land of the normal people. I won't be joining them.

Gabriel's right about one thing. People run from crisis. Janet is running. And dad, too. Like cows seeking shelter from thunder under the trees. We shouldn't run. We shouldn't hide. We should celebrate. Wow. Crisis. A chance to change. A chance to shed this old skin and start a new life. Thank you. Bless you. Embrace the fucking crisis.

Dad has stopped asking her if she wants to come to dinner. Now he's telling her she will. She says she can't. He says she can and she will. She's crying.

I better get ready. I hope I don't look too stoned. Our time in Africa is drawing to a close. This makes me sad. I love it here. I don't like the tour vans and the angry stares and the poverty. But there's something here. Something potent. Something about the beginning of the whole damn thing. I'm going to miss that.

Dad has just called to me from outside my tent. I can hear that Janet is with him. I guess we'll do the family dinner carnival one more time. You have to give us credit for trying. A lot of families would have packed up the plates and napkins and moved on. But not us. We're going to try again. See if we can't enjoy a good meal together. Have a few laughs. Swap stories. Yak it up. Get that Christmas morning feeling back again.

8:59 p.m.

Dad should never have brought mom to dinner. I could tell from the moment I stepped outside the tent that things were not right. She looked like a stray dog stranded at the corner of a busy intersection — the honking, the bumpers blurring past, the confusion, not knowing whether to cross. And the saddest part of all was how valiantly she tried to seem normal.

"Are you ready?" she asked in a cautious voice that would have been entirely appropriate had we been living in 1965 preparing to make a dash over the Berlin Wall.

The three of us made our way to the restaurant. Dad had obviously continued drinking in the tent because he stumbled twice. I talked about the elephant that had charged through the camp. Mom pretended to listen. I kept looking at dad to get a read on him. He had that distant, judgmental look. Like he was ready to chew up and spit out anything we said.

I became aware of the stares almost as soon as we sat down. People at the other tables kept stealing glances at mom. A small child in a Winnie-the-Pooh shirt was staring at her for so long that his mother asked him to stop. We were a circus show and mom was the main attraction. Dad was drinking another scotch and was too hammered to notice. I was still humming from my lines and my antenna was up, bent but not broken.

To the untrained eye, there was nothing dramatic going on. Mom had the same haunted expression she has worn the entire trip. Her fingers twisted like claws and picked at her nails. But all of this had been witnessed by diners before.

No, this was not a response to her physical state. These people knew. Everyone in that restaurant could see mom's soul weeping. They could sense despair beyond the boundary of normal comprehension, a place where genius and madness danced and spun, a place where mom was either going to be purified by the fire and emerge a goddess, or burn to ash and become a painful memory in the minds of her family and friends. There were no other choices. Goddess or ash.

I don't think anyone knew exactly why their eyes were drawn to this attractive, middle-aged woman. She was dressed conservatively in jeans and a pale, buttoned shirt. Her hair was combed. She was eating her meal like the rest of them. She wasn't sipping her soup with a fork or eating mashed potatoes with her fingers. And yet they stared. And mom was painfully aware of the attention.

I thought of Jackie Kennedy in her blood-stained dress, valiantly holding her own, trying to ignore the invasive eyes around her, imploring her to change her clothes.

Mom expressed her appreciation for the cool African night. She said that the salad was excellent. She commented that the rolls looked fresh and delicious. Dad had settled into sloppy, drunken silence. He wasn't noticing anything.

"Do you remember your suicide attempt when you were two?" mom asked me as she buttered her roll.

If she had wanted a safety line she had chosen a curious topic. But I was not about to let go.

"I don't remember that."

"I was vacuuming and the phone rang. While I was talking you somehow got the cord wrapped around your throat. By the time I came back you had crawled to the end of the living room, dragging the vacuum cleaner behind you. You were blue. I thought you were going to die."

Two years ago we all would have had a big laugh, well probably a small laugh. But given the present circumstances her story was met with a clumsy silence. I didn't really mind but I'm sure dad didn't want the subject of suicide perched on a chair at our table like a drooping vulture.

"That's funny," I said.

She was not too far gone to hear how hollow I sounded.

"You don't think so at all."

"Sure I do."

"You think suicide is funny?"

Twisted games. A safety line only works when both people hold on tight.

"No, I don't think suicide is funny. But your story was funny."

I was gripping the sucker with all my might but she was unfastening the carabiner at her end.

"Why?" she asked.

"Why? Because it wasn't really a suicide attempt. A two-year-old doesn't try to commit suicide. It's absurd. That's what's funny."

"How do you know you weren't trying to kill yourself?"

Dad had been tuned out. He tuned in. "Change of subject," he slurred.

"Why?" she asked innocently.

Dad staggered to his feet and grabbed her arm. "Let's go," he said. "Back to the tent."

"Am I embarrassing anyone? I'll shut up then."

"Let's go."

"I haven't finished my dinner."

He yanked again on her arm.

"Leave me alone," she said and seemed to look to me for help. I just sat there. Of course.

In spite of his drunkenness, dad didn't want to turn a small scene into a big one. So, he turned and lurched away from the table and created a big scene anyway.

He didn't see the small child in the Winnie-the-Pooh shirt standing behind him. Dad knocked the child to the ground with his knee, unintentionally, of course. But intentions mean nothing to a child when he's smacked to the floor, chin-first. He began wailing. Now we had the undivided attention of the entire restaurant. And not for invisible, psychic reasons. Normally, dad would have felt awful, stooped down to help the child and offered a thousand apologies to the parents. Well, at least one anyway. Instead he cursed. I think he said, "Damn you," (To mom? To the child?) and carried on. Just like that. Stumbled away, leaving the child to be picked up by his horrified mother. She shot me an angry glance.

"Don't look at me," I said. "I didn't do it."

I was angry. I know I should have said something to the woman but I was damned if I was going to apologize for his actions. Besides, it wasn't that big a deal. The kid got run over. He wasn't hurt. Dad should have apologized. But he didn't. That's what I was telling myself. The truth is, that I was just as disgusted as the mother. But I didn't want her or anyone else at the restaurant to know.

Mom took it upon herself to protect the Clark family's good name. She apologized. Her apology fell on deaf ears. The family just stared at her like she had shit in her hands. She was doing her best, goddamn it. I went over.

"She said she was sorry. And she didn't have to. She didn't knock your kid over. Can't someone nod? Can't someone say, it's okay? Anything?"

They all looked away. The whole fucking family. They wanted nothing to do with me or mom or dad. The world was turning its back on us. We were being banished from the tribe.

I wanted to tear that whole family apart. Rip into each and every one of them. Their bright, healthy, happy faces made me feel like I was back behind the bush, with spiders swarming up my legs.

Then everything got witchy. I had no idea what I was looking at anymore. I could see one thing for sure. The happy faces around that table had turned ghoulish. They were terrified. Their fear made me nauseous, furious. I felt a tug on my sleeve.

"Let's go, Richard," said mom.

Mom took me by the arm and steered me out of the restaurant.

She guided me back down the path, saw me safely inside my tent and told me everything was going to be okay. My mind was frozen. I'm not the one with the problems. She is. And maybe dad, too. But for that brief, black moment, I was the one who had to be helped back to the tent. Suddenly I was the one in the hospital gown.

Mom left me alone. I have been lying on my bed, staring at the wall, racked by thoughts and words that don't seem my own. There is silence in mom and dad's tent. I wish I could hear them screaming at each other. Then I could tell myself, *You see? It is them. You're okay, Richard. You're not the crazy one.*

Mom told me that I had a knife in my hand at Winnie-the-Pooh's table. She's lying. I never picked up any knife. I'd remember that. She's trying to shift the focus to me. She thinks if she does that then she can sneak out of going to the hospital. All I did was give that family a tongue lashing. I couldn't have had a knife in my hand.

It's so damn quiet out there. I am hyperventilating. Nothing is making sense. The words just don't work anymore. I have orbited the round edge of a glass with my thumb. I have tapped the glass against the wall beside my bed. And had thoughts. Freedom.

Sunday, August 21
6:35 a.m.
Shaba Camp
Tent 3
Kenya, Africa

Woke up at five o'clock this morning seized by fear. I felt like there were a lot of things wrong but I couldn't remember them right away. Slowly, I began to make out shapes in the darkness. The first thing I remembered was the knife. That was bad. And then the glass. I thought I would feel better about things once I had tangible objects orbiting in my mind. But I didn't. I was better off with the unknown fear I woke up with.

I lay in bed and tried to sort things out. The knife would have to wait. The glass was something I could figure out. I hadn't done anything. That was important. Lots of people have tried to kill themselves and failed. I wasn't even close to that. All I did was pick up the damn glass. It was a fleeting, momentary thing. It's not like I shattered it and had a shard against my wrist. I just picked it up, looked at it, thought about it and moved on. Who hasn't done that at least once in their life? No big deal.

The madness that came over me before I picked up the glass was a big deal though. I've never lost control of my thoughts like that. This was scary. Perhaps it was a delayed reaction to the lines. I smoked more than usual.

Last night was a night of firsts. It was the first time I've threatened innocent people with a weapon. It was the first time I've lost control of my mind. And the first time I've ever held a glass for something other than drinking.

The night was ugly but this morning has been no picnic either. In spite of my brief layover at the lip of the bottomless pit last night, I still had the strength to masturbate. I cleaned up with a tissue and left it overnight on the floor beside my bed. During the time I was stapling my mind back together after I woke up this morning, I got hard again.

I reached down afterward to get the tissue and wiped my belly. It was still dark so I couldn't see what happened next. But I could feel it. Hundreds of tiny tingles spreading out across my stomach like an angry, nervous stain.

I jumped out of bed, grabbed my flashlight and shined the light on my stomach. Ants! Up my chest, down my thighs, in my pubic hair, on my fucking dick! Christ almighty.

After I frantically brushed the ants off I realized that the little bastards had been feeding all night on the tissue and marching back to their nest with bellyfuls of my juice. I am trying to find some symbolism in this. But perhaps some things in the wild kingdom are best left in the realm of the unknown.

I found a beer that I hadn't opened. It is warm. I'm drinking it anyway. Now that I've rid myself of ants I need to chase a few bats from my belfry.

8:15 a.m.

I went for breakfast a little after seven. Mom wasn't there. She was sleeping. Dad was cold and distant. It was rare for him to be so moody first thing in the morning, even if the night before had been brutal. I could tell though that he hadn't yet been told about the knife. He would have said something right away. Nice to know that in spite of mom's madness she's still loyal.

Before I could take my first sip of coffee to wash away the bitter aftertaste of my beer, the camp manager entered the restaurant with two assistants.

I felt like Lee Harvey Oswald in the Texas Theater when the Dallas police showed up. And like him, I wanted to yell, "This is it," and bolt from the table. But Africa would be a lonely and dangerous place for a fugitive.

The manager arrived at our table and asked us to step outside. Dad was perplexed but unimpressed. I suppose he thought it was related to the destroyed tent. Boy, was he in for a surprise.

We assembled beside a steel garbage container behind the restaurant. It stunk of rotting food.

"The Carpenters have decided not to press charges against you," said the manager to me. "But, given the circumstances, I really have to ask all of you to leave . . . immediately."

Once I had confirmation of what happened I became light-headed. Part of me had been holding onto the possibility that mom had imagined the whole thing. All of me was then wishing Kurt and Alex were there to tell the principal I had nothing to do with it.

"What?!" asked dad, no longer unimpressed. "Who the hell are the Carpenters?"

I wanted to tell him they were a brother and sister who sang about being on top of the world looking down on creation, and that this damn manager had all his facts wrong.

"Your son threatened them last night."

At this point I started walking away. I didn't want to see dad's face change from confusion to rage, or worse . . . disappointment.

"Where are you going?" asked dad.

"I'll be in my tent."

I walked back with the same awful feeling I'd had before I got whipped. Although this time I didn't pinch my ass.

It wasn't the fact that I'd threatened the Carpenters with a knife that bothered me. It was that I didn't remember doing it. I remembered asking them to acknowledge mom's apology. But not picking up the fucking knife. This scared the hell out of me. To lose it like that, to black out, to have a fifteen-second gap there, where something else, something violent, took over.

What would happen next time? Would I "lose it" again and "come to" to find mom and dad, lying at my feet, hacked to pieces? Would I then look down and see blood dripping from a machete in my hand? Would I go to trial and spend the rest of my life in prison for a crime I didn't even remember? What a fucking nightmare that would be. But then, I could always get a good defence lawyer and plead temporary insanity. What a selfish bastard. I've got mom and dad lying in pieces and I'm planning my defence strategy.

I sat on my bed and waited for dad. I stared at the wall of the tent and told myself to calm down. It was okay. It was going to get better.

If I had been at home I would have started running. But there was nowhere to run. I thought about killing myself so dad would arrive at my tent to give me hell and find me hanging. That'd learn him a thing or two about wanting to yell at me. I told myself I wasn't serious. I was just messing around in my head. I told myself I shouldn't mess around like that anymore. Even joke about it. I was too raw. It was too risky. And then I got scared that I thought it was too risky.

None of this is any fun anymore. The excitement and drama of mom's madness is gone. Now it is me who has a touch of the fever.

I sat on the bed and I tried to surrender. Gabriel said it was just like falling in love. Bullshit. It felt like I was plummeting from the top of a high-rise. The pavement, flat and hard, rushed up to meet me. My feet hit the concrete. My hips dislocated and smashed upward, crushing my pelvis, rocketing up through my ribs, snapping them like celery sticks, until finally my hips met my shoulder blades. *Hello.* A once proud six-foot young man was now only four feet tall. Very painful. And all of it happened slowly in my mind. Again and again. Not a good visualization.

I had begun to sweat. It dropped off my forehead and formed tiny circles at my feet.

I thought I'd sweat it out. All that garbage in my head. All the nastiness. I'd sweat it out and it would be gone. Everything was starting to close in. I was hanging on with everything I had. I tried as hard as I could to remember where I was. I could do that. I was sitting on a bed in a tent in Africa. I tried to remember who I was. This presented a problem. I drew a blank. A big, horrible blank. I felt like an eighty-year-old boxer with brain damage; my day-care counselor asking me if I remembered my mother's name. I had to look at my legs to remind myself that I was still in a body. I heard someone approaching on the gravel.

Dad walked wordlessly into my tent. He took a seat and stared at me. "You want to tell me what the hell's going on?"

"Nothing."

"Last night was not nothing. The manager said you threatened that family. He said you picked up a large spoon and waved it at them."

"A large spoon?"

"That's what he said."

Momentary relief. Mom was wrong. It wasn't a knife after all. A spoon? I picked up a fucking spoon? Obviously, I didn't want to tell dad I thought it was a knife. That would only have made matters worse.

I had to think quickly to explain my surprise. I didn't want him taking aerial, reconnaissance photographs of the "don't you remember?" terrain. I wouldn't have had to deflect anything if I were talking to a regular dad. But this wasn't a regular dad. This was Dick Tracy. You had to cover your tracks.

"It wasn't a large spoon," I said. "It was a soup spoon."

"I don't give a goddamn if it was a teaspoon. You threatened them."

"I was defending you. I was defending mom. I only went over to say something to them after she had apologized and they were rude to her."

"What the hell are you talking about? Apologized for what?"

Permanent relief. He didn't remember knocking the kid over. Like father, like son. Blackout. God bless scotch. I was free. The sun shone down. I had the leverage now.

"You don't remember?"

"Don't play games. What happened?"

"You got up from the table, you knocked their kid over, he cried, you left, mom tried to apologize, they were rude, I got angry, I waved a spoon and that was it."

Now it was his turn to look confused and frightened. He racked his brain, trying to remember. Couldn't. He was extremely agitated. The word "blackout" was strutting around the tent and the emperor was not only naked, he was wagging his dick in dad's face. Alcoholics had blackouts. Dad wasn't an alcoholic so he couldn't have those.

"I don't remember knocking any kid over," he said. "So let's just f-f-f-f-f-forget the whole damn thing."

I had heard him cry in his tent. But to hear him stutter. And to have been right there. Jesus. I didn't know what to do. I knew to acknowledge it would have just made it worse. So I didn't. We both just sat there. He grinned like a fool. I tried to grin as well. But I got stuck on a grimace. Why the hell he was grinning, I don't know. Perhaps he couldn't control himself. Or maybe he was locked in a battle to maintain control. And like the idiots of villages past, his battle had ended in a grin, a perpetual smirk, that others would mistake for happiness.

I know why I grimaced. I was trying to match his expression, like a mirror, thinking this would somehow keep him from falling. I really didn't want to see him fall, not there, not then. Not so soon after finding ants where they're not supposed to be, not so soon after emerging from the vacuum of not being able to remember who I was. No. You needed time to rest after those mile markers.

It was awful. Neither of us spoke. We just sat there, frozen in this horrible moment. Grinning. Grimacing. He seemed afraid to speak, like he might stutter again. I was afraid to speak. I didn't know what to say.

I don't think dad's instability has been obvious to me. He's a very private man. But sitting there in my tent, looking into his startled eyes, I knew. I could see it. And he knew it, too. You don't need to be standing in an alley, eating dog shit and laughing at a black trash bag blowing in the breeze, to be unstable. You can be sitting quietly in a tent in Africa with your fists clenched on your knees. It's the eyes. The eyes don't lie.

Dad didn't say anything after he told me to "forget the whole damn thing." He did pull a mint out of his pocket at one point.

Looked at it. I saw shoulder-slumping despondency but dad shrugged off his despondency, unwrapped his mint and popped it in his mouth.

When he finally did speak he talked about our next stop, the Meru Mulika Lodge. He said we'd try to squeeze one more day out of the safari.

I did want to give him a chance to unload if he wanted.

"Are you okay?" I asked.

He looked at me like I'd asked him if he his name was Ted. "I'm fine," he said. "No more threatening anyone."

I nodded. And then we shook hands. Why? I don't know.

"We'll get through it."

He waited for me to nod. To agree with him. I didn't. I couldn't.

"Let's get packed up," he said and left.

The fact that I grabbed a spoon, not a knife, was great news at first. But it doesn't matter. I still grabbed something and don't remember doing it. It could just as easily have been a steak knife. I feel like a walking time bomb.

I should have felt some relief from the fact that dad was engaged in his own subterranean battle and couldn't summon the energy to judge me or be cruel or sarcastic. But I think I would have preferred this. That would have been familiar. I hope that what I just saw in dad is a one-time thing, not the first crack in a window that's ready to shatter.

2:20 p.m.
Meru Mulika Lodge
Room 65
Kenya, Africa

We all gathered at the van around nine-thirty. Gabriel could sense that things had deteriorated even more, not just with mom but with dad and me. Mom and dad both wore sunglasses.

I hate people who wear sunglasses. And those who wear them indoors? They really should be taken outdoors — and beaten. Even on the brightest, sunniest day I won't wear them. I don't care that I end up squinting the whole time. I don't care that I end up looking like Ho Chi Minh. The eyes are the great revealers. Even sophisticated liars can't shelter deception in their eyes. I don't trust people who wear sunglasses. I always think they're hiding something or trying to look cool. And I hate people who hide things and pretend to be something they're not.

I forgave mom and dad for the sunglasses. If I had owned a pair I might have thrown them on. I felt that raw. I think we all did. I'm sure Gabriel noticed. He was silent and nervous and distant and cautious. He saw the three of us climbing into the van, skinned alive, all red and squishy and gross.

I was happy to be getting the hell out of Shaba. I wished we were heading back to Nairobi and I think if I would have said something to dad, applied even the slightest pressure, he would have agreed. But I didn't want to be the one to crack, the one to scream out that I wanted to get off the ride. As it was, Gabriel punched the van into gear and we drove away, headed not for Nairobi but for Meru Mulika. I looked out the back and saw the camp manager standing there, making sure we were actually leaving. I waved at him. He didn't wave back.

We passed through a very rich, forested area this morning. The air smelled like cherries. The drive turned out to be very soothing. The bouncing motion. The comforting squeak of the van's battered shock absorbers.

Dad's head was turned slightly to the right so I almost missed what happened next. Gabriel began talking about the surrounding trees. Mom used to have a real interest in plants and that kind of thing so she kind of paid attention. I've never cared much for plants so I tuned out and kept my eyes on dad.

I thought it was sweat at first. But I quickly realized it was not. A teardrop had emerged below the bottom rim of his sunglasses like a just-bathed, naked baby crawling out of a coal mine. It reminded me of a tiny, red bird I had seen sitting on a giant buffalo at Maralal. It didn't belong there. Like seeing a white rabbit run across dead soldiers in the trenches of World War I. Like seeing a flower slide into the barrel of a gun. Like finding a frog fifteen thousand feet up a mountain.

It was a magnificent sight. In violation of this stern, severe face, with jaw muscles tight and shoulders so tense they caressed his ears, somehow this tear had escaped the prison. The guards must have been sleeping. The teardrop made it as far as the corner of his mouth before I looked away. I knew he would turn to see if anybody saw. Sure enough, out of the corner of my eye, I could see his head turn slightly toward me. I was looking in the other direction. When I turned back the tear had been dispatched. What had launched that teardrop?

Whatever it was, wherever he'd been, he didn't stay there long. He took off his sunglasses, massaged his eyes like he was tired and began a conversation with Gabriel about London. I reached forward and tapped mom on the shoulder. She jumped.

"Sorry," I said.

"What are you doing?" she asked.

"Tapping you on the shoulder."

"Why?"

"To ask you how it's going."

She seemed frightened of me. I remembered we hadn't spoken since the incident with the Carpenters. I leaned forward so she could hear me over the wind cutting in through the windows. *Leaning forward to tragedy.*

"So?" I asked.

"So what?"

"How's it going?"

"Pretty good."

"It wasn't a knife you know."

Mom turned and grimaced. She had no idea what I was talking about. I'm such a snapperhead sometimes. I assume that I am at the centre of everyone else's universe. I assume they are fretting about me. And they never are.

"Last night. It wasn't a knife."

Mom dragged herself from the passing trees. Her eyes registered the memory.

"Says who?"

"The manager."

"He wasn't there."

"No, but the family told him. It was a spoon."

"I saw a knife."

"They didn't."

"You can still hurt someone with a spoon."

"Not as much."

"You need help."

"You do too."

"Leave me alone."

"Okay."

Gabriel stopped at one point to take a pee. I got out with him. We unzipped and started. Well, he started. I can't pee with other people standing there.

"What's going on?" asked Gabriel.

"It's all coming down," I said.

Gabriel raised his eyebrows. "It's been coming down since you arrived in Africa."

"I know. But we're real close now."

"To what?"

"I don't know. Something bad."

"Maybe something good."

Gabriel zipped up. I was wishing he would leave so I could pee.

"Your dad seems troubled," said Gabriel. "Try not to be around him if he drinks tonight."

"What? Why?"

"I'm here if you need me."

Gabriel patted me on the back and returned to the van.

Cryptic bastard. *I'm here if you need me,* like I was fragile or something. Warning me about dad. I tried to pee but I couldn't. Dad shouted from the van, telling me to get a move on. This made it worse. I never did pee. I got back in the van with my bladder on fire.

The pain reminded me what a loser I was. What a total and complete failure. I caught my reflection in the side window. I was ugly. I was full of shit. I had opinions on everything. I thought I was so far and above everyone else. I deserved that pain in my bladder. I would never see Nicole. I would never find a twenty-dollar bill on the sidewalk. I would never hear my name called in a raffle.

My despair reached a point of frenzy in my head. I wanted to do something. Anything to relieve it. I took my lighter and began holding the flame to my finger. I had that wart on the side of my forefinger. I don't have it anymore. I held the flame against my wart and watched the skin start burning away. It stung something fierce but I held the flame steady until the wart was burned right off. I was still holding the flame against my skin but I stopped feeling pain. I think I burned right through the nerves. Pain has its limits. This brought me comfort. I also didn't have pain in my bladder anymore. I had pissed my pants.

"What the hell is that smell?" asked dad.

Mom turned around with a crinkled nose.

I wanted to tell them not to worry. It was just the smell of urine and burning flesh.

"I don't know," I said, and rolled my window down.

"Are you smoking pot back there?" asked dad.

"No sir," I said and lit a cigarette. My burned hand was twitching uncontrollably. I looked at the side of my throbbing finger. Black and pink. Good colours. I didn't have to worry about a wimpy scar on my elbow anymore. This would definitely leave a scar. A nasty one.

I spent the rest of the ride chain-smoking to hide the smell of urine. When I got to my room at Meru Mulika I puked. Too many cigarettes. I held my hand under the cold water of the bathroom sink. It was a nasty burn. I was able to cover it with two adhesive strips I got from the front desk.

Meru Mulika Lodge is almost worth all the trouble getting here. The accommodations are fantastic. There is a wonderful view of the land here. Very open. There are elephants, about fifty to sixty of them, grazing about five hundred yards from my room. Who am I kidding? Fantastic? Wonderful? Who the hell is writing this cheery shit? Obviously not the guy who just mutilated himself and peed his pants. I'm like a soldier dashing from the surf in Dieppe and stopping to admire an enchanting seashell in the sand.

We got into the lodge and went straight to our rooms. Mom and dad are in the room right next to mine. Again! I could hear them moving around but they weren't saying a word. I soaked my jeans and underwear in the sink.

We maintained our composure at lunch with superficial conversation. It seems that we are well past the breaking point. We are already broken. We'd have to crawl but we can finish the safari and make it back to Nairobi. All we have to do is keep the topics of conversation simple and breezy. Even me, Mister Depth and Dimension, didn't want to hear anything more than mom's instructions for sewing a button on a heavy plaid shirt.

Mom asked about my bandaged finger. I said I had cut myself. She wanted to see. I wouldn't let her. She knew I was lying. Moms always know when you're lying.

We go on a game drive with Gabriel this afternoon. We're supposed to see some rhinos.

7:10 p.m.

I am sitting in my room sipping coffee. We left for our game drive after lunch. My finger was throbbing so I took some aspirin. There was some puss starting to ooze out. I hope the damn thing isn't infected.

It felt good to be wearing dry underwear, although the seat still stunk of urine. I cracked open the windows right away. If dad said anything I was going to say that an animal must have snuck in and pissed in the van.

We arrived at a grove where other tour buses had already gathered. I was annoyed at first but then thought that Nicole might be in one of them. We got out and walked to a clearing in the trees. It is only now that I realize that mom did so without any trepidation. Oddly, it was dad who looked scared. He was the one who lagged behind. I checked the other vans. No Nicole.

I thought when Gabriel said we were going to see rhinos we would watch from the van. But this was not the case. There they were, with their impressive horns, standing motionless, with tourists milling about. Contrary to the accusations I hurled, Gabriel insisted they were not drugged. My image of the rhino as a dangerous animal was shattered. Why weren't they impaling us? Gabriel told us that not all the rhinos were like this but these ones had gotten quite used to human contact. I bet the other animals made fun of these rhinos after everyone left.

Normally I would have been disappointed. You can get that close to animals at prisons like the San Diego Zoo. But there was something thrilling about getting that close to a wild animal. I was just as nervous as dad. I kept expecting one of the rhinos to say, *Ha! Fooled ya.* And then start charging, sending us scattering like rodeo clowns.

We were even able to touch the rhinos. It was mom who took the lead. She reached her hand out and began sliding it over the skin. She did so without being told it was okay. Her fingers rubbed the neck of the beast and up over its horn. She stroked the horn itself.

To hear myself describe what she was doing sounds obviously sexual. But her movements were not sexual. God knows, I experience almost everything sexually. But this was not a pagan ritual with a phallic symbol.

She stroked that horn the way a knight might slide an admiring hand up the shaft of his sword before galloping into battle. Or the way an executioner tested the blade of his ax before hammering it down on a traitor's neck. There was purpose in her eyes. Dark purpose. I imagined she looked exactly the same when she fingered the bottle of pills before shaking them out onto her palm. Ah, who the hell knows. She may have been crying when she took those pills. But I know that dad was worried. He watched her carefully. He didn't like what he saw. I swear to god I heard the rhino groan under the scrutiny of mom's hands and eyes.

It was my turn to touch the hide of the rhino. I think you could have pounded a one-inch nail into the side of that horned beast and it wouldn't have felt a thing. In the end, the three of us had our hands tracing back and forth over the skin.

I am reminded of that Indian story of the blind men who touched different parts of an elephant and described what they felt. Each of them, including the idiot who thought he was touching a wall, thought they knew what they were feeling. I think if mom and dad and me could pull off our blindfolds and look at the mess of our family we might be on to something. Or not.

I don't believe much in personal energy and all that New Age crap but I was thinking that if humans do in fact give off energy then that poor rhino was getting a terrible dose from the six hands of the Clark family. It should have been enough to burst an artery or break a rib.

For one brief minute that rhino became our touchstone, our connection to one another. I guess it was appropriate that our animal was not a beautiful pony or something. No, the Clark family's common ground was a rhino, with a hide so rough you could sand a dining room table with it. *Gee, Richard, are you saying that this rhino's skin was as coarse as sandpaper?* I am indeed. *That's damn coarse.* Yup.

As ugly and rough and dumb as that rhino was, I will never forget it. It brought us together. Just before we left mom moved herself so she was right beside its massive head. I thought she was going to whisper something. But she leaned forward and kissed it gently behind the ear.

"I'll bet he's never felt that before," she said.

Mom smiled at dad and me and walked away. The rhino done good. For all of us. The sunglasses came off and the fires that threatened to consume us were, for the moment, brought under control. If this safari were a Hollywood picture show, it would have ended right then, with us walking away from the rhino. A family again. One of us would have cracked a bad joke. We all would have laughed, flung our arms around one another and strolled to the van. The composer would have scored a burst of loud, triumphant music. The last shot would have been of our trusty guide, Gabriel, with a smile on his face and perhaps a tear in his eye. Roll credits.

We chattered like sparrows on the way back in the van. Dad checked the rhino off his list and seemed really pleased that he'd done so. I forgot about the burn, and the urine, and the look in mom's eyes, and the tear from dad's eye, and the smell of baby oil, and the bottomless pit, and the swim across the river, and surrender, and madness and change. One of us could have started "Ninety-Nine Bottles of Beer on the Wall" and the others would have joined in.

In spite of our smiles and laughter there was one face in the van that was not happy. Gabriel's. He looked grim. I could see the side of his face. His jaw was set so tight a vein was popping out of his temple.

Dad asked him a few questions about our destination for the next day and only got one-word answers. Maybe the rhino didn't take our negative energy hit after all. Maybe Gabriel took it. Right in the forehead.

I hoped that Gabriel had something other than the Clarks on his mind. Maybe he was thinking about his bank account or perhaps some old girlfriend that had broken his heart. I didn't want to believe that he saw no happiness in the van. He watched us laughing and telling stories and he was afraid. More afraid it seems, than if we had all been vomiting on one another or shouting in languages not known to anyone. His fear brought my happy tongue to rest and I rode the rest of the way in silence.

We arrived back at Meru Mulika and the sun had just set. A shining full moon had risen up over the lodge. It looked big enough to swallow the Earth.

Mom and dad walked ahead of Gabriel and me. I tried to get Gabriel to talk. His mood was bothering me.

"Not now," he said and hurried away like someone leaving a beach after they'd been told a tidal wave was on the way. Not panicked. Not a full-out sprint. Because the wave hadn't appeared on the horizon yet. But a quick, sober exit.

Mom and dad entered their room without saying a word to me so I have no idea what time we are meeting for dinner. I am so tense right now. I don't feel like eating or seeing mom and dad. I'll tell dad that I don't feel well. Tonight is bad. It's a night when we should all just stay inside. I pulled my jude out from underneath the dirty clothes in my suitcase and thought about doing a single line. But I knew if I did one line I'd finish it all.

I have been so blindly wrapped up in myself that I just realized I have stopped calling mom Janet. I'm not going to switch back to Janet now that I have noticed it. She's my mom. She's not Janet.

I hear nothing from mom and dad's room. What the hell happened to all the chatter in the van? So it's not just me. They feel it, too. Whether they are conscious of it or not. The beach has been evacuated. Something bad is coming. Gabriel knows it. He wants nothing to do with us tonight.

Somebody just knocked at the door. It is dad. I wish he'd go away. Another knock.

The bats are flapping outside my window. There are lizards swarming on the walls of the building. And no, I am not hallucinating or being metaphorical. They are there and they are real. When I went to grab my coffee to bring back to my room I had to duck bats all the way and there were at least five lizards on my door. It's a creepy night. A night of bats and lizards. A good night to stay inside and whisper tales of ghosts and goblins, or at least admit the possibility of their existance.

Dad sized me up as soon as he stepped in. "What's the matter?" he asked.

"I don't feel well," I said. "I think it might be the flu."

He didn't seem all that interested in my answer and wandered over to the desk where my journal was lying open.

"You're still writing in this damn thing?"

"Once in awhile. Keeps me out of trouble."

He was glancing down at the pages.

"There's no 'a' in existence," he said.

I walked over and shut it. He grunted and walked away. *Wise guy. Asshole.*

"Just five more days and then we're home free."

He was definitely in a shit-stirring mood. He never planned that far ahead. Ever since the troubles with mom began, he had been taking it a day at a time. Now he was talking about five more. I wasn't sure I could handle one. He was making me nervous. Pacing back and forth.

"You think we can last five more days?" I asked.

"If your mother's up to it. I am. Are you?"

He was baiting me for an argument. I said nothing and returned to my desk and pretended like I was going to start writing again.

"They have laundry facilities here," he said. "Why don't you do a wash. Your clothes stink."

"That's a good idea," I said, without looking up. I was not in the mood for a clash so I was determined to tell him that all his ideas were good ones. There was a big pause. I was hoping the next sound I'd hear was the sound of the door clicking behind him. Or slamming. I didn't care. No such luck. Not on this night of bats and lizards.

"What's this?" he asked.

I turned slowly. He was standing beside my suitcase with my bag of jude in his hand. Dick Tracy had found my stash.

"What are you doing snooping around my suitcase?"

"I wasn't snooping around anything. Your suitcase was open and this was lying on top of your clothes. What is it?"

He held the sandwich bag up to the light like an animal researcher who had just found a rare species of butterfly. I had to answer quickly. To pause, to think, would have been incriminating. And this was Tracy. No stone left unturned. I gave him a quick answer. But not too quick. That would have looked suspicious. It was a good answer.

"It's foot powder."

"For what?"

"Athlete's foot."

"When's the last time you did something athletic?"

He opened the sandwich bag and smelled it.

"What's it doing in a sandwich bag?"

"The container broke."

That was a good explanation. I was impressed with myself. I wasn't choking under the pressure. I figured that an innocent man would surely comment on all the dumb questions. So I did.

"This is ridiculous," I said.

I walked over to grab the bag. He whipped it away.

"Is this cocaine?"

"I told you, it's foot powder."

"Hash?"

"Why don't you smoke it and find out? If it's a drug you'll get nice and high for about two hours and then when you come down, you can have me arrested. If it's foot powder, you'll turn purple, foam will come out of your nose, you'll suffer full cardiac arrest, and I'll call an ambulance."

"I've got a better idea," he said as he turned and left with the sandwich bag.

I would normally have panicked but my heroic journey on this trip made it possible for me to dismiss any repercussions that might have come from his discovery. I told myself that a captain of eternity couldn't worry himself about silly twists and turns like his father finding his heroin and spanking his little ass or telling him that he was now in double-dutch.

He was gone a really long time. I wasn't worried about what he would do to me. I was worried that he would tell mom. This might be the hack that finally broke her ankles. Finding hash oil was one thing but this was heroin. The big H. She would never understand. I kicked myself for leaving the jude on top of my clothes. Stupid.

I wouldn't have minded if he drove her to suicide but I was damned if I was going to be the one. I'd end up spending the rest of my life on long walks, standing on empty beaches, looking out at the ocean. There's certain family things you just don't get over. Killing your mom would be one of them.

When Nicole and I were together she had told me about a father who was taking his two teenaged sons fishing. The boys were talking too much for his liking so he told them if they didn't shut up he'd pull over to the side of the road and cut their heads off. I'm sure the boys thought that he was just being a goofball. So they didn't shut up. The father was not pleased. He pulled the car over and hacked off the head of the eldest. The younger one, about thirteen, watched. The thirteen-year-old survived because some passing motorists saved him. But who cares. You shouldn't be seeing something like that at any age, but during puberty? You've got a shrubbery growing between your legs, zits on your face and then you see your dad hack off your brother's head by the side of the road on the way to your favourite fishing hole? No way. Fuck therapy. Drive to a quiet park, hook up the hose, put a good song on the radio, ease the seat back, relax and breathe deep.

Part of me wanted to go out looking for him. To find out what the hell he was up to. But I was too scared to leave my room. Which had nothing to do with dad's detective work. It was just that silly old madness thing acting up again. Yup, I'm feeling mad again. Must mean it's gonna rain soon.

Dad came back. Didn't knock. Just walked in. He was all business but he wasn't angry. He didn't have the sandwich bag anymore. We picked up right where we left off.

"It was heroin," he said.

"Foot powder."

"I found someone in the lounge who knows about these things. He said it was heroin."

"And who was that? Keith Richards?"

"A pharmacist."

I would have had an easier time believing Keith Richards. "How is there a pharmacist out here in the middle of nowhere?"

"He's on safari."

"But how did you know he was a pharmacist? How did you know to ask him about it?"

"I asked several people. He happened to be one of them."

"I don't believe you."

"Go ask him. I just had a beer with him. He's probably still there. Grey beard. Blue shirt. Nice fellow."

"So what did you do? Walk around the lodge with my sandwich bag asking people what was inside?"

"It doesn't matter what I did. The fact is, I know it isn't foot powder. It's heroin. You're on heroin."

He stood there looking at me, a quiet satisfaction in his eyes, his crime solved, his quarry caught. I didn't have any fight left. I should have gone to the bar to check this guy out but I couldn't be bothered. And, actually, I could see him doing it. Not walking around with the sandwich bag but asking people discreetly whether they knew what heroin looked like. And he got lucky. He got a pharmacist on safari. It wasn't that unusual. He could have gotten a cop or a junkie jazz musician.

His first concern was not with my well-being, my future or even the fact that I'd lied to him. No. His first concern was with what he was always concerned with. Money.

"I'm not going to pay for university in the fall. But I will pay for you to go into a hospital to detox or whatever it is you do. You think about it."

With that he turned and left but didn't shut the door. A symbolic gesture? I shut the door. I suppose I should feel relief. My secret is out. But I actually don't give a shit that he knows. I'm not going to any stupid treatment centre. I will beat this thing on my own.

I lay in bed and tried to visualize myself somewhere high. I stayed away from buildings. I finally settled on a bridge. A really high bridge. An old bridge. A gothic, old bridge. And I envisioned myself hanging from it. I let go with both hands. And I fell. And I looked down and saw the boulders below rushing up to meet me. My eyes flipped open. Panic.

A full moon is a perfect night for a surrender but I have nothing I want to surrender to. Fucking icons. Fucking idols. Fucking crosses and temples and symbols and bullshit and bullshit and bullshit. I am not ready for a surrender. Someone's knocking at the door. Maybe it's dad with the African police. *It's for your own good, son. You'll manage just fine with one hand.*

8:45 p.m.

Mom was at the door, not dad with the police. She was beaming. And she was wearing the same short dress she wore on the night of baby oil. I guess to celebrate the full moon.

"Are you ready?" she asked.

"For what?"

"Dinner."

"I don't feel well."

"I don't want to eat alone."

"Where's dad?"

"In the lounge. He's in a mood. Do I look beautiful?"

"Stunning."

I stepped outside. The lizards were now not only covering the walls. They had spread to the sidewalk. I walked gingerly around them, not wanting to hear a squish. Mom had no time for gingerly. She paraded ahead of me.

I have a lot of images that will remain burned in my brain until I am an old man. But this will be one for the top three. There she was, clicking down the concrete path, bathed in electric blue light from the moon, moving her ass under her dress in a rhythm more appropriate for a high school tart — lizards to her left, lizards to her right, lizards scattering to avoid her high heels, bats flying above.

She talked excitedly all the way through dinner. I don't remember a word. I tried to force food down my throat. I knew if I didn't eat I'd really start to lift off and I was worried I wouldn't come back. We smoked and drank coffee after dinner.

"So, what do you think set him off?" she asked.

"I don't know."

"Let's go finish our coffees in the lounge."

"I'm pretty tired. I'm going to pack it in."

"Let's just sit with him for awhile. Let's not abandon him. Not tonight."

What the hell did she mean by, *not tonight*? Way too ominous. Gave me the slithers. I didn't want to go. I knew he'd be drinking.

"For me?" she asked. Her eyes sparkled.

I followed her into the lounge. We passed a grey-haired man with a beard and a blue shirt. I wanted to stop and ask him if he was a pharmacist. But mom was beside me. And if he was the pharmacist, I didn't want him saying, "Yes I am. Are you the boy who does heroin?"

Mom and I grabbed two chairs and pulled them up beside dad. He was staring at a roaring fire in a pit dug right there in the middle of the lounge. A blackened, steel flue hung suspended over the fire and channeled the smoke outside. If dad was a Buddhist, I'd have thought he was in a deep meditation. But he was just drunk, sipping scotch. He didn't acknowledge our arrival. Mom reached over and began massaging his neck. The last time I saw that we were in the station wagon heading for Custer's Last Stand in Montana.

I decided for tonight, in the interests of preserving the chunk of sanity that I gripped like melting ice cream in my fist, not to have any expectations. To embrace the unexpected. Mom continued massaging his neck. I expected him to fling her hand away but he didn't.

"Your family is worried about you," she said. "They think you should learn to relax."

Dad finally spoke. "Did you tell her?" he slurred.

I couldn't believe it. He was going to reveal his great detective work.

"Dad," I said, cautioning him with my eyes.

"Tell me what?" asked mom.

"Richard's not going to university."

The cruel bastard was going to drag it out. Start at the conclusion and work his way back to the suitcase with the pile of dirty clothes.

"Alright, enough with the games," I said. "You want me to tell her? I'll tell her right now. Dad was snooping around my room tonight . . ."

"And I found a pack of cigarettes," said dad with lightning speed.

What an idiot. For a crafty Dick Tracy, he had come up with something really stupid. It was fast. But it was dumb. Foot powder had been fast but smart. Cigarettes were stupid. Mom thought so too.

"So what?" said mom.

"So what? You think I want my kid smoking?"

Mom withdrew her hand from dad's neck. She looked highly suspicious. "He's been smoking the whole trip. What's the big surprise?"

Mom looked at me for an answer. I tried to stare at her blankly. "What is going on here?" she asked.

"Richard and I had a talk tonight. Right, Richard? You decided I'd be wasting ten thousand dollars a year because you're not really sure about what you want to do."

I wanted to scream. I realized what he was doing. He was going to hammer me in front of mom without delivering the knockout blow because he knew it would knock her out as well.

"That's right," I said.

"Yes, he's got a lot of things he needs to sort out before he goes to school. Isn't that right, Richard?"

"That's right."

Dad stood and pulled out the sandwich bag of heroin. Mom didn't see him do this. He made sure of that. But he made damn sure I could see it.

"Otherwise." Dad took the sandwich bag over to the fireplace and tossed it in the fire. "It'll all just go up in smoke." Dad staggered past us. "I'm going to bed."

He was gone. I wiped sweat from my lip. Quite a performance by the old man. But he wasn't as clever as he thought. Drunk people never are.

"What was in the baggie?" asked mom.

"What baggie?"

"The one your father just threw in the fire."

"I didn't see a baggie."

I left. I got back to my room and I cried. I cried myself into convulsions. I cried so hard I thought I'd give myself a hernia. I had looked over my shoulder before I walked away and saw her sitting there in her pretty dress, looking so small, so lost, with no answers, with no one to turn to. And I left her there. Because, under the circumstances, it was the kindest thing to do. I couldn't sit there and lie to her anymore.

10:29 p.m.

The lizards and bats and the full moon have taken their toll. I must write quickly. We are heading back to Nairobi. Tonight. We have an emergency. All of my fears about the night came true. The sign that the weeble was dragging by his teeth outside the Norfolk said *You will know the truth, and the truth will make you free.* The truth has been told.

I don't know how long I was back in my room before the shouting started. Mom had returned to their room and dad was crazed. That calm exterior, all that quiet talk about a treatment centre, that sober response to the heroin discovery. All that was smoke. He was erupting.

"I found heroin in his room tonight!" shouted dad. "You've ruined him!"

"You don't think I know that?" she cried, defeated.

I knew that dad was just getting started. And I had already heard enough. I ran from my room. The lizards were startled and darted helter-skelter. I threw open their door. Mom was curled up on the bed, holding up her hands to protect herself, not from his fists but from his words. Dad loomed over her, swaying slightly.

"Stop it!" I shouted.

Dad was startled at first to hear my voice. But he quickly recovered and turned his back to me.

"Go back to your room."

"Leave her alone."

I rushed him. Everything blurred into a primal mess of raw reaction. He was drunk and off balance when I shoved him. He staggered backward and fell into a chair. I was hoping he'd end up stuck there, too drunk to get up. But he looked like he was sobering up pretty quick. I raised my skinny arm and clenched my fist. It must have looked like a big peach hanging from a thin branch.

"You stay there."

He got out of the chair and put his fists up. His dad had taught him the art of boxing but he never passed it along to me. He was just about to give me my first lesson. He began circling, bobbing and weaving. I brought my fists up.

"C'mon you want to do it?" he asked. "Let's go."

"No!" yelled mom.

"C'mon hero. Take a swing. Let's see what you got."

He swung a hand out and slapped me really hard across the face. *Floating like a butterfly and stinging like a motherhumming bee.* I realized right then why I never liked fighting. It really hurts.

"Enough!" yelled mom.

That slap made my whole face numb. My fight had gone. Yes, I had my fists up — to protect myself. Yes, he was drunk and drunks were supposed to be slow and clumsy. But he was neither. And I've never had a clue how to fight.

There was also something else that was holding me back. If I retaliated where would it end? Would we kill each other? Would a tooth get knocked out? Would a nose get broken? Where would we get medical attention? Was it something mom needed to see? Dad wasn't troubled by internal questions, practical or ethical. He snuck a hand through again and slapped me hard. I was ready to burst into tears, ready to run from the room. But he slapped me again. The third slap was the charm.

I finally threw a punch. It landed solidly on the side of his face. I knew it hurt him because it nearly broke my hand. I was shocked. But not nearly as shocked as he was. I thought that was it. I had never hit him before. He would surely back down. It wasn't the punch that would send him from the room, it was the vibe — the vibe that his son had finally fought back. And on this night, under a full moon, at that precise moment, he would realize his son was right to fight back. But dad was never really into vibes very much.

He exploded. He picked me up like I was made of straw and hurled me against the wall. I don't know how many times he hit me. I lost count because the first punch knocked the wind out of me and

I went numb. But I know he kept hitting me in the stomach because I could feel my back slamming against the wall. There was no pain though. Like when I burned myself. There's a threshold.

He lost his grip on my collar. One of his stomach punches missed as I fell, caught me in the mouth and blood streamed down my shirt. Mom rushed over, pushed him away and covered me with her body.

"Leave him be!"

Dad was standing over us, eyes wild, fists clenched, ready for more. Mom must have thought I was dying. I thought I was dying. I couldn't breathe.

"So, now you want him," sneered dad. "Now you'll look after him."

"Leave us alone," said mom calmly.

"It's too bad you didn't feel this maternal and protective when you were pregnant."

"Not now."

"Hey Richard, you ever wonder where you got your cleft lip?"

"Let me!"

"Ever wonder what could have caused such a thing?"

Mom sprang at him with her nails aimed at his face. He'd been clawed before. This time he was ready. He fended her off and tossed her onto the bed.

"Ask her," dad said as he started for the door. "Ask her what she did when she was pregnant with you. Ask her about the bottles of sedatives and tranquilizers scattered on the floor when I came home at lunch. Ask her what the doctors said about tranquilizers and birth defects."

He bolted from the room. Mom appeared beside me. I was still labouring for breath. She took me in her arms and began dabbing a napkin on my bleeding lip.

"I'm sorry," she whispered. "I'm so sorry."

I was silent until my breathing returned to normal. The bleeding slowed enough that she stopped dabbing. And when the gasping of my breath faded from the room we were left in silence, me lying there with my head in her lap. I asked what should never have been asked. I should have given us more time. I should have let her continue rubbing my forehead, my temples, soothing me, comforting me.

"Is it true?" I croaked.

"I didn't know I was pregnant," she whispered.

Her fingers paused and then left my face. She slowly pulled away, got up and went to a chair by the window. She sat down and stared out at the cartwheeling bats chasing insects drawn to the light from the window.

I stayed on the floor for a long time. It had never occurred to me that she had tried to kill herself while I was in her belly. All dad had said was she'd tried to kill herself after Maggie was born. And there were eighteen months between Maggie and me. I had assumed that it had happened in the months before I was conceived.

I didn't hate her. She hadn't intended to disfigure me. She had tried to end her own life. Dad had come home. He wasn't supposed to. I went to her. I wanted her to look at me. I got in front of her and knelt down and put my hands on her shoulders.

"I believe you when you say you didn't know you were pregnant."

She gently traced her fingers down my nose, past my lip, off my chin.

"You wouldn't have done it if you knew you were pregnant."

"Does it really make any difference?"

She looked through me, past me, to the darkness. I got a whiff of that rubbing alcohol smell again. That same awful scent I was hit with just before that zebra got taken down at the salt pit. The smell cleared my head. I knew right then what we had to do.

"You wait here," I said. "We're going home."

I rushed to the lounge and found dad sitting alone with a drink.

"We're leaving tonight."

I pulled the glass from his hand and slapped it down on the table beside him. I grabbed his elbow and pulled him out of the chair.

"You go keep an eye on her."

Dad stood there, looking disoriented. His strength was gone. "She can't be left alone!" I shouted.

He staggered away. I rushed to the front desk and asked where the drivers were. I found the tiny room at the back of the lodge. I called out Gabriel's name. Some of the men were sleeping. They cursed at me. They said he was out walking. *At this hour?* I asked them to tell him to come to my room when he showed up.

I am back in my room. My things are packed. I am waiting for Gabriel. Where the hell is he?

11:20 p.m.
En Route — Meru Mulika to Nairobi

I am in the back of the van. I have a little overhead light like on an airplane. It's awfully bumpy. Gabriel eventually came to my room. He told me it would be better if we waited until morning. It would be too dangerous to travel at night. I said I didn't care. Mom's life was in danger. We were going.

I was filled with something potent. Don't know what it was but I wish I could have bottled it. Everyone was listening to me. Dad protested at first but eventually gave in. Same with Gabriel. I had taken over. I was calling the shots.

Gabriel tried to ask me what happened. I told him I couldn't talk about it right then. But I did say that the dark link had been exposed. He asked about my lip. I told him the tranquilizers had done it. He looked really confused. I realize now he was asking about my lip because it was fat and bloody from dad's punch.

Gabriel took my bags to the van. I went and knocked on mom and dad's door. Dad opened it. He didn't say anything. He was packing. I think he had started to feel a fragment of guilt for his savage handling of the family secret.

Mom was still at the window in her dress. I went and knelt at her feet.

"Hey, we're going now. Okay?"

Nothing. I could hear dad go into the bathroom and start collecting the toiletries he hadn't left with me. I had never thought much about mom's relationship to my lip. I started thinking about it. I studied every line on her face.

All those years. Every day. My lip. Her reminder. How could anyone live with that? Pick any day. Any moment. Me at five. That'll do. Coming down for a bowl of Shreddies. Her looking up. "Good morning, sunshine." And me eating, slurping. And her eyes falling absently on my lip. And the sliver of jagged wood, gouged under her fingernail would be reignited.

And the surgeries. My tears. Why my tears had brought her tears. Why my reluctance to go through the pain of a fifth surgery was so enthusiastically accepted and supported by her.

I wasn't her son. I was her curse. Her day-by-day, minute-by-minute curse. She might have been feeling really good, happy. But I was always around, somewhere, destroying her peace. Emerging from the basement. Coming home from school. Plopping myself down onto the couch beside her as she read her book at night. Because, after all, I was the evil myth, snakes flying out of my head, turning her heart to stone.

How wonderful it would have been to have been born a flower. A beautiful, proud, sweet-smelling rose, bringing smiles to people's faces, pleasant thoughts to their minds. Instead, I was born a disfigured freak. There's no hump on my back, no claw where a hand should be, no stump where a leg should hang. But I'm a freak nonetheless. Worse than a freak in retrospect.

I would never have been able to inspire anything but rage in dad's heart when his eyes looked, not at me, but through me, to mom. Like a prism refracting light. And when mom's eyes found me, her heart would have struggled to find that love she should naturally have felt for her son. But like grandpa's cat looking for her destroyed kittens, she would find nothing. Mom would not find love. Only guilt.

A prism of rage for dad and a trigger of guilt for mom. These are not the ingredients from which strong, healthy children are made.

And yet, and yet, as I knelt at her feet, and searched my heart for my hatred, I could not find it. I could only think what a terrible burden she had carried all these years. Perhaps she would have been relieved to have heard hysterical condemnations.

The truth had finally been born. But it was all fucked because she had not delivered naturally. The truth had been ripped from her belly with angry hands. She had not been ready to deliver. And yet there it was. At her feet. Sobbing. Bloodied. Horrible. Dad turned on the water taps in the bathroom to muffle my crying.

It was all wrong. I shouldn't have been blubbering at her feet. I was just making things worse. I would have felt better about crying if she could have acknowledged me in some way. Patted my head. Coughed. Anything. But she just continued to stare at the bats outside the window.

The last thing she probably needed right then was for me to be making a really big deal about everything. I mean, it was a big deal and all but I should have been stronger. She didn't need me collapsing at her feet. I think I pushed her further away. I wish I could have told her that my tears were for her. Not for me.

"Can I get you something?" I finally asked. "A glass of water?"

Her bottom lip quivered. At last. Something. Long pause. "I just want to go," she said, so quietly, I had to lean my head to hear her.

"We are. Right now."

I stood up and wiped my nose on my sleeve. Dad was still running the water in the bathroom. I didn't care that my outburst was inconvenient to him. He created it. He could deal with it. Or, if he couldn't, he could run water.

I walked over to a chair. Dad had neatly stacked some of his clothes. On top of the pile was his animal list. The leopard had been checked off and then scribbled over to make it look like it wasn't checked off. How dad. How sad.

"Are you ready?" I shouted.

He turned the water off and came out with his toiletry bag under his arm, eyes locked on the floor. We gave each other a wide berth as I passed him on my way into the bathroom. As I peed I looked at the sink. He had wiped it dry.

Used to drive mom mad back home. She'd rinse something in the sink and walk away. Within thirty seconds he'd appear from somewhere in the house. He'd stroll in and nonchalantly grab the dish towel hanging from the oven and wipe that basin dry. Fucking water drops. He hated them as much as schmeglies. Sometimes after he was through she'd go run the water again just to annoy him. They even fought about it once but I think mom realized it was stupid. He wasn't going to stop doing it.

The sight of the spotless sink actually gave me a little comfort. In spite of the bomb packed with nails that had exploded in that hotel room, some things were never going to change.

Dad dropped the toiletry bag in his suitcase and reached into his pocket. When I looked back again, he was standing there, shoulders sagged, staring at his hand. His face looked as though he'd pulled a dead mouse out of his pocket.

"I don't understand that," he said.

"What?" I asked.

He held a tiny, white mint with green swirls, wrapped in plastic, in the palm of his hand.

"I keep three mints in my pocket. Two cinnamon. One spearmint. Every time I pull out a mint, I get a spearmint. It makes no sense. You'd think I'd get a cinnamon more often than a spearmint. I like the cinnamon mints. That's why I keep two of them."

He looked distraught. He pulled two red cinnamon mints out of the same pocket and held them out for me.

"You see? Two cinnamon. One spearmint. But always the spearmint. I swear to god, I can go a month and not get a cinnamon mint first."

"Why don't you keep only cinnamon mints in your pocket?"

"I like the spearmint too. Just not as much as the cinnamon."

"So keep the cinnamon mints in one pocket and the spearmint in the other."

"I keep my keys in the other."

"Oh."

There wasn't much else to say. How do you tell someone it's perfectly okay to have mints and keys in the same pocket? You don't. You say, "oh."

"It's not the end of the world," he said. "And it seems silly now. It's just strange."

He tried to close the zipper on the suitcase and it got stuck. I knew his temper and I knew what a stuck zipper might do. He handled it at first and continued tugging at the zipper.

"No, it just goes to show you that sometimes things don't work out the way you planned."

"Here, I'll get that," I said.

He wasn't listening. He was now completely preoccupied with the zipper. I stood back. I stood back because I knew what was coming as he gave the zipper one final, violent tug.

"Goddamn thing!! Fucking bullshit! Fucking goddamn thing of a bullshit!!"

He tore the zipper off, ripping the fabric and flung the suitcase against the wall. I looked over at mom. She sat stoically at the window. He punched the suitcase.

"Nothing works out! Nothing ever works out!"

He smashed the suitcase one more time and stomped out of the room, slamming the door behind him. I tried to remember that expression. About the nut (son) falling from the tree (father), not landing that far from the base of the tree. Or something like that. *Nothing ever works out.* Too much going on. Way too fucking much.

Mom seemed unimpressed with dad's tantrum. She maintained her vigil at the window.

"Everything alright?" I asked.

Blank stare. I looked at her dress. "Do you want to change into some other clothes? It's going to be a long drive."

The blank stare again. Okay, that was going to be it for the questions. The broken zipper presented a problem. I wouldn't be able to carry all the luggage in one trip. The busted suitcase would have to be taken separately. I didn't want to leave her twice. And I didn't want to tell her where I was going in case she figured she had time to do something.

So I said nothing. I lifted the broken suitcase like a dead soldier and carried it out the door. I rushed as fast as I could to the van. Dad was already sitting in the front passenger seat. Gabriel was waiting at the rear. We loaded the suitcase.

"You want some help with the rest?" he asked.

I was going to say, "no," but I realized I might need help getting mom to the van. Gabriel followed me back. We got into the room and the chair by the window was empty. Of course it was. On this night of bats and lizards. It had to be.

The bathroom door was closed. I tried to turn the knob. It was locked. I hammered my fist on the door.

"Mom! Open the door!"

No response. Gabriel came up behind me. "I'll go get the manager to bring a key."

I looked at the door handle. "There's no keyhole. Mom! Open the door right now or I'm going to break it down. Do you hear me? I mean it."

I waited. Nothing. I leaned back and slammed my shoulder into the door. It didn't even rattle but I got a nasty shiver through my whole body. I kicked my boot as hard as I could. The handle rattled but that was it. Mom was in there, vein opened, blood spurting onto the tiles and I couldn't even knock down a fucking door. I felt like bread soaked in milk. Those movies where heroes knocked down doors were bullshit.

I decided I would make a run and throw all my weight into it. I walked back to the end of the room and ran at the door as fast as I could. I bounced like a bee off a windshield. I crumpled on the floor thinking for sure I had broken my collarbone. Gabriel looked down on me, concerned. "Are you okay?" he asked.

We heard the toilet flush. The door opened. Mom came out with her purse, didn't even look down at me. Walked right back to her chair, sat down and looked out the window again.

I got up and walked over to her. I signaled to Gabriel to grab the remaining suitcases off the bed. He did so and left the room.

"We're going now," I said quietly. "If you can walk, great. If you can't, that's fine, too. Either way, we're leaving."

She continued staring out the window.

"I'm going to pick you up and I'm going to carry you. Okay?"

I paused, so everything I said could sink in. I reached behind her back and tucked a hand under her armpit. It was quite damp. So she was scared after all. I snaked my other arm under her knees and lifted her out of the chair. I expected her to announce that this was all very ridiculous and she could walk by herself to the van thank you very much. But she didn't say a word.

We crossed the threshold of the door into the night like ghastly newlyweds, mom in her pretty dress, me stepping over lizards, bats flapping above our heads and the light of that moon giving us nowhere to hide.

I carried her all the way to the van with her arms wrapped around my neck and her purse tapping against my back. She was much lighter than I thought she'd be. Gabriel had the sliding side door of the van open and I eased her inside. I crawled to the rear seat. Gabriel slammed the door shut like a prison guard, started the engine and we were off.

I'm feeling a tremendous sense of relief. We are all safely in the van and within hours, probably just as the sun is rising, we will be arriving at the Norfolk Hotel in Nairobi.

Mom will probably have to be hospitalized in Paris. I can't see dad letting me take her back to Canada. I'll hang in Paris for awhile, maybe a week, make sure she is okay and then see about her returning to Canada with me.

I am really looking forward to finally touching down in Canada. I'll be a bit of star with the boys back at the patch with my African stories.

I was so excited to be heading back that I broke out in song. I started in with "Ninety-Nine Bottles of Beer." This was the last time we would all be in the van together. It didn't matter that the timing was entirely inappropriate. Needless to say, nobody joined in, but nobody told me to shut up either. I got thirty-two bottles of beer off the wall before I stopped. I was going to clear the entire stock but the hollow sound of my voice, piercing the dark African night, became too demoralizing.

Dad has pulled himself out of his cinnamon mint depression and is fumbling through his travel bag for his papers. I have been carrying the family for the past few hours and my shoulders hurt. It's time to hand the sextant back.

"Are we going to be able to get a flight out tomorrow night?" I asked.

"I'm going to try," he said. "I just hope they'll let your mother on board."

Christ, I didn't even think of that. That's why he's the skipper. What the hell are we going to do if we can't get her on? Mental ward in Nairobi? Holy shit.

I know dad is looking for the location of the airline office in Nairobi. He could do all that when we get back to the hotel. But he wants to be ready. He wants to know exactly where it is right now so he'll know exactly where he has to go. Otherwise, he'll start doing doughnuts right there in the seat.

1:20 a.m.

Soon after my last entry we hit some small patches of fog on the road. They appeared like dancing ghosts in the headlights of the van. I could see Gabriel's worried face reflected in the big side mirror.

The patches became more frequent until the entire road was enveloped in a thick fog. Gabriel slowed right down. He couldn't see a thing. He clicked on the wipers to clear the condensation.

Dad grabbed a roll of paper towels from the floor of the van and leaned forward in his seat, locking his eyes on the road, thinking this posture was assisting Gabriel in some way. He then tore off a sheet of paper towel and began wiping the inside of the windshield glass. He executed a few swooping, circular swipes and realized it wasn't helping.

Mom was unaffected by the fog. She continued to stare out the window. It didn't matter what the elements were doing. We could have been surrounded by fire and she would have stared out the window with the same expression.

I, for one, was not troubled. I've always loved fog. The mornings I love best in the oil patch are always the foggy ones. Show me a photograph of a foggy coastline and I'm at peace. Instantly.

I suppose I like the mystery that fog and mist represent. When the world is sunny and clear, all is obvious and boring, like people you suss out within a minute of meeting them. But in the mist and the fog great mysteries are hiding.

I feel closer to the supernatural in the fog. Like there is something beautiful and powerful shrouded somewhere in the mist. I guess it's the nearest I get to god. I've always suspected if a spirit world exists, it is closest to me when the elements become veils. Like fog or mist or a sunset or a sunrise. When things are there but not there. Here but not here. In between.

I popped the top on the roof and stuck my head through the observation hole. My face was damp within seconds. It was liberating. Soothing. I closed my eyes and let the fog caress me. It kissed my eyelids and filled my lungs. Hope thumped through my chest. I knew that everything was going to be okay.

I opened my eyes and watched the lights of our van slice through the fog. At one point, Gabriel almost hit a herd of goats. We stopped to let them cross the road. We passed a few Kenyans walking on the road. They emerged from the fog like phantoms and were swallowed up behind us.

I was telling myself, if I could live where it was foggy 365 days a year, I'd be a captain of eternity. I could have people up to my cave and explain things to them. They'd nod and call me a great man. I'd tell them to save their compliments and ask that they leave me money in a pot. I might fondle a few of them as well.

The fog finally cleared. Gabriel and dad were relieved. Mom didn't give a shit. I was disappointed. When the fog left, my peace went with it.

Suddenly Gabriel slammed on the brakes. I hadn't been watching the road so I had no idea what was going on. The van hit something heavy and there was a heart-piercing squeal that lasted only a moment. I was thrown forward against the edge of the observation hole and I fell back down into my seat.

"Jesus Christ!" I yelled. "What the hell was that?"

"Is everyone all right?" asked Gabriel, leaping out of the van, followed quickly by dad.

I grabbed my journal and jumped out to join them. (I was worried mom might reach around and start reading the damn thing, even though she was clearly in no state of mind for snooping.)

Dad and Gabriel were at the front of the van, looking down at something lying on the road, about two feet ahead of the bumper.

"That's a damn shame," said dad.

"I didn't see him," said Gabriel, looking sick.

It was a baby elephant. Dead. Internal organs crushed by the bumper of our van. I was glad mom hadn't gotten out. It wasn't like there was blood and stuff everywhere but it was a baby elephant after all. Not something you hit every day. I remember hitting and killing a dog once when I was stoned. Saw it bounce up off the pavement in my rearview mirror. I knew the owner, too. Some girl from school. But that was nothing. This was a fucking baby elephant.

They had enough trouble protecting these animals from poachers without tourists like us running them over. I think we all sensed the magnitude of what had happened. Gabriel most of all. He was in state of shock. I patted him on the back.

"It's not your fault. There's nothing you could have done."

Gabriel felt it first. His head jerked to the side. Dad and I felt it a few seconds later. It was the ground. It was shaking. And the shaking was getting stronger.

"Get in the van!" yelled Gabriel.

Gabriel ran to the driver's door and jumped in. Dad and I started walking back, a little confused, as Gabriel tried to start the engine. It wouldn't start. Gabriel tried one more time, grabbed his bag and jumped out.

"Get her out!"

Dad and I stood there like morons. Neither of us had any idea what the hell was happening. Gabriel yelled again.

"Get her out of the van and run!"

Dad and I dragged mom out. The ground was shaking even more. I had never been in an earthquake. And I couldn't understand why we were abandoning the van. But I figured that's what you did during an earthquake. You got the hell out of your car and ran like crazy. Dad dragged mom away and that's when I saw it wasn't an earthquake at all. It was worse.

The first elephant appeared, a large bull. He rammed into the side of the van with the force of a truck. It was enough to tip the van over onto its side. The rest of the herd arrived. They began to smash and crush the van. It started to flatten like a beer can. The elephants weren't interested in us. They were destroying the beast that had killed their baby.

In a matter of minutes the van was pancaked. It groaned and hissed but it didn't put up much of a fight. Where once had stood six feet of proud solid steel, there now lay one foot of conquered metal. Thank god Gabriel had gotten us out of there.

At the time we weren't concerned that it was night and we were in the middle of Africa and we no longer had a means of transportation. We were standing in awe of what these elephants had done to our van. Mom especially. She looked almost delirious.

A few elephants gathered around the dead baby. Their trunks tenderly slid over and around its still body. Steam rose up from the pile of twisted metal. If we had been wearing hats we would have taken them off. I had heard about elephants paying respects to the bones of their clan but to actually see them caressing this baby was too much. Gabriel was crying. I had tears in my eyes. Dad was a rock. And mom was smiling. Not a sympathetic smile. Or a demented smile. Or an isn't-that-amazing smile. I don't know what kind of smile it was.

Gabriel started walking into the grass and told us to follow him.

"Why aren't we sticking to the road?" asked dad. "Surely someone will come along and give us a lift."

"I want to get us away from the elephants," explained Gabriel.

"So why can't we walk down the road and do that?"

"Because they are blocking the direction we need to go. We will get back on the road further down. But I wouldn't get your hopes up for a ride. Not many people drive this road at night. It's too dangerous."

Dad shot me a look like it was my fault. Like I had panicked and gotten everyone riled up about getting the hell out of Meru Mulika. I couldn't get defensive because, of course, he was right. I had made a terrible mistake and I knew it. We could have waited until morning. It's not like mom was suffering from liver failure. A panicked person should never be allowed to make important decisions that will impact on other people.

The ship had been without a skipper for those few critical hours and I had assumed control. But instead of guiding the good ship Clark to calmer, safer waters, I had landed us in the middle of Africa, in the middle of the night, with no guns and nothing but our feet to carry us.

Any further discussion about leaving the road was stopped before it got started. One of the bulls spotted us, flapped his ears back and charged. He obviously felt that our attendance at the funeral for the baby elephant was entirely inappropriate. Gabriel, dad and I did what our instincts commanded. Survive. We started to run, forgetting that mom's survival glands were not secreting. She stood right where she was.

As I was running I turned around and saw the elephant stop about twenty feet away from her. He became very agitated, ears waving back and forth. A few of the elephants from the herd came up from behind and this seemed to give him courage. He started to charge again. And this time it didn't look as if he was going to stop.

Gabriel had seen what was going on and had circled back. He threw mom over his shoulder and ran. I was impressed with his strength. We kept running until Gabriel got tired. Which turned out to be a really long time. Long enough that nobody had a fucking clue where the road was anymore. Gabriel decided the best thing for us to do was to set up a camp and find the road in the morning. Mom did not want to be carried anymore and asked to be put down.

We walked for about twenty minutes until Gabriel found a spot that he liked. It was a grove of trees. He checked the branches first, probably to make sure there weren't any lions sleeping up there. We all broke branches for firewood. Even mom pitched in. With the wood gathered, Gabriel started a fire. Thank god he was there. We would have been lost without our guide. But then again, we got lost because of our guide. Well, I suppose the charging elephant had something to do with it. Within minutes we had a respectable fire.

Even with the fire it is damn cold. The bag that Gabriel snagged from the van has a few things that will help us get through the night. He had a heat blanket in there. It looks more like a giant roll of aluminum foil than a blanket. Mom refused to be wrapped in it. She said it looked ridiculous, said she'd feel like a baked potato if she climbed inside. There was a container of water, which we all passed around and drank from. All except mom. She refused. And chocolate bars. I ate a chocolate bar.

It wasn't the possibility of roaming big cats or hyenas that got me tense. It was when I took out my pack of smokes and saw that I only had three left. This was bad. I would have to ration myself. I didn't want to smoke in front of mom because she might ask me for one. I would have shared anything with her but I was damned if I was going to share my smokes.

I ended up lighting one anyway. But I retreated from where she was sitting and turned my back. Take my clothes. Take my shoes. Take my last drop of water. But don't ask me to share a cigarette when I only have three left.

As soon as I stubbed out my smoke I saw her making her way over. She stood over me and flicked a strand of hair from her eyes.

"You got a light?" she asked.

She pulled a pack of cigarettes out of her purse. She had her own. We'd have enough to get back to Nairobi. My mood brightened instantly. I gave her my lighter.

She lit her cigarette and sat down beside me. She didn't make a very good effort to keep her knees together. I saw she was wearing white panties. I tried not to look again. Her bare feet were dirty. Her face looked rugged and worn like a farmer's wife after a dust storm.

"Do you know the mistake I made?" she asked, as she handed my lighter back.

"Not running from the elephant?"

"Letting you ruin my life."

"Thanks."

"When I found out I was pregnant with you I felt like I had been rescued. It was a miracle. Then your father came to see me. He told me that the doctors had said there was a possibility of a birth defect, maybe brain damage. He wanted me to think about an abortion. I had just found my one reason to live and he wanted me to kill it."

The smoke swirled from her mouth and blew through her hair. She looked really severe, almost scary. "Don't ever make another person your reason for living."

I looked over at Gabriel sitting by the fire. I thought he'd be watching us. He wasn't. He had his hands held out to the fire. *Warmth, comfort, protection, mother.* I gulped on a throat filled with sorrow.

"I forgive you for taking the overdose."

"No, you don't."

"Don't tell me what I do or don't!" I spat. "I fucking forgive you."

She looked at me with kind, loving eyes. Her voice was soothing and quiet.

"You can't. Not now. Not tonight."

Mom got up and kissed me on the top of the head.

"You were never a burden, Richard."

She walked back to the fire. Sitting there alone I was suddenly stung by a memory I had long ago forgotten — dad had his boss and his wife over for dinner. A framed picture of me that sat with other family pictures above the fireplace ended up turned around, facing the bricks. I think I was eight but the picture was taken when I was six. My nose looked really flat and you could still see lots of scarring around my lip. I was proud of that picture. I knew I looked different than other kids but that picture made me look brave, spirited, in spite of everything. I thought the picture had been turned by accident.

As I looked at mom sitting beside the fire I realized who had turned that picture around. My blood started to boil. I got up and paced. My brain began retrieving images, moments, words from my childhood; not that I'd forgotten all of them but I was suddenly seeing them through a different lens.

I walked over to Gabriel who was standing under one of the trees looking up at the stars.

"One of us has to stay awake."

"I know," said Gabriel, looking back at mom. He could sense that I was ready to blow. I was.

"Why don't you sit down and relax? Nothing's going to happen."

"I can't relax."

Dad had been watching us talk. He came over. "What are you telling him?"

"Everything."

I was cruising for a bruising. Stumbling around the smoky bar, looking to pick a fight.

"It's none of his business."

"You almost got him killed tonight. He should probably know why."

Gabriel raised his hands to stop it. "He wasn't telling me anything that happened. He wants one of us to stay awake." Gabriel turned on me. "That's all you said. So cut it out."

Gabriel walked away and sat with mom. The scrap was on and he wasn't having any part of it. Dad wagged a finger at me. He was still back on my accusation that he almost got Gabriel killed.

"I'm not the one who got him behind the wheel to drive us across Africa at midnight."

"And why did I do that?"

"Because you overreacted. And I had too much to drink."

"Is that your excuse for destroying mom?"

"I'm not responsible for that."

"Why did you tell me?"

"You had a right to know."

"Not like that I didn't."

"I don't want to talk about it. Not with Gabriel here. This is a family matter."

Dad started walking away. I moved in front of him and ended up walking backward.

"You thought I'd hate her didn't you? That's what you wanted. You didn't want to drag that dirty skeleton out of the closet so we could all get on with our lives. You wanted everything to fall on her shoulders. That way you could come through squeaky clean. And I'd end up blaming her for my miserable life."

I stopped backing up. He was forced to stop or he would have bowled me over. I touched my lip. "You see this? This is skin. And there's bone underneath. I've hated this fucking thing since I knew it was there. But let me tell you something, what she did is nothing, nothing compared to what you've done."

I slammed my fist against my chest.

"You want to talk about scars? Let's talk about the ones in here."

"Will you stop being so goddamn dramatic?!"

"Why did you turn that picture around?"

"What picture?"

"The one of me, over the fireplace, that night your boss came over."

"I have no idea what you're talking about."

"You don't remember doing that?"

"No I don't."

"Do you remember how happy I was in elementary school?"

"No."

"I'm not asking as a question."

"You asked me if I remembered something. I'm saying I don't."

"It's a rhetorical question. I wasn't asking you, expecting to get an answer."

"I'm not an idiot! I know what a rhetorical question is. And I'm telling you, I don't remember you being any more happy in elementary school than you were in high school."

"Well, I was."

"I'll take your word for it."

"I was happy. I felt good about myself. In spite of this stupid harelip, I actually thought I was okay. I had friends and nobody teased me. Or, if they did, I took it in stride and didn't make a big deal out of it. I teased them back or I fought or sometimes I even made fun of myself. I felt like I belonged. I felt good about myself. Do you remember what happened at the end of grade six? Do you remember that play my class put on?"

Dad just stared at me.

"Do you remember the play?"

"Is this another rhetorical question?" he asked sharply.

"No. I'm asking if you remember the play I was in."

"No, I don't."

"It was in June. You and mom and Maggie came? About four hundred other parents?"

"I don't remember."

"All the grade six homeroom classes put it on. I played a gingerbread boy and was running around in brown leotards. You don't remember any of this?"

"No."

"I climbed into an oven made of cardboard. But the oven was too close to the edge of the stage. And it fell off with me inside. I jumped out and when everyone saw I was okay they started laughing. And I laughed too because it was pretty funny. And that was that. The play ended. Everyone clapped. Twenty of us, up on stage, bowing, thinking we were pretty hot stuff. Met you and mom and Maggie in the parking lot afterward. You didn't say a word all the way home. I could tell right away you were pissed off about something. Mom and Maggie kept talking about what a fun night it was. But not you. You said nothing. Before you trudged off to bed I asked if you had a good time. And do you remember what you told me?"

No response.

"That's not a rhetorical question," I said.

He was seething.

"You told me you had never been so embarrassed in all your life."

He didn't deny it. His face told me he remembered.

"I was twelve, dad." My voice was cracking. I was doing my best not to break down in front of him. "Your opinions on things mattered. I didn't know if you were embarrassed about me being in leotards or because I fell off the stage or because of this."

I slapped my face, hard enough that my lip started to bleed again, not a lot but enough that I could feel blood dribbling down my chin.

"But I'll tell you what. I stood at the bathroom mirror that night and I looked at myself. I looked at my lip and my nose. I started to think that those parents were laughing because I looked funny, not because I fell off the stage. In the time it took you to say one fucking sentence, five fucking seconds by my count, you made me feel like I was a freak."

His eyes were wild. He raised his hand. I thought he was going to smack me. I didn't care. But he didn't hit me. At least not with his fist. He poked two fingers into the my sternum. It hurt like hell.

"You listen and you listen good. I made some mistakes. I admit it. I wasn't the best father. I was narrow-minded and stupid at times. But if you're going to stand there and blame me for all your bullshit, all your failures, then you're always going to be a freak. And I suppose if your arm gets tired from whipping me you can always start blaming your mother."

He reached inside his pocket. I thought he was digging around for a mint. He pulled out a folded piece of paper towel. A white flag of surrender? An olive branch? I thought he was going to hand it to me so I could wipe some of the blood off my chin. I was waiting for the offer so I could refuse it. But he didn't hand it over. He blew his nose in it.

"You're not a boy anymore," he said with a slow, measured voice and stuffed the paper towel in his pocket. "You're a man. Your guess is as good as mine when you'll start acting like one."

He walked away. I started pacing around. I was totally trapped. I finally went and sat near the fire. Gabriel got up and walked away. I was still all pumped up, blood dripping from my lip, surging through my ears. But I heard mom's voice behind me.

"He does love you, Richard."

I looked to my right. Dad was standing against a tree with his back to us. He looked broken, like a scarecrow after a storm. And mom behind me, in her pretty dress, waiting for the next elephant to charge. And me, the skinny addict, dabbing my bloody mouth on my wrist, mainlining bullshit to myself and everyone around me. Three lonely, broken people. With nowhere to hide.

I am writing by moonlight. And there is a lot of it. I'm so goddamn tired.

I'm fighting the temptation to smoke another cigarette. I don't want to have to ask mom for any. With only two left, I need to save one for later and still have one for the morning. I'm trying to stare at the fire to calm myself down. It's not working.

I've decided I don't like our fire anymore. It's too connected with rage and burning. It reminds me of my finger. My burn is dirty but I can't clean it. The only water we have is for drinking and we don't have much of that anyway. The fire also reminds me of how itchy my legs are. My spider bites have scabbed over and I've been scratching the hell out of them. So much so that I've drawn blood. I've got to stop scratching. And I've got to stop looking at the fire.

Gabriel just brought the water around like a boxing trainer between rounds. We all refused. He took a couple of small sips, saving the rest for us. What a huge fucking sacrifice. It's not like our plane crashed in the Australian Outback. We'll find our way back to the road at sunrise and be at the hotel three hours after that, where they have plenty of water. And beer. But still, it was a nice gesture.

Gabriel has walked over and is standing beside dad at the tree. I can't hear what they're saying but Gabriel just patted dad on the back. He touched dad and dad didn't yell at him. I'm impressed. Mom has closed her eyes. She's still sitting up so I know she's not sleeping.

I can see to the horizon in every direction. Rocks and trees are silhouetted against the moonlit sky like black jewels. If we had planned this as a camping trip it would be quite beautiful. Perhaps the gods are being kind. To have surrounded us in darkness for this night would have been cruel.

I have moved away from the fire and I'm sitting with my back to everyone. I feel better under the cool, blue light of the moon than I did beside the hot, yellow fire.

I'm staring out at the grasslands. I can't remember a single word of the exchanges I had with mom and dad. I want to analyze them. Dissect them. Sort things out. Was I too mean? Did I say too much? I am trying to remember what was said but it is gone. Of course, I could always read what I wrote but that would be cheating. I want to remember on my own.

I am trying to think of the coming days. Paris. Hospitals. Canada. Job. New Hampshire. Nicole. But I can't do it. I am stuck in the present, my butt in the dirt, with the grasslands stretched out around me.

Most people spend their lifetimes trying to experience *the now, the present*. They meditate and they chant and they work, work, work at it. I am experiencing the present. But not by choice. I feel like I am sitting on a swing set with no arms and legs. I try to get myself swinging back and forth but I'm not going anywhere.

I want to roll around in the past like a hog and get dirty. I want to view images of tomorrow to give me something to look forward to or even something to be afraid of. But I am stuck on the swing, held fast by the light, the grass, the sky, the sound of the wood cracking in the fire, the smell of the smoke. It pins me down and says, "You're not going anywhere. Stay here. Stay right here."

Tonight my spirit is on the prowl. I see beyond good and evil to the bubbling nectar that waits silently, the bubbling nectar that ends, dissolves, destroys all opposites and the confusion they create. I see the beginning and the end. And I hear what Jesus said when he told everyone he was the alpha and the omega.

I see the shape of something beyond the beginning and beyond the end. The shape of the spirals that I saw inside the animal and human figures on the wall of Crocodile Man's cave. Something that just keeps going round and round and round. Never beginning. Never ending. If I have a soul, if it is true that we all have souls, then it makes sense that these souls are eternal. And we are all connected in some way. You and me.

I have had these thoughts before but it has not had much of

an impact upon me. I'd think, that's great but I'm horny and I feel like masturbating or that's pretty cool but I just smoked a huge bone and I feel like eating four glazed doughnuts. I am impressed that my mind can capture something so elusive when it isn't swimming in chemicals.

I have come to a startling conclusion. If the present moment, meaning this moment right now, is real, and five seconds ago is not real, and five seconds from now is also not real, and there really is no good or evil, and I am really not my body but the soul that inhabits my body, and there really is no beginning or end, only eternity, which means that my soul is eternal, which means even when my body dies, I will not, not the thing humming inside this organic costume, sitting in the dirt, looking out at these grasslands, and if all this is true, I mean really fucking true, not some bullshit at a meditation seminar that I paid two hundred and fifty dollars for, or not some nonsense passed along to me on Sunday by a man with a white collar who wants too much in exchange for his message, but just fucking true, absolutely true, then, then why the fuck should I worry if I only have two cigarettes left? Why the fuck should I worry if I go to get a large coffee and the store closes five minutes before I get there? Why the fuck should I worry if a turning car doesn't yield to me as I am walking across an intersection? Why the fuck should I worry if I never find Nicole? If mom never finds forgiveness. Or dad never finds compassion. Or I never find courage. Or Dorothy never finds her red shoes. To really swallow this medicine means that there's not a fucking thing to worry about. Not one.

I am so happy, I just lit one of my two remaining cigarettes. I don't care if there isn't one for the morning. I have captured a magic toad. With no help from Jesus or Buddha or Vishnu or Muhammad or Timothy Leary or Reverend Moon or Billy Graham or Shirley Maclaine or Jim Jones. Fuck them all. I caught this one on my own. Ugly and small. But it is mine.

Gabriel just came over. I was sure he was going to tell me I should forgive dad and try and get us to shake hands or something.

But he didn't. He just said he was really tired and was going to shut his eyes for awhile. He knows we have to watch mom so he said I could wake him up when I wanted to sleep. I told him I wasn't tired at all. Liar, liar, head on fire. Told him he could sleep for as long as he needed.

He asked me how I was. I was going to tell him about my night prowl but it would have sounded stupid. You just can't put this stuff into words. I mean, I know I just wrote it down and everything, but to speak it would have been so lame. It's like, yeah, yeah, yeah, I've heard all that crap before. So I didn't tell him anything. I just said I was fine. He did say that my eyes looked clear, that I looked peaceful. That was nice to hear.

Gabriel returned to the fire, said something to mom that she did not acknowledge, curled up on the ground and put his jacket under his head. Mom has not moved during the time I've been chasing my toad across the burning grasslands. Dad looks tired and is now sitting at the base of the tree. I wonder if he is cold. He could go sit by the fire but he obviously wants to be left alone. I want to say something to him but I can't. There is such a heavy silence hanging over all of us. It is a sacred night. I don't want to disturb it with an apology. We are all exactly where we need to be. And we have all said exactly what needed to be said. There is no need for conversation. Just wind. Crackling wood.

I'm afraid that my moment of clarity will not last. I fear it will not be long before an itch in my nostril, a bowel movement, a shattered dream, an erection, a coffee stain on my shirt, will wrench me down from my celestial sky.

I also fear that I'm not really ready to live a life of eternal bliss. I like my pain too much. I like the dirt too much. I like the confusion and the fear and the highs and the lows and the tears and the laughs and the sick, infantile things that make me smile.

What I really want to do is walk. The plains look so inviting. I have never seen a full-moon night so radiant. I don't know if it is just me and my bright-eyed and bushy-tailed spirit or whether the night is just as incandescent for the others. Maybe my life will be this bright from now on. Maybe the others just see a pitch black night. Maybe this is what that Blake guy meant when he talked about cleansing the doors of perception and that when they were cleansed everything would appear as it really was — infinite, eternal, or something like that. Maybe dad read Blake in college and when he got older he got windows confused with doors. Maybe he was searching for eternity when he cleaned the patio window every Saturday.

I'm really trying hard not to overanalyze and destroy what has happened to me. But I can't help myself.

I got my ideas about the soul from some book and my vision of eternity from some other book. I am only regurgitating stuff someone else has said or written. Even that doors of perception crap. That isn't my idea.

My, my, my, I can fuck this up good. Toss that dead toad back and get me a refund. Nothing is original. I can't even avoid a trite spiritual experience. I haven't really awakened at all. I was just hungry, got light-headed, needed a cigarette, threw on some hand-me-down underwear, got seduced by the moonlight and thought I'd stumbled onto the grail.

Dad's head is slumped against the tree. And I hear the familiar snoring I knew as a boy when he passed out on the couch.

I just walked over to lay the heat blanket on him. He was farthest from the fire so he'd need some warmth.

I saw his sleeping face. A person's face is supposed to look peaceful when sleeping. But his was all wrinkled and tense. And there was another sound to accompany his snoring. The grinding of his teeth. As I laid the blanket I felt real sympathy for him. Even sleep is not a reprieve from the hounds at his heels. But then again, what the hell do I look like when I am sleeping? Mom knows. I don't want to know.

I went to the pile of wood that Gabriel had made and tossed some pieces onto the fire. It is my responsibility to make sure that everyone is snug and secure. I feel like a counselor at a Girl Guide's camp. Everyone is asleep. Except mom. She is just pretending to sleep. And everyone has their own space. Dad has the trees. Mom and Gabriel have the fire. If I knew mom was sleeping I would go sit by the fire but it makes me uncomfortable knowing that she is faking. There is nowhere for me to sit down so I am back where I was before. Out here on the perimeter.

Monday, August 22
3:08 p.m.
Norfolk Hotel
Nairobi, Kenya

There is nothing to do but pick up from where I left off. My back began hurting so I dropped down on my side and propped my hand up like I was lying on a couch, watching television. I wasn't going to wake anyone up to get my own nap. I stayed like that for quite some time.

Saw a shooting star. Watched a small cloud blow across the sky. Scooped dirt and let it run through my fingers.

At first I thought my eyes were playing tricks on me. Something was moving, way off in the distance. I sat up. If it was an animal I wanted to be ready to alert the others. At least we had the trees. We could climb up into them if need be. And then I saw it wasn't an animal at all. It was a person. But a person with what looked like a really big head.

I stood up and got ready to wake Gabriel. For a second, I thought it was Crocodile Man. As it turned out, it wasn't Crocodile Man. But it was a man. And my eyes weren't playing tricks on me. He did have a really big head. Not just bigger than average. It was easily three feet across and two feet high. I thought for sure it was a mask. But as he got closer I saw that it wasn't. It was his real head. He was naked. But he had no genitalia.

He walked right up to me. I stood there numb. He opened his

mouth and belched loud and long in my face. It smelled like summer sausage. It was hideous.

"I need a drink," he said and walked over to where Gabriel was sleeping. He grabbed the container and guzzled our remaining water. I couldn't believe that the man's voice hadn't woken Gabriel up. The man with the big head tossed the empty water container on the ground. And still nobody stirred.

I did a serious evaluation of myself. I knew I wasn't stoned. And I knew I wasn't exaggerating what I was seeing. He started rummaging through Gabriel's bag, his big head bent over. I thought the weight was going to pull him into a forward somersault.

"You got anything to eat?"

He dumped everything on the ground. We had eaten all the chocolate bars. He raised his big head again.

"This is pitiful," he said, and stalked back toward me. "That's a nasty harelip. You should grow a moustache."

And with that he walked away. I watched him until his big head disappeared over the horizon.

It was about that time I felt a tickling on my hand. I thought it was spiders again. Or ants. I didn't want to look at my hand. I couldn't handle seeing anything swarming there.

I realized then that my eyes were closed. When had I closed them? Maybe after the big head disappeared over the horizon. I slowly opened my eyes. I was lying on the ground. Did the big head knock me down? It took me awhile to orient myself and realize I may have been dreaming. I think because my dream had taken place there at our campsite, I didn't understand right away that I had fallen asleep.

I finally looked down at my hand. There was something curled up inside my fist. It was a 3x3, black-and-white photograph. My eyes were still drowsy so I couldn't focus very clearly. At first I thought it was a picture of one of those trained chimps that made funny faces and was laughing with its mouth open. But then I saw that the skin wasn't black, it was white. The thing, whatever it was,

was being held by someone. It was curled up in the nook of an arm. And a face was looking down on it. The smiling face of a woman. A really loving, warm face. A young face. A face caught cooing something silly and sweet. But the thing. What the hell was that thing in her arms?

Sleep had affected my logic. Had I looked at the photo on a rainy afternoon after a strong cup of coffee I would have known immediately what it was. Or at least within seconds. But it took these long, confused seconds for everything to tumble into focus. And when they did, I felt like Sharon Tate must have felt when she realized that Tex and the girls weren't in her house to use the phone.

It was mom. And she was holding me. The thing. The chimp. The freak. The newborn. The harelip. Or, in proper medical terminology, the cleft lip and palate. Or, in proper emergency ward terminology, a face that looked like it had been dragged behind a moving car for two blocks. Or, in proper circus terminology, a face that would launch the construction of a tent and the undivided attention of a hundred spectators. Or, in proper hackneyed terminology, a face that only a mother could love.

I couldn't believe what I was looking at. This was fresh. This was right after delivery. This was before the surgeries. This was a fissure, no, a gap, no, a pit, a black pit between lip and nose that was wide and gaping, like the exit wound in John Kennedy's head. I understood immediately why there had never been any baby pictures lying around on coffee tables or sent to family and friends. Or why the few that had been taken were probably hidden away, wrapped in a towel, stuffed in a dusty shoe box, and pushed into the far corner of the attic.

I realize now that she put the photo in my hand, not to hurt me or scare me, but to show me. Not how I looked. But how she looked. That her eyes were not afraid. They were not ashamed. They were not disgusted. They were glowing with love. A glow in a mother's eyes that only a newborn baby could inspire. A glow that no man, no matter how brilliant, could inspire. A glow that no sunrise, no matter how glorious, could inspire. The glow of a mother's love for her baby. That's why she gave me the photo. To see her. To see her looking down at me. With that glow.

I also realize now that mom may have brought the picture to Africa to show me. To tell me. To confess. Maybe she was just waiting for the right moment. And dad beat her to it.

I eventually looked over toward the fire. I expected to see mom sitting there, waiting for my response. I was going to walk over and hug her and thank her for showing me that her love did not see a deformed creature. Her love saw a baby boy. *That which takes place out of love takes place beyond good and evil and pity and disgust.* But she wasn't there. Gabriel was there, still curled up by the fire that wasn't burning anymore. There were only small traces of smoke curling up into the air. Not only was the fire not burning but the sun had started to rise. I stood up immediately. I had thought I had only shut my eyes for a few minutes. Clearly it had been longer than that.

I rushed over to where dad was lying, still snoring. Mom was gone. Damn it! I had fallen asleep. I had volunteered to stay awake. I had blown it. Then I saw her clothes. They were piled neatly beside his legs. Her shoes. Her dress. Her bra and panties. I took one quick look around. Even looked up in the tree, half expecting to see her sitting up there, naked, having a giggle at my expense. Would have given anything to have seen that.

She had done it before when I was in junior high. The tree part. Not the naked part. She'd climbed the big tree in front of the house while dad was at work and had sat in it for several hours.

Dad was furious when she told us about it at dinner. He yelled at her. Told her she was nuts. Asked her if she cared at all what the neighbours thought. Kept asking her *why, why, why*. She just smiled bravely but she looked hurt, being ridiculed in front of her kids for something she thought we'd think was pretty neat. She didn't know why she did it. She just did it. For no good reason. What a thing for dad to have yelled at her like that.

I shook dad's shoulder. "Get up! She's gone!"

Dad bolted awake and was instantly on his feet. Gabriel had started to stir. Dad saw the pile of mom's clothes. He swore. I don't know if he was more upset that she had disappeared or because she was obviously wandering around in the nude.

I ran to different sides of the camp and screamed for her. I had seen this before in movies and thought it looked stupid. But it felt like the right thing to do at the time. Dad also started calling her name. The tickling in my hand was what had woken me up. She couldn't have gone that far.

Gabriel found a small set of binoculars in his bag. I grabbed them from him. I was the one who fell asleep. I was going to be the one who found her. I started scanning the grasslands. Gabriel joined dad and started screaming for her. Hearing others shouting her name helped me realize why this was futile. If she was off doing what I thought she was off to do then hearing people calling her name from a distance was not going to magically turn her around. But you do what you can do.

I walked around the camp perimeter looking out at the grasslands. The binoculars made me dizzy. Her white skin was actually a good camouflage in the tall grass. But eventually I found her. She was walking buck naked through the tall grass. She looked like she was out for an afternoon stroll around the block. She playfully swatted a hand at a stalk of grass and threw her head up to the sky. I couldn't tell if she was laughing or crying.

"There she is," I said.

Dad and Gabriel rushed over. I started jogging in her direction. I turned to make sure that Gabriel was coming. He wasn't. He looked at me and shook his head. I don't know if he was saying, "Don't go, it's too dangerous" or "No, I'm not going." Either way, he stayed where he was.

Dad ran beside me. He pointed in the direction I had started jogging. "This way?" he asked. I nodded and he was off. Not jogging. Sprinting. As fast as he could. At first I didn't think I'd have to run full speed to keep up with him, being a former high school football player and all. But I quickly discovered that even when I was running as fast as I could, I wasn't gaining ground. In fact, I was losing ground. I had no idea he could run so fast.

He began shouting her name. I cursed at him but he didn't hear me. We were best catching her by surprise, tackling her if need be, bundling her up and carrying her back to the camp. If she heard we were coming she'd start to run.

The sky was blood red. The tip of the sun had just come up over the horizon. My sides were killing me. My head was pounding. My lungs were burning. My legs were going as fast as they could.

I came over a hill and saw that dad was closing in. And he was still screaming her name. She finally heard his voice, turned and did what I was afraid she was going to do. She started to run. If dad had been closer he could have caught up to her. But he was still too far away. Still, I figured that with his speed, it wouldn't be long before he caught her. But if dad's speed was surprising, mom's speed was shocking. She broke into a frantic sprint like she had a gold medal waiting across the finish line.

The pursuit continued for quite some time. Mom in the lead. Dad behind her, gaining ground, surely but slowly. And me, the two-pack-a-day man, eighteen months removed from my last football practise, running for Team du Maurier, bringing up the rear, coughing up bits of phlegm and other red squishy bits I hoped were not pieces of lung.

Mom finally found what she was looking for. There was a small grove of trees off in the distance. I thought perhaps we had come full circle and would arrive right back at our camp. Mom would stop, out of breath, and wait for dad and me to arrive, then look at us like we were crazy for getting so upset about her going for a naked run, at dawn, in Africa, something she had always dreamed of, and had finally done. But these were different trees. There were six or seven female lions resting at the base of these trees.

Dad was still ahead of me. When he saw the lions he slowed down. Common sense commanded this. But he only slowed for a moment. A very brief moment. And in that brief moment he made his decision. And he continued to run.

The lions had picked up mom's scent and started to rise. Their movements, which before had been lazy and vague, were now coiled and precise. Mom sprinted right toward them. They weren't used to having their food run at them like that. In fact, it would be safe to say that none of them had ever seen anything like this before. Their mothers had not taught them what to do. They got nervous the closer mom got. They started moving around, tails twitching. Not sure what to do. Yeah, it was morning, it was feeding time and all that, but what the hell was this naked woman doing? Elephants sometimes charged lions. Two-legged, 120-pound animals did not. The scent would have confused them as well. I'm sure they knew the scent of a gazelle, the scent of an elephant. But the scent of a suicidal woman?

The moment of truth arrived. Mom ran right into the pride. And you know what they did? They scattered. Sure, a few of them snarled and looked mean and nasty. But they scattered. They wanted nothing to do with her. I don't mean they tucked their tails under their bellies and ran for the hills but they did get out of her way. I know there are animal experts who will never believe such a thing could happen. But I would ask them, "When was the last time you ran at a pride of lions without any clothes on?"

I could almost see the frustration on mom's face. That was supposed to be the end. That was supposed to be her door slamming shut on the madness, her finest moment. She slowed down a bit and looked over her shoulder like a lonely woman in a short skirt who had walked unnoticed past a group of idle construction workers.

The lions hadn't seen dad yet. They were still focused on mom. The scattering of the lions had stopped dad in his tracks. He was just as confused as they seemed to be. I was just about caught up to where dad was standing when we both saw mom double back on the lions. She came at them again. Only this time she was screaming. I couldn't make out what she was saying. She ran through the lions again. This time they weren't as nervous. They didn't lunge at her. But they didn't move either.

I started thinking that this would be mom's ultimate punishment. Life. Continued life. Resolution with me and dad, or insanity. But not death. Not on these grasslands. But mom was smart. After her second aborted pass she kept running. I think she figured out that lions weren't used to prey running at them. They were used to chasing. And so she kept running. And this time she didn't look over her shoulder.

I was just about caught up to dad when he started to run again.

One of the lions finally resolved her nervousness and confusion. And she began to gallop in pursuit of mom. I was still running after dad.

The lion took her down like I'd seen them do an television. A paw to the back leg, so it crossed over the other and the animal tripped. The lion was on her as soon as she fell. But before anything could happen, dad was on the lion. He grabbed the beast around the belly and with a display of strength that seemed grotesque, pulled her off mom. There was no hesitation in his actions. No concern for himself. He had one thing on his mind. And that was saving her. Because ultimately, when all was said and done, and putting aside the scolding for sitting in a tree, and the drinking and the rage, and the taunts to commit suicide, putting all that aside and more, and recognizing all of it as blisters and pimples and corns . . . deep down he loved her. And he was going to protect her.

Dad's courageous struggle with the lion ended when the rest of the pride arrived. They weren't afraid anymore. It was morning after all — feeding time. And they were hungry. The pride moved in quickly and forcefully. That's one thing about lions. When it's time to eat they don't mess around. There's not a cruel bone in their bodies. No teasing. No games. Things would be over mercifully quick.

It was all a blur. Images of tails, back legs taut, muscles rippling. No screams from mom or dad, only a few moans, and the occasional snarl from one of the cats. A whirlpool of blood and teeth and claws. A vortex. And I was drawn. I kept running. I knew this was it. This was the whole deal. I felt like I did before ejaculating for the very first time. It was intoxicating. Exhilarating. Seductive. I wanted to dive into that vortex and feel the waves of that shuddering mystery consume me.

At the time I didn't know why I stopped. Perhaps all the romance of death spilled as quickly from my mind as the blood from their bodies. Maybe I was winded from too many cigarettes and not enough exercise. But then again I suppose I could have found the strength to make a final, desperate dash to the pile and throw myself on top. Somehow that didn't seem right. What mom did seemed right. Same with dad. I suppose I might have been thinking how stupid I'd have looked rushing up late and jumping in there. What if I wasn't eaten? What if they tossed me aside, teased me, ignored me? What a bunch of shit. I don't know why I stopped. Hope? Cue the burst of uplifting music. Maybe some horns and piano to underscore my change of heart? No way. Maybe I just chickened out.

So where does that leave me? Why'd I run? Why'd I stop? For no good reason I guess. Wish it was more clear. Wish I could nail it down.

I was doubled over, trying not to puke, when I noticed the white safari buses. Three of them. Not too far from where mom had been brought down. People were watching in silence from the vans. Perhaps they had been screaming before but now they were silent. One man was videotaping what was happening.

I dropped to my knees. My head was bowed for quite some time. I must have looked like I was praying, but I wasn't. I kept my head bowed until I heard the grass rustle in front of me. And I heard breathing. And I knew I wasn't alone. I looked up.

And there he was. Ten feet away. Sitting on his back legs. The male lion I had seen when we watched the giraffe being eaten. The male lion with the scar. The male lion that had watched me so intently. He blocked my view of the feeding pride. Not that I think that he did this on purpose. It just worked out that way. I couldn't

understand why he was not attacking me. Perhaps I was too skinny.
Not worth the effort.

The wind blew his mane to the side. His eyes were red and
matched the sky. But what I really noticed again was the nasty gash
that ran from his upper lip to the bottom of his eye. It wasn't open
or oozing or anything. It was healed. But he'd have it for life. A scar
like that would be something. I don't have a scar like that. But I do
have something in my life that he doesn't have in his. Mirrors.

I can see now that the root of all that is harmful in this world
is not money. It is mirrors. The reinforced illusion that what I'm
looking at in the mirror is me. When it really isn't. Not the real me
that slumbers deep inside my body. This attachment to my body will
be a tough bond to break. Perhaps the toughest. But it has to be broken, especially at times of crisis, especially when loved ones have
been eaten alive by lions.

The mirror reinforces the selfishness that poisons everything.
The vanity. *How do I look? Do I look good?* The false pride. *I am so
fucking cool I could spit.* The *me, me, me,* and the *I, I, I.* The mirror lies.
It tells me that I am ugly. It tells me that you are pretty. It tells me
that I am me and you are you and it will not let me find that real me,
that real you, which is not really a me or a you at all but a place where
the you and the me collapse in on each other like two tired dancers
and spin in a circle, shooting suns and stars and burning dust in
every direction. The place that addicts chase and lovers grace and
astronomers, bishops and senators will never see.

The lion didn't sit for long. He rose up, lifted his tail and sprayed
urine into the air. Some of it caught the wind and hit me in the face.
I got up off my knees and backed away slowly. I didn't need to. He no
longer had any interest in me. He rumbled over to the pride and
cleared a spot so he could feed. He may have been a symbol of inspiration but he was still a lion. I remembered I had one cigarette left,
which I pulled out and lit. I turned, walked away and didn't look back.

Some might think me insane for leaping from lions to mirrors.
Some might think me insensitive to my parents. After all, while I am

making ambitious leaps of thought from one seemingly unrelated hill to another, my parents were, only hours ago, devoured. I know the lion wasn't some magic animal. Like everything else in my life that has any semblance of hope or happiness, it was all in my head. But I guess it is far better for me to create a fantastic formula for salvation than it is to reminisce about dad's intestines being sucked into a hungry mouth like wet spaghetti.

One of the safari vans pulled up beside me. The people were staring. I felt like I was in the zoo on the other side of the cage. The guy who had videotaped the attack was now videotaping me. The other tourists were hanging outside the windows. I stopped and was going to get in.

"She almost made it," one of them said.

"What?" I asked.

"To the vans. She almost made it."

It hadn't occurred to me that she might have changed her mind and was making a run for the vans after her second pass through the pride. Nah, it was tragic enough. I couldn't stomach the possibility that, ultimately, she wanted to live but was tripped on her dash to safety. I hated that fucker for putting that idea in my head so I punched him. Not hard. But hard enough to knock him back into the van.

I wasn't done. The guy with the video camera was leaning out, catching it all on tape. In one swift motion I grabbed the camera from his hands and began walking. He yelled at me, called me names. The driver asked me to get in the van. He didn't want me walking. I took the tape out and dropped the camera. I cracked open the cartridge and began yanking the tape, letting it trail behind me like a black ribbon.

The owner of the camera jumped out of the van. I was hoping he was going to come after me. I would have killed him with my bare hands. And I would have had an excellent defence. Shock and trauma, etc. He quickly grabbed his camera and rushed back to the van. It wasn't the lions he was scared of. He yelled one more curse at me. I don't remember what it was. Soon after, the sound of the van's engine was gone.

I didn't want to litter so I wrapped the unspooled videotape around my wrist. I probably should have gotten in the van. It would have made getting back a hell of a lot easier. But riding in that van, being stared at by those creatures, would have damned my soul.

I walked for a long time. Long enough to wind 246 metres of videotape around my wrist. I felt completely immune to danger. Nothing more could happen.

I came over a small hill and saw Gabriel standing near some trees. He started walking in my direction. He saw the ball of videotape wrapped around my wrist and thought it was a crude bandage.

"Are you hurt?" he asked.

"No."

"You didn't come with us," I said. "But then again, we run pretty fast for a white family."

I kept walking. Good old Gabriel. He didn't need to ask, "So, are they dead?" or even, "What happened?" He knew. He came up beside me and put his arm around my shoulder. That was all. He kept it there for a short time and then he let me go. No big hugs. No big scenes. Things had been too big, too much. He knew I needed something small. Something brief. Just a nice, gentle hug.

We arrived back at the campsite. I tossed the videotape on the blackened wood and set it alight. It burned quickly, sending grey smoke into the air. I found mom's clothes over by the trees. I walked back to the burning tape and placed the clothes on top. It took a moment but eventually they ignited and began to burn. I didn't want to leave any evidence. I didn't want any strangers wandering through and finding mom's clothes. That wouldn't have been right. And I was damned if I was going to tuck them under my arm and walk them back to Nairobi. The last thing I tossed in the fire was the picture mom gave me. I'd seen it once. That was enough.

Gabriel came over with the water. I almost told him not to bother, that some guy with a big head had drunk all of it last night.

This thought made me remember I had fallen asleep. Which made me think, if I hadn't fallen asleep, I wouldn't have to be burning mom's clothes.

I stopped myself. No room for that. If I couldn't carry mom's clothes, if those were too heavy, I sure as hell couldn't make it back to Nairobi with the weight of my nap on my skinny shoulders. No, there just wasn't room for that. Later. When my shoulders were stronger. I focused instead on lifting the water jug to my mouth. I had one swallow and realized how thirsty I was. I began guzzling. Gabriel told me to finish it. So I did.

I picked up my journal and threw mom's purse over my shoulder. Gabriel could see I wasn't comfortable with the purse so he offered to put it in his bag. I accepted. I wasn't uncomfortable because it was mom's. I was uncomfortable because it was a purse. There's no good way for a guy to carry a purse.

We managed to find our way back to the road. Our pancaked van had been moved off to the side like a flattened milk carton kicked into the gutter. I knew I had some packs of smokes somewhere in my suitcase. But I couldn't get to them in the wreckage, although I tried. I didn't feel right about opening mom's purse and smoking hers.

It seemed wrong to leave everything in the van but we didn't really have a choice. And everything was crushed anyway. Gabriel said he would make a call and get the stuff delivered to the hotel when we got back.

Gabriel and I started walking. The first car approached and I held my hand flat and dropped it up and down in the way I'd seen everyone else do. The car whisked by. They weren't stopping for no tourist.

The next vehicle came along. Gabriel snagged it. It was a Happy Taxi. It wasn't a car. It was more like a small bus. An old, dilapidated bus. There was no room inside so Gabriel and I had to climb onto the roof. We both just about tumbled off the back when it accelerated. The roof had small wooden slats along the surface. We held onto these for dear life.

The Happy Taxi was true to its promise of always having room for one more. Gabriel and I were joined by several other men, women and children along the way. All local Africans. They had mastered the art of roof-riding and had no need to grip the wooden slats. I think they enjoyed my panicked expression whenever we hit a big bump. This happened, much to my discomfort, every hundred feet or so.

The travellers who joined us on the roof tried to include us in their noisy conversation. It helped to keep my mind off the obvious. The chaotic rhythm of the vehicle was also a good distraction. The key was going to be to stay mobile. When the bus eventually stopped I would have to start walking and keep walking until I passed out. Then, when I woke up I could start walking again. I couldn't think about stopping.

One of the women on the roof brought out a loaf of bread and began offering pieces to everyone. I refused. Gabriel shot me a look that said she would be offended. I wanted to shoot a look back that said, "My parents have just been eaten by lions and if I don't want a piece of fucking bread then I don't have to have one, buddy." But I didn't know how to make that face. So, I took the bread. It actually tasted really good.

I felt bad that Gabriel had no idea what happened to mom and dad. He had been through a lot on this trip as well and deserved the facts. But I couldn't bring myself to go into it. Gabriel was smart enough to figure it out anyway. We were in Africa, after all. Three of us ran off. One of us came back. Lions, leopards or hyenas . . . what fucking difference did it make?

Gabriel did his best to make our trip back to Nairobi as normal as possible. He continued his role as guide and pointed out a few animals and points of interest. I stared blankly at whatever he was pointing at. I knew what he was doing and I appreciated it. But, to me, it felt like the earth's surface had been covered by a layer of jelly, fifteen feet deep, and we were driving through it. Everything moved slowly and Gabriel's voice was hard to hear.

He leaned forward and said something to me. The wind. The chatter of the travellers. The groaning of the engine. The smothering effect of the jelly.

"What?!"

"You should be able to let go now," he said.

I pulled my hands from the wooden slats, held them in the air and started tumbling back. Gabriel caught me with his hand. "Not right this second," he said.

I turned to him and he had his hand out. It looked like he wanted to shake my hand so I tried to give him a soul handshake. He didn't want a soul shake. He wanted a regular vanilla shake. Our hands got all twisted up. We eventually got untangled and ended up doing a regular handshake. He shook my hand until I looked up into his eyes. They looked moist, like he had been crying but I don't think he had been. Perhaps it was the wind that made them shine so. Perhaps it was the jelly.

"Everything's going to be okay," he said. There was tremendous confidence in his voice. It gave me a chill. In a good way. Those would be the last words I would hear from Gabriel.

At one point, the people on the roof began to sing. It was really quite awful. I didn't understand the words and the tones and keys were all foreign and crazy to me. I suppose there are people who would have felt privileged to have been present for something like that. Might have even told some friends about it. But the singing started to make me dizzy. I stuck my head over the side and began to puke.

I don't know how long I held my head over. A minute. A half hour. I don't know. Between the damn singing and my puking, I lost all sense of time, and space for that matter. When I finally pulled my head back up, mom's purse was beside me, and Gabriel was gone. Vanished. Poof! Perhaps he got off while my head was hanging over the side. I think we stopped once or twice. But to get off without saying good-bye. What the hell was that? I couldn't even ask anyone if they saw where he went because nobody spoke English. I take that back. One of them may have spoken English. But being a narrow-minded hillbilly from Canada, who was travelling through jelly in a state of shock I assumed they didn't and never asked.

The Happy Taxi dropped me off right in front of the Norfolk Hotel. By that point, enough passengers had departed that there was room down below. But I stayed on the roof, even through the busy streets of Nairobi. I got a few stares from tourists at the hotel as I slid down to the sidewalk. I hope they were staring because I was on the roof, not because I was carrying mom's purse. Although I wasn't carrying it by the strap. I was carrying it under my arm. Like a football.

I looked for my weeble friend with his "truth will set you free" sign. He should have wobbled by, right on cue, towing his sign behind him. That would have been a defining moment. A character moment. A moment where I pieced it all together and nodded appreciatively. But he was nowhere to be seen.

My quiet anonymity lasted until I got to the front desk to get a room. When I told them my name, the response was immediate. Within five seconds I was Elvis Aaron Presley. Everyone wanted a piece of me. I was whisked into a small conference room. The parks department was there. Three reps from Wimpole Tours. The hotel manager. The local police. And an officer from the Canadian High Commission.

The Canadian officer inquired, with a voice barely above a whisper, whether I needed anything. I asked her if she had any du Maurier cigarettes. She didn't. I asked if anyone smoked. Silence. Finally, one of the guys from the police department, an inspector, pulled out a pack of cigarettes. The hotel manager said there was no smoking in that room. The inspector didn't give a shit. He handed me a cigarette and lit it. One of the Wimpole Tours reps dashed out to get me an ashtray. I was still Elvis.

Once my cigarette was lit, I gave them the raw, detached details. Mom had been depressed. Suicidal. We made a dash for Nairobi. Crashed the van. Spent the night in the grasslands. She took off in the morning. Dad and I went to get her. She died. Dad died. I didn't.

There were several follow-up questions, which I answered coldly and quickly, including the fact that the crashing of the van was not Gabriel's fault, it was mine. Wimpole Tours wanted to hear that part twice. The inspector asked where Gabriel was. I said I didn't know.

I feel bad about one detail. I made it seem like it was only mom who ran to the lions when in my heart I knew it was all three of us. But I also knew if I mentioned anything they might have had me committed for a short time and I had one goal: to get out of Nairobi as soon as possible.

The parks department, the gal from the Canadian High Commission and one of the two police guys left the room. The inspector stayed behind and talked to me about what to do with the bodies. Yes, the bodies. Or what was left. I told him the remains should be sent back to Canada. I would make arrangements with my sister. Then it hit me. Maggie didn't know. And Maggie might have just had her baby. Fuck me.

I would have to call her. Jesus. What the hell would I say? *Maggie? It's Richard. How are you doing? (pause) Boy or girl? (pause) That's great. (pause) Oh, I'm (pause) I'm okay. Listen, I've got some bad news. Mom and dad are dead. (pause) That's right. (pause) No. Lions. (pause) I'm not joking. I'll be home tomorrow. I'll explain it all. Bye.*

I coordinated with Wimpole Tours about sending the remains to Canada. I thought I should go to Paris first and get things settled there. Shut down the apartment, banks, all that crap. But that didn't make any sense. What about Maggie? She'd have to deal with the remains. That wasn't right. I was shaking. I had to stay with the remains. That was right. Canada. Book a flight to Canada. I would go with the remains to Canada. Do all the funeral stuff and then I could fly back to Paris and get things settled at the apartment.

That done, Wimpole Tours took off to make arrangements. I think I could have asked them to wash my underwear by hand and they would have done it.

The inspector told me about the van. Said they had already

loaded it onto the back of a platform tow truck and were bringing it back to Nairobi. He split.

Ten seconds later a dapper man with a red tie walked in. He introduced himself as a lawyer for Wimpole Tours. His hand was sweating. He had a statement for me to sign. The statement absolved Wimpole Tours of any liability for the fatalities. He handed me a pen.

The door opened and the inspector came back in. He told me not to sign anything and told the lawyer to get out. The lawyer left but he wasn't too happy.

The inspector asked me for a second time if I knew where Gabriel was. I said I didn't. Apparently, Wimpole Tours was worried that Gabriel's conduct may have contributed to the fatalities. I lit into the guy, even though he was just passing along information. Told him Gabriel was the only reason we got as far as we did without someone dying. Told him Gabriel was a prince. Told him the whole idea of investigating Gabriel was a pile of shit. He wrote everything down.

The inspector asked me what I knew about Gabriel. I told him I knew he was from Nairobi. Knew he studied medicine in London. Knew he was a hell of a safari guide.

The inspector told me that Gabriel was indeed from Nairobi and had indeed studied medicine in London. But he had also been picked up by the police near Covent Garden for creating a public disturbance and appearing disoriented and incapacitated, and subsequently spent a month at St. Mary Abbott's Hospital in the psychiatric ward. The inspector said he'd take my word for it that Gabriel was a good safari guide.

I asked him if he knew what happened at Covent Garden. He looked through a stack of papers he was carrying and tried to read the tiny print on a paper that looked like a job application form. (Apparently one of Gabriel's job application references from London had ratted him out. He got the job with Wimpole anyway and I guess this is what they were worried about. I didn't give a shit about that.) The inspector said the incident at Covent Garden had something to do with a dead bird and an argument with a cab driver.

I can't say I was shocked to hear that Gabriel had spent time in a nuthouse. I had started to think he might have been an angel, what with his guiding hand, his name, commanding presence and his mysterious disappearance. I'm kind of relieved he was a little crazy not divine.

The inspector told me he thought I should find out more about Gabriel before I signed the liability waiver. I signed the damn thing anyway but I wrote a condition at the bottom that they couldn't fire him.

The inspector was first class. He tossed me his pack of smokes when he left. They were Embassy Kings. Not du Mauriers but what the hell.

I've been writing since I was left alone in the room. It had all been settled pretty quickly. But now I've got a new set of problems. What the hell am I going to do with the rest of the afternoon? Sleep? Read a book? Go to a movie? Go for a walk? Decisions. So many fucking decisions. I've been sitting here for a really long time.

The hotel manager just poked his head in and gave me a key card to my room. He said it was a non-smoking room, but, given the circumstances, he wouldn't mind if I had one or two. What a hero. My mind was spinning too fast to come up with a snappy reply. So I told him to fuck off. He did.

Back to my dilemma. What the hell am I going to do with my afternoon? Wimpole Tours has just told me they have booked me on a flight to Canada. It leaves at midnight. It connects through Hamburg and Toronto. Two connections? They'll lose the remains. Wimpole Tours said there was a more direct flight leaving the next day. No, it has to be tonight. Book me for tonight. Done. Gone. Alone in the room again.

The burn on my finger gave me a reason to get my ass moving. I went to the shop in the hotel to buy some cream and some bandages. They only had suntan lotion. I bought two packs of cigarettes instead. I was told about a store around the corner that could help me with the cream. The gal at the cash register recommended vitamin-E oil.

I didn't want to leave the hotel. I was a big, open wound. I couldn't see myself walking out into the bright sunshine of the afternoon and subjecting myself to the unpredictability of strangers. To possibly have one of them stop me and ask me something, like what time it was, or directions for somewhere, or for money.

I forced myself to walk outside and around the corner, prepared to encounter untold conflicts. Nothing bad happened. I grabbed twenty-nine millilitres of vitamin-E oil and some bandages. They were put in a little brown bag. I returned to the hotel feeling like a conquering hero.

I found my room and shut the door behind me. I stood there with my back against the door. I felt safe. I dropped the little brown bag, my journal and mom's purse at my feet. And started to cry. Not about mom and dad. It was too soon for that and I wasn't even thinking about them. Just cried. I think I would have stood there crying for three days had there not been a knock.

I opened the door. A hotel staffer was standing there smiling, with his elbows sticking out at awkward angles. At first I didn't know what he was carrying under his arms. Makeshift wings stolen from a history of flight museum? Then I realized. Our luggage. They had obviously managed to extract our battered suitcases and bags from the wreckage.

I almost told him to go away and throw everything in the garbage. But he looked so proud. Like he was doing a really good deed and would be disappointed if I did not accept them. I should have been overwhelmed with memories. Overwhelmed that such an effort had been made to return them. But the damn things looked so fucking stupid, all flattened like that. What started out as a giggle soon became a laugh and then a harsher laugh and then spasms. I was laughing so hard I was wheezing and my eyes were tearing. It was hysteria, plain and simple. He came in and carefully laid the pieces on the bed, stacked them like giant pizzas. I gave him the rest of my African money, about seventy dollars worth. He tried to hand some back but I refused. He left, thanking me over and over and over.

I had no desire to try and open the luggage. That could wait. I knew that something could pop out. Like mom's toothbrush. Something that would detonate the explosives at the base of the dam.

The luggage reminded me that they had not returned anything from dad. Like his wallet. I started thinking about that wallet. Maybe the lions had eaten it. This led to my thinking about the lions eating his butt. I didn't want to think about the lions eating his butt. But I was worried about the wallet. What if the lions hadn't eaten his wallet? What if one of those fucks in the safari vans had taken it? Or someone at the mortuary? They could use his credit cards. I guess if they ran up the cards to their limits I'd just refuse to pay. Explain the circumstances and refuse to pay. That would work. Still, I was hoping the lions had eaten the wallet, that way I wouldn't have to deal with all that. I'm sure they ate the wallet. Why the hell wouldn't they? Sharks eat all kinds of stupid things. Like licence plates. But lions weren't sharks. They weren't indiscriminate eaters like that. Maybe the wallet was lying out in the grass. Maybe some African kid would find it and make earrings out of the credit cards. That would be alright.

I took off my clothes and ran a bath. I was really looking forward to the sensation of having my body caressed by warm water. I emptied my pockets. Old habit. Unnecessary. Out of the breast pocket of my shirt came the rose that Nicole left me. All dried and withered. I had forgotten it was there. I hadn't wanted it in my suitcase. I was worried it would get crushed.

Damn, that rose made me smile. I stuck the stem into the frame surrounding the bathroom mirror. I searched my pockets for the twig I had brought back from the other side of the river. It wasn't there. I couldn't remember if I had put it in one of my bags. I'd find it later. It wasn't that big a deal anyway. Be nice if I found it but it didn't seem as important as it had the night I grabbed it. Certainly not as important as the rose. That was something special.

I clicked off the bathroom light and climbed into the tub. The water swirled around my legs. I slowly slid my shoulders under the water. God, it felt good. The sound of the faucet dripping. The soft water. The only illumination in the bathroom was a shaft of light coming in from the other room, falling across the tub.

I was being completely selfish. I still hadn't called Maggie. I told myself I would. After my bath. I wasn't thinking of mom or dad. I would. After some time. I wasn't thinking about Gabriel. I knew I would. One day.

I rested my head on the edge of the tub and looked up at the rose. I thought about Nicole. I thought about university. I thought about my job. I thought about jude and Jack Daniels and hash oil. I thought about what I wanted to do. Where I wanted to go. Who I wanted to be.

If I wanted to find Nicole, I could. If I wanted to go to university, I could. I could do that. If I wanted to go back to the oil patch, I could do that, too. If I wanted to grow a moustache, I could do that. Nah. Moustaches are stupid. I'll never grow a moustache. If I wanted to have my fifth and final surgery, I could do that. If I wanted to think about stopping the booze and the drugs, I could do that, too. There was a lot I could do.

I rubbed the red welts on my legs. I looked at the burn on my finger. I was looking forward to the vitamin-E oil and the bandages. I touched my swollen lip. It reminded me of dad so I pulled my hand away. The cut on my elbow was scabbed over. I sure had my wounds. They were good wounds. I felt like a warrior. No, I felt like a mortal who had journeyed to the land of the gods, gotten his ass kicked and was now soaking in a tub of ambrosia.

I found myself drifting, tumbling, softly spinning, seeing that old bridge. The bridge I discovered after dad found my jude. An old, gothic bridge. A bridge from a time long ago. I think I heard Celtic pipes off in the distance. Horses and carts clopped above me. I was hanging from underneath the bridge. Hanging by my hands. Below me were clouds, or mist, or fog, I don't know which, perhaps all three. It was not scary anymore. I looked up and watched as I released my hands from the bridge. I fell. Fear threatened. But only for an instant. When I looked down, I saw, not boulders rushing up to crush my bones, but swirling clouds of fog. I was suddenly enveloped. And the sensation of falling was replaced by the soothing touch of the cool mist. It covered me from head to toe. It dampened my skin and put drops on my eyebrows. It filled my lungs. My hands disappeared when I extended my arms. But I felt safe. The boulders that had rushed up before were scary. But this . . . this was good. And then it dawned on me. This wasn't just good. This was really good. This was not only a place to drop into from time to time but it was something I could see myself surrendering to. Mystery. Fog. Mist. A place in between. A place that didn't pretend to have any hand-me-down answers but also a place that didn't ask any questions. A place that didn't necessarily offer truth but a place that didn't tell any lies either. A place where faeries and even the occasional beastie crept through the mist and fog. No, my place did not have stained-glass windows and organ music. It did not have burning incense or sand gardens. But it had fog. And mist. And it was cool, refreshing. And it was mine.

The oil felt nice. I did a lousy job with the bandage. Not a neat wrap at all. But the burn is oiled and covered. I got a pot of weak coffee from room service and called Maggie. No answer. I'll try again from the airport. They have just knocked at the door. It is time for me to go. *Kwaheri/Asante.* (Good-bye and thank you.) Gabriel taught me that. But you know what? The snapperhead took off on me and I refuse to end this day's entry with something he said.

The driver is waiting impatiently outside the door. I don't care. Let him wait. And let me say, for the sake of argument, that the truth is like the sun, and it makes everything clear and obvious, and makes you put on sunglasses, and allegedly makes you free. I want nothing to do with it. Mom and dad have shown me that true freedom is found not in the lotus position, and certainly not in the revelation of dark, buried secrets, but in the jaws of a lion. And even that freedom doesn't lead to much. Just piles of dung in the grasslands.

I know it is possible that right now, as I write, their spirits, their souls, are humming sweet songs and rejoicing with the sensation of being free again. But I don't know that for sure. It's nice to think about. But I don't want to waste my time anymore thinking about an existence I don't know.

Give me the moon, partially hidden by clouds. Give me the mist. Give me the fog. Give me the mystery. It may not make me free. But I think freedom and truth are overrated.

ABOUT THE AUTHOR

Robert Sedlack was born and raised in Calgary, Alberta. He attended university in New York City and chased overdue invoices for a soap company and then a chocolate company in London, England. He was also an enthusiastic but ineffective housekeeper at Helena Bonham Carter's family home in London.

He is a writer and documentary filmmaker involved in a number of fiction and non-fiction projects, including an ongoing video documentary of Brent Dodginghorse, an aboriginal hockey player trying to make it to the NHL. *The African Safari Papers* is Sedlack's first novel. He currently lives in Los Angeles with his cat, Molly, where he is working on his second novel.